A DANGER DESTROYED

A DANGER DESTROYED
CHRONICLES OF AN URBAN DRUID™ BOOK 15

AUBURN TEMPEST
MICHAEL ANDERLE

This book is a work of fiction. All of the characters, organizations, and events portrayed in this novel are either products of the author's imagination or are used fictitiously. Sometimes both.

Copyright © 2022 LMBPN Publishing
Cover by Fantasy Book Design
Cover copyright © LMBPN Publishing
A Michael Anderle Production

LMBPN Publishing supports the right to free expression and the value of copyright. The purpose of copyright is to encourage writers and artists to produce the creative works that enrich our culture.

The distribution of this book without permission is a theft of the author's intellectual property. If you would like permission to use material from the book (other than for review purposes), please contact support@lmbpn.com. Thank you for your support of the author's rights.

LMBPN Publishing
PMB 196, 2540 South Maryland Pkwy
Las Vegas, NV 89109

Version 1.00, April 2022
eBook ISBN: 979-8-88541-276-6
Print ISBN: 979-8-88541-277-3

THE A DANGER DESTROYED TEAM

Thanks to our JIT Team:

Christopher Gilliard
Deb Mader
Dave Hicks
Diane L. Smith
Dorothy Lloyd
Jim Caplan
John Ashmore
Micky Cocker
Rachel Beckford
Kelly O'Donnell
Paul Westman

Editor
SkyFyre Editing Team

CHAPTER ONE

"Hurry! Hard, hard, hard." I'm squatting at the end of our backyard ice strip calling the play, laughing as Nikon sweeps in front of my stone and Dillan creates a shield to defend against magical attack. Curling gets crazy when you're playing with empowered folks. "Whoa. Get off. Right off. Yeah. Leave it. Leave it."

My stone sails over the pebbled surface of the ice, closing in fast on its target.

I stand and watch as my shot rock *cracks* against the exposed edge of Calum's stone and stays in the rings. His, on the other hand, gets knocked spinning out of the back of the house.

"That's how you do it, bitches." Dillan high-fives Nikon and Dionysus at the other end.

Jackson, Imari, and Meggie cheer, waving their foam fingers and whacking each other with them.

I jog a couple of steps and stand on one foot, pushing myself along the ice with the other. Oh, if the kids in my high school curling elective could see me now. Back then, I was on my ass more than my feet.

Feline Finesse for the win.

When I get to the other end, I grin at the rocks still sitting inside the colored bands. "The Brushoffs score three. Tie game. Broomzillas, you're up."

Sloan kisses me as I glide by and winks. "Are ye ready to concede, *a ghra?*"

I laugh. "In your dreams, hotness. If you want to claim a prize in this family, you've got to earn it."

He bites his bottom lip and gives me a look much too intimate for the company. "Challenge accepted."

I laugh and push him back toward his team.

"Irish! Irish!" Calum, Eva, and Aiden chant.

Sloan picks up his first stone of the end and goes over to confer with his teammates.

I leave them to their strategizing and check on the kids. "Are you guys having fun?"

The three of them look up, and they're all smiles and hot chocolate mustaches. "Yep," Jackson says, grinning. "Can we go in the grove and get warm with our friends?"

The forest of our family grove runs the length of our two adjoining properties and is magically larger within. It's also insulated against the chill of winter to keep our fae friends comfortable and warm year-round.

"Of course. Remember to stay away from the hot springs pond, be gentle with the Ostara rabbits, and be quiet near Pip's and Nilm's home tree. They have a new baby, and we don't want to disturb them."

Jackson rolls his eyes at me. "I know, Auntie Fi. I'm not a kid anymore. I'm almost six."

Technically he's closer to five than six but why call him out in front of the girls?

"My mistake. If you know the rules and abide by them, you're good to go."

"Thanks." Jackson takes off his foam finger and sets it in his lawn chair wedged in the snow.

Imari and Meg do the same, and the three of them hurry off and disappear into the trees.

Aiden looks at me from the ice and lifts his chin. "All good?"

"Yep. Just opting for a warmer climate and new distractions."

He nods and returns his attention to the game.

I move over to stand with Nikon and Dionysus to study the rocks at the far end...or rather the lack of them. "What did I miss?"

"Sloan placed a guard, and I cleared it," Nikon says.

"Calum's likely going to try something tricky," Dionysus says. "He's shiftier than he looks, that one."

I laugh at the seriousness in his tone. "We Cumhaills are a strategic bunch, for sure. He'll likely place a high guard and try to force Dillan to tuck in behind it at the top of the house."

Dionysus frowns. "Sneaky."

I chuckle, about to say more when movement inside the gate raises my alarm. My instincts flare, and I turn, hands raised to assess the danger of the intruder. "What the—"

"Hey, babe. Looking good."

How Jordan got from the gate to me in no time flat is a mystery but what's more mind-boggling is why he grabbed me, and his tongue is pushing to gain entrance into my mouth.

I resist his hold, but he's way too strong to escape. Then it hits me. He's empowered.

Huh. You learn something new every day.

I call *Bestial Strength* and shove him hard, forcing him back with a pulse of power. He staggers back, but his disheveled surprise only makes him look more attractive.

I tug off my glove and wipe my palm across my mouth, my ire fully engaged. "What the hell, Jordan? Have you ever heard of a lady's choice? That was not okay."

The ruckus has drawn attention, and the gang is closing in. "Everything all right, *a ghra?*" Sloan asks, his voice uncharacteristically icy.

"I think so." I dry my hand against my jeans and regain my composure as I pull my glove back on. "I don't know what the suckerfish routine was about, but I'm sure Jordan is about to explain."

"Jordan," Dillan repeats. "Was that her sexy valet?"

"No, that was Jacob. Jordan was her sexy chef," Aiden corrects.

"No, that was Jared." Calum joins in. "Jordan was her sexy musician."

I roll my eyes as my brothers revisit my catalog of exes. "Jordan is a musician, yes. He's not mine, and there's no need to comment on his rate of sexiness or lack thereof. The question at hand is what the hell is with the mack attack? Why are you here?"

Jordan shrugs as if he finds this entire exchange amusing. "I saw you boldly kicking ass on a video on Faebook and looked you up on Witchipedia. I didn't know you had gifts. That would've made you so much more interesting."

I snort a laugh and send an apologetic glance at Sloan. "Well, no harm done. My lack of appeal led me straight to where I was meant to be. Everything worked out as it was supposed to."

Jordan follows my gaze and assesses Sloan. They are both over six feet, both broad-shouldered and hot, but where Sloan is *GQ* chic and fine lines, Jordan is all *Sons of Anarchy*, rule-breaking rough edges.

He frowns at Sloan and rakes his fingers through his long hair. He was always big on wearing a bunch of silver rings. Between that, the hair, the biker image, and the guyliner, he was part of my heartthrob rebel phase.

Add to that him playing the guitar and singing…yeah, he was a memorable period in my life.

I hold up my palm and run my thumb over my Claddagh band to draw attention to it.

Jordan's eyes widen. "You're *married* to this guy?"

Sloan stiffens and steps forward, but I move in front of him and cut off the advance. "Not married in the traditional sense, but very much together and not available for tongue swapping."

He eyes up the crowd and tilts his head toward the gate. "Can we talk?"

I stand my ground and cross my arms. "Right here works. There's nothing you need to say to me in private that you can't say here."

He looks over my family and friends and seems less than impressed. "Fine. Well, once I saw the video of you taking out nixies in the aquarium, I did a little recon. You're the Guild Governor for Toronto Druids."

"Correct. I am."

"Well, I didn't share this with you because I didn't know you were empowered, but I'm Moon Called. I'm a griffin."

I look at him again with that information in mind and yeah, a few things fall into place. He was always a different kinda guy, bulky, strong, long mane of hair.

Moon Called makes sense.

"Cool. I'm close with Garnet. You're lucky to have such a strong alpha."

By the tightening of his expression, I'm not sure he agrees. "Griffins are more exotic than lions. I hate to sound conceited, but I'm one of the most interesting members of the empowered world. After seeing you in action, I thought I'd come to give you another chance."

I bite my bottom lip to keep from laughing out loud. "That's thoughtful but not necessary. I'm good. Thanks for thinking of me and dropping by though."

I grip the sleeve of his jacket and turn him toward the gate before giving him a push.

He doesn't budge. "Don't be hasty, babe. You're a bit famous now, but that will fade. You should consider how you want to position yourself going forward."

I chuckle, unable to take this seriously any longer. "A social media video of me tidal waving a bunch of nixie assholes doesn't make me famous. Even if it did, I'm good with that spotlight fading."

My answer surprises him. He glances around at the folks gathered and flashes me a conspiratorial wink. "I get it. I interrupted your afternoon. I'll let you think about it. Having powerful allies will be more important than ever in a few weeks, and we don't want you regretting a rash decision."

I take a step back, surrounding myself with my clan. "I'm flattered, Jordan, but I'm good. Thanks for noticing me in that video and thinking about me. Honestly, my life is full, even without a griffin boyfriend."

He doesn't look convinced, so I go one step further. "As for me needing powerful allies." I lift my finger and point around my circle as I name people off. "I have my druid soul-mate who rocks my socks every day of the week, a Greek immortal, a Greek god, an Angel of the Choir, a mythical battle bear, a couple of amazeballs dragons, and those are only the allies here right now."

Bruin, Dart, and Saxa have come out of the grove to see what's going on. Rory flies overhead and lands on Dillan's shoulder, pegging Jordan with an icy gaze.

He looks at the group and the dragons, and when Bruin lumbers over to stand next to me, my bear calls forward his battle armor.

I fight not to laugh at the look on Jordan's face.

He always did think a lot of himself.

Too bad for him that in my circle, there's no room for self-inflation.

He's getting the picture, so I give him a break. "You're right about bonding together in the troubled times to come. If you and yours need anything or fall into any trouble, don't hesitate to reach out. The next couple of weeks will test all of us, and we need to stand together to fight for Team Light."

He casts a look over the crowd and brushes his fingertips

down my cheek. Shrugging, he flashes me a look that suggests he's bored and done with this conversation. "I doubt that will happen, but thanks. I'll check in with you later once you've had a chance to think about us."

"Yep. Nothing to think about. I'm good." I wave goodbye.

"Is good really good enough when you can have more? I don't think so." He backs away pointing at me with dual finger guns.

My brothers burst out laughing behind me, but I can't look, or I'll lose it. I escort him to the gate, and when he's through, I click the latch, securing the wooden fence behind him.

Maybe it's time to change our three-foot white pickets for six-foot iron bars. Not that they would keep out empowered folks any better than the warding on the property already does, but it might keep out the riffraff.

I walk back to the group, ready and waiting for the peanut gallery to weigh in. Once I'm standing in front of the crowd, I curl my hand toward myself in the international gesture of bring it on.

The ones who weren't already laughing break out in a fit of laughter. I take the hits for a few minutes. My questionable choice in men. My fame from flooding out nixies. How I need to consider my position before my favor fades and people forget me.

Once I've let them have their say, I hold up a finger. "So, I'm confused. Am I two-timing Sloan and dating a griffin now or did he get the picture?"

Cue another fit of laughter.

When it seems they aren't winding down, I roll my eyes. "Let he who hath no bad exes cast the first stone."

That shuts them up quickly.

My phone alarm goes off, and I pull it out and shut it off. "This is the last end of the tournament, folks. I've got a baby bear to get home in thirty. Whose turn is it?"

"It's you, babe." Sloan wraps his arm around my hips and yanks me tight to his chest. "It's all you."

He leans close, securing me against his body. "Is this the part where I shove my tongue down your throat? Just asking because I don't want you to miss out on anything. I know how women like bad boys."

I press my fingers over his mouth to keep him from trying. "I'm not missing out on anything. Thanks for the offer, though. I appreciate it."

CHAPTER TWO

Garnet Grant, the Moon Called Alpha and Grand Governor of the Lakeshore Guild of the Empowered Ones, owns a swanky home in midtown Toronto. It sits on a couple of acres of land and has a long driveway that winds behind a line of hedges. The screen of cedar offers ample space for us to portal there without anyone on the street below seeing it happen.

Sloan *poofs* Imari and me there, and we pass through the magical archway. After the flutter of a screening spell determines which house we're welcome at, the subtle pressure of magic *pops* around us, and we portal again—this time to the private compound of Garnet's pride in the African savanna.

"Home sweet home, chickie-poo." I unbutton my winter coat as quickly as possible and peel off my layers as we walk through the gate and into the yard.

Imari does the same and takes off along the flagstone pathway that leads to the house. "Hi, Mommy!"

"Hi, baby!" Myra waves from where she's sunning herself on a lounge chair over by the oasis swimming hole. "Did you have fun?"

"Tons of fun." Imari races inside.

Sloan and I are moving at a much slower pace. It's a jarring change in climate from Toronto to Africa, but honestly, between the dry heat and the exotic fragrances coming off the colorful blooms growing around the compound, I don't care that I'm overdressed.

The heels of our winter boots *thunk* against the stone walkway, and we stand under the shade of a swaying palm while Myra gets up and pulls herself together. The breeze is lovely against our skin and stirs the air enough that the temperature doesn't become overwhelming.

My gaze is stuck on the vibrancy of color and growing things. "Look at this place."

"Look at what?" Garnet asks, coming out of the house with a tray of glasses and an icy pitcher of pink liquid. "Can I offer you a drink?"

I toss our winter things over the glass railing that borders the portico and the yard and pull off my hoodie.

A tank top and jeans are as good as it's going to get.

"I was commenting on how everything looks lusher and greener than usual. Did you get a new landscaper?"

Garnet arches a brow at me. "I never know if you're asking me a straight question or if you're being sarcastic."

I chuckle. "It was a straight question. Don't you think the oasis looks even more paradise-y than usual?"

He glances over at the swimming area surrounded by large sunning rocks and swaying trees. "I can't say."

I shrug. "I guess when you see it every day you miss it. Trust me, it does. So, what are we having?"

"Oh, it's my new favorite thing." Myra's sheer pool wrap flaps around her like an elegant tropical cape in the breeze as she joins us and slides onto one of the six seats around a stone table. "Pink lemonade icy."

Garnet pours for the ladies first, and Myra scoops a little spoon into a bowl of raspberries and blueberries, dropping them on top. "Good and at the same time good for you," she says, handing me an aluminum straw.

I give it a try and sputter a bit before swallowing it. "Wow, those are strong."

"But yummy."

I chuckle and watch as Sloan sips his with a mask of emotion that gives nothing away. No fair. I warned him.

I take a second sip. "Yes, they're very yummy, but did I mention strong?"

Garnet chuckles. "I make them exactly as instructed. If you have complaints, you have to take it up with the lady of the house. She's our mixologist and knows what she likes."

Myra waggles her eyebrows and grins. "Yes, I do."

I take another sip and wowzers. It won't take long before this hits. "So, by the wide smiles and flirty talk, I take it Mommy and Daddy had a nice afternoon all to themselves."

Myra swoons to the side. "It was glorious."

The subtle smile curling Garnet's lips tells me he's pleased with that review.

Imari rushes back outside. She's stripped off her warm clothes and has a sundress on and a carrot in her hand. "Daddy, can we take Contessa a treat? She hasn't been feeling good."

"Anything you want, kitten. Lead the way. I want you to tell me all about your day."

"May I join you, Imari?" Sloan sets his drink on the table. "If the Contessa is feelin' poorly, perhaps I can help. Healin' is one of my gifts."

Imari gives him a nod of approval and the men get up to leave us. "Do you want to come too, Mommy?"

Myra sinks deeper into her chair and sips through her straw. "I think I'll have a drink of pink juice with Auntie Fi and will go with you to check on Contessa tonight before bed. Is that okay?"

"Yep. Hasta la pasta, baby." She skips off with Sloan, hand-in-hand.

Garnet looks back at me and blinks. "Why is it that every time she spends a day with your family there's some new colorful saying we get treated to?"

I laugh. "Considering it's my family we're talking about, hasta la pasta isn't bad. It could've been worse."

Garnet rolls his eyes and turns to catch up with Imari and Sloan. As they strike off across the green lawn stretching from the oasis to the plateau behind the house, Myra and I settle in with our pink juice.

"Thanks for taking Imari, Fi. It was a much-needed adult day. We truly appreciated some quiet time."

I hook inside a raspberry with my straw and lift it into my mouth. It's cold and tastes both of berry and pink lemonade icy. Delish. "Not a problem. We had fun. Thanks for trusting us enough with her that we didn't end up with a full-detail shifter security squad at our house for the day."

Myra laughs. "He is a little over the top protective of her, I'll admit, but his heart is in the right place."

"It definitely is." I take another long sip and smile. The more I drink, the less I notice how strong it is. That doesn't bode well for me later.

"How are things with your dad?" Myra asks.

"Another good reason to drink."

She clucks her tongue. "Aw, I'm sorry, duck. I know how that hurts you."

"It does, but I still believe I did the right thing. He's cutting himself off and wallowing in his loss. I get that everyone grieves in their way, but it's been a year and a half and he's getting worse, not better."

She reaches across the table and squeezes my hand. "Losing a child isn't something anyone can truly understand unless they've suffered it themselves. Yes, it's about the loss, but it's also about so many other things. Your father's guilt might not make sense to you, but that doesn't negate it."

I sigh. "I get that...I think I was more scared for him than anything. We're losing him."

Myra's smile is so achingly sad it hurts my heart. She and Garnet lost their son, then lost each other to decades of loneliness and grief.

"Okay, new subject. This is Fun, Family, and Friends Day. Let's not lose sight of that."

"Right you are." Myra nods.

With the buzz of alcohol draining away the tension of the times I live in, I watch Myra drinking across the table. "You look really good, girlfriend. Are you doing something different with your skincare?"

"Nope. Same as always." She reaches up and grabs the pitcher's handle, pouring until we're both topped up. "Maybe it's an afternoon of skinny-dipping and lion-man jungle loving."

I chuckle. "I'm not discounting it, but my instincts tell me it's something more. Everything about this place seems lusher and more vibrant than usual."

She considers that and nods. "Now that you mention it, I have noticed something but didn't want to bring it up."

"No? Why?"

"Well, remember when you first accepted your heritage powers and built your grove?"

"Yeah."

"Remember how I could feel the shift in the magic level before most of the other races and sects?"

Oh no. "Did we bugger something else up? Are empowered races going to come gunning for us again?"

She shakes her head. "Quite the opposite. Ever since you came back from that prana island in Ireland, I've noticed a steady increase in the magical energy both in the city and here. It's in the air, the water, the grass, and the trees. It's like the natural world got a boost."

"Because it did. I didn't realize it would affect you here, but there was a boost to the prana, and the ley lines carry that energy everywhere. It makes sense you're feeling the rebalancing of that."

Myra sobers. "That's the problem, duck. It isn't rebalancing. So far, it's a steady increase without leveling off. Just more and more power offered to the natural world."

I take another long sip and sigh. "Why do I feel like this won't be a good thing?"

"Likely your keen instincts and sharp intellect."

I chuckle. "Yay me."

After an afternoon at Myra's compound and a third pitcher of pink lemonade icy, Sloan *poofs* us into the carriage house at Casa Loma. The Gothic Revival mansion located in midtown is no longer the private estate of financier Sir Henry Pellatt. The castle is rented out as a party venue and movie set and is home to the swanky BlueBlood Steakhouse.

Sadly, tonight we're not here for the prime rib. Instead, the vampire community that lives in the secret U-boat bunker built under the carriage house during WWII expects us.

When we materialize, we remain still for a moment to give any nearby vampires a moment to adjust. I've battled vampires enough to know I *can* match them in a fight, but I also don't want to.

It's better to err on the side of not pissing them off.

"Do ye feel that?" I whisper, my shield warming against my back. Even though my early warning system has saved my bacon more times than I can count, I don't need it to tell me something wicked this way comes.

The hair on the back of my neck tickles, and my skin rises in a rush of goosebumps. Frozen in the shadows, my powers coil within me ready to engage.

Sloan lowers his chin in answer to my question, his gaze narrow as he scans the isolated outbuilding.

Following his lead, I drop the glamor that hides my fae vision and release my goddess-given nocturnal sight. Searching the darkness that surrounds us, I see nothing. No auras of people hiding in the shadows. No heat signatures of people approaching. Nothing.

Maybe the stress of coming events is getting to me.

Paranoid much? "Fiona and Sloan are here," I say, to ensure we won't startle anyone.

Taking out my phone, I text Benjamin we've arrived.

Sloan takes my hand, and we head through the carriage area toward the horse stalls. As we pass, I scan each historic horse stall but get no sense of who or what was setting off my alarm bells.

A squeal of delight breaks the tension, and I wave at my friend as she and her vampire companion climb the staircase hidden in the floor of the last stall. "Yay, you're here. I'm so glad to see you."

I smile at my high school teammate and friend. "Sorry. Are we late?"

"No. I don't think so. I'm just excited. Thank you again for doing this, Fi."

I wave away her gratitude and smile at the vampire closing in. "Hello, Benjamin. How are you?"

He seems a little embarrassed by the question, but my concern is genuine. We recently arrived at the scene of his attempted final death, so yes, I worry.

"I'm doing better, thank you. And thank you as well for all your time."

"It's not a problem, *sham*," Sloan says. "Anything we can do to help. I'm sorry your moments can't be more private."

Me too. When we first started coming over to check on Laurel, Sloan offered his ring to Benjamin so they could have some private time. The ring won't work for him. We're not sure if it's because he's not a druid or because he's a vampire, but for whatever reason, these visits remain a spectator event.

"Has Xavier had any luck with the witches?" I ask.

The last time we were here, Sloan suggested the witches or wizards might have a way—similar to his ring—to help make Laurel visible and audible to him.

Seeing how Garnet and I are not currently popular with High Priestess Drippy Face or Andreas Markdale, we suggested Xavier handle that personally.

Benjamin frowns. "Nothing yet. Xavier says they're still jostling in the politics of it all. He's not sure if they can do it but is being cautious about what it might cost him."

"That's disappointing," I say.

"But reasonable," Laurel adds. "With the Culling so close, it's not the time to mix alliances and make promises that they might use against us in the days to come."

"I get that, but your window of choice is closing. Maybe it's selfish, but I want more for you than to be invisible for the rest of your existence."

Laurel sighs. "Trust me. I'm not a fan either, but the way I see it, I would've aged, died, and been taken away from him as his companion feeder anyway as a mortal. Now, if we can figure out a way to bring me to the foreground, I will be as eternal as he is. We can spend our centuries together like we always dreamed."

"Not like we dreamed." Benjamin frowns and holds Sloan's other hand. "As much as I don't want to lose you, I agree with Fiona. You deserve more than to be a ghost following me around. You deserve happiness too."

"I will be happy," she insists. "Maybe not right away, but in time, maybe months, maybe years, we'll figure out how the magic of Sloan's ring works, and we'll recreate it so we can be together."

I sigh. "Not to be indelicate, but being seen and heard is only part of living in a seethe. What about physical contact and feedings? Vampires are known for voracious appetites. Neither of you can wish that hunger away. That will be hard for you to watch and for him to endure if he knows you're here and less than whole."

Benjamin rubs a hand over his face and growls. I'm not sure if he hadn't thought of that or simply doesn't want to think about it, but it's true. The guy will need to feed and fornicate, which will be awkward with the ghost of his love standing in the corner of the room wishing it was her.

"Nothing needs a decision tonight," Sloan says. "Merlin and I are still working to isolate the enchantment on my ring and Xavier will cut through the politics of the witches and wizards, no doubt."

"No doubt." Benjamin forces a smile.

"We'll figure it out," I say. "Eva is working on it from her angle as well."

Laurel wraps her arms around herself and sighs. "Thanks, Fi. You guys have been great."

"Go, Trojans." I raise my fist and call our team's name.

Laurel raises her hand too. "Go, Trojans."

CHAPTER THREE

We get home around six o'clock, and despite an afternoon with friends, I can't shake the feeling that something is way wrong. Well, maybe not *wrong* so much as off. The surge of growth at the compound, the dark energy I sensed from the vampires...what's next?

If bad things happen in threes, there is a stiletto poised to drop close by, and I don't want to get it through the eye socket.

Even with Myra's assurances that the magic she senses is well within acceptable ranges, I can't get rid of the feeling that the rebalancing of the fae power is building up to bite us in the ass.

Yeah, there goes that paranoia again.

"I want to talk to Merlin and see what he thinks." I take off my boots.

Sloan hangs his jacket in the closet and extends a hand for mine. "I'm not sure why this has you so unsettled, luv. We knew reestablishing the connection to the Source would increase the prana in the ley lines."

"I know, and I was expecting that. This is different. My instincts wouldn't be firing like this if it was only a matter of fae power leveling up. Something's not right."

"Ye've never been an alarmist, so I don't doubt your instincts. Still, I don't know that there's anything to be done to ease your worries. Reestablishing the link between the island and the Source was a tactical decision made by not only us but with the guidance of Fionn and Bodhmall."

I'm fully aware of the tactical decision.

It cost me Emmet.

I swallow, giving Sloan my back, and stride off toward the kitchen before he sees my pain.

It's not like Emmet is dead—I get that—but having him commit to being the guardian of Emhain Abhlach means I don't have him here with me anymore.

Unless there's an empowered network I don't know about, I can't call him or FaceTime him behind the veil of the hidden city. He is truly leading his own life.

I don't want to think about that.

I tromp into the open concept living/dining/kitchen and stop in front of the Christmas tree. I took a few of the family ornaments that meant the most to me last year, but for the most part, our tree is gracefully bare with twinkling white lights and the potential to make our own holiday traditions.

Only…I don't feel much like celebrating.

Sloan's arms come around me, and he sets his chin on the top of my head. "How can I help ye, *a ghra?*"

I turn in his arms and press my cheek against the solid plane of his chest. My eyes are stinging, and I wriggle my nose to keep from crying. "First Brenny, then Da, and now Emmet. Who's going to leave me next? Promise me you're not going anywhere. I don't think I could come back from losing you too."

His arms tighten, and he brushes a kiss against my ear. "Ye won't lose me. Even if the next few weeks don't go our way, and I have to have Eva bind our souls, I'll not leave ye. I promise."

I draw a deep breath and exhale.

I'm about to thank him for that when Dillan jogs down the

stairs with a duffle over his shoulder and Eva smiling behind him. "Hey, little sista, I'm glad you're back. Listen. We were talking to Tad, and since Em and Ciara have moved out, he's got that big house all to himself. He invited us to—"

"No!" I point up the stairs. "No, you can't move across the road. You just got here. Put your stuff back in your room, right now."

The tears I'd been trying to hold back fall freely, and I swallow against the clog in my throat.

Shocked horror spreads across his face.

I swipe my sleeve across my cheeks and rein in the cray-cray. "Sorry. Obviously, you're grown and can do what you want, but I don't want you to go."

"Noted." He still looks a little shell-shocked. "What the hell, Fi? What's going on?"

Sloan squeezes my arm. "I'll start on dinner. Eva, would you care to join me?"

"Of course, although I've only ever mastered toast."

The two of them step away and leave Dillan to handle my breakdown. Now that the tears are falling, I can't get the dam back up to stop them. "I feel like our family is breaking apart and we're losing people one by one. I can't lose you too. Please, stay, D. I need you here...at least until this is all over."

Dillan lets the strap of his duffle slide off his shoulder, and it hits the floor with a heavy *thump*. "Done. I'm here. I'm not going anywhere. I thought you and Irish might like your privacy. You're a couple building a life in your own home and—"

"Well, we don't," I snap, another round of moisture rolling down my cheeks and freefalling from my chin. "You guys have always been my foundation, and right when the world is falling apart, you're disappearing. I can't take it, D. I need you here."

"Then right here is where I'll be."

He opens his arms, and I fall into him. "It's so much. I don't know how to keep it all from crumbling between my fingers most days."

He rubs a strong hand over my back. "You hold on tighter, ask for help, and make it known what you need. And yeah, if you need to lose your shit and pull a *Misery* moment, you do that too. I promise we'll pay attention."

I chuckle at the *Misery* moment comment. "I promise not to hobble you, no matter how much I want you to stay."

"I believe you, but I'm still going to hide the sledgehammers for my peace of mind."

I laugh and hug him again. "Is it stupid that I miss how things were? I understand that the world evolves, people grow up, and lives change, but it seems so final these days. Like I'm losing everyone."

He eases back, and I stare into the depths of his new teal eyes. "I won't lie and say I don't feel it. I do. It hurts, and it sucks, and I know it's not fair to point fingers, but it all started with Brenny."

"Da always said I'm the touchstone of the family, but I don't think that's true. Brendan was our joy, our whimsy, and our soul."

Dillan blinks, and now his eyes are glossing up. "We lost him, and the missing piece seemed to loosen the fit of all the rest of the pieces in our family puzzle."

Yeah, that's exactly how it feels.

Dillan steps back and tugs me toward the couches. "Da dropped the ball, Fi. There's no denying it, and it's not your fault that he's pissed and won't talk to you. That's all on him. I'm happy he's happy with Shannon, but it pisses me off that he up and moved on."

"Except he didn't move on. He only moved away. He's hiding. Wallowing in the loss."

Dillan nods. "I'm not trying to slag the old man or judge how he should deal with his grief, but where I think he failed us is not realizing he didn't stop being the head of our family because

Brendan died. It's like...destiny dealt the father in him a blow, and he packed it in."

"I shouldn't have eased his grief, but I didn't know what to do to help him."

Dillan waves that away. "Nah. Don't beat yourself up over that. Your heart was in exactly the right place. It's in our nature. We see someone suffering, and we try to help. It's the Cumhaill way."

"It is the way," I say in my best *Mandalorian* voice.

"It is the way," Dillan repeats. He leans toward me on the couch and hugs me again. "We'll figure it out, Fi. The family might have been our foundation to get us this far, but we gained a shit-ton of other sources of strength over the past year to patch the cracks."

Magic, incredible friends, powerful loves.

"True story." I draw a deep breath. It wavers a bit in my chest, but it's steadier than ten minutes ago. "Thanks, D. I needed this."

He holds his knuckles up for a bump. "Anytime, day or night. I'm here for you, baby girl."

"Now that my *Misery* moment is over if you and Eva want to move to Tad's, I'll deal. After all, Calum and Aiden are both next door neighbors. I can deal with you being across the road."

Dillan arches a brow and chuffs. "Oh, no. It's too late now. You're stuck with us."

I can't help the grin that spreads across my face. "Good. I'm happy to be stuck with you. If I had my way, we'd build a big castle here in the city, and everyone could live under one roof."

Dillan laughs. "Irish, you better see if Casa Loma is going up on the market. Fi might be growing out of this place."

Sloan chuckles, setting a hot chocolate on the coffee table for me. "If it's a castle she wants to fill with family, I happen to own one already."

"In Ireland." I chuckle too. "It makes the daily commute to work a little outrageous."

"But not impossible." There's a ring of truth in his tone. "Besides, at some point, yer destined to take Lugh's place as a Master Shrine-Keeper of the Druid Order. It seems gauche to have a castle here too."

I laugh, but there's a nugget of truth in that statement. I am Granda's heir, chosen to be the next Master Shrine-Keeper. I gave him my word that if he allowed me time to live with my family and learn my powers, I would assume my place one day.

Once again, my worldview expands.

And not in a good way.

After dinner, Sloan *poofs* us over to the drag club, Queens on Queen and we climb the narrow stairway to the door to Merlin's loft apartment. The first time we came here, the glitz and glam of Merlin's feminine persona, Pan Dora dazzled and amazed.

Now we understand the biggest influence on that fabulousness was Empress Cazzienth, the dragon he's bound with.

I knock on the door and wait.

"Who is it?" Merlin's voice has an odd tone to it, and I look at Sloan to see if he picked up on it too.

He did.

"It's Fi and Sloan."

There's a soft *click* of locks on the other side of the door, and when the door doesn't open, we let ourselves in. I haven't even stepped inside when the stench of some foul torture assaults me.

I hold my breath to keep from inhaling as I rush to open the closest window. *"Gust of Wind."*

Calling a rush of crisp December air into the loft, I raise my hands and create a gentle cyclone to trap the stink. When I can breathe again without gagging, I send it back outside and close the door.

Shivering, I grab a fuzzy zebra print blanket off the back of the couch and wrap it around my shoulders. "Chilly is way better than stinky."

"No argument, *a ghra*," Sloan says. "But that fetor can't be a good sign."

No shit. "Merlin? Where are you?"

"In my lab, but I warn you, it's not pretty."

I chuckle at the frustration in his voice and wonder what could shake the unshakable Merlin?

"Where's his lab?" I ask.

"This way." Sloan leads the way through the loft and into a section of the apartment I've never been to. Knowing the layout of the building, I figure we must be over the soup kitchen now.

The lights are flickering, and the energy snapping in the room makes the hair on my arms stand on end. Whatever happened here had a lot of oomph. We come into the open space and check out the round table in the center of the room.

It's a massive, wooden antique with an ornate English rose carving in the center and looks like it could fit a dozen people around it, maybe twice that. I step closer and run my fingers over the worn paint at the edge. There is a definite pattern to the old script, and I wonder if they indicate a place setting.

Leaning over, I try to make it out. L.A.N.C—

I straighten and blink at Sloan. "No way. Is this the Round Table of King Arthur's court? Like, *The* Round Table with a capital T?"

Sloan grins. "Aye, I believe so. I asked him about it once, but he didn't seem inclined to discuss it."

"You knew? You knew the Round Table was in my city and you didn't tell me?"

He laughs. "I didn't know ye cared. Ye've never taken much interest in my passion fer antiques. I didn't realize ye'd find it so incredible."

"Well, I do. How cool is this?"

"Very cool. Now, back to the point of our visit. Where's Merlin?"

"Right here," he says, close by.

Sloan and I glance around. I see shelves crowded with ancient books and labeled containers of all shapes and sizes, some antlers, bones, a dozen bundles of dried herbs and plants hanging on the walls, feathers from a bunch of different birds, but no Merlin.

"I take it ye've had a bit of a foul-up with tryin' to make Laurel visible," Sloan says.

"Foul-up is one way to put it," Merlin agrees. "Thoroughly cocked-up is another. On the other hand, if either of you wants to know how to make yourself invisible, I think I've mastered that."

I bite my bottom lip to keep from laughing and search the air where Merlin's voice is coming from. "I'm so sorry. How can we help?"

He lets out a long grumble and sighs. "It should wear off in a day or two. Potions are different than spells. With potions, it comes down to the accuracy of details and ingredients. With spells, it's more about harnessing intent. Without knowing exactly what we need to make a ghost visible, there's bound to be some trial and error."

It's unnerving to know Merlin is standing five feet away and I can't see him. Him saying the effect of the experiment gone wrong *should* wear off doesn't make me feel better.

"Well, sometimes learning what ye need to do is aided by learnin' what not to do," Sloan offers.

"Right you are, Mackenzie." I try to highlight the positive. "Now if we can't help you fix this, maybe you could help me understand what's happening in the world of magic. Things are happening, and I have a bad feeling I might have a cock-up to deal with too."

CHAPTER FOUR

"Right this way, boys." I release the security protocols on the doors to the Batcave the next afternoon and usher in my elves. Calum, Kevin, and Nikon each have their arms full and are carrying in my holiday cheer. "On the table is fine. I'll take it from there."

Following my instruction, they carry the boxes to the long conference table in the center of the room and set them down.

"What have we here?" Andromeda comes out of her office to greet us. She leans close to her brother and peers into the box he was carrying. "Oh, nice."

I nod. "I've been in a bit of a funk and figured that since the world is going to hell over the holidays—"

"—not if we can help it," Calum says.

I grin, catching his meaning. "Right, no, not going to hell—Light shall prevail—but since there will be holiday interruptus with all the Culling chaos, I'm moving up the seasonal celebration so we can enjoy our family and friends time without missing out."

"Excellent idea." Andy pulls out an evergreen wreath. "It will be different for you guys this year without Emmet home."

I draw a deep breath and check that all my crumbling on that topic is locked down. Thankfully, it is. "Yeah. This year we'll be missing Emmet, Brenny, and likely Da. It seems there's no holding back the change of time no matter how much I want to."

Andy squeezes my shoulder. "As someone who's seen more change of time than most, I feel for you, Fi. It's hard. The thing to remember is that you shouldn't mourn all change. Sometimes new traditions, new challenges, and new friends bring a rush of happiness you never expected."

I hear the subtext in her voice and appreciate the sentiment.

"Well said, sister mine," Nikon says. "Our mother always said that with lives as long as ours, we needed to release the loss of individual moments and focus on the blessings of ages to measure our happiness."

It's not easy, but it's worth a shot.

"I absolutely count my blessings, but I'm afraid for what's to come. We're less than two weeks from the Culling. Ready or not...here it comes."

"How's the request to get an audience with the goddess?" Andy asks.

"Sloan isn't convinced Sarah is giving it her all and his father needed him for something at Stonecrest anyway, so he *poofed* home this morning and will state our case in person."

"Do you think Sarah would stall you on purpose? You said she's a white witch, didn't you?"

"She is, but dark witches killed her coven because of us, and there was a messy breakup between her and Emmet. We're not sure where the stopping block is."

"Then an in-person approach is best." Andromeda looks into the box in front of her. "Holly. Mistletoe. Fir. Did you bring any olive branches?"

"In my box." Calum opens the flaps of the box he set on the table. "Nikon insists we needed them to hang on the entrances."

"Absolutely." She frees several two-foot branches from the

box and holds them in front of herself to inspect. They're covered in long waxy leaves, are hanging with green olives, and smell freshly cut. "Mmm, did you pop off home to get these from the vineyard?"

Nikon holds up his palms and grins. "I know better than to half-ass a tribute."

She grins, looking thoroughly pleased. "To our people and us, olive branches are a strong symbol of peace. As Nikon said, there's no sense half-assing it when calling for good fortune."

I guess not. "You believe in them?"

"Do you know Virgil's *Aeneid*?" Andromeda asks.

"Nope, can't say that I do."

She takes the branch over to the door and hangs it on the metal clip at the top of the frame.

> *"Resolve me, strangers, whence, and what you are;*
> *Your business here; and bring you peace or war?*
> *High on the stern Aeneas his stand,*
> *And held a branch of olive in his hand,*
> *While thus he spoke: The Phrygians' arms you see,*
> *Expelled from Troy, provoked in Italy*
> *By Latian foes, with war unjustly made;*
> *At first affianced, and at last betrayed.*
> *This message bear: The Trojans and their chief*
> *Bring holy peace, and beg the king's relief."*

I clap at the end of her oration. "Very poetic. Let's hope hanging that here brings us holy peace in the weeks to come and long after."

"Leave nothing to hope or chance, Red. We'll make sure of it." Nikon takes the other olive branch and hangs it on the door that leads into the back where the holding cells are.

Kevin and Calum pull out a long garland to string one over the tops of the monitors on the monitor wall, while Nikon hangs three more over doorframes leading into Garnet's, Maxwell's, and Andromeda's offices.

"Much cheerier." I grin at the festive improvement, trying not to dwell on how much Emmet would've enjoyed this. My heart is still aching in his absence. It's only been a couple of weeks. There's still time for my world to right itself.

Maybe then the pressure on my chest will ease.

For now…it's fake it 'til you make it.

I spot the red Santa hats and pull one on. "Merry ho-ho, one and all."

Andromeda chuckles. "Druids have Yule traditions, not Saint Nick."

I unpack a couple of poinsettias and set them on the table. "Yes, but I've been a druid for one year and a believer in Santa for twenty-three before that."

Calum snorts. "Really? You believed in Big Red until last year? That has to be a record."

I stick my tongue out at him, but it feels good to tease and be teased. "How about I believed in the spirit of Big Red and his holiday of giving?"

Andromeda holds a sprig of fir up to her nose and inhales deeply. "Fair enough. Traditions are so mashed together now there's no saying any given holiday belongs to one group or another. All that matters is the eat, drink, and be merry aspect."

There's a *snap* of energy in the air, and my favorite Greek god appears in the middle of the room. "Did someone chant my mantra?"

I chuckle. "Were you eavesdropping, Tarzan?"

Dionysus glances around at the greenery, and his eyes glass up. He presses a flat hand to his chest and gives me a look that melts my heart. "You remembered. Thank you, Jane."

He rushes over to hug me. The decorations so genuinely touch him that I'm not sure how to ask what he's talking about.

In ancient times, December was when the Greeks celebrated the birth of Dionysus, Nikon says directly into my mind. *Our boy here was known as our divine infant. When we were kids, Papu used to take us to Dionysus' temple with garlands and small trees as an offering. It's not a tradition in practice anymore.*

It seems he misses it, Calum says, also on the private wavelength. That's a bonus from Fionn's crown, which I now wear more often than not given everything going on.

It seems so, I add.

Not wanting to burst his bubble, I gesture at the garlands and the olive branches. "What would make your offering more special, Tarzan? How would you like us to celebrate you?"

"Need you ask?" He grins, fanning his hand over the table as a feast of food and wine appears—a platter of turkey, a glazed salmon, a roasted pig. The air suddenly fills with succulent scents and my stomach growls.

Nikon chuckles and rounds the end of the table. "Allow me to open things up to breathe so we can get started on our celebration."

The simple joy on Dionysus's face is addictive.

"Happiest of holidays, Tarzan. We are so honored to have you as one of Clan Cumhaill. We heart you hard." I form a heart with my fingers and hold it against my chest.

"Yeah. Mad love, my man." Calum holds his fist up for a bump.

"Glad to know you and lucky to call you friend," Kevin adds.

I accept the glass of red wine Nikon hands me and sip. It's fruity and full-bodied and goes down *waaay* too easily. I check the time on my Fitbit and chuckle. "This wine is too good for three o'clock."

"Day drinking!" Kevin raises his glass.

"Day drinking!" Dionysus, Calum, and Nikon echo.

I meet Andromeda's gaze and shake my head. "I'm in trouble. Sloan's not in town to rope me in and adult me."

Andy barks a laugh and sips from her glass. "Oh, my, then yes, you are in trouble. This is much too tasty for our good."

I swallow again and set my glass down to visit the buffet. "If this is Dionysus Day, I need to lay down a solid base and eat something."

Calum laughs. "On that note, Kev and I are off. His parents are expecting us for dinner, and if we stay much longer, we won't have the willpower to leave."

Dionysus frowns. "Will you come over later tonight? I'll make a party."

I chuckle to myself and fill a plate. *Make* a party. Dionysus needs only to say the words and the party people will come. "Can we keep the invitees to a shortlist of actual family and friends?"

Dionysus holds up his fingers in the Boy Scout's salute. "On my honor."

I snort. "Well, that makes me feel much better."

"Sounds great." Calum grabs their coats from where they flung them over the back of a chair. "We'll let Dillan and Eva know. Fi, will you be there?"

I nod. "Only if someone promises to take me home when things get wild and unruly. Sloan's not here tonight, and I know how I get."

Calum and Kevin grin and I can only imagine what moments of my highlight reel they're revisiting.

Nikon holds up his wine glass and winks. "I will escort you home and ensure you make it to King Henry with your reputation and virtue intact. Don't you worry about that."

"Excellent. Then it's a solid yes from me." I stack a wad of juicy meat and several types of cheese onto a flaky croissant. "I might need to run my truck home first. I wasn't expecting a drinking day, and I have stuff to do tomorrow morning. Honestly, maybe I shouldn't. I never know when something's going to happen, and I might need to get somewhere fast and be official."

Calum snags a plate of sliders and grabs some napkins to go. "If Nikon can chauffeur you for the day and is getting you home tonight, Kev and I can take the Hellcat to the in-laws and drive it home."

I turn to check with the Greek.

"It's all set." Nikon grins at me. "Consider me your sidekick today, Red. Let's see what mischief we can manage."

Nikon and I finish sprucing up the Batcave and snap upstairs to Dionysus' loft to have a couple more glasses of wine with him. Andy has work to finish but will join us for the party later. She hasn't seen Evangeline in a while and wants to catch up with her.

I sometimes forget that she was the one who brought Eva to Dionysus' housewarming party the night she and Dillan met and got together.

I love when the universe works out like that.

The three of us have a fun couple of hours playing in the VR room, and I'm riding the crest of a nice wine wave when my phone goes off, and the *Lion King* theme song brings reality crashing back.

Jogging over to the coatrack inside the new foyer room Dionysus invented for me, I grab my cell and swipe green. "Hey, boss man. How are things in the land of sand? Anything new since yesterday?"

"That's why I'm calling. I'm trying to track down Nikon. Andromeda said you're spending the day with him."

"True story. He's here with me now. Do you need to speak to him?"

"Both of you, if the two of you are available. We're having a Greek issue I'd like to get an opinion on and need you to come to me."

Garnet's voice sounds funny. It's not anger exactly, but he's certainly not happy.

"Are we in trouble?" I eye up Nikon while racking my fuzzy brain.

"Should you be?"

Okay, that's a loaded question...and one I'm not sure I want to answer while altered by quality red wine. "We'll be right there."

I hang up and pull my coat off the hook. "Okay, duty calls. Garnet requires the presence of the Mischief Marauders."

"Are we in trouble?" Nikon has the same look of contemplative confusion on his face that I do.

"I don't think so, but with Garnet, there's no telling. His exact words were, we're having a Greek issue, and he needs an opinion."

"Why'd he call you?"

I shrug. "He called Andy first, and she directed him to me."

Nikon upends his glass, hops off the couch, and pulls his phone out of his pocket. "My phone's dead."

"Mystery solved. Are we good?"

"Yep, give me two seconds."

While he jogs off toward the loo, Dionysus snaps his fingers and has his boots and coat on.

"Are you coming?"

"Garnet said it was a Greek issue, right? Well, I'm Greek too. Can't I come?"

"You absolutely can. I only meant that you were getting ready to have a party."

He checks his watch and shrugs. "Just text on the family chat line that Garnet called us to duty. Everything is set up. They can start without us."

"I'm quite sure no party is the same without you."

He grins. "That goes without saying, but it doesn't matter. I'm part of the Team Trouble family and Garnet's pride. It's my duty to respond when called. Besides, I have gifts for Myra, Imari, and Garnet."

"That's very thoughtful of you."

He scratches the back of his head and shrugs. "This is my first Yule with a real family, and I wanted to do it right. Don't worry. I have gifts for you too."

I drag a deep breath in and sigh. "I'm sorry the Culling and all that craziness will overshadow your first Cumhaill Christmas. We'll do it up right next year, I promise."

Dionysus glances toward his dining room and raises his palms. A moment later, he's holding three fabric-wrapped boxes with gold rope ties.

Aww…he even wrapped them.

Nikon is back, and I hand him his leather jacket. Once he pulls himself together, I lace our fingers and give them a Tabitha nose wiggle. "To Garnet's house, Greeks. There's an issue that needs your attention."

CHAPTER FIVE

The three of us arrive at Garnet's African compound, and the peeling of clothing begins the moment we materialize. If it weren't for the driveway through the archway part of the journey, I wouldn't bother with a coat, but since I must brave the elements, I'm not willing to snap here in shorts and a tank top.

I shed my layers, and Dionysus chuckles as he holds out his hand to take my jacket and scarf, then my hoodie, and the flannel button-up I'm wearing over a white muscle shirt.

"So, this is the key, is it?" he asks.

I read the amusement swirling in his eyes and shrug. "The key to what?"

"The key to getting you undressed. I've been flirty, sexy, and naughty and gotten nowhere. Apparently, all I need to do is ply you with wine, portal you to the grasslands of Africa, and you'll do the honors."

I chuckle and glance down at my undershirt and yoga pants. "Sadly for you, this is the extent of the clothing removal. Even for all the heat in Africa, I'm not getting down to the naughty bits."

Dionysus shrugs. "Maybe I need to turn up the sun and test that theory."

When he glances up at the amber ball of fire in the sky, a fleeting moment of panic strikes.

He can't affect the sun, can he?

"Garnet, we're here," I call, searching the grounds with a sweeping gaze.

"Good." Garnet ducks out from under the shade of the portico. His stride is swift and deliberate as he navigates the path.

His footing slows as he sees Dionysus.

He arches a brow at me, and I know what he's thinking, but I couldn't exclude him. He's so excited about being part of the team.

"We were with Dionysus when you called and thought one Greek is good, but two is even better." I point at the chair on the other side of the railing, and Dionysus drops my clothes off. "So, what's the issue that needs consideration?"

He hooks his finger in the air for us to follow and strikes off toward the side of the house. "Myra told me the two of you were discussing how the increased fae power might be altering things here."

"Yeah. You guys might not realize it, but the grass is greener, the oasis is lusher, and there's something different about the air. I can't quite put my finger on what it is, but it's noticeable."

He draws a deep breath and points into the corral for Contessa McSparkles. "Could your change have caused this?"

I scan the interior of the pen and don't follow. The only thing I see is Imari's unicorn.

Contessa McSparkles' coat is mauve, pink, and white and swirls in pastel whorls. When she moves, the golden light of the savanna makes her coat glimmer and glisten with sparkles—thus her name. Also, of course, there's the two-foot horn sticking out of her forehead.

"Caused what?"

He flashes me a smartass grin. "Contessa, Fi stopped by with that friend I told you about."

I'm about to comment on Garnet having conversations with unicorns when Contessa turns her head and trots over. *"Geia sou file mou."*

I blink and look from Garnet to the unicorn to the Greeks. "I didn't know Contessa McSparkles can talk."

"Not only that, but she also speaks Greek." Nikon gestures at the latch on the gate. "May we go in?"

Garnet nods. "Please, that's why you're here. It's not every day a unicorn starts speaking in ancient tongues."

I laugh. "It's not every day you hear someone say something like that."

"That's because she's not a unicorn," Dionysus says, following Nikon.

I snort and point. Sticking two feet out of the front of her forehead is a horn that corkscrews in a smooth swirl like a never-ending soft-serve ice cream cone.

"Maybe you missed the very tall, pointy, swirly lance on the front of her head."

He grins and shakes his head. "No, but I'm pretty sure you missed the ten-foot iridescent purple wings she's about to stretch open."

I glance back and study the barrel bulge of her sides. They don't look any different than any other time we've come to visit. They are sparkly, swirly, pink, white, and mauve but no wings.

"How much wine did you drink, *adelphos*?" Nikon arches a brow.

I laugh at the absurdity of that. No. Wine wouldn't do it. "Were you experimenting with happy pills again?"

Dionysus grips one hand into Contessa's mane and swings his leg up to mount her in a move more controlled and graceful than I imagined possible. Sitting atop her back, he leans forward, straight-backed, and hugs her muscular neck.

He says something in Greek. Then she lifts her chin to the sky and a wave of magical energy pulses out from them. A moment later, she is, indeed, unfolding and stretching out powerful feathered wings on either side of her body.

"Huh...would you look at that?" My mouth is hanging open, but there's no helping it.

Contessa whinnies and the two of them take to the sky.

"What exactly did he say to her?" I ask.

Nikon blinks up at them looking almost as shocked as Garnet and me. "Nothing, really. He said, 'go ahead and show them, beautiful.'"

I raise my hand to shelter my eyes from the brilliance of the day as I try to make sense of it. "Do you think this is why she hasn't been feeling well?"

Garnet offers me a blank look. "Am I my daughter's unicorn keeper?"

"Sort of, yeah."

"Well then, I have no idea. If you don't mind, I'd like to blame you."

I laugh. "*Me?* Blame me for what?"

"For making her unicorn sick and turning her into a pegasus."

"I think it's awesome. Sure, blame me."

"It won't be awesome if this means the end of the Imari and her dancing unicorn love affair. If this changes things between them, she'll be heartbroken."

"So, why blame me?"

"Imari loves you. If I explain to her Contessa is a magical creature, and you and your family helped her find her wings, she might like that and be less sad."

"Scapegoating me is the cowardly lion approach."

He ignores me, scowling at the sparkling unicorn dipping and diving through the blue, cloudless sky above. "What do you think this means going forward?"

"Imari's horseback riding lessons just got much more complicated?"

He chuffs. "I meant on a more global scale. Contessa

McSparkles can't be the only creature altered by the change in energy."

"Maybe we'll have a resurgence of a pegasus population as we have with dragons?" I think about that and groan. "Damn, it'll be impossible to keep the worlds of the fae a secret if I keep making giant flying mythicals."

"True story," Nikon says. "No matter how much Imari loves Contessa, if she's sentient and mythical, she can't be kept penned up in a backyard if that's not where she wants to be."

I sigh. "No. I don't suppose she can."

"So, what the hell do I do about it?" Garnet snaps.

"How about we wait until she lands, and we can talk to her before we let our pessimism run wild. If she's sentient, odds are she can tell us what she wants."

Garnet sighs, his amethyst gaze pivoting as he scans the sky. "Okay, where the hell did they go?"

After an hour of us sipping pink lemonade icy under the portico, Nikon and I give up waiting for Dionysus to return. My stomach is growling, and although Garnet and Myra are offering to make dinner, we have all that food back at the loft and people coming, so we take our leave.

When we get back to Dionysus's place, Dillan, Kevin, and Calum are already there.

"Welcome to Dionysus's party," Calum says, holding up a full plate of food. "Where is our host?"

I take off my coat, and Nikon collects it to hang on the rack. "Funny story. You know how we altered the world's fae prana?"

"Yeah?" Calum's brow pinches.

"Why do I get the feeling we're going to hate this story?" Dillan asks.

"Life experience."

"Yeah, that's it."

I chuckle and head over to the feast table. "You're not wrong. We came from Garnet's compound where Contessa McSparkles sprouted a twenty-foot purple wingspan and flew off with Dionysus riding bareback."

Dillan scowls, and I follow his train of thought.

"Ew, don't go there. No. He climbed onto her back with no saddle, grabbed her mane, and they flew off into the sun."

"I thought she was a unicorn," Kevin says.

"So did we all, but either we were wrong, or she leveled up once we brought the island back online."

Dillan joins me at the food table, and instead of making plates, we pick up veggies and dip them. "Do you think it's an isolated event or is the surge of power to the ley lines going to start mutating our normal world?"

I crunch an orange pepper. "No idea, but knowing my penchant for magical mayhem, I'd guess this is only the kickoff to another rollicking adventure."

They all get a laugh out of that.

Nikon pours me a glass of the wine we were enjoying this afternoon, and I take a mental inventory of my buzz. I was feeling good heading over to Garnet's, but Myra's special concoction has tipped me closer to drunk than tipsy.

I accept the glass but slow my roll until the spinny-swimmy settles a bit. When the world is going wonky, there's no telling what I'll need to be ready for.

As if the Fates are mocking me, there's a melodic whinny, and the building's sidewall begins to morph.

"What the actual fuck?" Calum shouts, rounding the table to stand next to me. "Are we under attack?"

Nikon freezes with a meat skewer in his mouth and his eyes wide.

"Not an attack," I say, almost certain of it. "My shield isn't flaring, and I sense Dionysus' magical signature. I think this is him making some sort of grand entrance."

Calum snorts. "Grand entrance. I see what you did there, Fi. Good one."

I wasn't referring to the construction in progress, but yeah, that works too.

"Why does he have to transform the side of my building?" Nikon asks.

The wall reforms. He's taken the foyer area he made for me and turned it into an outdoor balcony entrance with a huge barn door.

"Hello, family." Dionysus clops in on the back of Imari's unicorn. His long brown curls are windblown, but it only adds to his charm. "See, Contessa, I told you they'd be here waiting to welcome you."

"Holy wings." Calum stares. "How did you miss those?"

Dionysus frowns, swinging his foot back and dropping to the floor as he dismounts. "Calum...the lady is a little self-conscious about the wings. Let's not stare."

"Uh...sorry." Calum meets Kevin and Nikon's wide gazes and chuckles. "I was stunned."

"Did you enjoy your flight?" I'm not sure where to take this convo.

"Absolutely. It's been millennia since I've ridden the skies on a pegasus." Dionysus gestures toward the table. "See, we have food, milady. What would you like?"

Contessa says something in Greek and Dionysus answers.

Nikon jogs toward the den. "I can do that."

"Do what?" I ask.

Dionysus grins. "Contessa is thirsty. She would like a large bowl of something fruity."

Contessa speaks again.

He nods. "Preferably mango-flavored."

"Here you go." Nikon returns with a *Finding Nemo* children's pool Dionysus uses for Jell-O wrestling. He sets it down on the floor, Dionysus points at it, and it fills with a pale peachy-orange juice.

Contessa McSparkles clops forward and drops her nose to the surface of her refreshment. She drinks a bit and lifts her head, licking her lips.

"Do you like it?" Dionysus asks. Whatever her response is, Nikon looks surprised, and Dionysus bursts out laughing. "A lady after my own heart. Of course, we can."

"Can what?" I'm thoroughly dazzled.

"Can make things a little more interesting." Dionysus produces a bottle of Grand Marnier and another of tequila. He pours them in and when they're empty, stirs with the necks of the bottles.

Then he holds his hand toward the bar to call a large bottle of lime juice. He finishes his bartending duties and gestures for her to take another drink.

Contessa dips her velvety nose into the pool a second time and lifts her head, shaking her mane, then stomps her hoof a couple of times.

"I take it she likes it," I say.

Dionysus laughs and scrubs her forelock. "She does. Mango margaritas all around."

My phone rings and saves me from yet another dive into another drink. Man. Drunk Fi doesn't have a chance of slowing down with the Fates today.

I jog over toward the massive new door and find my coat on a hook mounted to the inside of the balcony wall. My fingers aren't listening to me, and I fumble while trying to retrieve my cell. When the call drops, my phone goes silent.

With the pressure off, I take my time.

A *ping* follows as someone posts to one of the WhatsApp chatrooms.

I figure out I'm searching in the wrong pocket as my brothers curse behind me. For the sake of expedience, I turn to them. "What's going on?"

By the look on their faces, it's not good.

Calum speaks up. "It's Aiden. Jackson's missing."

CHAPTER SIX

The six of us snap to my family home and are standing in the front hall less than a minute later. Calum and Kevin run upstairs as Nikon, Dionysus, and I start searching for answers on the main floor.

There's no sign of Aiden or Kinu in the living room or the kitchen. I'm about to run downstairs when Aiden bursts through the door from the backyard. Other than the red patches on his cheeks from running outside in the cold, he's white as a sheet. "He's not in the grove."

My skin tingles. "Are you sure? It's huge, and with the new dragon lair there are tons of places for him to hide."

He shakes his head. "I don't think so. I mean...I looked but... why the fuck would he get out of bed and go out there? He was so excited to have Bizzy here for a sleepover."

I glance around the back entrance and frown at Jackson's cubby and hook. "His coat and boots are here. I doubt he'd go outside in his socks in December."

"I'll go grab my cloak and take another look." Dillan rushes past us to run into the backyard.

"Has he ever sleepwalked?" Nikon asks.

Aiden shakes his head. "No. Never. He's a sound sleeper. If anything, we have a hard time getting him up and awake in the morning."

It's true. Jackson is a champion sleeper.

Calum and Kev jog downstairs. "Aiden, you need to be with Kinu. She needs you. We've got this. If you think of anything, call us."

Aiden doesn't budge. He's a protector and a father. It's obvious by looking at him that handing over the reins to find his missing child doesn't sit well.

"Calum's right." I back him up. "Kinu needs your support, at least right now. Go calm her down and reassure her. You know we won't stop until we've figured this out. We'll find him."

He exhales with a curse and runs rough fingers through his hair. "Fine. I'll stick close to Kinu, but I need updates. A lot of them."

I pull out my phone and check to see if Dad or Emmet has chimed in on Aiden's post. I see the missed call from earlier and don't recognize the number. "Aiden? Was it you who called me?"

Aiden frowns. "When?"

"When you texted the family channel. You didn't phone me right before?"

"No. I hit you all up at once."

I ponder that with twisting insides while Calum hugs our older brother and pats his back. "Try not to panic. The little monkey is probably safe and sound and tucked away somewhere we haven't thought of yet."

"From your lips." Aiden heads upstairs.

When the creaks and groans of the century-old wooden floorboards place Aiden in the master bedroom above, I explore my thoughts. "Nikon, see if Merlin is in town this weekend and if he'll scry for us. If not, I'll do it, but he's much better at it than me."

"On it." Nikon strides off toward the front room, pulling out his phone.

"Bruin, I need you to start in Jackson's room and see if you can track a scent leading anywhere. If not, search the forest."

"I don't think he'd leave the property and wander off," Kevin says.

"Neither do I, but we need to consider all possibilities. Maybe he woke up confused. Maybe he forgot his favorite stick in the forest during a walk. With a five-year-old, we can't be sure."

Bruin leaves me in a powerful rush, and I move to the next thought.

"What can I do?" Dionysus asks.

I scrub my fingers over my face trying to think through the alcohol haze. Damn it. I knew I needed to slow my roll. "I don't have a job for you yet other than being here as my transporter the moment we figure out where he is. Then you can help us rescue him."

"Rescue?" Kevin asks, eyes wide. "Don't you mean find him?"

"I don't think so, no."

"What aren't you saying, Fi?"

I sigh, not wanting to go there. "Jackson is a good sleeper. It's only ten o'clock. There's no way Kinu and Aiden would miss him walking downstairs and out the door. We've all lived here and know every creak this house makes."

The back door opens, and Dillan comes in looking winded and defeated. He reaches up and pulls the hood of his enchanted cloak off. "Nothing. There's no sign of him. Dart and Saxa haven't seen him and the fae friends in the forest haven't either."

"Sadly, I'm not surprised." My worst fears grow stronger. I step in closer and lower my voice. "Someone had to have portaled in and taken him."

The horror shared in the gazes around the room echoes everything reeling within me.

"What about the warding?" Dillan hisses. "Our property is

damned secure. With our spells and Merlin's reinforcements and Dart and Saxa's dragon magic sealing the deal, nobody should be able to get in here and get to the kids."

I shrug. "Jordan got into the backyard yesterday. The warding didn't stop him."

"The spellwork specifically blocks people with ill-intent. He wasn't looking to cause trouble. He wanted to make out with you."

I roll my eyes. "Okay, then, maybe whoever got in here doesn't consider taking Jackson an act against us. I don't know. No system is perfect. We've learned time and again that nothing is for sure. Look at Dionysus's god powers when Loki messed with him. My impenetrable armor has been breached twice by beings more powerful than me."

"Who would want to take Jackson?" Calum asks. "He's only a little boy."

"I know, but anyone who knows how we operate knows our family ties are both our greatest strength and our greatest weakness."

"You think this is about an enemy gaining a foothold for the Culling?" Dillan's face is twisted up like he's tasting sour milk. "That's disgusting."

"I look forward to being proven wrong, but I don't know what else it would be."

I check my phone again and realize why Da and Emmet aren't responding. It's three a.m. in Ireland.

Nikon snaps back with a bag in his hands, and at first, I'm not sure if Merlin is with us or not.

"Still invisible?" I glance around.

"Still invisible," Merlin repeats, "but that shouldn't affect my powers. I'm only visibility challenged. Otherwise, all systems are functioning."

I breathe a sigh of relief. "Thank you for coming."

"For you, cookie, always." My arm squeezes under the gentle

grip of our invisible wizard and druid mentor. "Where can I set up?"

"Let's use the kitchen table." I gesture at the room on my left and lead the way. Calum and Kev hurry around me and clear things off.

Nikon places the bag on the chair at the end of the table, and it's like we're living in a B-movie when the zipper opens, and the altar cloth, Tarot cards, and pendulum unpack themselves and float through the open air to settle on the table.

"That's freaky as fuck," Dillan says.

"Sorry boys and girls," Merlin replies. "If you want me, you gotta take what you get."

"We want you," Dillan says. "Freaky or not, you're the bomb."

"Fi. I need something that will carry Jackson's energy in large quantity."

I glance around and grab Spiderman, Thor, and Optimus Prime. "Here, try a few of his action figures."

Each plastic toy lifts into the air and settles back on the table. "Yes, they'll do fine."

I take a step back, and Nikon is there with a comforting smile. He opens his arms, and I accept the hug.

"He's only a little boy," I say.

"I know, Red." He rubs a hand over my back, and I suck in his strength. "Listen. If we can take on the worst of the worst and come out on top, we can find Jackson."

He eases back from the hug and pegs me with a look so filled with confidence that it steadies my panic.

"Thanks."

"Anytime. The point is not to think the worst. Maybe there's a simple answer that doesn't involve dark and dastardly intentions."

"I hope so."

My phone rings and I pull it out and sigh. "Hey, hotness. I guess you got the message?"

"I woke with a bad feelin' and checked my phone. Have ye found him?"

"Not yet, but Merlin's here, and he's about to scry for his location. Hold on. I'll put you on speaker." I hit the button to include Sloan in the night's drama and set the phone on the table.

Dillan and Calum light the ivory pillar candles Merlin brought and distribute them around the kitchen. Kevin unfolds the map of Toronto, presses out the creases, and shifts it across the table.

Merlin adjusts the map on the black satin altar cloth and spells it to straighten perfectly flat. Then he holds each of the three action figures again and settles on Thor. "Everyone focus on Jackson and where he is."

I do. *Where are you, buddy? Help us find you.*

All eyes lock on the gentle sway of the crystal pendant suspended in the open air. Dangling over the map, it moves in a lazy swing over the paper but isn't indicating anything.

Merlin utters a throaty grumble, and I've worked with Dora and Merlin enough to know their sound of frustration. Whatever energy he's getting back from his scrying, he's not happy about it.

"Goddess of the moon and sun,
Our child is lost, our hearts undone.
The circumstances yet unknown,
We ask the location to be shown.
So mote it be."

"So mote it be," we all repeat the refrain.

For the next few minutes, we're all focused on the gentle sway of that pendulum, waiting for something to happen—hoping for anything to happen.

"It's not working," Kevin says. "Not like when you found Emmet."

Merlin exhales heavily. "That's because he's not here to find."

"What does that mean?" Dillan snaps, horror clouding his

bright teal eyes. "Are you saying?" His voice cracks. "Do you think he's…"

"I think he's not in Toronto. That's all." The map lifts off the altar cloth and refolds along the creases. "Where is that large atlas we used for Emmet? I want to start with a global scope and work backward to country and town."

My mind trips on that one. "Global? You think he's been taken out of the country?"

Merlin sets his pendulum crystal down on the table. "Let's just see what the magic says, girlfriend. No need to borrow trouble."

"Fi, take me off speaker, luv," Sloan says.

I jump, hearing Sloan's voice, and shake myself. After making the call private, I press the phone to my ear. "Hey, Mackenzie. Sorry, I forgot you were on the phone."

"That's all right, *a ghra*. I wish I was there with ye. Once Merlin is finished scryin' with the atlas, maybe ask one of the Greeks to come get me. I hate ye facin' this alone. I know ye've been feelin' abandoned lately."

Calum is back with the atlas from our basement man cave, and we're ready to try again.

I meet the hopeful gazes of Nikon, Dionysus, Kevin, Calum, and Dillan. Merlin takes the large book from Kev, flops open the cover, and starts flipping the oversized pages to find a world map to work with.

The air around me swirls, and I feel Bruin's presence, welcoming him to bond with me. *Sorry, Red. There's no sign of him. No scent to follow—his or anyone else's. It's like he simply vanished.*

Thanks for trying, buddy. Hopefully, Merlin will have better luck with the scrying.

Nikon comes over and laces his fingers with mine. "Was that Bruin who blew in here?"

"Yeah. He found no trace."

He bumps my shoulder with his and smiles. "The scrying is going to work, Red. I know it."

I draw a deep breath and circle back to Sloan's comment. "It's okay, hotness. I'm not alone. I've got my support system here, and you're here too. Besides, it's silly to be worrying about me when it's Jackson, Aiden, and Kinu this is really happening to."

As if drawn by my words, the floorboards above our heads creak, then the stairs flex with the weight of someone coming down to join us.

It's both of them.

I wave for Aiden to bring Kinu through so she can see what Merlin's doing.

When they arrive, I hug Kinu and try to offer her an optimistic smile. "Good timing. Merlin's about to search for Jackson's energy signature using the atlas. If he can get a lock on him, Nikon and Dionysus will portal us straight there, and we can put an end to this."

"Merlin?" she asks.

I glance at the open space between the boys and the pendulum hanging in the air. "Yeah, that's another thing altogether. Merlin's invisible at the moment after helping us with the Laurel problem."

Kinu doesn't seem to care, and I don't blame her. "Do you think he'll be able to find him?"

"He found Emmet in the South Pacific, and when we worked with the white witches of Blarney, we found the dark witches in Limerick." I leave out the part about how they backchanneled our scrying and blew us up.

Why add to the stress of the moment?

"Okay, quiet folks," Merlin says.

We all fall silent to let him focus and do his work.

"Goddess of the moon and sun,
Our child is lost, our hearts undone.
The circumstances yet unknown,
We ask the location to be shown.
So mote it be."

"So mote it be," we repeat for the second time.

This time, the energy of Merlin's spell takes hold almost immediately, and the easy sway of the pendulum pulls with angled deliberation. The tip of the crystal points toward the upper right corner of the glossy page.

I adjust my stance as the crystal gets the opportunity to seek out its target. When it stops, it's hovering quite obviously over—"Ireland."

Calum points at the map. "Not just anywhere in Ireland. That's the countryside of Kerry. Could he be at Gran's and Granda's?"

"How?" Aiden asks.

A frisson of energy rushes through me, and the hair on my body stands on end. "First we find him. Then we'll figure it out. Kev and Calum, can you stay and watch the other kids?"

Calum nods. "Yeah, just go."

I press my phone against my ear and dash to the back hall. "Give us a minute to grab our coats and boots, and we're coming your way, hotness."

"I'll meet ye there, luv."

I hang up and pocket my phone. There's a mad scramble for everyone to get ready to leave at the back door. I tuck Jackson's coat and boots into a shopping bag in case he needs them and take Kinu's hand.

Then, I reach out to Dionysus with my other hand. "You're up, Tarzan. Let's go find our missing monkey."

CHAPTER SEVEN

We arrive on the back lawn of the druid shire a moment later and fan out.

"I'll check Gran's place." Dillan jogs toward the sleepy stone cottage with thatched hats for roofs. Under the silver light of a four a.m. moon, it looks even more like we've been transported behind the faery glass and are looking at a fantasy.

"I'll search the treehouse," Dionysus says a split second before snapping out.

Aiden and Kinu seem frozen and unsure which way to turn. There are now three homes on the property, and if Jackson *is* here, he could be in any one of them.

"He's not in there." Sloan comes out the back door of Gran's place before Dillan gets inside. It seems the distance between us is too much for his patience because instead of walking over to me, he *poofs*.

His arm is around my shoulders the moment he materializes, and he kisses my forehead. "Hey, Cumhaill. How are you doing?"

"I'll do better if we knew where our boy is."

"It's your father's place," Kinu says to Aiden. "His happy

thought before he went to bed was going to Granda's house for a sleepover. He misses him terribly."

Dillan jogs off in the opposite direction of the treehouse toward the little love nest cottage Dionysus created for Da and Shannon.

"What's a happy thought?" Nikon asks. "Is it magical? Like a wish?"

Aiden shakes his head. "No. Each night we ask the kids for one thing they're thankful for and one happy thought. We want those thoughts to be the last thing they think about before falling asleep."

"He's a wayfarer." Sloan blinks. "It makes perfect sense. It happened the same for me...and funnily enough, my powers brought me here too. I bet that's all it is. He's come into his druid power."

Oh, could it be that simple?

"Got him!" Dillan waves his arm from the front porch of Da's home.

Aiden and Kinu run through the snow, and I turn to hug Sloan. "Thank the goddess."

My heart is thrumming beneath all the layers of winter coat, and I draw a deep breath of crisp air and try to settle. "How about you *poof* us over to Da's? I don't think my legs will take much more excitement. I'd rather not flop in the snow."

Sloan chuckles against me and kisses the side of my head. "As ye wish."

By the time we take off our coats and boots and step inside Da's and Shannon's place, everyone seems to be calming down. Shannon has a thick sweater over her flannel pajamas and heads to the kitchen to make tea. Da still looks half-asleep with his russet-red hair sticking up off his head like a rooster's comb.

And there he is.

Jackson is sound asleep in Kinu's lap on the couch, with Aiden curled around her and their son.

"The little turd doesn't even realize the panic he caused." Dillan chuckles.

"All's well that ends well, I suppose," Da says, his words dragged out in a yawn. "Another wayfarer in our midst. Fer it bein' an uncommon gift, to have three in our circle is remarkable."

My mind catches up with things, and I pull out my phone. Nikon has already texted on the chat page that we've found Jackson and all is well.

I glide my thumbs over my screen and add to the text chain.

A huge thank you to Merlin. You came through for us yet again, my friend. I heart you huge.

Mad love, Calum texts.

Truly in awe of you, man, Dillan adds. **And while you're invisible too. Bonus points for delivery.**

You have our undying devotion, Aiden finishes. He straightens and comes over for a hug. My oldest brother might be big, brawny, and able to take down gun-slinging robbers and drug dealers, but he's shaking and looks like he's about to collapse.

"Why don't you and Kinu take your boy home and focus on your family? You look like you've had enough excitement for one night."

"For a lifetime." He exhales. "Thanks for putting the pieces together, Fi."

"It was Merlin who found him. I'm just so freaking relieved it was something as benign as an amazing power awaking in him."

Aiden chuffs. "You see amazing. I see us watching him day and night so we don't lose him again."

"We'll chip him like Sloan chipped Fi." Dillan grins, pulling out his phone. He reads a text, smiles, and responds before returning his attention to our conversation. "I don't know many five-year-old boys who wear Claddagh bands, but maybe a pendant or something with a dragon on it."

"Like our Team Trouble pendants." I like this idea. "We can make it cool and tell him it's his first step to being a druid dragon rider. I bet he'll never take it off."

Aiden frowns. "I don't want him to be a druid dragon rider. I wish you wouldn't encourage him."

I pat his shoulder. "He doesn't need any encouragement. I simply don't *dis*courage him."

"A fine distinction."

Kinu sends a pleading look at my brother, and I push him toward his wife. "Take them home."

"I've got them," Dionysus says. "I just remembered I was having a party tonight, and Contessa is settling into her new home."

"About that," I say, unsure how to broach that situation. "Are you sure having a mythical pegasus living in your loft is the best answer for her?"

Sloan's brows are creased, and I raise a finger to cut off his questions. "I'll catch you up on that in a minute."

I swing back to Dionysus and squeeze his hand. "I know the two of you hit it off, and you speak the same language and all, but—"

"Her dialect is different than mine, but yes, for the most part, it's the same language."

"Right, but doesn't she want to go back to Imari and eat grass and live in the wide open?"

"Not even a little. As much as she likes Imari, Myra, and Garnet, she's not happy there. She says it's much too hot and they make her dance and feel stupid."

Oh, dear. I've been part of more than one of Contessa McSparkles' dressage recitals, so I've contributed to the dancing issue. "All right. For now, I'll tell Garnet she's exploring her options, but I still think she might be happier on a farm or somewhere she can run and graze."

He chuckles. "Silly Jane, she runs in the sky. That's what a pegasus does."

Aiden flashes me a look, and I wave the conversation away. "Okay, not tonight. Yes, Tarzan, please see Aiden, Kinu, and Jackson home. Thank you. Love you. I'll check in with you tomorrow."

I wave at Kinu as Aiden scoops a sleeping Jackson off her lap and the three of them get ready to portal home. Once Dionysus snaps out, the world seems to exhale a deep breath.

"Contessa McSparkles is a pegasus?" Sloan asks.

"Yeah. Today, two ten-foot purple wings sprung from her sides, and she started speaking ancient Greek. We think the flux of prana power in the ley lines is causing an imbalance and affecting latent or dormant magical energy."

"Like transforming a unicorn into a pegasus."

"It's hard to say what happened with Contessa. Technically, she was a djinn wish and wasn't real."

Sloan seems to have moved on from that thought now and frowns. "If Contessa sprang wings out of nowhere, maybe this prana power flare is what triggered Jackson's wayfarer ability to surface."

"Yeah, that and the fact that he's missing his Granda," I say unapologetically loud. Da's already mad at me, so why should I pussyfoot? "Kinu said Jackson's been missing you terribly."

Da lowers his mug from his lips and sets it down on the table behind the sofa. "I realize I haven't handled things as well as I might have, kids. I'm sorry about that—truly, I am—but as well as bein' a da and a granda, I'm also a man. Fallible, vulnerable, and imperfect."

He's looking at me, but he's directing his comments to the entire room.

"I don't give two shits if you're perfect or not, Da. I just want you to be around. Since Brenny died, you've made a slow and steady withdrawal from our lives. That's what sucks."

He crosses his arms, and the muscle in his jaw starts to twitch. "Am I not allowed to have a life of my own? Shannon and I are newly married. Is it wrong fer me to want to focus on buildin' our lives?"

The heat of my hurt and frustration blooms in my chest. "You say that like we weren't already a family. Shannon was ours too, and you both left. Liam might be too busy taking over everything at the bar to lift his head, but he feels the same way. It's like the two of you decided after a lifetime of parenting us that we don't exist."

"That's not fair, Fi," Shannon says. "Ye know we want to be closer to our parents now that they're in their twilight years."

"No one opposes that. Da taught us love is never finite—the more you give, the more you have. Except when you guys got married, and we were all supposedly becoming a family, you both buggered off and cut ties."

"Yer exaggeratin'," Da says, annoyed.

"No, she's not." Dillan purses his lips. "If you two are happy here, hiding away in the forest and visiting your parents for the next two or three decades, that's great, have at it. But while you've been here building your lives together, you cut us out."

Da frowns. "That's ridiculous."

"You may not have meant to, but you have. So, build your lives. We wish you every happiness. It's just too bad it doesn't include us anymore."

Dillan turns and heads for the door.

I blink against the sting in my eyes and follow him. "Sorry to interrupt your night. I'm glad it was something as simple as Jackson missing his Granda. If it wasn't, it would've devastated us all. I guess we'll see you when we see you."

"Och, don't be like that," Da snaps. "Yer grown now, so pull up yer britches and stop bein' children."

"But we *are* your children, Da." I turn, my tears getting away from me. "That didn't stop because Brendan got shot. We lost him too. You're not alone in your pain."

"Feckin' hell, don't ye think I know that?"

"No. I honestly don't think you do."

The room erupts as Da, Dillan, I, and even Shannon get into it. The buildup of a lot of hurt feelings and months of disconnection comes to a head of steam.

Sloan and Nikon step back and look like they can't decide whether to step in to break it up or run away.

One thing about Clan Cumhaill. We love fiercely, but when we fight, it's with the same passion. I wouldn't be surprised if we wake up Gran and Granda in their house across the property.

The room is loud, the four of us shouting over one another, Dillan and I digging in about how we feel, and Da and Shannon opposing us without considering that we might be right.

Which we are.

"Don't you see, Da? I'm fighting to save the world, and you're pretending none of it is happening. I need you, and you're screwing the pooch on this."

"Och, watch yer mouth in my house, missy," Da snaps. "Ye may be grown, but I taught ye better than—"

A loud shrill whistle cuts the air. "What the fuck, you guys? What the hell did I miss?"

Evangeline is standing in the center of the room. I take one look at the guy at her side, and my entire body begins to shake.

"Brendan? How..."

My dead brother doesn't look dead.

Can the others see him? I glance at Dillan, Shannon, and Da

and by the terror and shock on their faces, the answer is yes...yes, they can.

It can't be but...

"How?" I gasp, throwing my hand out to catch my balance. Sloan's there in an instant, and it's a good thing too, because I'm about to ruin my brother's reunion by ass-planting on the floor. "Are you really here?"

"Yeah, and this isn't the welcome I expected."

"How, Angel?" Dillan asks, his voice choked.

She looks confused, and her dimples fade. "I texted you I was coming and had a surprise for you. I told you it was going to make you very happy."

"Yeah. I thought you meant like a private, sexy kind of a surprise, not the ghost of my dead brother."

"I thought you'd all be happy. When you and Fi were crying, you said your family puzzle fell apart when the Brendan piece got lost."

Dillan exhales a heavy breath. "Yeah, that's true."

"Well, since Death is breaking the rules and using me, I decided I'd break the rules too. What good is it being an Angel of Death if I can't flex my wings?"

"So, yer sayin' this is *really* Brendan?" Da asks, pointing at my brother. "My Brendan? My boy?"

She looks from Da to Dillan to me, confusion clouding her sunshiny smile. "Of course. Was I wrong to bring him? Did I mess up again?"

"No, babe." Dillan rushes forward to hug her. "No. It's just shocking."

"Are you real? A ghost? What?" I ask.

Brendan holds his hand out and turns it over to examine it. "I feel real. I'm not sure how long it'll last, but I think I'm here."

"You are here." Eva is smiling again. "There's a good chance Death will be angry and will put you back in your final resting place, but for the moment, you can say what you need to say and heal your hearts. Maybe fix your puzzle."

"You're amazing, angel." Dillan grips her cheeks and lays one on her better than any leading man in any movie.

I don't care how she did it or how long we have. I close the distance and wrap my arms around him. "Dammit, Brenny, I've missed you like crazy."

Squeezing him, I breathe in his scent and decide if this is a dream I'm good not waking up. Ever. The tears of anger and frustration morph into tears of sheer joy.

"Can I get in on this?" Dillan wraps his arms around both of us.

"Us too," Da says, bringing Shannon to join the family huddle.

A moment later, Calum and Aiden are there too, and they pile on. I wonder how that's possible, and Nikon winks at me. "Mischief managed, Red. I've got you."

CHAPTER EIGHT

The night slips into the dawn of day with a lot of laughs, and our family crowded around Gran's and Granda's kitchen table. We don't know how long we have with Brendan before Death weighs in on his resurrection, and we want him to meet our grandparents.

"I can't stop looking at you." I run my hand over his arm.

"Or touching me." He laughs. "I don't remember you ever being so tactile, baby girl."

"Sorry. It's been really hard. I never got to see you. I never got to tell you I love you."

He grunts. "I didn't need you there to tell me, Fi. I knew. From what I hear, you were here in Ireland, kidnapped and missing."

"Kidnapped by Baba Yaga and locked down in the dragon lair until the Wyrm Dragon Queen's eggs hatched."

He rolls his eyes. "You always had a way of getting into your own kind of trouble. Even for you, that's nuts."

He's not wrong. "Yeah, a lot has changed since you've been gone. On the plus side, I've become an all-powerful female and have matured spectacularly."

That gets Aiden, Dillan, and Calum laughing.

Brenny studies the faces of our family, and his smile fades. "A lot changed and at the same time, nothing changed. Despite that scene I interrupted when I arrived, we are a family. I never wanted that to change because of losing me. I'm really pissed and disappointed things are falling apart."

"*Were* fallin' apart," Da says. "There are a great many things I'm not proud of, son, but the fault is mine. Yer brothers and sister were simply tryin' to carry more than their weight and get it through my thick skull that I was feckin' things up. I'm sorry, kids."

I snag the last of Gran's cluster squares and take a bite. "If it's over and you're going to be our dad again, you're forgiven."

Maybe I shouldn't put a condition on my forgiveness, but hey, I want it known he needs to do better.

In truth, we *all* need to do better.

"Fresh start then." Dillan reads my mind. "Whether Brenny's with us for hours or days, we need to keep it together when this bonus time ends."

"I don't want to think about it ending." I grip Brenny's hand and squeeze. "I'm not ready."

Brendan winks at me and leans in for another hug. "There are no guarantees, so let's not think about it."

Good plan. Let's not. "So, what now?"

Brendan smiles. "Now, I want you all to stop looking at me like I'm going to disappear suddenly. Go to bed, all of you—or back to bed for those woken up so rudely."

Gran clucks her tongue. "Don't ye fret about that, luv. Yer granda and I are more than happy to be woken up to meet ye. Sloan should've woken us up when he was lookin' for wee Jackson."

Sloan shrugs. "It was a quick sweep through the house and off to meet Fi and the others. If we'd not found him right away, ye know I would've circled back to fill ye in."

Granda nods. "Aye, that's true. Now we have the return of two boys to celebrate. We're ever so pleased to have ye at our table, son."

I yawn and shake my head. "Sorry. Yeah, maybe Brenny is onto something. An hour or two of sleep might be a good idea."

"Of course, I'm right. I'm always right. Now, go on. Get some real sleep. This was amazing. If I'm here when you get back, it's a blessing. If not, let's be thankful for what we had tonight."

I press a hand against the tightness in my chest. "It kills me that Emmet didn't get to see you."

Brendan chuffs. "Don't give up on me yet. Tomorrow, when we're all refreshed, if I'm still here, we'll go to his secret island and surprise the hell out of him."

"Best prank evah!" Dillan chuckles. "I can't wait to see his face."

Brenny nods. "For now, I need to lay my head down as much as the rest of you. Being alive is tiring."

"Ye can take the spare room if ye like, luv." Gran gestures toward the bedrooms.

"Or Emmet's room in the treehouse," Dillan offers.

Da purses his lips. "I'd really like it if ye stay with us, son. I'm not ready to let ye out of my sight. Call me over-reactive, but I've not been whole since ye died. I can't bear to part with ye yet."

"Sure, Da. That sounds good." Brendan stands, and the rest of us get to our feet too. "Good night, guys. I love you all."

We take time to hug and kiss Brendan goodbye. Even though I don't want to, I have to let him go.

Da and Shannon escort Brenny out of Gran's kitchen and across the back lawn. I watch them out the window above the sink, three silhouettes against the gray light of dawn. After they disappear into the trees where Da's cottage sits, I'm still a little lost.

Sloan hugs me from behind and turns me to face the room. "Are ye all right?"

"I'm not sure. Did tonight truly happen? I'm numb."

"It happened." Dillan pulls Evangeline against his side and kisses her cheek. "Thank you, Angel. This was an incredible gift."

Eva grins. "I colored a little outside the lines, but as your guardian angel, it's my duty to protect you from harm. The loss of your brother was affecting your family and your ability to embrace what is coming. I consider that a danger to you all."

"I agree." I'm next in line to hug our guardian angel. She's a great hugger and smells faintly of vanilla. "We'll never be able to thank you enough. Even if all we get is the time we had tonight, it was an amazing gift."

Eva grins. "I'm glad I got it right."

"You nailed it." Calum kisses her cheek.

"You did," Aiden adds.

By the looks on my brothers' faces, they're all as discombobulated as me. Calum yawns, and it starts a chain reaction through the group.

"On that note." Dillan shakes his head like a wet dog, "Who's going where, and how are we getting there?"

Aiden raises his hand first. "I'm heading home if Nikon doesn't mind taking me."

"Same," Calum says. "It happened so fast that Kev got left behind. I want to catch him up and bring him tomorrow if, you know, Brenny's still here."

"And Liam," I say, my heart racing at the idea. "Liam has missed Brendan terribly. No matter what, we need to visit Emmet as soon as possible."

Nikon nods. "Consider me at your disposal. I'll take everyone home now, and we can reconvene at what, around one? That gives us all six hours of sleep."

"Make it two and give us seven." I hug Nikon and sink against him. "Thanks for all of your support. You really are a rockstar."

He kisses the side of my head. "Get some sleep, Red. Tomorrow promises to be another exciting day in the life of you."

I step back so they can leave. For the first time in a long

time, the proposition of an exciting day in my life makes my cells fire with positive energy instead of apprehension and dread.

I hug my grandparents, say goodnight, wrap my arms around Sloan's back, and rest my cheek against his broad chest. "Anne Boleyn is calling my name. Take me to bed."

Sloan's arms tighten around me. "As ye wish, *a ghra*. To bed it is."

My stomach wakes me up before my body wants to rise, but there's no helping it. You gotta feed the beast. Sloan and I shower and head down to the dining room of Stonecrest Castle to share lunch with Wallace.

"I can't tell ye how pleased I am fer yer family, Fi." Wallace flips the toasted brioche crown off his burger to add his fixings. "Please give yer father my congratulations. I can't imagine the pain of losin' a son, and it does my heart good to know that pain has lifted if even fer a short time."

The way he glances at Sloan, I know he's thinking about the dark months when his son would have nothing to do with him. Thankfully, he turned things around, and they've been able to patch things up.

"I love the new furniture." I gesture at the ebony sideboard and matching table and chairs set. "You have wonderful taste."

"Thank you, Fi. In truth, an old friend of mine from uni is an interior designer. I invited her to help me reinvent myself, and she's grabbed the baton." By the smile that warms his expression, I take it she's grabbed Wallace's baton both figuratively and literally.

"I'm happy for you. Tell her to keep up the good work. The smiles look good on you."

While Sloan and his father talk more about the renovations

and redecorations, I pop a few sweet potato fries into my mouth and check my phone.

I admit I'm not very attentive to the conversation, my mind whirring with questions about Brendan. When I first woke up, I was afraid to check my phone for an update on whether or not he was still with us.

Now, the need to know has grown too strong.

I pull out my phone, and there's nothing in the family chat. Is that a bad sign? Maybe they're still sleeping. No way. Da is an early bird no matter what time he gets to sleep and it's after twelve.

Brenny?

My message is quick and thankfully Da messages back immediately.

Present and accounted for. Sleeping and snoring like nothing ever happened.

Sloan reaches across the table and squeezes my hand. "Everything all right, *a ghra*?"

I blink up at him, and his beautiful face is lost behind a wall of moisture. "Oh, yeah, sorry."

"No need to apologize. What's happened?"

I dry my eyes with my cloth napkin and laugh at myself. "Nothing. Brendan is still with us and is currently snoring away like old times."

"That's a relief, I'm sure." Sloan hesitates, pulls his phone out, and reads a message. "It's Sarah gettin' back to me. She's been away on coven business and didn't get our messages. She says I can come straight away to meet her and explain what we need."

"Awesomesauce. First Brenny and now Sarah. Maybe our luck is changing, and Team Light is finally catching some breaks."

Sloan finishes his Coke, wipes his mouth, and sets his napkin on the table. "I'm sorry to eat and run, Da."

Wallace waves that away. "No need to apologize. I'm thrilled to see ye no matter how short the visit is. The two of ye have taken on so much. I couldn't be prouder."

"Aww, thanks. That's sweet of you to say." I pop a few more fries into my mouth, then wipe my fingers on my napkin and join Sloan.

He takes my hand and smiles. "Where to? Do ye want to go to yer family or Blarney?"

The need to be in two places at once is real.

Except…my need to be with my family is purely selfish while speaking to Sarah could affect our position in the Culling and, in turn, the world's safety.

Choice made.

"I'm with you, Mackenzie. I gotta keep an eye on you around pretty single ladies. Elbows up. Claws out. I haven't forgotten you and she had a special friendship before me."

He rolls his eyes at me. "Yer ridiculous."

"I know. I said that to make your dad laugh."

"Mission accomplished." Wallace is chuckling. "Now, off ye go, kids. Love ye. Be safe."

I wave goodbye with my free hand as Sloan *poofs* us to Blarney to meet up with our white witch.

Sarah Connor lives in a quaint eighteenth-century stone cottage in the historic part of Blarney. The last time we were here, she was rooming with two of her sister witches, Yasmine and Erika. The three of them, and the other witches in their coven, were instrumental in saving Sloan's life when he was hexed by Moira's witches and dying from festerbug poisoning.

Without their help, Sloan wouldn't be with me now.

I am forever grateful.

"Is it wrong of me to wish Sarah had been the one Emmet fell for instead of Ciara?"

Sloan glances down at me and arches a brow. "Privately, ye may think that fer maybe one minute a year. Other than that, ye need to keep yer opinion to yerself and let yer brother and his betrothed live their lives."

"One minute a year. That's all I get?"

"Aye, that's it."

"Well then, this is my minute. Sarah is lovely, has a great heart, and cares about the people around her. Sure, maybe Emmet found her lifestyle too tame back then but look at him now. He's completely settled down and bound to spend his time in one city pretty much for the rest of his life."

"Yer point?"

"My point is I don't think Ciara's right for that life with him. Do you see her making him happy living there, secluded, no Internet, no shopping, no one fawning over her except my brother? No. I don't see it working out."

"All the more reason fer ye to keep yer opinion to yerself. Let them work that out. They're handfasted. In the next four months, they'll re-evaluate their commitment and decide if they want to stay united. No one but the two of them should weigh in."

I breathe in and exhale. "I guess you're right."

"I'm one hundred percent right. Remember how it felt to have my parents injecting their opinions about the two of us dating? It destroyed our relationship."

That's true, and I certainly don't want that.

"Yer one minute is now up."

I'm about to respond, but he hooks his elbow with mine and tugs me up the driveway. His expression is stern, and his stride is quick and clipped.

"I lurve you, surly."

He grunts but his mood softens. "Of course, ye do. I'm the

best thing that ever happened to ye. If not fer me, ye'd be playin' tonsil hockey with Jordan the griffin and complimentin' his manly biceps."

I burst out laughing. "You didn't hear him sing and play the guitar. Those are his best qualities."

"Well then, maybe we'll have to invite him fer a night of singalong at our next backyard bonfire."

I snort and hug tighter around his arm as we arrive at the side door. "Hard pass. I'm happy with my choice. No need to revisit past mistakes."

Sloan winks at me and knocks on the door. "Good then. It's nice to know my spot at the bonfire is safe. If needed, I could portal my piano out to the backyard and tickle the ivories fer ye. Maybe play ye some Niall Horan if it solidifies my standing."

I'm about to respond when the door opens, and Emmet's ex greets us. Sarah has always reminded me of a hippie Cinderella with a swinging ponytail and colorful peasant skirts.

"Fi and Sloan. It feels like donkey's years. Come in. Come in. I'm happy to see ye."

The two of us step inside, and after the hugs, she leads us down the hallway, past the dining room, to the little family room off the kitchen.

There's a tray of sweets set out, and the kettle is whistling. Sarah goes over and pours the water into the teapot. "Can I get ye both a cuppa while we chat?"

"Aye, that would be lovely," Sloan says.

Sloan and I take the loveseat and leave the two floral armchairs vacant. The hand-woven rugs, the myriad of ivory pillar candles, and the tendrils of smoke rising from stained-glass incense burners all add to the ambiance of Sarah's home.

"Do Erika and Yasmine still live here with you?" I ask to make conversation.

"Erika does, aye, but Yasmine married Paul, and they bought a place not far from Dublin. So, it's only the two of us…well, three. Erika's man is here more often than not."

She brings the tea tray and sets it on the large, tufted ottoman. "The messages ye left mentioned a matter of some urgency. I apologize fer not gettin' back to ye sooner. The Council of White Witches called a forum on a lovely island in Greece. I stayed a few extra weeks because I enjoyed bein' cut off from the world fer a bit. The past year has been tryin'."

I shake my head. "Not your fault. I get it. If I could unplug and enjoy a Greek island for a few weeks, I absolutely would."

"But yer home now," Sloan says.

Sarah nods. "Aye, so what can I help ye with?"

Over the next half-hour, we fill her in on what we know about the Culling, how Fionn and Bodhmall had Mother Nature as their sponsor to favor Team Light, and how we wondered if she kept in touch with her or knew how we could contact her.

"Well, the answer is both yes and no, I'm afraid. Ever since our battle with the dark witches, our Lady has watched over our wee coven. She's given us a helpin' hand now and then. She seems to know when she's needed, and that's when she comes to us. Nothin' I do makes it happen. She simply comes."

Sloan swallows a sip of tea and sets his empty cup on the tray. "Could ye maybe pray or burn a candle with the intent to speak to her or call an invocation? Do ye think if ye actively requested an audience ye could get one? It's very important."

"I can try."

Neither Sloan nor I move.

"Oh, ye mean right now. All right. I can't make any promises, but we can give it our best effort."

CHAPTER NINE

Before we start with our attempt to contact Mother Nature, I check my phone for the latest update.

Brenny?

Still sleeping, Da texts back.

Are you sitting there watching him?

Maybe.

I chuckle. **I don't blame you. We're in Blarney chatting with Sarah about getting in touch with Mother Nature. Let me know when he's up. I don't want to miss anything.**

FOMO is real, Dillan texts.

True story.

With a smile on my face, I catch up with the conversation

already in progress. Sloan and Sarah are chatting and gathering supplies: wide ivory pillar candles, a hand-woven mat rolled into a tube, a jar of raw honey, a freshly baked scone, a can of root beer, an antique serving set, some wooden matches...

"Are we going on a romantic picnic?" I ask.

Sarah grins. "No. Sloan is plainly yers. We're lookin' to attract another wee fella. A messenger of sorts."

Oh, cool.

Erika jogs down the stairs, and her expression tightens when she sees us. "Are ye here with good news or bad this time around?"

I understand her caution considering the first time we met her, our dark witch drama killed almost everyone in their coven and the second time was when those same dark witches hexed Sloan, and he was barfing festerbugs.

I hold up my hands. "This is solely a fact-finding mission, I promise."

Her tension eases, and I'm happy to see she's not as apprehensive about us as I feared.

"I love your hair." I gesture at the bright curls. "It's awesome."

"Thanks. It's new." She swings her head to make the magenta curls sway. Erika is a lovely, athletic girl and the color pops against the dark brown of her skin. "So, what are you doing?"

Sarah opens the hall closet and pulls out a plastic grocery bin. "We're going to talk to Merriweather. Want to come?"

"Aye, I do. I owe him a gemstone from the last time. Give me two minutes." She hurries to the door leading to the basement and is gone a second later.

"Grab the tent while yer down there," Sarah shouts.

"Aye. I will."

"Who is Merriweather?" I ask.

"He's a forest gnome who lives in the parkette two streets over. He's a bit of a crusty oul coot, but if ye promise him a shiny stone, a gem, or a crystal, he's more than willin' to overlook ye botherin' him fer a favor."

"What favor are we asking of him?"

"Well, his home might be beneath the grand oak, but he lives in the Earth world of Fae. He can carry a message to our Lady as quickly and easily as a stroll through the park. I'd much prefer to start with a request than an invocation if it's all the same."

"That's fine," Sloan says. "Whatever yer comfortable with works fer us. Thanks."

Sarah takes a last look at the items packed and seems happy with the collection. "Now, do ye have a crystal or a gemstone yer willin' to part with? I'd offer one, but the request isn't comin' from me. It's best not to cross intentions when dealin' with such things."

The only gemstones I carry are my druid casting stones, and I'm not willing to part with any of those. I look at Sloan. "I don't. Do you?"

He considers that for a moment and nods. "Back in a flash."

He *poofs* out, which leaves Sarah and me to finish getting ready. I take the grocery bin to the door and set it down while I sit on the bench to slide my boots back on. "Thank you for helping us. I hate to say it, but I was worried you might not."

Sarah arches a brow, and a knowing smile lights her eyes. "Because of what happened the last time? With Emmet, I mean."

I stand and claim my jacket from where it's hanging on the hook. "Yeah, Em mentioned that there was a kerfuffle the last time the two of you spoke."

"Och, I don't hold Emmet responsible fer the venom that spews from the mouth of the bitch who latched onto him." She catches herself and swallows. "Sorry. I don't mean to offend."

"No offense taken. I'm sure your opinion of Ciara is firmly rooted in experience. I've had my run-ins with her too. I understand where you're coming from."

Sarah pulls her hair out from the back of her jacket and sighs.

"It's a shame, is all. Emmet is a good soul, kind, and cares fer people. He's a fixer. Maybe the two of them are a good match, and I'm just bitter, but my gut tells me no amount of Emmet's efforts will fix selfish and vicious."

No. I suppose that's true.

"I can't comment. If Emmet is happy, I'm happy for him. With everything that's happened with him over the last month, he needs our support."

Her expression darkens as she fixes her attention on me. "Oh? What's happened?"

Sloan interrupts that thought when he *poofs* back and joins us in the entranceway. "What do ye think of this? Will it do?"

He holds up a blue diamond the size of a small marble. It's suspended in the center of a silver spiral pendant and catches the light and sends out a thousand shimmering prisms.

"Is that real?" My eyes must be bugging out, but holy schmoly, I didn't know Sloan had the Hope Diamond's baby sister in his possession.

He looks at me like I'm crazy. "Of course, it's real. My mother bought it fer me fer my graduation gift. I hated it then, hated it when she chastised me fer not wearin' it, and hate it more now that she's shown her true colors and fucked off."

Yikes, no unresolved anger there.

"Okay, so we've established that you hate the lovely blue diamond. Does that mean you need to give it away? It must be worth a small fortune."

Sloan lifts a shoulder as he buttons his jacket. "A very sassy redhead once told me it's more important to care about people, not money. I think savin' the world from darkness and those who thrive in it is more important than the cash value of a blue rock."

I can't argue with that. "All righty then, we have our gemstone."

The parkette a couple of streets over is one of those quaint, gated private parks for the tenants who back onto it. I didn't know that was a thing until I watched *Notting Hill* and fell in love with Anna Scott and William Thacker. Funny movie.

"So, which tree is his?" I ask.

Erika points at the largest oak standing in the center of the long, rectangular band of green space. "Merri's magic is what made that tree grow so big."

Yeah, that and probably a couple of hundred years.

We arrive at the tree's base, and Sloan and Erika make quick work of putting together the tent. It's a simple A-frame with a nylon cover that drapes over the two sides and one end. The other end is slitted down the center to leave two flaps for a door.

Sarah sits cross-legged on the woven rug, about eight feet from the tree, facing the wide trunk. She's set up the serving set in front of her and has unpacked the grocery bin to lay everything out.

I lower myself to my knees facing the little picnic. "I take it Merriweather likes a little snack while he chats?"

"He does. The way to most fae species is through their vices. Most often those are food and collectibles of some kind. The trick is to pay attention and learn what they like."

"Where do ye want the tent set?" Sloan asks.

Sarah lifts her hands and makes a point over her head, bringing her arms down to the sides. "Right over the top of us, thanks. The door toward the tree."

The two of them lift the frame over us, and I laugh. "Oh, I didn't notice the cutesy kittens in party hats before. Oh, are those squirrels eating pizza?"

Sarah grins. "The outside is plain so it doesn't attract too much attention from the people in the park, but the inside is all about fae whimsy."

Sloan and Erika step inside, hunched over, and lower themselves to sit with us. Sloan sits opposite me and Erika next to him. At first, I wonder how we're going to fit, but once we're settled, there's more room than I thought.

Sarah pulls one of the long matches out of the box. "All right. No sudden movements, no touching Merri, no reaching for his snacks, and no making promises ye don't intend to keep. Forest gnomes have deep roots in old magic. They believe in a code of honor, but if ye snub one, ye'll find yerself in a world of discomfort because they also have a long memory and a sadistic side."

"Good to know." I blink. "The only gnome I've come into contact with was in a village in the fae realm, and she was quite lovely."

"Likely an arcane gnome. They live in villages and are quite a bit more sociable. Forest gnomes are different. They're odd folks but good-spirited if ye respect them."

Sloan nods. "Then we'll have no issue."

Sarah looks us over and checks the layout of everything in front of her. When she's satisfied all is ready, she pinches the long, wooden match in her fingers and lifts it in front of her mouth. A gentle breath ignites the match head, and she lights the wide pillar candle.

"Merriweather, if it be yer will, we have a favor to ask and a favor to give."

She shakes the match to extinguish the flame and picks up the teacup. Holding it in the center of the tent, she extends the thumb of her free hand over the cup. Erika does the same. When she nods at us, Sloan and I follow suit.

The four of us sit, arms extended so our thumbs are over the dainty cup.

"Project yer intentions," Sarah says. "Envision the outcome yer here to secure. Merri will taste the truth of yer convictions in our oath."

I'm not sure what that means until she speaks again.

"Sanguis iuramentum." As the Latin words fall from her tongue, her spell takes hold, and a quick sting slices the pad of my thumb.

The belly of the teacup catches the blood that drips from the wound along with the blood of the others.

"We pledge a blood oath, on our honor, that Merriweather of the Grand Oak will come to no harm and we will not ask him to do anythin' beyond his will."

She sets the teacup down and opens the can of root beer, pouring a tiny bit into the cup to dilute the blood. "Yer feast awaits, my friend."

Sloan and I heal our thumbs as Sarah sets the scone onto a sandwich plate. Then she opens the jar and drizzles honey over it. When the table is ready, she rests her hands gently in her lap and closes her eyes. "Now we wait. Merri can sense anxiety, so try to clear your auras."

Well, crap. That would've been good to know.

I'm stressed about most things most days. Sloan's been working on meditation with me, but I'm hopeless.

Still, I try.

I stretch my neck and become mindful of my breath and my state of mind. I must manage a decent result because about five minutes later, there is a rustle of leaves outside the tent.

I open my eyes slowly and meet the gaze of the little man peering between the loose flaps of the tent door. He studies me, smiles at Erika, scowls at Sloan, and his smile returns when he looks at Sarah.

Not more than ten inches tall, Merri resembles the garden gnomes decorating many flowerbeds but differs from them too. He has lacey green dragonfly wings that extend past his brown velvet vest and a shaggy mane of silver hair that falls to his slim waist in a chaotic tangle of curls.

"Welcome, Merriweather of the Grand Oak," Sarah says. "We are honored ye made the time to visit with us today. Our blood oath awaits yer approval."

His steps into the tent are hesitant. Leaning forward, he glances into the teacup. He sniffs the air and approaches the cup with the utmost caution. After another round of sniffing, he lifts the offering with both hands and *glug-glug-glugs* the contents down.

Tossing the cup to the grass, he takes flight and backs up so he's once again at the flaps of the door. The rhythmic buzz of his wings is the only sound as he flutters back and forth at the tent's exit.

The four of us remain completely still.

"It's okay, Merri," Sarah says. "Ye know ye can trust us and Fi and Sloan are our friends. They have a request and bring a very special sparkly to exchange."

That catches his attention.

"More brown fizz," he snaps. "Strange magic makes my tongue all tinglies."

Sarah tips the can of root beer again, this time filling the cup three-quarters to the rim. "Yer used to our magic, but Fiona and Sloan are druids, not white witches. I'm sure their power signature tastes different, but what's important is the oath. Are you happy with our intentions?"

"Fine, fine. Strangers fine. No ugly, sneaky snakes."

Sarah smiles. "Sloan, would you like to present Merri with your token of favor?"

Very slowly, Sloan extends his closed fist, turns it upright, and uncurls his fingers. The moment Merri sees the blue diamond, he races so fast to snatch it, he leaves a cloud of gold motes puffing out behind him.

Merri holds the silver pendant up and eyes the blue diamond inside. "This sparkly is for *Merri?*"

Sloan nods. "It will be if ye promise to deliver a message to the Fair Lady right away."

His gaze narrows on Sloan as if the tall, dark stranger is about to pull a fast one on him and steal his new treasure. "What message?"

"Simply that Fiona Cumhaill requests to speak with her. It's very important."

Merriweather the forest gnome purses his lips and gives Sloan a wash of stink eye like I've rarely seen. "That all?"

"That's all."

"Then the sparkly is mine?"

"Aye. Give us yer word, and the diamond is yers."

He pulls a leather thong out from the collar of his shirt and hooks the pendant on. The diamond looks massive against his chest, but it's no bigger than the smile on his face. "Deal is made. Now eat so no take-backs."

Sloan tears off a piece of the scone and pops it into his mouth and Merri picks up the rest and goes to sit between Erika and the door. He takes a big bite and smiles like a Cheshire cat. "No take-backs."

CHAPTER TEN

When we leave Sarah's house, it's almost two o'clock. I hope we haven't missed anything good with Brendan and the family. Pulling out my phone, I call up the family chat.

Is everyone awake? Where are we meeting?

Dillan responds a moment later.

We're hanging out in the treehouse, shooting the shit.

Perfect. On our way.

Sloan *poofs* us there.

"Good morning, family...well, afternoon." I rush over to the breakfast stools and hug Brenny where he's sitting at the island counter. "How did you sleep?"

"Like the dead." He waggles his brow and flashes me a wide grin.

"Boo. Let's *not* make you being dead into a joke."

"Too soon?"

"Much too soon." I lean in and hug him again. "Sorry. I can't stop."

He chuckles and hugs me back. "It's fine. It's nice to know you missed me."

"We did." The tingling of emotion in my sinuses is a sign I need to change the subject, so I turn and pull Sloan into the conversation. "You met him last night, but I want the two of you to get to know each other."

Brenny stands to shake Sloan's hand. "I hear great things about you, my man. It seems you've already earned the Cumhaill seal of approval, so I'll just say welcome to the family."

Sloan inclines his head. "I've heard great things as well. Ye left a hole in the lives of a great many people when ye passed."

Brendan winks at me. "Yeah, well, I always told them they'd miss me when I'm gone."

I shake my head. "No. Stop."

He mock-punches my shoulder and bites his bottom lip. "Geez, Fi, you used to have a better sense of humor about things."

"Maybe, but after living through the past eighteen months, there's nothing funny about you getting shot."

He waggles his ebony brows and makes eyes at the room. "Well then, I guess that tells me. When did you get so grown up?"

"Likely right around the time people started trying to kill me."

Brenny grunts. "Da filled me in on things this morning. I don't like the idea of the darkness of an empowered world gunning for you."

Sloan chuffs beside me. "Sadly, the sentiment of not likin' it doesn't change a thing."

I wave away their concern. "I'm fine. Did Da happen to mention my druid animal companion?"

Sloan shakes his head. "He's not."

I flick my hand at Sloan and laugh. "He's an animal and my

companion. Hush now. We've been over this. It's not your story to tell."

Sloan chuckles and heads over to the coffee maker.

"So, my animal companion?" I continue.

Brenny shakes his head. "I've met Dillan's little dragon, Rory. Is your companion like that?"

"Similar, yeah. Bruin lives within me like Rory does with Dillan, but he's a little different. He's shy. Would you like to meet him?"

"Yeah, of course."

"Awesomesauce. Okay, come over here and get on your knees so you're not so big and scary."

I catch Dillan snickering and pulling out his phone but avoid looking at him or I'm going to laugh.

Brendan gets down on the floor and sits back on his heels. "Is this good?"

"Yeah, perfect. One sec, I'll let him out." *Are you ready to meet my brother, buddy?*

I'm ready for anything, Red.

Good. Then materialize right in front of him, standing on your back legs, looking really big and scary.

Should I wear my battle armor?

Oh, yeah, for sure. I didn't even think of that, but that's awesome.

Bruin flutters around in my chest adjusting his position. Then I release him.

My bear solidifies three feet in front of Brendan, reared up on his back legs, and battle-ready. His roar rattles the glasses in the cupboard and makes even my heart skip a beat.

Brendan screams and throws himself back, sliding on the floor as he uses his heels to kick and put distance between him and Killer Clawbearer at his finest.

I bust up laughing, and Dillan moves forward to improve the angle of his video.

The moment the prank is over, Bruin drops to all fours and

releases the kickass armor Manannán mac Lir awarded him for taking down the sorceress last month. "Is he all right, Red? I didn't break him, did I?"

"No, buddy. Brenny is the Cumhaill king of pranks. He's good. Aren't you, bro?"

Brendan drops flat on his back, his chest heaving. "I'm good," he pants, pounding his sternum. "Or, I will be once I finish having a coronary, and I can get my heart started again."

Sloan offers him a hand to pull him back up to his feet. "Ye don't know how long she's wanted to do that to ye. It's ridiculous."

Brendan waves that away. "No, she's right. That was next-level. Well done, Fi. I never saw it coming."

I bow my head with a little curtsy. "Thank you."

"Yeah, I never expected you to try to kill your brother on his first day back from the dead."

I laugh, not falling for it. "Yeah, yeah. So, do you think I get an Oh Henry! for that one?"

He chuckles, patting his chest. "I'll pick a dozen up the next time I go to a store. Oh, wait…do I have money?"

"You have as much money as you need. Your police life insurance was big. I've bought a few things for the family on your behalf, but you're rich, buddy."

"For as long as I'm undead and unless anyone from the force sees me."

I wave that away. "Anyway, Brendan, this is Brunior the Brave, my battle bear, protector, warrior-in-arms, and dear friend."

"It's good to meet ye," Bruin says.

I relay that for him, and Brendan starts to reach out but hesitates. "He's not going to bite off my arm or anything accidentally, is he?"

"Nope. He's fully sentient, wise beyond his years, and housebroken."

Bruin chuckles. "Housebroken? How about 'has excellent taste in whiskey?'"

"He also has excellent taste in whiskey and is a Casanova with the lady bears," I add.

Brenny runs a hand over Bruin's shoulder and gives him a gentle pat. "Whiskey and women, eh? Well then, he fits right in with this family."

The air snaps and Nikon arrives with Calum, Kev, Aiden, and Liam. My brothers gaze at Brendan with visible relief while Kevin looks stunned, and Liam appears shaken to his very foundation.

Liam stumbles forward first. "Is that really you, B?"

"Could there be any other?"

In three quick strides, Liam and Brendan are chest-to-chest. Liam back-claps him and stays there, in no rush to step back and save face.

He doesn't have to.

In Clan Cumhaill, everyone is safe.

When the two finally ease back, Liam swipes under his eyes and lets out a long exhale. "Fuck, it's good to see you, brother."

Brendan musses Liam's hair and laughs. "I get the feeling the party wasn't the same without me."

"Not even a little."

"I heard we are officially brothers now, too."

"Yeah, your dad and my mom."

Brendan makes a face. "That's not weird at all."

I snort. "Says the guy conveniently absent when that awkwardness first surfaced."

Brendan barks a laugh. "Conveniently absent? I believe I was pushing up daisies."

"Like I said. Convenient."

"Aw, come on. It couldn't have been that bad."

Now it's my turn to laugh. "Sloan *poofed* us home from Ireland after the hobgoblins tried to kill me and Liam stepped in front of the bullets. Needless to say, the two of them were upset and not expecting us to transport home so soon."

"Sloan's father is a wonder in the magic doctoring department," Liam interjects.

I nod. "That is true. So, Sloan *poofs* us home from Ireland, and we go upstairs—"

"—I wanted to make my bullet casing into a necklace and Fi has all that jewelry-making stuff."

"Right," I say. "So, we jog up the stairs and blew the whole sexcapade wide open in the upstairs hall."

Brendan laughs, and Liam rolls his eyes. "You wouldn't think it was so funny if you were there. Mom barely covered in a towel comes out of the bathroom and screams."

"That brought Da running out to greet us as naked as the day he was born."

Liam shakes his head. "We froze in place, and there was no escape."

"Especially since Sloan *poofed* off and left us standing there. Talk about awkward parental moments."

Brenny's still laughing and man, it does my heart good to hear it.

A notification goes off on my phone and Sloan's at the same time. Do we have any shared notifications?

He pulls his cell out to see what's what.

I shuffle over and pull my phone out too. "What is it? What does Alarm NG mean?"

"The alarm Samuel put on the Newgrange tomb to detect Mingin's return went off. He's here in Ireland."

"Shit. Family reunion interruptus. Who's with me?"

There's a moment of scrambling as Dillan pulls on his boots, grabs his cloak off the hook, and whistles. Rory wakes up from where she's curled up on the back of the couch, and when Dillan pats his chest, the small dragon flies across the room and gets absorbed into his body.

Calum unzips his coat and hands it to Kevin. Straightening, he flexes his hand, and his bow appears in his hand while his quiver materializes on his back. "Love you." He gives him a quick kiss.

"Be safe, Robin Hood."

"I'm in." Aiden stretches his neck from side to side, his vertebrae popping. He ditches his winter coat too and calls forward his sword and buckler.

Sloan, Nikon, and I gather close and everyone intending to join the battle puts their hands in.

"What the fuck is happening?" Brendan asks.

Liam steps in beside him and smiles. "Didn't you hear? They're magically empowered crime fighters now. Go get 'em, guys. Kev and I will take care of Brenny until you get back."

Nestled in a bend of the Boyne River, Newgrange tomb is a marvel of architecture. Older than Stonehenge and the Egyptian pyramids, it took generations of ancient Irish farmers to build. It's a massive, rounded mound of earth with walls made of white stone and heavy boulders engraved with swirls and patterns all around.

We materialize in the vacant pasture down by the river and take stock of the situation. "Do you think he's still inside?" I text Dionysus, Samuel, Ahren, and Quon Shen. "Do you think the notification spell worked?"

Sloan frowns at the ancient tomb. "I can't say from here. If it did, and he's trapped inside, it will go a long way in aiding our fight to have him removed from the opposition."

My gaze locks on the shadowed entranceway in the distance and I wait for my shield to weigh in. "I wish we knew more about Samuel's spell. Did tripping it signal Mingin that we caught him in our snare? Is Melanippe in there with him?"

"I don't know, luv."

My phone buzzes in my hand and I glance down to read the texts. "Samuel is in a hotel in Turkey. Quon Shen and Ahren are back in Greece."

"Get the addresses, and I'll bring them," Nikon says.

I request the added info and call Dionysus while we wait. It rings a couple of times, but he doesn't pick up. When it's time to leave a message, I give him our location and a quick recap of what's going on. He's our fifth shaman, and we'll need all hands on deck if we're facing either one or both of our old enemies.

By the time I end the call, I've got addresses for the Hunter-gods. "Here, Greek. I'm sending you the deets now."

Once Nikon has the information on his phone, he snaps off.

"While we wait, let's get a bit of intel," Dillan says. "Fi, let Bruin out to survey the land. At the same time, Sloan can *poof* me to the far side of the tomb so I can look around."

I release Bruin as he suggests. "Did you get that, buddy? Ghost around and see what you can find out. For the moment, don't go into the tomb. We don't want to tip Mingin off and lose our element of surprise."

"Assuming we have one," Calum says.

"Yeah, there's that."

With all my focus on the tomb in front of us, when I sense a surge of power behind us, I jump and spin. Raising my hands, I'm about to defend myself when I recognize the goddess rising from the river's depths.

Her hair is dark as a night sky and flows behind her like an ebony cape. As the light catches the silky strands, they shimmer purple in the breeze. "Merry meet, cousins. Welcome back to my land."

"Welcome to the party, Boann," I say. "What brings you to the surface?"

Boann almost seems to float as she crests the riverbank and strides forward to join us. I can't see her feet beneath the hem of her long, flowing gown, but it wouldn't surprise me a bit if she wasn't touching the frozen ground. "I felt the power in the tomb shift. There is an evil presence with us today."

"That's why we're here too. We set a spell to notify us if one of our enemies chose to return. The alarm went off about five minutes ago, and we're preparing to investigate."

"I'm blessed to have such brave and handsome kin workin' to keep the balance."

I smile at my gathered friends and family. "We'll do our best to contain the intruder. Unfortunately, it's a volatile time."

"Aye, the Time of the Colliding Realms. A volatile and dangerous time," she says. "When rays of first morn's light warm the depths of the sacred tomb, the powers of dark and light will hold their ground or seal their doom."

"Cheery poem," Calum says.

No kidding. "I'm more of a limerick girl, myself. There once was a man from Nantucket…"

"There once was a man from Leeds…" Calum adds.

"There once was a boy named Harry…" Dillan says.

Boann casts a glance toward the entrance of the tomb and frowns. "Whoever is inside is gainin' power. I fear the time for investigation has come to a close, cousin. If ye intend to take yer stand, make haste."

The moment Nikon snaps back with Samuel and the others, we portal onto the tomb's roof. Between us and the ritual chamber below lies twenty-five feet of earth and stone.

From here, we can act quickly, not be seen from the mouth of the tomb, and survey the situation.

I'm not sure where Dionysus is, but there's no time to wait for him. Three Hunter-gods originally banished Mingin. We have four, plus a backup. It'll have to do.

"So, here's how we're going to play this," Samuel says, pointing at the ground around us. "Sloan will portal Fi, Calum, and I into the east chamber. Nikon, you've got Quon Shen,

Ahren, and Dillan and will materialize in the west chamber. Bruin and Aiden, we need you to come in through the passage and block Mingin's escape path."

"I thought the whole point of your spell is that he can't escape," Dillan says.

"I don't think he'll be able to negate my spell, but with Melanippe's help, I can't be sure. She knows my magical signature and the way I do things. If they've reconnected and are both in there, this will be a fight."

"Bring it," Dillan says.

I share Dillan's enthusiasm to bring this to an end, but don't like not knowing what we're walking into. Calling my body armor forward, I draw a deep breath and take a moment to appreciate everyone who's here to stand beside me and fight.

"Be careful, everyone. I torched Riordan, but we don't know who Mingin is inhabiting now or what their powers might be. Take nothing for granted."

The ten of us gather into our groups, and when Aiden closes the distance to the tomb's entrance, he nods.

"Take care of him, Bruin." I pat my boy on his furry butt.

"With my life, Red. Take care of yerself, aye?"

When Bruin ghosts out and Aiden drops to the ground, we move out.

CHAPTER ELEVEN

The passageways within the giant dome of Newgrange tomb resemble the shape of a sword. A long, sixty-foot passage runs straight back through a round, main chamber dissected with small eight-foot antechambers on the west, north, and east.

That's where we materialize.

Sloan's energy is still tingling over my skin when reality sucker punches me in the boob.

We didn't trap Mingin in the main chamber.

It's *sooo* much worse.

"Morgana."

My skin tingles with cold chills as I study the woman suspended in the air before us. Her long, dark hair flows out behind her, caught in an invisible cyclone of power. She's raised her arms to the sides and tipped her face back to stare at the vaulted part of the chamber's ceiling.

She's not alone.

A dozen glazed-eyed soldiers in uniform are here as her backup. Judging by the green camo, berets, and service rifles, I'd bet they're an Irish squadron missing from one of the local barracks.

They don't seem to be cognizant of our arrival, but I'm not sure how long that will last. "How did she trip Samuel's spell? What is she doing here?"

"Why the fuck is she smiling like that?" Dillan asks.

I have no idea, but it's a horrible look for her. Releasing my fae sight, I see things with perfect clarity. "Holy shitballs. Guys, this is bad."

She's pulled apart the veil's seam, and the fissure releases dark smoke tendrils. The banished souls of the Neitherlands are seeping free from the seam and swirling around inside the main chamber.

What came out the last time amounted to four or five souls. If that measure holds true, there must be dozens leaking. Worst of all is that she's consuming them.

One by one she's directing her magic and catching the whisps. Sucking them into her mouth, she inhales until the dark soul is within her.

"Is soul-eating a thing?"

Sloan turns his bone ring and scowls up at the ceiling line. "What do we do?"

"What do you see?" Samuel asks.

Right. When we battled the souls of the Neitherlands last time, we were on the astral plane so we could see what we were dealing with.

That's why a Hunter-god needs to be a shaman.

"Sloan, help him see."

Sloan grabs his wrist and Samuel curses, raises his hands, and magic surges from his palms. "Cumhaills, stop Morgana from feeding on the banished souls. Hunters, we need to seal the seam and proximity now!"

Bruin, Nikon, and my brothers rush toward the main chamber. The moment they contact the soldiers, they react. "They're running on autopilot," Nikon says. "They're possessed or something."

I agree. "They're innocent. Try not to kill them."

"Autopilot doesn't change the fact that they're trained soldiers and heavily armed." Dillan grips the rifle of one soldier. "They'll still kill us."

"Just try," I say. "If there's nothing to be done, save yourselves."

Sloan frowns, looking trapped standing there holding Samuel's hand. With a grunt, he pulls off his ring and hands it to Samuel. "Test that it'll work fer ye. It doesn't always play nice with others."

Samuel nods that it does, and Sloan joins the fight.

"I want to stand with them—"

"Fi, we need to stop her from ingesting any more souls," Samuel snaps.

"I agree, but how? We didn't set up for the ritual. We can't lie down at Morgana's feet and leave our bodies to police the astral plane while her zombie army is here and able to fill us with bullets. What's our play?"

Samuel considers that and frowns. "We'll have to do it from this plane. You and I can see the souls that have already breached the seal. We need to take our positions and create a circle. That will contain them while I patch the seal."

"And make it easier for Morgana to suck them in."

He curses. "One problem at a time. First, we cut off the supply of souls. Then we address the soul-sucking."

Hearing him say that boggles my mind.

This is my life. I scan the chaos in the main chamber. For me to get to my position to create a magical circle, I need to get around to the mouth of the passageway. That means I need to get past everyone battling.

"Here goes nothing." Pushing off, I run along the chamber's interior wall. Bruin is roaring and knocking men around like bowling pins. Aiden's sword is flying. Sloan, Quon Shen, and Ahren focus on Morgana and cast like magic-wielding fiends.

Dillan, Calum, and Nikon fight head-to-head with everything they've got.

As I run, I shoot balls of faery fire to knock Morgana's magical minions out of my way until I'm in position. Unfortunately, they're still in their trance. I have a feeling if they were aware of what's happening, they'd lay down their arms.

On the other hand, we'd have a major exposure breach to deal with if they knew. It's lose-lose.

If we'd set up our ritual pentacle properly, Samuel stands in earth's position.

Which it isn't.

While he works on the proximity bubble, I work on keeping the fugitives from being inhaled by Morgana.

She seems oblivious to the efforts Sloan, Ahren, and Quon Shen are making to bring her down. Their magical and physical attacks bounce off her with no effect. Meanwhile, she stares up at the ceiling with that crazy smile.

She must love consuming banished souls.

That's not a good sign.

My shield has been stinging hot since we arrived, but as each of the smoky, inky globs of Neitherland fugitives get sucked into Morgana's body, the intensity of my alarm bells turns up. "That's it. You're cut off."

The last time we took on these fugitive souls, I learned Birga cuts straight through the smoke. I raise my hands and go a different route. *"Whirlwind."*

A gust of wind builds around me, and I raise my arms. The souls are pulling themselves together into a form resembling a dementor, and if I'm lucky, they've gained enough physical form to blow them back.

Sort of. Not really.

"Maelstrom." I send my second spell out, and thankfully, that seems to twist them into smoggy whisps and prevents the dark escapees from gathering themselves into a solid form.

Focused on the ones in front of me, I miss a couple when they scatter and get behind me.

My shield bursts into a full flaming warning.

"Fi, down, now!"

Dillan's command leaves no room for question. I drop to the dirt and stone and roll to a crouch. The thundering tat-a-tat-a-tat of assault rifle gunfire is a shock.

I continue to roll as the *thwip-thwip-thwip* of arrows race over my head.

My hair is in my face, and it takes a moment for me to flick it out of my eyes. I get back to my feet and frown at the human porcupine lying ten feet behind where I'd been standing a moment ago.

I blow my brothers a kiss, reclaim my position, and check in with Samuel.

He nods and raises his hands.

As he begins, I fish out one of the two silver pendants I always wear. Squeezing the ebony etching of Dionysus's face, I hope he gets the call and decides to join us.

"Come on, Tarzan. We could use the help."

Samuel's spell to create a proximity bubble is underway and seems to be keeping the escapees contained as well as preventing them from materializing more fully.

Thankfully, the spell is primarily his responsibility. He's the expert. He learned how to do it from Melanippe before she switched sides. Quon Shen, Ahren, and I are simply here to balance the power, represent the other elements, and look good doing it.

Sadly, without Dionysus, we're missing fire.

The four of us stand in our positions around the seam and raise our palms toward one another. Samuel speaks in tongues, and I try to troubleshoot while he does his thing.

Morgana draws her hand through the ebony tendrils of evil as darkness seeps through the split seam and coils around her wrists like serpent armbands.

The intimacy of it sends a shiver down my spine.

I frown at the rip. The veil between worlds is thinnest during the time of the solstices, and this is the Time of the Colliding Realms. I don't know why I'm so surprised someone decided to take a run at releasing the dark souls of the Neitherlands to strengthen the power of Team Dark.

The snap of power beside me brings Dionysus into the mix, and he looks around like he's trying to catch up.

"Take fire and help us close the seam," I shout over the fight's chaos.

Dionysus snaps into the represented position of the pentacle's fifth element. His power links with ours, and the balance shifts.

"Yeah, baby." I breathe deeply, grounding myself in the turning of the tides. "Glad you joined us, Tarzan."

"Sorry. Clouds don't have a cell signal."

No. I suppose not.

The surge of light magic in the air eases the oppressive cloy of darkness, and the seam begins to knit back together. The flow of dark souls escaping from it slows.

"It's working. Keep doing what we're doing, guys."

With no souls left to consume, Morgana's focus shifts to assess the room. She scans our group and locks her sights on me. "You! Slayer of my son!"

Well, crapballs.

Morgana throws her hands toward me, and my shield ignites to a red alert. I drop my focus from erecting a perimeter bubble to not getting dead.

"Impenetrable Sphere."

The spell she casts at me hits and then it's on.

The world explodes in a powerful light show as Morgana's rage is directed straight at me. Yes, I struck her son down with a bolt of lightning, but in my defense, Yvain was in the middle of a cosmic prison break and tried to kill me first.

Her energy rattles my teeth and leaves a bad taste in my mouth. I expected her to be incredibly powerful but hoped she'd be like Voldemort and have to take time to regain her strength after being gone for centuries.

Or maybe that's what the soul-eating is about.

Does consuming the souls of dark powers increase her power? I have no idea, but from the assault I'm fighting to hold off, I think it does.

The force of evil energy bombarding my sphere of protection is incredible. I've got my hands up and am shaking from the violence of fending off her barrage of attacks. In the back of my mind, a little voice says having Morgana focus on me is a good thing.

It's giving Samuel and the others a chance to close the seam while she's working out her vengeful fantasies of revenge.

"Enjoy your last breaths, wench," she screeches. "Your end has come." She seems super committed to that statement—overly committed in my opinion.

I hope taking one for the team doesn't go much further than this.

Sweat drips into my eyes as I make continuous adjustments and corrections to keep my sphere around me. I blink against the sting, trying to keep my vision clear when a flash of light illuminates the inner chamber and forces me to close my eyes.

It's never a good idea to close your eyes in a fight to the death, but there's no helping it.

My shield flares as my impenetrable sphere fails and the blast knocks me back into the air. I hit the stone wall of the tomb's interior, and the little birdies are still circling when Sloan dives over to me.

"*Wall of Stone.*" He tackles me to the ground with a *thud*. I grunt, winded from the rough landing.

A moment later, a stone igloo encases the two of us. I sink against the floor and heave for breath.

"Are ye hurt, *a ghra?*" He presses a hand to my chest, and the warmth of his healing energy opens my lungs and allows me to breathe deep.

I inhale and shake my head, clearing the cobwebs. "Only my pride. That bitch has a lot of power for being dead for centuries."

"Maybe banished souls are the Power Bars of the dark world."

I bark a laugh. "Maybe you're right."

"Are ye ready to get back in the fight?"

I take a quick inventory of myself. "Yep. Everything seems to be in working order. Ready when you are."

The world outside our stone dome falls silent, and someone knocks on our shell. "Olly olly oxen free."

Sloan releases our protective barrier and helps me off the tomb's floor.

I am happy to see that other than superficial wounds, everyone is upright and in good spirits. "Did we win?"

Calum chuckles. "Well, we didn't lose."

I glance around the interior of the ritual chamber and take in the carnage. "So, what did I miss?"

Dillan smiles and lays a heavy arm across Eva's shoulders. "Our guardian angel arrived and tipped the scales. The moment Samuel sealed the seam and Eva and Dionysus turned their power on her, Morgana bugged out."

Eva is wearing an uncharacteristic frown. "Don't try to flatter me. You were supposed to notify me when everyone woke up. I finished my training, and when I went to the treehouse, Brendan and Kevin said you already left to battle without me."

Dillan sends her an apologetic smile. "Honestly, it was minutes after everyone arrived this morning that the alarm tripped. We rushed here and Boann said there was no time to waste, so we stormed the gates."

Evangeline props her hands on her hips and frowns. "How can I be a guardian angel if I have nobody to guard? I'm supposed to be with you guys."

Dillan lowers his chin in defeat. "You're right, angel. Our mistake. It won't happen again. On another note, you were awesome."

CHAPTER TWELVE

I leave Dillan to make things up with Eva and to work out the rules of how she should be involved in our lives. Samuel and the Hunter-gods are checking the bodies of the dead minion soldiers and sorting through the destruction. "How are things here? I lost track of things when Morgana targeted me."

Samuel looks tired but pleased. "With Dionysus's help, we stopped the exodus from the Neitherlands and patched the seam. I can't say how well it will hold with the veil so thin nearing the winter solstice, but we'll stick around and see what else we can do to strengthen it."

"Well, good. I'm not in the mood to track fugitives all over the hills of Ireland with glowing rocks today."

"Then consider the crisis averted."

I scan the faces of the soldiers. "If you're talking about the seam, yeah. What do we do with these guys? Can we drop them back to an army base or will that raise too many questions? And what does it mean that Morgana was consuming banished souls?"

"I'm going to say, not sure, yeah, and nothing good in that order," Calum says.

"Your wisdom never ceases to amaze me, bro." Dillan chuckles.

I step over to hug Dionysus. "Thanks for the help. I felt the tides turn the moment you joined us."

He frowns and looks around as if expecting the sudden appearance of someone. "You can't say things like that, Jane." He glances up at the ceiling. "I didn't use my powers in any way that unduly changed the natural course of events. I just helped as one of the many."

I chuckle and look up at the ceiling with him. "Have the Fates been giving you a hard time?"

He shakes his head. "No. Not yet. Eros made a few comments last night at my party about me stepping over the line. He was drunk and laughed it off, but he thinks I'm too invested in the outcome of the Culling. He said I should stop playing house with the humans and go back to being a god."

"Eros is a self-important jerk."

"Most gods of the pantheons are."

"Do you think he'll cause trouble for you?"

He shrugs. "I think he'd gladly cause trouble for *you* and that's enough to make me worry. I know I'm not the only Light member with mad skills, but I don't want to get benched because another god is jealous and bitter."

"That's the story of your life, isn't it?"

He frowns. "My old life, yes."

I hug him again, and I'm not sure if I'm reassuring him or me. "Maybe avoid Eros until the New Year's Eve party. By then, everything will be over, and he won't be able to screw anything up."

Dionysus perks right up. "New Year's Eve party? Are we having a party?"

"Of course, we are. I figure the Culling will ruin our Yule celebration, but it'll be over and done by the week after. We'll have the traditional Cumhaill dinner and resolutions celebration, and we can all snap over to your loft for a party. Sound good?"

He leans back and raises his palms. "Good? It sounds amazing. Can I pick the theme?"

I chuckle. "It's your party. Make it however big and flashy you like. No matter how this stupid Culling turns out, we'll need to unwind. You are the god of good times, so I leave it all to you."

"Hey, Dionysus," Dillan shouts from across the chamber. "Any chance you're helping us clean up this mess? Newgrange is open for business these days. Imagine the surprise of the tour guides tomorrow morning when they come in here and find dead bodies."

Yeah, that would be bad.

"What's the plan for the soldiers?" I ask.

Dillan straightens and shrugs. "Return them to the embrace of the earth? Whatever Morgana did to them, the moment she left they dropped dead. We can't send them back looking like this."

I study the spider-veining creeping from their ebony eyes outward onto their cheeks. "No, you're right. That's hard to explain."

I consider his suggestion of giving them to the ground, but my instincts take me in a different direction. "Sloan, can you *poof* me to Drombeg? I want to check something out."

Sloan and I *poof* to the Drombeg stone circle, and I glance around the ancient druid grounds. Also known as The Druid's Altar, the axial circle of the remaining seventeen standing stones is the original site our Toronto circle is modeled after.

It's where we performed the Ostara ritual.

It's also the portal gateway Dart and I use to travel between Toronto and Ireland.

After a quick call back home to Kinu, a second to Patty, and a text in the Heirs of the Order WhatsApp chatroom, I tuck my phone away and study the scene.

"Yeah, this will do. *Poof* back and bring the bodies of the fallen here."

"What have ye set into motion?" Sloan asks.

"It's a three birds with one stone idea. Let's see how well it works."

After verifying I'll be all right on my own for a few minutes, Sloan *poofs* back to the Newgrange tomb. Yes, it seems silly to ask a grown woman if she can stand alone in the countryside of Cork without getting into trouble, but reality has proven it's a fair question.

While I wait, I walk a withershins circuit around the stones. Circles are important in the magical world.

Doing magical work within circles sets an area of focus on the energy of intent. It helps not only to refine the magic of a spell but direct its intent more clearly.

Thus, Samuel's need for us to create a circle for him to contain the banished souls of the Neitherlands.

The perimeter keeps random magical energy from entering and interfering as well as the desired energy contained so it can't dissipate.

We also use circles for protection. If I'm within the circle, I could spell it to keep magical beings or harm out and away. Conversely, if I'm outside the circle, I can spell it to keep magical beings contained within if I want to trap them for safety or questioning.

The rumble of the earth beneath my boots starts as a gentle tremor and grows until I press a hand against one of the ancient stones for support.

Outside the stone circle, a sinkhole drops into the ground, and a stunning red dragon digs through the surface. Breaching the depths, she climbs out onto the wintery grounds.

Riding on the back of Scarlett is my favorite leprechaun and dear friend. Patty lifts his hand and gives me an easy wave before releasing the neck frill of the wyrm dragon. He toddles to her ribs, slides down her round body, and lands on the frozen ground. "Good to see ye, Red. When did ye get here?"

"About three this morning. We had a bit of family excitement and ended up with an unexpected trip."

His smile dims, and he studies me. "Are ye all right? Ye look like ye've been in a tussle."

"The family excitement turned out fine. Jackson's wayfarer abilities unlocked last night, and there was a frantic scramble to find where he'd gone. He was sound asleep at Da's and Shannon's. No harm done. Then, Eva surprised us and brought my brother Brendan for a visit."

His gaze narrows. "Isn't he the one shot and killed?"

"Yeah. Imagine our surprise to have him standing in the living room looking as whole and healthy as ever."

"Eva, ye say? That's Dillan's reaper girlfriend?"

"Yes, although she's working on becoming a guardian angel instead. She's currently assigned to assure the safety and well-being of our family. She used that as a loophole to give us a bit of time with Brenny."

"I'm pleased fer ye, Red. How does that get ye covered in dirt and lookin' like someone dragged ye through one of Scarlett's holes?"

I pat my chest and Scarlett swings around, drops her chin, and pushes her forehead against me. I rub my gloved hands over the scales on her skull and pat her frill. "That came later."

I've almost finished relaying the tale of Morgana opening the seam of the Newgrange tomb when another round of tremors brings our attention to the hole where Scarlett emerged.

The Western dragons in Dart's brood have arrived.

They emerge like eight colorful firecrackers shooting out of the ground, straight up into the air where they spread their wings and shake themselves free of dirt.

Green, blue, red, green, green, red, blue, green.

At the same time, a surge of magical energy erupts, and the standing stones burst into a ring of glowing golden orange. The portal link takes hold and Dart and Saxa fly up from the center of the Drombeg stones and into the air to join the others.

"The gang's all here." I smile at them greeting one another. "Wow, they're all getting so big."

Patty adjusts his hat and tucks in an escaping tuft of snow-white hair. "They are. I've mentioned it before, but it's gettin' hard to keep them happy stuck in the lair. It's in their nature to want to be out and flyin'."

I grin. "That's part three of my plan. Come on. Let's get things started, and I'll tell you what I'm thinking."

Over the next half-hour, the ten dragons play in the sky above the prehistoric monuments. When my brothers and the Greeks portal the dead over, they're invited to enjoy a crunch and munch delight.

"Do you think it's wise to give them a taste for humans?" Dillan asks.

I hadn't thought about that. Do dragons get a taste for things and go on a feeding spree? "That's a problem for tomorrow. The good news is the tomb is clean, and we patched the seam before the tourists return in the morning."

"Keeping the secret world a secret is getting harder by the day," Calum says.

Sloan nods. "Samuel said they'll reset the alarm on the tomb and make sure all traces of the battle are gone. He's still expecting Mingin to make a run at the seam, and he wants to ensure Morgana is truly gone."

"How did she set off the alarm in the first place?"

Sloan takes that one. "I wondered about that too, luv. It's only a theory, but I'd bet that after bein' a disembodied soul banished to the spirit realm for centuries their energy would carry many of the same characteristics. I'm not sure what parameters Samuel used for his spell, but if he targeted a powerful banished soul, Morgana would indeed trigger the alarm."

"That makes sense, although I have no idea how banishment to the spirit realm works."

Eva brushes a hand over her ivory coat, and the blood splatter from the battle disappears. "The structure of the spirit realm is similar to the mortal plane. Picture it like the continents of this world. Depending on who you are and how you got there, souls reside in boundary areas. There are the idyllic and utopic afterlife locations for different pantheons, races, and religions—"

"That's where I want to go," I say.

Dillan grins. "You're the one with dragon longevity, so we'll meet you at the afterlife pub."

"Sounds good." I chuckle and meet Eva's gaze. "Sorry. Go on. I don't suppose it's all Valhalla."

"Not at all. To everything, there is a balance. The banishment areas are for those removed from the physical plane for one heinous reason or another. As well, there are the punishment areas for those destined to be contained and controlled."

"The souls are segregated well enough that people stay where they're supposed to?" I ask.

"Oh, my, yes. The powers that be ensure no crossover. Could you imagine the chaos if that happened?"

I think about Brendan spending the past eighteen months in his afterlife location, and I'm thankful for the hard division. "Morgana spent centuries banished. So, there's a possibility she bumped into Mingin. Maybe she came to Newgrange to release him and have him join her cause?"

"What is her cause?" Nikon asks.

"Lady PacMan'ing all the ghosts?" Dillan offers.

I don't know. "Maybe there was someone specific she wanted

to release, or she simply wanted to power up on the strongest, most vile fugitives of the Dark."

"Maybe Merlin would know," Dillan says. "He knew her for years, and they were close at one time."

"I'll text him and ask if he has any ideas." I pull out my phone as a notification hits, and my cell vibrates in my hand. I read the message and smile. "Okay, perfect. We're onto part two of my plan. Road trip!"

"Where are we going?" Dillan asks.

"To Emhain Abhlach."

The mythical and mystical island of Emhain Abhlach seems innocuous at first glance. It brims with beauty as the Irish Sea ebbs onto the rocky beach, the tall grasses sway wild and untouched, and water plunges from cascading waterfalls down toward a dense green forest that seems to go on for miles.

It is all those things, but after being here more than a dozen times over the past month, it's much more.

There is a reason why every power-hungry faction of civilization has tried to gain control of this island's energy.

It's a primal source.

The island radiates raw fae prana in such a concentrated form you can feel it with all your senses. It permeates your lungs when you breathe. It tingles in your cells when you move. It buzzes as a soft white noise in your ears. And it fuels a druid's core energy and strength as if you've sucked back a case of Red Bull.

Sloan *poofs* Calum, Dillan, Eva, Patty, and me to the shoreline. Dionysus descends from the air on the back of Contessa. The Heirs of the Druid Order stand together awaiting our arrival. Almost simultaneously, Nikon arrives with Da, Brendan, Kevin, and Liam.

"Welcome to Emhain Abhlach." Fighting the urge to smother

Brendan—because I totally want to—I jog over and hug the brothers Jarrod, Darcy, and Davin Perry, then Eric Flanagan, and Tad McNiff. "Thanks for coming on short notice, guys."

Eric grins. "Anytime, Fi. Yer always good fer a change of pace and a few life-altering surprises."

Jarod nods. "He's right. When ye send us an invite fer anythin', there's usually a better than fair chance we'll be rollin' up our sleeves and gettin' down to it."

I'm not sure that's the reputation I want to be cultivating with my peers. Not that they're wrong…but still. "Sadly, we've already fought today's battle, but I have an idea that might fit into the life-altering surprise category and will be a change of pace."

"What's that?" Tad asks.

I turn back to the Perry twins, my excitement building by the moment. "Did you bring them?"

They step apart and gesture at the stack of dragon saddles lying on the ground.

I tilt my head back and close my eyes, focusing on my connection with Dart. *Ready when you are, buddy. Come join us.*

One moment the sky is clear and blue and the next, it's speckled with ten awe-inspiring dragons swooping and flapping above. Dart initiates his descent and Saxa follows close. The rest of the brood follows suit.

Once the dragons have landed, I waggle my brows and smile. "Spread out and introduce yourselves, fellas. Oh, and welcome to your first dragon flying lesson."

CHAPTER THIRTEEN

"Are ye sure this is a good idea?" Brendan asks from where he's standing at Dart's second spike.

I grin back at him and nod. "Don't worry. I'm a professional. You're perfectly safe. Just don't let go."

Brenny's emerald eyes are practically glowing. "Trust me. The last thing I'll do is let go. I've only been back from the dead for twelve hours. I'm not ready to get myself killed again."

"Good to hear," Dillan shouts from the back of Esym, a green female dragon. "I'm not sure if anyone has mentioned it, but you getting yourself killed didn't work for the rest of us."

Brenny sends me an apologetic wink, but I know if put in the same situation, he'd sacrifice himself again.

That's who he is.

So, for as long as we have with him, we'll consider it a gift and a huge win on the closure front. Hopefully, he can work out whatever has been eating at Da.

I check in with the red boy on my left. Sloan is a natural as a dragon rider, but Liam's looking a little green around the gills at the second spike. "How you doin', bestie?"

Liam casts me a withering glare and releases his middle finger from his grip on the handle to answer me.

I laugh. "Come on, dude. Where's your chutzpah?"

"The last time I stepped out of my lane in one of your druid adventures, I got shot twice. Been there, done that, got the brass casing pendant to prove it."

Does he hate it that much?

I study his expression, trying to determine if I've grossly misread his limitations when he sighs and shakes his head. "Fine. It's not totally horrible."

"What happened to you in the past two years?" Brenny asks. "Where's my partner in crime?"

Liam shrugs. "Like Dillan said. You getting dead didn't work for the rest of us. That and almost getting dead myself made me re-evaluate."

Brendan snorts. "That was your first mistake. Don't worry. Brenny's back now. I'll pull those granny panties off you and help you find your balls again."

I chuckle. It's so good to have Brendan time.

Rory swoops happily around Dillan before flapping her wings to resume flying with Eva's dove.

Eva dips her wing, soaring gracefully on the crest of the wind. She's majestic in her dove form, and the rays of golden light streaming down from the heavens to fall on her strengthen the image.

I check on the others as well.

Calum and Kev seem to be having the time of their lives riding Abeloth—the largest of the red dragons. I'm glad he's behaving especially after the fiasco of him kidnapping Dillan as a Quidditch snitch.

Eric looks comfortable riding Chezzo, a blue boy like Dart.

Darcy and Davin are on Cadmus and are having the time of their lives. Their time studying the lost art of dragon care has given them the most experience with the dragons, but that didn't include dragon-riding.

Until now.

Patty and Da, on the other hand, look as serious and apprehensive as usual.

"Come on, oul men. It wouldn't kill you to crack a smile and enjoy the moment. We're riding dragons!"

Patty frowns at me from the first spike saddle on Kaida, a blue female. "The warding on the island isn't to be underestimated. Are ye sure we should approach this way?"

My hair flips wildly in the wind, and I pull it out of my face to see him. "I'm not underestimating the warding. Dart and Saxa portaled in during the battle last month, and Dionysus is not only a god but also duty-bound to the island. They'll be able to lead us in."

"I hope yer right, Red. In all the time I lived in the city, no one ever arrived who didn't pass through the test of the shifting forest."

"Dare to be different, oul man. This is a new age for Emhain Abhlach. Besides, I want to create bonds between the dragons and potential riders."

Not all dragons take riders, Dart says into my mind. He pumps his wings and tilts his head toward Saxa.

His girlfriend is a brilliant sunshiny yellow with dark gold wings and a blunt snout. Raised in Merlin's sea cave far below Tintagel Castle, Saxa is a free dragon and fought hard to stay that way in a time when men revered dragons as mindless beasts of burden.

I know, sweetie. That's why I didn't ask Saxa to wear a saddle or offer to carry anyone. I respect each dragon's choice. If one of your brothers or sisters agrees to carry one of us and train for the Culling, that doesn't mean they have to unite with the rider with a permanent bond as we did.

Thank you.

Of course.

"Fi, tell me the truth," Eric shouts, from the back of Chezzo, on my left. "Is that a pink and purple pegasus, or is Dionysus screwin' with us?"

I chuckle, taking note of our path of entry into the small, protected valley where the hidden city of Emhain Abhlach is. "Contessa McSparkles is a pink and purple pegasus, yes."

He laughs and shakes his head. "See, always a life-altering adventure."

I'm about to explain that Contessa being a pegasus has nothing to do with me when Dart's magical signature ratchets up and tingles over my skin.

Dionysus is in front of us, and I feel his power too. "Welcome to Neverland, boys."

A sudden sense of foreboding strikes me, and everything within me wants to turn and forget the whole idea. It's invasive and pervasive.

I fight to come to grips with it when a round of the shakes hits and my stomach swirls.

Hold on, Fi, Dart says. *It's only the warding. It'll be over in a moment.*

I close my eyes and focus on his words. It's only the warding. It's only the warding. I squeeze the center handle of my saddle with both hands and breathe through it.

Passing through the warding is like breaking through an invisible field. It grows steadily more resistant. Tightens around me. Compresses my lungs.

Then—*snap!*

The tension releases like a snapped elastic band, and I gulp a deep breath to fill my lungs and settle my traitorous stomach. "Okay, Patty. You were right. The forest entrance is much easier on the mind and body."

I glance around, and everyone seems to be recovering as

rapidly as I am. Lifting my face, I let the wind coming up over the scaled plate of Dart's head calm my nerves.

Once I feel more grounded, it's smooth sailing, and we're looking down at the glistening golden dildo of the hidden city.

Should it be called the hidden city now that we can see it?

Davin and Darcy burst out laughing as the dragons descend toward the grassy meadows by the pink prana river. "Does anyone else think the tower of Emmet's palace looks like a giant, golden willy?"

There's a round of shared laughter, then Dart's wings reverse to give us backward thrust, and we're settling on the ground.

We disembark as a group, and I drop off Dart's elbow to land on the lush, green grass. Unlike the outside world, this magical place is warm and thriving with life.

"What do you think of this place, kids?" I ask the dragons.

The excited grunts and posturing make me think they like it but without an internal bond to them all like I have with Dart or the ability for them to speak our language, it's hard to tell.

"They are curious why you ask." Dart answers for them.

"You're growing every day. Patty says even the new lair isn't enough space for you to stretch your wings. I realize you have the ability to glamor now, but I thought maybe living on an enchanted island with an open sky, endless space, and the power of prana to feed your strength, maybe it's a place you could call home without having to hide."

There's a great deal more excitement now and a lot of tail-smacking.

"Cadmus and Abeloth want to know about food," Dart says. "What will they eat?"

"We're still working on that. The system the druids put in place to keep you fed is still the best option but getting it to you through the warding of the island on a regular basis will be prohibitive."

A rush of grunting and jostling ensues.

Patty chuffs. "Och, stop yer bellyachin' ye wee babies. She said we're workin' on it, didn't she?"

I bite back the urge to giggle. Patty sounds like Da did while he was raising us. "Yes, I'm working on it. I was thinking—"

"No, ye can't hunt wild in the countryside, ye thick-skulled adolescents," Patty snaps. "That's the opposite of livin' in secret. Isn't it?"

Exposure is happening more and more often, but I won't let my dragon kids be part of that fiasco. "Patty's right. You can't hunt freely, but if you prove to us you can live here with less supervision, we could let you fly to Gran's and Granda's a couple of nights a week, and we can ensure there is food for you."

Patty frowns at something said and shakes his head. "Did ye hear the part about provin' ye can live here without constant supervision? That means if ye *don't*, ye'll be back in the lair with Queen Smotherer motherin' ye until yer two hundred."

I chuckle at the horror on their faces. "No need to panic yet. We're going to head into the city to visit my brother for a few hours. Explore the valley, discuss it among yourselves, and when we get back, we'll talk more about you staying here."

They rush forward, and I'm swept away and lifted to body surf like we're in a dragon mosh pit. I giggle and navigate the ride for a bit before I reclaim my independence and drop the ten feet to the ground.

Patting Esym's blunt snout, I catch my breath. "Go play and explore. Don't burn down the city and don't push past the warding. There's plenty of space for you to enjoy right here. You stay on the island. Got it?"

I assume they do because the eight of them launch off and are cartwheeling through the sky a moment later. I scrub Dart's center horn and smile up at his siblings. "We're not going anywhere, buddy. If you want to go play and explore, have at it."

"Rory wants to come too." Dillan grins at the pseudodragon perched on his shoulder. "Keep an eye on her, will you?"

Of course. But in truth, this island is her home. She grew up here, Dart says.

I relay that to Dillan, and he chuckles. "Right. I forgot about that."

Dart spares a moment to look at Saxa, then the three of them launch into the air and pump their wings to catch up to the others.

Contessa whinnies and gallops off as well.

I watch the aerial acrobatics for a minute and shift my attention back to the two-legged members of my family. "All righty then. That was phase two of my plan for today. On to phase three."

"What is phase three, *a ghra?*" Sloan asks.

I grin. "Seeing Emmet's face when he sees Brenny."

CHAPTER FOURTEEN

Our procession moves away from the fuchsia river of prana and through the two massive golden gates set into an ebony stone wall. The streets of the hidden city lay beyond and up the steep slope that leads to the palace. While the building is massive and palatial, there is no denying the phallic architecture of the golden tower.

"I can't believe any of this is real." Brendan gazes around at the multicolored houses stacked in tiers and rising with us as we climb.

I hug his arm, and I know I'm being touchy-feely, but man, I can't stop. "The first time we came here with Fionn, Bodhmall, and the Fianna warriors, the houses were all so vibrantly painted and glistening with magic and ornamentation I couldn't believe it myself."

"That was when you traveled back in time?"

I see the struggle of Brendan's mental hamster in his eyes as he tries to process it and totally sympathize.

We've all been there.

"Yep."

"That's happened to you more than once."

"Yep."

"And since you were here back then, the city got locked away and unplugged from the Barbie juice, and you guys resurrected it and juiced it up again."

"That's the gist of it. But unknown centuries of being locked away and forgotten left the city a little worse for wear."

"What about the people who were here?"

"No idea."

"What happened to lock it away?"

"Another mystery."

He glances down the side streets and up toward the balconies. "Emmet is the king of this island?"

I shield my gaze from the sun. The light reflecting off the tower is blinding. "During one of our early battles he was knocked into a river of power much like the one back there, and it altered him."

"Funny, not funny," Calum says. "Shortly after that, he turned into a kangaroo."

Brendan barks a laugh. "Okay, now I'm sure you're shitting me."

"Not even a little." Dillan pulls out his phone. "Look, I took pictures."

Brendan accepts the phone and laughs as he scrolls through Dillan's gallery.

"Huh, my brother can turn into a kangaroo. I never thought I'd say that."

"Wait until you see what Fi turns into."

Brendan shakes his head. "Nope. Not ready for that. I need my baby sister to be Fi...at least until I can wrap my head around any of this. It's bad enough she's living with a guy and moved out. Too much too soon."

I roll my eyes. "I only moved next door."

"Calum and Kev moved beside you, and Aiden and Kinu moved the kids into our house."

"There are four monkeys now, not two," I add.

"Yeah, Aiden mentioned that."

I get the sense that he's overloading, so I let the conversation drop. We walk for a few minutes without saying anything.

"Emmet chose to leave everything and live here? I can't wrap my head around that. The last time I saw Em he was in the academy and excited about being a cop. Now what? That's over?"

"Officially, he's been reassigned by the SITFU task force we all work for. If he comes back, he'll always have a place, but for now, he feels his powers brought him here for a reason, and he swore an oath that bound him as the guardian of the island."

"What are his powers?"

"Honestly, we don't really know yet. But it's going to be good. Mother Nature even said so."

"Mother Nature," Brenny repeats, chuckling. "This is whacked."

"Welcome to our world," Calum says.

We climb the city's slope, making our way toward the palace sitting high above the meadow and prana river where we landed. The dragons are flying above us, playing, twirling in the air, and blowing fire at each other in a game of tag.

"That was the bar where Betrys and I had our meeting and got to know each other." I point up to the balcony overlooking the street. "That's where Sloan stood and glared at me."

He arches a brow. "Only because ye refused to keep quiet about events yet to come and I didn't want ye cockin' up the future."

"Och, and there she be." Patty grins at the faded purple house down the next side street. "If ye don't mind, I'll catch up with ye. I'd like to spend some time with the ghosts of my past."

"Sure, Patty." I smile at him. "But be careful. Brendan brought up a good point. We don't know what happened here, where the people went, or how the reboot of the city will affect things now."

I stare at the draperies hanging in the windows and the

wooden doors dangling off hinges. Maybe I'm paranoid and inviting trouble, but I've got a weird feeling that the city isn't as dead and abandoned as it seems.

"Bruin, keep an eye on Patty for me, will you?"

I release my bear, and he materializes in front of me. "Sure, Red. On it."

Brendan jumps to the side and collides with Liam. "Fuckety-fuck. I don't see me getting used to that."

I laugh. "Bruin's not a *that*. He's a *him*. Sack up, Cumhaill. Did being dead make you into a Nancy boy?"

Brendan laughs. "So, we're past the gushing part of the reunion and settling in, are we? Nancy boy. Rude."

Liam pushes him upright and laughs. "Don't feel bad. The first time I saw Bruin, I nearly jumped into mom's lap in the front room of your house."

I laugh. "You did, but Dillan was the best. He jumped so far back he ended up on the back of the couch pressed against the wall."

Dillan flashes me his middle finger. "This is fun and all, but why the fuck are we walking up the hills of San Francisco when four of you can portal?"

"An excellent question," Dionysus says. "Shall I end the suffering?"

The suggestion seems to be popular with the majority, so I give him a thumbs-up. "Yeah, Tarzan. The main foyer would be great."

Dionysus snaps us inside the massive double doors of the palace, and I glance up at the swaying chandeliers over our heads. When we first came here with Kyna, they were lit with incense and filled the entire entrance hall with a lovely scent.

In the two times I've come in the past month, that has been lacking. "Noice. He's got these working again."

"I was thinking the same thing," Calum says, smiling at the ceiling.

"Yo, Emmet! Mighty King of the Enchanted Isle, we humbly request an audience!"

Dillan's voice echoes through the space, up the curved stone staircase to the second floor, and bounces off the golden beige stone of the walls.

I pinch together my finger and thumb and press it under my tongue. Letting out a sharp whistle, we wait for the returning sound.

When it comes, we strike off through the entrance hall and into the picture gallery across the corridor. We take a left and walk through the long, rectangular room and into what Emmet calls the deadheads corridor.

It's some kind of ancestral memorial room with oil paintings and close to fifty marble busts.

"That's a lot of carved heads," Liam says.

"I know, right? Look, this is one of the cat people that were here way back when."

"I believe feline folk is the appropriate term, luv," Sloan says.

We exit the deadheads corridor, cross through the dining room, and enter the servery. "Yeah, you're right. My bad."

"Feckin' hell, this place is monstrous," Jarrod says.

I laugh. "What part of the word *palace* didn't you understand, Perry?"

Calum cups his hands around his mouth and shouts, "Marco!"

"Polo!" Emmet's voice comes back to us from off and to the right.

Leaving the servery, we pass the pantry rooms and turn right toward a rear staircase. Jogging up the curved, stone steps, we emerge on the floor where Kyna set us up with a room when we flipped back a thousand years.

Is he on this floor or do we keep climbing?

"Marco!" I call.

"Polo!" Emmet calls, a hum whirring along with his reply. He's getting closer and definitely on this floor.

Brendan tucks in behind Calum and Dillan, and I chuckle, anticipating what's coming next. Sure, Brenny has been dazzled and overwhelmed today, but he's hands-down the most off-beat comic relief of our family.

Emmet rounds the corner in ripped jeans and a wild flamingo shirt unbuttoned and catching the breeze behind him. Doc is sitting on the back of the skateboard, a huge smile on his face and his warm brown fur rustling in the breeze of their travels.

When Emmet sees us, he drops his back foot to propel his board, racing faster toward us.

The playful image of him rolling along reminds me of when we were kids. Only back then, we had to share two beat-up old skinny skateboards—not the cruiser board he has now. We also didn't have a fraction of the track in our house he has here.

As they slow down, Doc jumps off, does an acrobatic roll in the air, and lands in what I can only guess is his attempt at a superhero stance.

It's hard to tell with a pine marten.

They're very low to the ground to begin with.

Emmet stops in front of us, stomps his kicktail, and the board pops up into his hand with a showman's flair. Straightening, he sweeps his free hand through the air. "Welcome to Fantasy Island."

He grins at Da. "Good to see you, oul man. What do you think of the new digs?"

"I'd tell ye not to skateboard in the house, but I suppose ye can do what ye want in yer own palace."

"Nice, right?"

"What happened to the Segway I brought you?" Dionysus asks.

Emmet frowns. "It seems EMP stands for EM on Prana. Being here juices me up and everything I touch fritzes out. My phone, laptop, the Segway...all dead. I've temporarily stricken modern from my daily routine."

"Do you think it's the island and not you?" I ask. "Maybe being here was shorting you out."

"Nope. It's me. I can feel the fae energy pulsing off me, fighting with the circuitry before it fritzes out. I'm too much to handle."

"No argument there." I chuckle and gesture at the group. "So, we brought some friends to say hi."

Emmet lifts his chin and smiles at the heirs and the Greeks. Then Dillan and Calum move apart, and Brenny steps into view.

"What the fuck?" Emmet's eyes blow wide, and he steps back, tripping into a stumble. He regains his footing and straightens. We all share the pale complexion of our Celtic heritage, but he's gone ghost white.

Ha! I suppose it's literally ghost white...although I'm not sure Brendan can be considered a ghost.

Emmet looks from Brenny to me, then to Da. "What's happening? Someone, please catch me up because I'm about to either wet my pants or lose my shit."

Brenny laughs. "Don't do that, Smidget. Kings of enchanted islands don't look good in pee pants."

Emmet groans as Brenny calls him by the childhood pet name the older brothers always teased him with. "Are you really here? How?"

Brenny laughs and opens his arms. "I'm going for the Oh, Henry! grand championship. Surprise! Best prank evah. Not dead. Kidding not kidding."

After we get Emmet caught up and the appropriate crushing hugs and tears of joy happen, I explain to Emmet why we're here.

"Dragons?" Emmet exhales. "How do I feed eight adolescent Westerns without livestock or any way of getting them what they need?"

"I'm working on that."

"I suppose you didn't wait to talk to me before putting this plan in motion?"

"Sorry, your cell reception hasn't been the greatest since you moved behind a veil of enchanted magic."

He can't argue that.

"Okay, when should I expect them?"

"They're getting the lay of the land as we speak."

"Of course, they are. Why am I not surprised?"

"You're not? And here I thought gifting you the guardianship of dragons would be a big surprise."

He offers me a droll stare. "Har-har. Fi's so funny."

"Hey, Em," Brendan says. "I heard ye ran off and got hitched. Geez, I wasn't dead that long."

Calum chuckles. "Em's always been an impulse shopper. It took Kevin and me ten years to get there."

Emmet shrugs. "If your death taught me anything, bro, it was that life is short. We grabbed the reins of happiness with both hands and seized the day."

Brendan grins. "Well then, I'm happy I was part of the happy day at least. Where is my new sister-in-law? Ciara, isn't it?"

Em's smile fades. "It seems the flames of passion aren't enough in the end. Ciara isn't keen on living in a magical bubble, and I need to be here. We're still good and love each other, but I want her to be happy, and she misses her old life."

"I'm sorry, Em." I rush forward to hug him.

"Good one, Fi. You sound sincere."

"I *am*. I want you to be the happiest of happy, no matter how that looks to you. I'm sorry it didn't work out the way you hoped."

He shrugs. "S'all good. We had nine amazing months together and parted the best of friends."

Da steps up and hugs him next, and when he eases back, he kisses his cheek. "That's what matters, son. Every experience adds to the building blocks of who we become. The time ye spent together was important to ye both."

Emmet looks like things are getting a little too real for him, so I divert the convo. "Now it's your turn to spend time with Brenny. We don't know how long he'll be able to stay with us, and I was panicked he'd be taken back before you got the chance to say hi."

That puts a smile back on Emmet's face. "Damn, I've missed you. I talked about you all the time with Ciara. Every time something came up and I thought of you, I'd tell another Brenny story."

Brenny squeezes Emmet's shoulder. "It's good to be worshipped. Not everyone can handle the adoration and remain humble. It takes a special kind of special."

"Yes, it does," Dionysus says. "How about we celebrate while the dragons settle in? Then I can show Em *my* little surprise."

Emmet arches a brow and chuckles. "I've been around you enough to have seen your little surprise more times than necessary, Greek. I'm good."

Dionysus grins. "There's nothing little about that, and don't pretend there is. No, my little surprise has wings and flies."

"Is it a pig? Do pigs now fly?"

Dionysus chuckles, his face warming with a sly smile as if he considers pigs as Emmet's first guess.

Emmet looks over the group and laughs. "It's really good to see all of you. Yeah, let's have a Dionysus celebration feast out on the grand balcony. We can enjoy the sunshine, check on the dragons, and Dionysus can show me his surprise."

CHAPTER FIFTEEN

The Dionysus celebration is, as always, a huge success. There is plenty of food and wine, laughter, and catching up. With him, any excuse to drink and be merry is a good thing. From the grand balcony, we can see the dragons soaring up from the meadow below the city, swooping through the sky in wide, graceful arcs.

"That's pretty spectacular." Emmet smiles out at the scene. "Do you honestly think I can provide a good home for them, Fi?"

"I wouldn't have brought them if I didn't. I know I joke about being the Mother of Dragons, but I sorta am. They look up to me like that, and although the Queen of Wyrms is their dragon mother, I get to be the fun one."

"It's always good to be the fun one," Dionysus says.

I chuckle as he passes, topping up everyone's wine glasses. When he moves on to check on the Perry brothers, I lean in and whisper, "Are you really okay, Em? I hate the idea of you being here all alone, and now that you can't play a computer game or anything, you must be so bored."

"Not even a little. Doc and I have been having a riot exploring the city, we have three libraries full of books, and now we've got dragons. We're good."

Doc brushes my feet, and I bend to pick him up. "Exploring the city, eh? So the two of you are Indiana Jonesing it?"

Doc brushes his whiskers against my cheek, and I kiss the top of his head. "Yesterday we went to the cantina and played old-time saloon. It was fun."

"The big yellow building on the main path toward the gates?"

"No. This was a blue building over by the city wall."

"Well, I was in the yellow one. It has a bar on the main floor and an open balcony on the second floor where you can sit and watch what's happening in the streets."

Em chuckles. "Which is nothing at the moment."

That makes me sad for him. "I'm sorry, Em. Truly. I want you to be happy however that looks."

"Thanks, Fi. It means a lot that you tried as hard as you did. I honestly didn't think it would matter where we live. Love is love, amirite?"

I think about Sloan and his comment about living in Ireland one day to take over as the Shrine-Keeper. Whether it's here or Toronto or anywhere in the world, I would love Sloan as much.

"You're right. When the stars align, and you're with the right person at the right time in your life, nothing else will matter."

While he thinks about that, I think about my words. Standing there with my belly full, my family whole once again, and watching the dragons play, I'm truly at peace.

Sure, there are a dozen crazy things about to go wrong in the world, but for this moment—all is well.

"It's nice, isn't it?" Em asks.

"I was thinking the same thing."

Sadly, as much as I'd love to stand here forever, life moves on, and our love-in ends.

"So, do you want to go ride one?" I ask.

Emmet turns to me and grins. "Hells yeah. If they're offering, I'm accepting."

I chuckle. "With what's about to go down in the coming days, I thought having druid dragon riders would be a great offensive force."

"Not to mention really freaking cool. I want to be a druid dragon rider. Who wouldn't?"

I laugh and turn to the others. "How about we take this party down to the meadow for Dragon Training 2.0? There are plenty of Merlin's lessons I can pass on to you. Then, we can get the man out here himself in the next day or two, and he can give the Mastery Course."

Dillan snorts. "Maybe by then, he won't be playing the part of the invisible man."

"Fingers crossed. He figured the misfire would wear off soon enough."

Emmet looks at me and barks a laugh. "Seriously? Merlin had a spell misfire and is invisible?"

"A potion, and yeah, we're still trying to figure out how to help Laurel and Benjamin."

"Then we should for sure invite him here. I want to see him invisible."

Calum laughs. "You do know what the word invisible means, don't you, Em?"

We all get a chuckle out of that.

With Emmet's heart hopefully a little lighter, I call everyone to order. "So, boys who portal...can we transport the group down to the meadow, please? We've got dragon-riding to do and only so much sunlight left."

"Don't forget my surprise," Dionysus says.

"And Emmet can see Dionysus' surprise."

"Which is not a flying pig," Dionysus adds.

The second dragon ride of the day goes off with as much excitement and enthusiasm as the first. Bruin and Patty join us down in the meadow, and after we do some basic maneuvers, the guys get gradually more adventurous.

I make it clear to the dragons the dangers we'll face in the coming weeks and tell them they don't have to be involved.

That doesn't deter them in the slightest.

With that settled, I explain that taking a rider can be as temporary as needed for the Culling. I'm not asking for anyone to extend invitations for bonding.

That said, I'm hoping a few of the dragons might *want* to bond with our crew because they're all good people, and secretly...if a dragon bonds with Sloan and my brothers, they'll get dragon longevity too, and I won't have to lose them.

No pressure.

"Can I play dragon tag too?" Bruin asks as Da, Brenny, and I watch the aerial hijinks overhead. "Remember when I bounced from dragon to dragon cutting down riders during Morgana's tournament at Tintagel? That was fun but more difficult than it looked. I think I should practice that more."

"Sure, buddy. Have fun."

Bruin takes off in a powerful run and disappears to ghost into the air and up to the dragons above.

"I can't believe this is your life." Brendan shakes his head. "Or that I've missed all of it."

I press a hand over my sternum, feeling Brenny's druid spark burning brightly within me. "I have something of yours...in here. When all this happened, Da and the boys voted that I keep your share of the family magic, but now that you're back, you should have it."

Brenny presses his hand against mine and shakes his head. "No. You keep it. We don't know what time we've got and when Death takes me back, I'll wish you still had a piece of me."

Part of me—a totally selfish part—is relieved. I love always having a piece of Brenny with me. "Thanks, B."

He steps beside me and hugs me tight to his side. "So, Ciara and Emmet have split before I even meet her. That's a shame."

I say nothing.

"By Emmet's surprise to hear your consolations, I take it the two of you didn't hit it off?"

"No, but we called a truce for Emmet's sake, and we both tried to coexist on good terms."

"Ye did yer best to put yer animosity to bed fer yer brother's sake," Da says. "I watched ye take it on the chin a dozen times to keep things civil. Sometimes people just don't get along."

True story.

In a flurry and flap of giant, purple wings, Dionysus lands and joins us. "Brendan, would you like to ride the skies on Contessa? She's very gentle, and Fi told me once how much you enjoy riding horses."

"I do, very much," Brendan steps over to admire her. "Although it's been years."

"It's like riding a bike, only it's a horse with wings."

"Got it." Brendan chuckles. "You don't mind?"

"Not at all. Sharing and putting other people's happiness ahead of mine is part of being in a family."

Brendan glances at me, looking a little boggled.

"Dionysus is an honorary Cumhaill of the first order. He's never had the kind of family love we offer and has proven himself worthy at every turn. I have no doubt you'll enjoy getting to know him as much as we have."

"Thank you, Jane." In a snap of magic, Dionysus shifts from being mounted on Contessa McSparkles to standing right in front of me. "I heart you."

"Right back at you, dude."

Brenny laughs and shakes his head. "Your life is crazy; you know that? Yet, somehow, it suits you."

"Crazy good you mean. Hells yeah, it does."

Brendan approaches Contessa and Dionysus goes over to help with the introductions.

"He's right, ye know," Da says beside me. "All of this suits ye better than it ever suited me."

I turn to meet my father's gaze, pleased we're back to speaking to one another again. "I love this life. I'm sorry you didn't find the same joy in it and that you got dragged back into it without a say. I feel bad about that for you and Aiden."

He shakes his head. "No regrets on my behalf. Enough things are comin' at ye that are beyond yer control. Ye don't need to carry the weight of guilt fer me or anyone else. Everythin' happens as it's meant. My parents sent Sloan to test my children to save Da's life. Ye stepped up and found yer purpose and yer partner in life at the same time. I wouldn't want it any other way."

That makes me feel better.

"Can we promise not to fight anymore? The world is going to shit, and you are the strength in my foundation. I lost my footing when you pulled out of our lives. I can't do all this without you."

"Well, I never meant fer ye to find out I'm not as perfect as ye think I am."

I roll my eyes and let out a soft chuckle. "Nice try. No one thinks you're perfect."

"Och, well, then I'm not doing my job." I hear the teasing in his voice, and I'm relieved.

I've missed it.

His fingers close around my wrist, and he turns me to look at him. "I'm sorry, *mo chroi*. Ye were right, and I was too caught up in myself to see it. That's over now, I swear."

I hug him and let out a breath I've held for much too long. "Good because I've missed talking to you."

He eases back and studies me. "Same."

"Clan Cumhaill is back on track and just in time, too. We've got a shit-ton to do and no time to do it."

"Indeed," a woman says before us. "There's very little time. I am pleased you finally reached out."

Da, Sloan, and I stiffen as the air beside us shimmers, and we're left blinking against the white glow of two women stepping through the open portal. When the brilliance dims, I blink and lower the hand shielding my eyes.

Mother Nature is a voluptuous woman wearing a leafy green skirt with animated images of forest animals running and hopping across the pattern. Her peasant blouse is ivory lace, flowy, and looks lovely against the warm, chestnut brown of her skin and the stunning Caribbean turquoise blue of her eyes.

She's utterly resplendent.

"It's lovely to see you again, Goddess." I bow my head. "Thank you for coming."

Da and Sloan have dropped to one knee and have their gazes fixed on the ground.

"What a reverent welcome," Mother Nature says. "If I remember correctly, I received a similarly warm reception the first time we encountered one another. Rise, gentlemen, please."

"It's an honor to meet yer acquaintance, milady," Da says, his hand fisted over his heart. "Blessed be."

Sloan has his hand over his heart too and lowers his head. "It's a pleasure as always, milady."

Mother Nature winks at me. "It never gets old, having handsome men of moral standing flattering me. It's one of the perks I enjoy the most."

Sarah Connor stands next to her, casually scanning across the skies at the dragons, Bruin, and Contessa playing in the clouds.

"Thanks for helping us connect, Sarah. It's much appreciated.

Oh, and welcome to Emhain Abhlach, or as Emmet calls it, Fantasy Island."

Sarah chuckles and scans the lush green meadow, the fuchsia pink river of prana, the dragons flying above in abandon, and the hidden city glistening behind us. "It's breathtakin'. I didn't know such a place existed."

Mother Nature smiles at the surroundings. "It did, then it didn't, and now it does once again. That is largely due to the Cumhaills—and of course, dear Emmet's selfless sacrifice."

She tips her gaze up to the late-afternoon sky and raises her hand. "Emmet, will you come down and join us, sweet boy? I wish to speak to you."

The words have no more volume than I'd use to speak to anyone standing three feet away, yet Cadmus swings in a wide arc and pumps his wings to return to the meadow.

"Emmet rides dragons now?" Sarah asks.

I grin. "This is his first attempt. Patty mentioned the Westerns are restless in the lair. I thought moving them here so they could live out in the open and fly without worry of consequences was an idea worth pursuing. They've only been here a few hours."

"They seem to enjoy it here," Mother Nature says.

"They do. They're very excited. The only stumbling block is how to ensure we keep them fed in such an isolated location."

"Can't they hunt?" Sarah asks.

Oh, the chaos that would cause. "They would love to, but if large stretches of the Irish countryside suddenly get razed, and dozens of sheep go missing, farmers will get upset. If it happens three times a week, they'll be more than upset. They'll start waving their pitchforks."

Mother Nature frowns. "Is that why you called for me, child? You wish for help feeding the dragons?"

"No, ma'am. We'll figure that out. We have a system of attaining and delivering dead animals from poaching, die-offs from farms, and roadkill. We can still do that, but the island's shielding makes things a bit more of a challenge. All we need is easier access."

"You asked me here to make access to the island easier?"

"No, ma'am," I repeat, feeling a little silly that this has become a guessing game. "We asked you here because we believe Death is supporting Team Dark during the Culling. We wondered if you will grant us your favor as you did for Fionn and Bodhmall during the last Culling?"

"If it be yer will," Sloan adds, bowing his head. "Any support yer able to offer would be very much appreciated."

Cadmus lands over by the orchard Gran created. Emmet releases the handle on his first spike, runs, and pitches himself into a forward aerial to dismount.

It's not only incredibly coordinated, but it's also damn impressive. I think simply being here has given him more confidence...which Emmet never lacked in the first place.

His cheeks are flushed pink when he arrives, and though his smile stiffens a little when he sees Sarah, I know it's nothing more than worrying about a confrontation after the bruised feelings from their most recent exchanges. "Hello, ladies. Welcome to Fantasy Island."

Da chuckles softly and shakes his head. "Ye like to say that, don't ye?"

"Yes...yes, I do." Emmet grins and turns back to Mother Nature and Sarah. "So, welcome. Do you want a tour? Can I get you something? What can I do for you?"

Mother Nature smiles. "Since you asked, I do have a favor to ask."

CHAPTER SIXTEEN

Sloan *poofs* the six of us back to the grand balcony of the palace, and Da offers everyone a glass of wine. "It's a very good vintage. Dionysus has impeccable taste."

Sarah chuckles. "I suppose he would."

There is still half a feast left, and Mother Nature seems intrigued by the spread.

"Help yourself to food," I say. "There's plenty."

She leans closer to the table and inhales. "It smells divine. You don't mind if we eat while we speak?"

"Of course not." I select a plate off the stack at the ready and hand it to her.

"Do ye always go all out like this?" Sarah asks.

"Not at all. We were celebrating having my brother back with us."

Mother Nature chooses a spring roll and spears a few meatballs. "Brendan, yes. Evangeline relocated him from his final resting place to bring him to you."

"You know about that?" I'm about to ask how when I clue in. *Right. She's Mother Nature.* "We hope the decision doesn't get her into trouble with Death. Our family was struggling, and she believed we'd be better prepared for the battles to come if we had closure."

Mother Nature scoops a spoonful of plum sauce and swirls the end of her spring roll through it. "Everything is a balance. Life and death. Good and evil. Chocolate and strawberries. As much as we might want things to evolve without consequence, it rarely happens."

Sadly, that doesn't make me feel better about Brenny or Eva.

That's not why we're here.

I make eyes at Emmet and tilt my head toward our guests. Mother Nature said she has a favor to ask of him.

Let's get that out of the way first.

He licks his lips and takes my cue. "I...uh, thank you for your reassurance the last time we met, Goddess. I was terrified about being Kangaroo Jack for the rest of my life. Your words calmed me down a great deal."

Sarah chuckles. "Oh, that memory is fun fer me."

He shrugs, laughing. "In hindsight, it was pretty cool. Since then, I've been able to transform into a bunch of other animals."

I laugh. "Not all by choice, but that's another story. My favorite is still the red panda. So cute."

Emmet grins. "Anyway, I'm thankful for all the blessings you've given us. What can I do for you?"

She crunches the end of a carrot stick and chews for a moment before speaking. It's surreal to be standing here munching and chatting with Mother Nature.

"I asked Sarah to work with you on bringing parts of this city back to life," she says.

Back to life?

Emmet looks as confused by that as I am. "You want us to welcome people immigrating to the island? Like, to repopulate?"

"No, sweet boy, it's not about people living *in* the city. I'm talking about the city itself. The hidden city is enchanted, and since the island is coursing with power once again, it's time to awaken it."

Hubba-wha?

Emmet's eyes widen. "When you say alive, you mean more like it has a quaint personality and not like *Hill House*, right?"

"I mean the city is enchanted with life, charm, and while I wouldn't say its personality is quaint, it can be whimsical at times."

"And at the other times? What are we talking?"

She gives him a patient smile. "I would like for you and Sarah to help it rouse. It's been asleep a very long time and will need some coaxing."

"That's where our partnering comes in," Sarah says. "With my white magic and your connection with the island and buffering ability, our Lady believes we can bring the city back to its original state."

Emmet swallows, and I can tell it's a struggle for him to get on board with resurrecting the spirit of his new home. "Sure. Cool. Looking forward to it. We've always been a good team."

Mother Nature bites a meatball off a toothpick. "Good. It's settled. Thank you both for your efforts. I look forward to the city lighting up and bursting with life. Now, to the other matter." Mother Nature turns to me and smiles. "I believe you have something you wanted to ask me, Fiona?"

That's my cue. "I do. From what Fionn and Bodhmall said when we last spoke with them, there is a guiding power behind Team Light and Team Dark going into the Time of the Colliding Realms. We hope you will honor us with your favor."

She grins. "I will. What is it you would ask of me?"

Me ask *her*? Am I supposed to make a request? I look at Sloan and frown. *Help.*

"What sort of aid are ye permitted to offer?" Sloan picks up without a beat. "Surely there are restrictions and limitations to the influence yer help can affect. As ye say, everythin' is a balance."

She winks at Sloan. "Right you are, young man. Death and I see things differently but understand the birth and nurture of my realm can only exist with the withering and death of his. Both are integral to the health of our worlds. The Time of the Colliding Realms isn't about Light winning over Dark or the other way around. Your purpose as my guardians is to strike a balance so neither side overshadows the other."

"*What?* We're not supposed to win?" My voice is higher-pitched than I intend, and I spit a little.

If she noticed, Mother Nature doesn't show it. "Not in the sense of dominating, no. Team Light, as you call yourself, is supposed to toe the line. Push back the opposing forces to ensure the darkest impulses of greed and power don't overtake justice and morality."

My mouth drops open. "This is blowing my mind. All this time, we've been gearing up for the fight of the millennium, toiling with how to overpower Mingin, Melanippe, and now Morgana. Now you're saying we're not supposed to win?"

Mother Nature offers me a patient smile. "No, child. Of course, you must stop evildoers bent on disrupting the balance. Absolutely, take your stand and force them back to their banishment and take them out of power."

I pat my chest, getting my heart beating again. "Okay, good. I thought I wasted a year of training heading down the wrong path."

"Not at all. My point is darkness on the whole comes in many forms. It is not your task to destroy it, simply to ensure it doesn't overwhelm and overshadow the light."

"Because we need the balance," I say.

"Exactly right." Mother Nature finishes her glass of wine and sets her goblet and plate down. "Now, ask your favor, and I will do what I can. Remember, I can't exert undue influence. I can only guide you."

My poor hamster is spinning in his wheel. "Then I humbly ask for our favor to be what we need most to ensure the best outcome for Team Light."

Sloan arches a brow.

Yes, I'm sure he had a dozen ideas of concrete things we could've asked for, but my instincts tell me Mother Nature is the best judge of what we need.

Besides, she seems pleased with my request.

"In that case, I give you this and wish you well." She hands me a piece of parchment folded in half with a little ribbon tying the top edge together. "Good luck, my guardians. Make me proud."

With that, a brilliant flash of light erupts, and she's gone.

Emmet blinks as my eyes adjust. "Show's over folks. Mother Nature has left the building."

The moment Mother Nature vanishes, I pull the ribbon on the parchment she gave me and practically tear it open to see what it says.

"What is it, Fi?" Emmet rushes in behind me to read over my shoulder.

"I'm not really sure? There are three things. The first is a spell. The second seems to be a bunch of GPS coordinates. The third is a little rhyme. It says, 'In the darkest moment of battle and plight, the path to victory is the team for which you fight.'"

"Oh, a riddle," Em says. "Nikon is wicked good at riddles. I bet he'll know what that means."

It's true. He is.

"May I take a look, *a ghra*?" Sloan asks.

I hand Sloan the paper and wait. Me saying he's the smartest person I know isn't hyperbole. The guy is crazy smart. If Mother

Nature thinks these three things are the keys we need to hold the dark side at bay, he'll figure out how.

He puzzles over the parchment for a moment, then steps over to my father to talk to him.

While they chat, I check in with Emmet and Sarah. "So, looks like Mother Nature has set you guys on a mission. That's exciting."

Emmet arches a brow. "Or horrifying."

"I doubt she'd set you up to unleash a haunting on you. Maybe it'll be like *Key House* and you and Doc will have adventures to unravel."

That calms him down a bit. "Yeah. That would be cool. Hey, if my city is a living entity that's even cooler." His focus shifts to Sarah. "Are you sure you want to do this? I know you're pissed at me right now."

"Och, I'll survive. I want to do as the goddess asks and she's never steered me wrong. If she thinks we're the best two fer the job, I'll not be the one to argue."

"Yeah, good point."

"So, if yer all right with the idea, perhaps Sloan or one of the others can portal me home to pack a bag and collect the things I'll need to awaken a city."

"I'm sure Dionysus or Nikon won't mind," I say.

"A bag?" Emmet asks. "You're going to stay here?"

Sarah nods. "I can't portal, so I'm not sure how I'd get here otherwise. Besides, it'll take time to get the job done. It's a big city."

"Yeah, right. I hadn't thought it through."

"Look. If yer worried about upsettin' yer girlfriend, I can stay in one of the houses outside the palace and stay out of yer hair as much as possible."

"No. That's not necessary. It's a big palace and only Doc and I live here, so you're more than welcome to claim one of the bedrooms. Hell, you can claim a wing."

Sarah's blonde brow crooks up and disappears under her bangs. "Just you and Doc? I thought—"

"Ciara moved back to her parents a few weeks ago to find her own path," Emmet says. "The island didn't suit her."

"Fi? Can ye join us, luv?" Sloan asks from across the room. "I have a question or two if ye don't mind."

I'm thankful for the excuse to step back and let the two of them speak privately. Crossing the room, I grab another brownie off the table and pop it into my mouth on the fly. "Sure, what do we know?"

Sloan and Da are sitting at a cleaned-off corner of the table and are studying the parchment. "I've taken a picture of the spell and want to send it to Merlin fer him to study but have no service. Also, these are GPS coordinates, but without the Internet, we can't pinpoint where they fall. I'm not sure what the answer to the riddle is, but I think it's fair to say we need to go so we can find out."

Funny. I love the idea of being unplugged from the bustle of the world, but it's such a pain not to be able to plug back in when we need to.

"Okay, let's call everyone in and head back to Gran's and Granda's. At least from there, we can see what we're dealing with."

"Toronto, Montreal, New York, Atlanta, New Orleans, Paris, Copenhagen, Berlin, Rio de Janeiro, and Hong Kong."

I type the cities into my phone as Sloan and Granda call them out and text them to Garnet.

> **We have reliable intel that these will be the cities hit hardest by Team Dark during the Culling. I'm forwarding the actual coordinates of where to focus our forces.**

Who is the source of this reliable intel?

Mother Nature.

Shit. That sounds credible. I'll work on getting teams organized for those areas. Well done, Lady Druid.

I like that he still calls me that now and then. "Okay, Garnet is on it. He'll rally the forces and have a heavy Team Light presence at the points of the coordinates. What's next?"

Sloan straightens from where he's scanning the pages of one of Granda's old spellbooks. "I sent Merlin a photo of the spell, and he's verifying a few of the ingredients. At first blush, he thought it was the answer to the visibility enchantment we've been working on."

"Why would the first thing Mother Nature gives us to help us in the Culling be a visibility spell we need to help a friend so her vampire boyfriend can talk to her?"

"Maybe it's not for her?" Calum says. "Maybe we're supposed to help someone else be seen?"

"In the next two days? How many invisible people do we know?"

Da looks over the parchment one more time and shrugs. "Fer now, go help Merlin work on the spell. If it is Laurel yer supposed to help, the reason will become clear, I'm sure. Things happen as they're meant."

Yeah, I believe that too.

"Okay, next question." I check in with the others. "Where are we supposed to dig in, Ireland or Toronto? What are we protecting?"

Da frowns at the list of sites. "I'd say yer meant to be in Ireland, *mo chroí*. Garnet can pull together an army of supporters to keep Toronto's dark ones in line. That's his job as Grand Governor."

"But it's our city and our homes are there."

Da nods. "True, but there are two sites listed here in Ireland. One is Newgrange, and the other is yer brother's island. I think yer needed here more to fight the battles only we can fight."

That makes sense. "When you say, 'only we can fight,' you mean it'll likely be our big baddies at those locations, right?"

"Aye, that's what I'm thinkin'."

"Don't forget," Dionysus adds. "Nikky and I can have you guys anywhere you need to be in a flash."

I flash him a warm smile. "Oh, I haven't forgotten, Tarzan. I'm counting on it. You two are the aces up our sleeve."

Nikon chuckles. "Secret weapons, are we?"

"Abso-Greekin'-lutely," I say.

Dionysus laughs. "I like that."

"Okay, for now, that will be the plan. We'll go home for the final prep and return to Ireland before dawn on the twenty-first when all hell breaks loose."

CHAPTER SEVENTEEN

"Hey, Merlin, it's good to see you." I hug him when he opens the door to his loft. "You don't look any the worse for your experience."

"Thankfully, not," he says. "Honestly, I don't know that I would've jumped back onto that spell if it hadn't been Mother Nature herself who gave it to you."

"I get that. I'm sorry you had the whole invisibility mishap in the first place."

"Not your fault. I spent centuries letting my skills fall away and pretending not to be who I was. The universe is bound to want to even the score a little. The past always comes back to bite you in the ass if you don't deal with it."

I unzip my jacket and toss it on the foyer table as we head inside. "Uh…speaking of your past coming back, I have some bad news."

He stops and crosses his arms. "I'm going to hate what's coming next, aren't I?"

"Yep."

"Okay, give it to me."

"While we were in Ireland, we got called to Newgrange

because someone had broken the seal to the Neitherlands and was siphoning power from the escaping souls. Turns out, it was an old girlfriend of yours."

Merlin's expression darkens. "So, I guess that's our answer then. She did escape her banishment that night with Yvain."

"Yep. She's powering up, zombifying soldiers, and sucking souls to regain her footing."

Merlin mutters a few curses in a language I don't understand, but the intention is obvious. "All right, so Team Dark got a bonus player. I suppose forewarned is forearmed."

"It is, but it also got me thinking."

"That's always dangerous," Sloan says.

Merlin chuckles and continues to escort us back to his magic lab. "Thinking about what, girlfriend?"

"The Culling runs over four days long and can be fought anywhere in the world. That puts Team Light on a defensive strategy, and I'd rather be playing offense. Mother Nature has gifted us with the locations to focus on, but again, if we're standing around at Newgrange or Emmet's island, we're still on our back foot."

"As opposed to what, *a ghra?*" Sloan asks.

"What if we could set our stage and get all the players we're worried about in one place at a time when we're ready? Wouldn't that be a bonus?"

Merlin smirks and lets us into his private workspace. Thankfully, it doesn't stink like it did the last time we were here. "So, you want to schedule the war between Morgana and us?"

"Sort of."

"I don't think she'll go for it. She was never one for keeping to other people's timelines. I doubt six centuries in magical purgatory has made her more amiable to things like that."

I roll my eyes. "I wasn't thinking about sending out gold-embossed invitations or anything."

"Then what were ye thinkin', luv?" Sloan asks.

"I wondered if there was a way to draw them to one place. Like a lighthouse in their darkness. Like a beacon or the bat signal."

Merlin's gaze narrows. "Go on."

"So, our biggest known enemies will be Melanippe, Mingin, and Morgana, right?"

"Right."

"There will likely be others we're not expecting."

"Agreed."

"So, if we could draw them away from the innocents of towns and cities and have our battle somewhere isolated, that would save lives."

"I'm with you. Where are you thinking?"

"Honestly, I'm wondering if Mother Nature gave us Newgrange and Emhain Abhlach as the two places in Ireland where we'll fight battles, that maybe it was a hint we should make it happen."

"Like a self-fulfilling prophecy?" Sloan asks.

"Yeah. So, it got me thinking. Is there a way to make the fae power of the island attract the powerful dark players so that's where they end up?"

"Like setting out honey for flies," Merlin says.

"Exactly. Is there a way to sweeten the ambient energy of the fae prana to make it irresistible to the dark leaders looking to increase their power?"

"We'd need it in the next two days," Sloan says.

Merlin chuffs and gives us a look.

I hold up a finger to stop him from telling me it's impossible. "In truth, if the Time of the Colliding Realms lasts for as long as sunlight reaches the belly of the Newgrange ritual chamber, any time in the next two to six days would still work."

Merlin looks off at the far wall, and I can see his mental cogs spinning. "Let me think about that. For now, I need Sloan's hands to help me finalize the visibility enchantment, and I need something to tie the enchantment to. Something of Laurel's would be best because it would already hold her energy."

I nod and rise on my toes to kiss Sloan's cheek. "On it. You two have fun with your spellwork. I'll get a ring or something for you to bind it to."

I leave the two of them to do their thing and grab my coat at the front of the apartment. Pulling out my cell, I call up Nikon's contact.

Do you have time to escort me from Merlin's apartment to Casa Loma and back?

Sure. Now?

If that works.

On my way.

I slide my arms into my jacket and shrug it on. Nikon quietly knocks a moment later. Opening it up, I step outside and meet him at the top of the stairs leading down to Queens on Queen.

"All set?" he asks.

I take his proffered hand and lace my fingers with his. "Thank you, Nikon. I know you give far more than you get out of our friendship, but I want you to know I am thankful every minute for everything you do for me."

Nikon squeezes my hand. "Nonsense, Red. I spent over a thousand years enduring a life devoid of love and relationships, knowing that one day a spitfire redhead named Fiona Cumhaill would risk everything to set me free. Papu never told me more than that. I spent countless centuries envisioning who you'd be and how you'd do it. Then, there you were."

"Did I live up to the hype?"

The look he gives me is so sweet I melt a little. Then his teasing smile returns. "Meh, you're all right."

I laugh. "Well good. I'm glad I'm not a colossal disappointment."

"No. You're good. Although, I'm still not over you putting pineapple on pizza."

I bump his shoulder with mine. "How about a trip to the carriage house of Casa Loma? Then we'll grab a few pizzas and go over it again."

"Sure. Sounds like a plan."

Nikon snaps us into the first horse stall in the carriage house, and my shield tingles the moment we materialize. It's not a duck and cover kind of tingle. It's more a warning that something lurks in the distance.

I squeeze Nikon's fingers, and he remains still and silent at my side. *Everything okay, Red?* he asks directly into my mind.

I'm not sure. My shield woke up, and the last time I was here with Sloan I got a similar eerie feeling.

Well, your feelings are usually damn accurate.

They are. Still, I have no idea what it means.

After a few more minutes, nothing has happened, so I figure it's safe to move on. I pull my phone out of my pocket and text Benjamin.

> **Upstairs. Can you meet us and bring a ring of Laurel's or a bracelet or something she wore a lot? We need it for a spell we're working on.**

> **Need it how? Will I get it back?**

Yes. We're working on tying an enchantment to something she can wear to bind to her.

Got it. Give me a minute.

I fill Nikon in on that and make my way out of the horse stall and into the central corridor. With more caution than I usually exhibit, I lead the way deeper into the old stables toward the one in the back, which the vampires use to enter the underground bunker.

You okay, Red? Nikon asks.

Not sure. Something is giving me the willies. I just don't know what it is.

My shield burns hot at the same moment a blur rushes out of the shadows, and a steel fist knocks me flying. The hit comes fast and hard from the side, and the force of the impact sends me sailing in the air and into the wooden wall.

The world blinks out of focus and the violent growl of an enraged vampire echoes all around me.

Tough as Bark. As my bracers activate and cover my skin with armor, I roll to my knees and try to get my wits working.

Before I can push up to my feet, Nikon falls to the ground next to me with his throat ripped wide.

I scream and release Bruin, my bear bursting from me with the force of ten immortal warriors. The gore of Nikon's condition is too much. I grip around his throat to try to staunch the bleeding, but then someone hooks an arm under my belly, and I'm thrown ten feet in the air.

My back hits the wooden rafter above, and it knocks my breath from my lungs.

As I plummet back to the floor, I see my attacker for the first time. *Fucking Oli.*

Has he lost his mind?

Bruin is dealing with two vampires down the corridor, so dealing with this asshole is all me.

Good. That's the way I want it.

Birga responds to my call without hesitation, and I manage to catch his meaty arm with a swipe as I fall. A vampire's skin is almost as tough as steel, so Birga's marble tip glances off without causing damage.

That's fine. I'd rather be facing him when we battle anyway. *"Bestial Strength."*

I drop to my feet, and now that adrenaline, fury, and the strength of my spell are kicking in, I'm in this.

"I've waited a long time for this, bitch." He throws a fist at me, and I catch it in front of my face and squeeze with everything I've got.

The *snap* of knuckles is music to my ears, and I twist his wrist, hoping to rip his hand off and leave him with a stump. "Too stupid to wait another two days, eh?"

I release his hand, bringing up both forearms to block my face from the crowbar in his other hand. "Why put off to tomorrow when I can kill you today?"

The impact on my arms is incredible. Damn, I hate fighting vampires. "If you had, you could've claimed your right as part of the Culling. Now you're only a brute asshole."

He gets a lucky blow to my shoulder, and I miss the backspin as he stretches out his arm and cracks me on the side of the face.

The impact snaps my head around like I'm an owl, but thankfully my body comes with me. I drop to my knees, and a sadistic laugh rips from my throat as he rushes me.

Gripping his junk with everything I've got with one hand, I use the other to slide my grip up Birga's staff and ram her spear into his side.

He roars with fury, his eyes glowing red, his canines extended and gleaming in the dim light.

"What the fuck is going on?" Benjamin shouts.

Oli ignores him and lunges forward. He knocks me onto the floor, and his mouth grips my throat.

Thankfully, he doesn't have the sire's power, and his teeth don't penetrate. When Xavier pinned me down, there was nothing I could do to stop him. Still, the pressure on my jugular is intense.

A moment later it's gone.

Another feral roar fills the air, but this time, it's not Oli, a.k.a. Oscar. That roar holds far more power and belongs to the King of the Toronto Seethes.

With Xavier taking care of my welcoming party, I scramble across the floor and kneel beside Nikon.

"Greek? I'm here." I lace my fingers with his and hug his arm against my chest. Blood and filth slick my hands and my heart is racing. "You can go now. I'm safe. Don't fight. I'll see you soon."

His usually bright gaze is glossing over. I know he's immortal, but I hate the fear and pain in his eyes.

"It's almost over, sweetie." I brush my fingers over his forehead to move his blond spikes from his eyes. "Not long now."

With a final, unnatural noise, he falls still.

"What can we do?" Benjamin asks me.

I shake my head, still clinging to Nikon's hand, my emotions building in my chest. *C'mon, Greek. Back to the vineyard same as always. You've got this.*

"Lady Druid?" Xavier says, a gentle hand squeezing my shoulder. "He's gone, Fi. I'm so sorry."

I force my throat to swallow past the tightness. "Just give him a minute."

C'mon, Greek...

I feel the surge of his essence before his body disappears. I've always thought it should glow or rise or something monumental, but it doesn't. When Nikon dies, his body disappears and resurrects at the family property on the Isle of Rhodes.

"What just happened?" Xavier says, eyes wide.

I accept the hand he offers and steady myself against Bruin's round rump. When my adrenaline rush recedes, it leaves me with a case of the quakes. "He's immortal. He'll be back."

I don't give them any details because that's Nikon's business, and at the moment, vampires aren't my friends. "Where's that piece of shit coward you call a bodyguard?"

"He's been detained until I speak with you and find out what happened."

"What happened?" I hold my hands out and look down at myself. "What happened is I came here because we're making headway with helping Laurel and I need a ring to enchant. Nikon and I came here to wait for Benjamin to come up. Your rabid dog was hiding in there and attacked us without so much as a hello."

Xavier's expression darkens. "There was no altercation beforehand?"

"No. Nikon and I were chatting and minding our own, then I was flying through the air and slamming into that wall." I point at the spot where I hit, but it's not necessary since the centuries-old wood has collapsed to the shape of my body.

"What about the two your bear beheaded?"

"I hit the wall and fell to the floor. Before I could get to my feet, Nikon dropped beside me with his neck torn open. I released Bruin and called my armor purely out of self-defense."

Xavier is looking angrier with every passing moment. "Did he say anything to you?"

"Only that he's waited too long and been looking forward to putting me down."

"It's got a hold on him," Benjamin says. "I know you don't want to give up on him, but Oscar is a danger to himself and others like this. Lee and Saint were young. They probably had no clue."

I follow his gesture, not following what he's saying. "Had no clue about what? What's got a hold on him? What are you two talking about?"

Xavier ignores my questions and curses at the vampires Bruin expired further up the corridor. "Dom and Chang, take the bodies to the incinerator. I want a family meeting before anyone goes out tonight."

"You're going to put him down, right?" There's no remorse or sympathy in my voice. I don't have any to spare. "He's feral, and I'm sick of it. Either you do it, or I'll go through channels and call for action through the Guild."

Xavier stiffens. "Don't threaten me or my family, Lady Druid. You're worked up about Mr. Tsambikos, but as you said, he's immortal."

I point at the pool of blood on the floor. "Yes, *he* is, but if Sloan had escorted me here tonight like he has a dozen times this month, he would be dead on the floor, not Nikon. And Sloan is *not* immortal."

Lightning cracks nearby as thunder rolls loud up above. My fingers are throwing off sparks like holiday sparklers, my entire body alive with power.

Xavier meets my gaze, and his eyes are cold. "It wasn't Sloan, so you need to get hold of yourself and calm down."

My hair flies up behind me as a cyclone of wind churns outside our speaking circle. "He ambushed us, and one of my best friends had his throat ripped out without cause. Don't tell me to calm down. Tell me that you'll put down the British mongrel who incited this."

Xavier lifts his chin and grows rigid. "*I* am the King of Toronto Seethes, Ms. Cumhaill, not you. *I* decide the fate of my people and won't bend to your will simply because you throw a few lightning bolts and demand it."

I scream and throw my hands out to the sides, knocking vampires tumbling to the walls as I stomp out of the carriage house.

Stupid fucking vampires.

CHAPTER EIGHTEEN

After all I've done to work with Xavier and his family, he won't get on-side for the Culling, he won't acknowledge he needs to put that asshole Oscar down, and he has the nerve to imply *I'm* the problem here?

The winter wind hits me as I storm out of the carriage house and onto the frozen grass of Casa Loma. The fresh air is a good thing to clear my head, but it also reminds me I have no ride home.

I grab my phone out of my pocket and send Sloan a text.

Trouble with the vampires. I'm fine but need a pickup ASAP.

"Fiona, wait," Benjamin calls while running behind me. "Please. You came here for a reason. You said you've almost figured out how to help Laurel."

"Yeah, for all the goodwill that earned me," I snap. "Despite what your sire says, I don't go around giving leaders orders, but that motherfucking guard dog of his almost killed me and did kill Nikon."

"*A ghra?*" Sloan's there the next second, studying me in all my bloody mess. "What the feckin' hell happened? Are ye all right?"

I take a moment to fill Sloan in on the attack and Nikon's death and end with a shiver racking me as my tears break free. "If it had been you instead of Nikon, there would be no resurrecting. I would've lost you."

As the words hang in the cold night air, my fury morphs into panic, and I start to shake. Sloan moves to pull me against his chest, but I resist. "No. Don't. I'm covered in Nikon's blood and will ruin your coat."

"I don't care about that. Needin' a new coat is an excuse to go shoppin'."

That makes me laugh. "As if you need an excuse."

"As if."

"Um…I hate to be insensitive or come off as self-serving, but are you still willing to help Laurel? Your fight with Xavier doesn't change that you and Laurel are friends, does it?"

I draw a deep breath. "Of course not, but honestly, I don't think Xavier understands what it means to be friends. Otherwise, he wouldn't treat me like a bug under his shoe every time something happens."

Benjamin says nothing, and I don't blame him.

"Yeah, I get it. You're inside Xavier's circle, and I suppose I'll always be on the outside. Point made yet again."

"I don't know anything about that, Fi. I'm sorry."

I wave away his apology. "Not your fault. So, do you have the ring?"

Sloan holds up a finger to pause Benjamin's answer. "Actually, havin' Laurel there would speed things up if the two of ye wouldn't mind comin' with us fer a bit."

Benjamin's face brightens. "You mean you're *that* close to figuring it out?"

"We are. Since Fi has had enough of bein' here fer one night, how about ye join us? We'll see if we finally have the spell we need to get this done."

Benjamin holds out his hand. "Yes, let's."

Sloan smiles. "I'm afraid I can't portal Laurel. Do ye have a car? I'll give ye the address unless ye know where the club Queens on Queen is?"

Benjamin nods. "The companions took us there on one of their monthly outings."

"Twenty minutes? I'll pop Fi home to change and wash up first, and we'll meet ye there."

"Laurel's here?" Benjamin asks. "Does she know to stay with me and get in the car?"

Sloan nods. "She does. She's very excited and says she'll see ye soon."

Benjamin grins. "See you soon, beautiful."

In the twenty minutes between leaving Casa Loma and the vampires and going to meet Benjamin outside the club, I strip out of my bloody clothes, get washed up and changed, and call Papu to ensure Nikon arrived and is regenerating as expected.

"Please tell him I love him, and I'm so sorry trouble follows me."

"I'll tell him, Red, but he knows it," Papu says.

"Is he all right?" Sloan asks.

"Thankfully, yes. He's there. Papu has him. He's all right."

"That's a relief."

"It is. I've been thinking a lot about Nikon lately," I absently say as I slide my feet into my sneakers.

"Should I be alarmed or offended?" Teasing is thick in his tone.

"No. You shouldn't." I finish with my shoes and stand, shifting to slide my arms into the coat Sloan is holding open for me. "I've been thinking Nikon is great with a sword and has a few basic magic tricks, but he needs an offensive power."

Sloan blinks at me and smirks. "I don't think ye can simply decide someone should get powers, luv. Nikon was born a human. The fact that he's immortal is pretty incredible."

"It is, but if he had an offensive power, maybe he wouldn't have to die so often."

"I don't mean this to sound as harsh as it will, but I don't think he did die often until he met you."

I frown at him. "That did sound harsh. Ouch, surly, you hurt my feelings."

He presses a soft kiss to my lips and squeezes my shoulders. "I only meant he didn't need offensive powers while simply livin' his everyday life."

"I know what you meant. Still, I'm going to hope for an offensive power for him."

"That sounds grand. You do that and let me know how it goes."

I don't care how much he's teasing me. The fact that I nearly lost Nikon tonight is still vibrating in my cells. "I love you, Mackenzie."

"Right back at ye, Cumhaill."

When the black SUV parks in the Queens on Queen lot, Sloan opens the back door to let Benjamin inside.

"Thank you again for doing this," he says. "I've been thinking about it all the way over here, and you're right Fi. You've done everything you could to help us and be a good friend to Xavier. I'm sorry he let you down tonight."

I shrug. "It's not your fault."

"No, but it's not yours either." He pauses and purses his lips.

"If I tell you something in confidence, will you make sure it doesn't get back to Xavier?"

"Sure. Of course."

He nods. "Xavier is protective of Oscar because he has a genetic condition. He thought things were under control, but obviously, they weren't."

"What kind of condition?" Sloan asks.

"It's very hush-hush in the vampire world, but it deals with a decay of behavioral filtering and an inflated tendency for violence."

"Yeah, I'd say Oli is two for two. So, if Xavier knows he has this condition, why let him out to wreak havoc on people?"

"Because when he's with us at home, he doesn't display any of those tendencies. You won't believe me, but Oscar is a great guy."

"You're right. I don't believe you."

"No. I don't suppose you do. In any case, Xavier kept him as his bodyguard as much to utilize the increased violence as to keep a close eye on him."

"So how did that end up with him hiding in the shadows and ripping Nikon's throat out?"

"Sometimes vampires who suffer from this condition develop a fixation on something or someone. Once that happens, paranoia sets in."

I see where this is going. "He fixated on me."

"Oh, he did. He talked about you all the time and would get some of the others worked up too."

Sloan straightens, a murderous fury clouding his eyes. "Are ye tellin' us that Xavier allows his charges to badmouth Fiona and plan violent acts against her?"

"Allows them? Absolutely not. Xavier has made it painfully clear that you and your family and your circle of friends are to be treated with respect and given our support if ever needed."

I scoff. "It didn't feel like that tonight. It was exactly the opposite. He was Team Psycho Vamp tonight and screw my dead companion and me."

Benjamin frowns. "In the heat of the moment, it might seem like it, but you backed him into a corner."

"*Me!* How did this become my fault?"

"Not your fault, Fi, but you demanded a course of action. Xavier's a very proud man in a position that demands unwavering loyalty. Bowing to your wishes makes him look weak in the eyes of other vampires. If someone deems him weak, that puts everyone in his line in danger."

"That's overly dramatic. We were discussing the fate of one vampire. One demented and dangerous vampire who tried to kill me. How could that put everyone in danger?"

"Because in a vampire coup for the throne, the entire siring line meets their final death to stop any chance of retaliation."

"That's both horrifying and incredibly efficient."

Benjamin sighs. "So, you calling him out in front of other vampires put him in a tight spot."

"Fine. I see that, but there should've been no question about his course of action. I knew he needed to put Oli down before you told me about his condition. It's even more important now."

"Then leave it to Xavier to reach that decision and don't challenge him."

I hear everything Benjamin is saying and though backing down isn't my strongest skill, I see his point. "Okay, enough about Oli and him wanting to kill me. How about we get upstairs and see if we can end the night on a happier note?"

Benjamin pulls out a silver ring with a square sapphire. "That's the best idea I've heard in months."

By the time we get upstairs, Merlin is waiting on the ring and a helping hand to get the spell finished. Sloan takes off his bone ring and gives it to me so we can check in with Laurel. Then, he takes the sapphire ring with him into Merlin's lab.

"Is this really happening?" Laurel bounces on the balls of her feet as she stares toward the lab.

"It is. Considering how we got the spell, I'm confident it will work."

"Where did you get the spell?" Benjamin asks.

I spend the next five minutes filling them in on the excitement of asking Mother Nature for her guidance going into the Culling and how this spell was the first thing on our list of things we'll need.

"What do you think that means?" Laurel asks.

"I don't know. There were no explanations, only the parchment with the three favors."

Laurel seems to be lost in thought over that for a long while before nodding. "I think she meant for you to help me so Xavier would change his mind about remaining neutral and supporting the good guys."

"You realize how ridiculous that is, don't you?" Benjamin asks. He's sitting on the couch with me, holding my hand so he can see and speak to Laurel. "Xavier is king of the vampires in Toronto. How do the vampires hold their place in the empowered world?"

I chuckle. "I realize asking the head of a crime family dealing in drugs and guns to support Team Light is a bit ironic, but maybe don't look at it like good guys and bad guys. Maybe it's more about justice and honor."

"Xavier is very serious about honor," Laurel says.

"I know, so maybe our objectives aren't so far out of line with him and the vampires."

Benjamin frowns, shaking his head. "It'll never happen. He's already getting persecuted for not actively joining in on the plans for taking over the city. Being neutral is costing him a lot."

I didn't realize that.

Damn it. I want to be mad at Xavier and stay mad at him. Why does he always have to be such a pain in the ass when beneath it all he's a good guy?

He's like a modern-day Mr. Darcy making arrangements behind the scenes to keep Elizabeth and her family from becoming social pariahs.

I exhale. "I suppose I should apologize to him."

Laughter bursts from Laurel. "Definitely don't do that. Vampires don't apologize, Fi. No. The best thing to do is simply pretend you didn't lose your mind, and he didn't piss you off, and the two of you didn't part in a cloud of dark smoke."

Benjamin nods his agreement. "That's exactly how vampires handle things like this. They pretend it never happened."

I shrug. "Fine by me. I'm not really sorry anyway."

The three of us are still cozy in the living room when Sloan and Merlin stride out to join us. By the hopeful excitement on their faces, I take it things went well with this new spell.

"Since there's no stench of explosion and I can still see you both, are we in business?"

Merlin holds out the silver ring and shrugs. "Only one way to find out."

"May I?" Benjamin reaches for the ring. "I want to be the first to look into her eyes."

Aww, so sweet. I hustle around the metal coffee table and hold Sloan's hand so he can see Laurel with me.

"Where is she?" he asks.

I point at where Laurel is standing beside him, and he turns, propping the ring in the air for her to slide her finger through. "This is our moment, beautiful."

"Please let this work." Laurel reaches forward. "Please, please, please."

The ring slips over her knuckles and rests perfectly in place.

The world seems to hold its breath. I want this so badly for the two of them. Benjamin is frozen, staring straight ahead. Did it work? Can he see her?

I take off Sloan's ring so I can tell.

"Yes!" I throw my arms around Sloan's shoulders and kiss him. "Success."

Next, I hug Merlin and kiss his cheek. "Amazeballs. You rocked it."

Merlin hugs me back. "Minus a few missteps."

I chuckle and ease back. "Gotta break those eggs to make an omelet."

Merlin waggles his dark brows and tilts his head toward Laurel and Benjamin. "My question is can she also be touched and heard?"

"I'm afraid to find out," Laurel says.

"Well, that answers half the question," I say. "We can hear you."

Laurel raises her hand and presses it against the smooth skin of Benjamin's jaw. At first, I'm not sure if she's touching him or if her palm is simply in place as if she wants to.

Then, Benjamin's eyes roll closed, and he leans into her touch. "You're not warm like you were, but I can feel you."

"That, my friends, is a triple header, grand slam," I say in my best announcer's voice. "We can see you, hear you, and touch you. The crowd goes wild!"

I wave my hands enthusiastically, and everyone chuckles.

Benjamin is hugging Laurel, and they've now lost interest in interacting with the rest of us in the room. I don't blame them.

"Thank you for all you do," I say to Merlin, giving him one last hug. "Congratulations, you two. I suppose you'd like to get back to the carriage house so you can catch up privately."

Laurel steps away from Benjamin and hurries over to hug me. "Thank you, Fi. I'll never be able to thank you enough. You've given me back my life."

"You've given *both* of us back our lives," Benjamin says. "We owe you a debt."

I wave that away. "I'm a sap for a happily ever after. Be good to one another, and we'll call it even."

We walk Laurel and Benjamin back to the parking lot and head home ourselves. It's close to nine, and we haven't had dinner. I'm tired. I'm hungry. My emotions are still raw from being attacked and watching Nikon die…again.

"What can I get ye, *a ghra?* Name it. Whatever yer heart desires, I'll make it happen."

I plop down on the bench in the back hall and stare at my boots. "A grilled cheese. Would you mind?"

He chuckles. "It's the work of buttering two slices of bread and sandwiching them around some cheese. I think yer worth that much at the very least."

"All right then, slap a slice of ham in there too, and we'll get fancy."

"I need to show ye what fancy looks like."

I wave that away. "No need. Grilled cheese with ham will be heaven."

Without asking, Sloan kneels in front of me and unties my sneakers, pulling them off at the heel.

"Oh, thank you. I wasn't sure if I would be able to get those off tonight or if I'd be stuck here until morning."

"Anytime, luv. Come now. Let's get you sorted out and up to bed early. We've got a big day tomorrow."

I let him tug me to my feet, my curiosity piqued. "Why? What's tomorrow?"

"Tomorrow we lounge around and rest and carb-load as much as we can before heading back to Ireland for dawn."

I slide in against his hip and rest my cheek against his shoulder. "It's finally here, isn't it?"

"It is."

"Do you think we're ready?"

"I think we're as ready as we can be. The rest will happen as it's supposed to, and we'll deal with it then."

I exhale a long, slow breath. "Then I guess we pull up our big-boy pants and get ready for whatever comes."

"Sounds like a plan."

"First we dine on fancy grilled cheese and sleep for twenty-four hours."

CHAPTER NINETEEN

"*Aghra*, time to wake up."

I feel the nudge against my butt and groan, pulling the covers over my head. "Five more minutes."

"That's what ye said twenty minutes ago. Come now. The world's waiting to look up to their Lady Druid and yer gonna have sleep lines on yer face."

I glance bleary-eyed at the time on my phone and curse—five-forty-one. Who the hell gets up at five in the morning? The importance of Sloan's words leaks through my sleepy haze, and I get a jolt of realization.

The Culling.

"Okay, I'm up." I roll onto my back and blink up at my guy. "You're so much better than an alarm clock."

He chuckles. "It's nice to be appreciated. Thanks."

I wipe my palm over my mouth to make sure there's no drool, then run my fingers through my hair. "Give me ten to pull myself together, and I'll be out to rally the troops."

"I'll pour you a coffee so it can start to cool." He leans in and kisses my forehead before heading back out to the treehouse living room.

Right. The Culling.

The Time of the Colliding Realms is upon us.

My shower is quick but hot, and by the time I head out for an early bird breakfast, I feel almost human. Sloan and I have spent so much time sleeping and lounging in the past thirty hours it's incredible.

That's the good news.

The bad news is we don't know when we'll be able to sleep or eat next.

"Good morning, family. How goes the first hours of the coming of the apocalypse?"

Dillan snorts and sets down his coffee. He's dressed for battle in a long-sleeved black thermal shirt and black flak pants. His green Cloak of Concealment is hanging on the back of his chair, and Rory is curled up on the couch snoring. "That's quite a good morning, baby girl. Feeling a little punchy?"

I hug him from behind and press my cheek against his damp hair. "Nah, I'm just kidding. We're going to kick this Culling in the cooter."

Kevin chokes on his juice and sets his glass down.

"Well, I guess that sets the bar." Calum pats his husband's back. "It's a good goal. Maybe a little graphic, but admirable."

Sloan slides a plate with a Western sandwich, taters, and roasted tomatoes toward the last spot at the breakfast bar and I climb onto the stool. "Thanks, Mackenzie."

"My pleasure."

"Knock-knock." Da steps in from the balcony. "Is this where the party is?"

"You know it." Dillan gets up to vacate a spot. "What do you need, food, java, extra weapons? We've got it all."

He's not kidding. While druids use nature as a weapon, not everyone on Team Light can. So, the mass of weapons that arrived at our home last night before we came here is a boon.

Da looks over at the hockey bag full of guns and whistles between his teeth. "Did ye raid an armory?"

"Not exactly," I say.

Sloan arches a brow. "Fiona got into a heated argument with the king of vampires. This was his peace offering."

Calum laughs. "Does everyone get the irony of the gun-running vampire giving us a fuck ton of guns and munitions as a peace offering? Only Fi could manage that one."

I swallow my tater tots and sip my coffee. "Vampires don't apologize like normal people."

Kevin picks up an AK-47 and strokes a gentle hand over it. "Apology accepted."

The air snaps with energy and Dionysus arrives with Aiden. "Women and children are secured in the main house. Take what you need with you because when we leave, I'm locking the entire property down with an impenetrable bubble."

I know he's not supposed to affect the outcomes of mortal society, but having him give Gran, Shannon, Kinu, and the kids full god protection makes everything in me feel better. "Thank you, Tarzan."

"My pleasure. To be sure no one tries to undo it, I spoke with Clotho, Lachesis, and Atropos last night. They say I'm walking a fine line but have deemed me keeping my family safe as a personal matter more than influencing the outcome of lives."

"You rock, Greek." Calum extends his knuckles for a bump. "We'll all be able to focus better knowing everyone here is safe."

Kevin's scowl tells me he's still pissed about staying here when we leave. Doesn't matter. It's non-negotiable.

"Where's Nikky?" Dionysus asks. "If we're going up against Melanippe, I'd think he'd want to be here. The two of them really didn't like one another."

I finish my sandwich and wipe my mouth. "I spoke to him last night. He had a bit of an accident and is still recovering."

"Is he all right?"

"He will be. He was pushing to get back to us today, but this is a multi-day event. I told him to rest up for one more day and join us tomorrow."

Evangeline arrives in a mist of golden sparkles and looks badass in white leather.

"*Helloooo* nurse," Dillan says, in his best Yakko Warner voice. He closes the distance between them and pulls her against his chest. "Where have you been hiding this outfit?"

Eva chuckles, relaxing into his embrace. "I have an entire wardrobe of battle gear. If I knew I'd get this kind of a reaction out of you, I would've dressed up sooner."

Dillan laughs. "You need to move that wardrobe into our room as soon as this is all over. Then we're having a fashion show. A very private one."

I take my plate to the sink, rinse it off, and set it in the dishwasher. This might be the morning of the Time of the Colliding Realms, but there's no need to leave the house a mess. "Everyone grab what you're bringing, and we'll take it down to the back lawn. Gran wants to say goodbye before we go."

Bruin and Manx are already down on the lawn when we get there. They're decked out in their battle armor and look wicked deadly.

"No one's going to want to mess with you boys." Aiden gives them a nod of approval. "You make our party look good."

Manx bows his chin, grinning. "Good of ye to notice. We're goin' fer brutal intimidation."

"Nailed it."

I chuckle and let them chat about that while I go over to hug Gran and the others. "When we leave, Dionysus will put a god-powered whammy on the property to keep you all safe."

"If something happens and you need help," Dionysus holds

out his hand, and a pendant the same as mine appears. He opens the chain's loop and hangs it around Gran's neck. "If you press it, I will come."

Gran gathers his cheeks between her hands and pulls his face down to kiss. "Yer such a sweet boy. Take good care of our family, lad. I mean it. I'm dependin' on ye to watch out fer them."

"I will Gran. I promise."

I hug Gran next. "Don't worry. This will be over before we know it and it'll be all rainbows and fun family dinners going forward."

"From yer lips to the goddess' ears, luv." Gran steps back and pegs us all with a serious gaze. "Take care of each other. There's no sense fightin' fer a world if yer not around to enjoy it."

Granda nods. "Whatever happens, it's more important that yer around to make it right in the long run."

Da kisses Shannon's temple and nods at the rest of us. "Ready and steady."

"Right and tight," Dillan says.

"Randy and handy," Dionysus adds.

I laugh at the expression on Da's face and go with it. "All right. Since we haven't heard from Merlin about the evil beacon idea, we'll have to try to track down evil as it hits. Everyone check your comms and make sure you're connected."

While they do that, I take out my iron crown and set it on my head. Between that and the earpiece, I should be able to stay connected to everyone.

When the shuffle of checking things out ends, I get back to it. "Granda and Kevin will be running intel. The Elders of the Order are positioned across Ireland and will relay anything they see or hear through him and to us."

"It's an essential part of our defense." Calum pegs Kevin with a look.

Kevin doesn't seem convinced. "Brendan is as mortal as I am and he's with Em to defend the island."

"Brendan is a trained cop. He will be armed to the teeth and is technically already dead. He wants to use the time he has left fighting the fight like always."

"And I don't?"

Calum sighs. "Please, stop. Stay here with the women and children. Snuggle Daisy. Be with Bizzy. Protect our family. Help us by being our eyes and ears."

A moment passes where the two of them are locked in a stare, then Kevin relents and rolls his eyes. "Fine, but you are *soooo* making this up to me."

Calum leans forward and claims his mouth. When he pulls back, he winks. "I look forward to it."

With that settled, I continue, "Dionysus, take the island team to Emhain Abhlach. The heirs will have the young dragons out on the beach and be ready for you. Sloan will take the Newgrange team to the tomb, and we'll meet up with Samuel, Quon Shen, and Ahren. Dart and the free dragons are meeting us there."

"Is everyone clear on the plan?"

Dillan rolls his eyes. "Fi—we've gone through it enough times."

"All right, testy boy." I drink in the faces of the people I love so dearly. "Be safe, everyone. Gran's right. There's no sense fighting for a world if you're not here to share it with us, so everyone survives. Agreed?"

"Agreed," they respond.

"All right. Let's getter done."

Sloan *poofs* us to the open meadow between the River Boyne and Newgrange tomb. I don't see Samuel, Quon Shen, or Ahren, but they confirmed last night that they were spending the night here to secure the tomb.

According to my Fitbit, it's just before eight a.m. and forty-three minutes until sunrise. I open the search on my cell and confirm the sunrise prediction.

"It won't change, *mo chroi*."

"No, I suppose not. I want to be ready."

"Yer as ready as yer gettin'. Now we have to take things as they come."

"Where are our men on the ground?" Calum asks. "Weren't the Hunter-gods supposed to meet us here?"

"They said so." I pull out my cell and check that I haven't missed a message. "I've got nothing."

The ambient magic in the air intensifies, and the goddess Boann rises out of the morning mist. As always, she floats over the ground as she approaches, her long, dark hair flowing behind her in the morning breeze.

Man, it must be nice to be a goddess.

To have grace and an air of beauty like that.

"Merry meet, cousins," she says as she joins us. "Here we are again."

"Here we are again," I repeat, nodding at the truth of those words. "Hopefully, we'll all be healthy and well for countless more adventures after this week."

"Nothing would please me more." She doesn't stop advancing when she arrives at our location. She continues to walk across the frosted ground toward the tomb, and we fall into step.

Sloan matches her stride and gestures at the tomb. "We had men here overnight, but they didn't meet up with us. Do ye sense anyone other than us here, goddess?"

"Yes. The three were here in the tomb overnight, but others arrived in great numbers some time ago. They seized the tomb and cloaked their presence."

Oh, no. I search the exterior of the tomb for any sign of them. "Do you know where our men are?"

"Within the tomb. They have been subdued and are captives."

"Well, they know how to bait a hook because now we're even more determined to get in there. All right. It looks like our first battle of the Culling will be to take on whoever took our friends hostage."

"You inspire me, cousin. You, my kin, have proven time and again your aim is to protect what's mine. Therefore, I will aid you to the best of my ability to protect what is yours."

"Are you allowed to help us?" Sloan asks. "The pantheons don't usually approve of interfering in the lives of man."

"Unlike other deities, I answer to no one. Being the goddess of the river and this land is my punishment and therefore all I have. I am within my rights to protect what is mine."

I link my arm with hers and smile. "Thank you. In return, we'll do our best to keep evil from opening the seam and releasing darkness over your lands."

"Yes, please do." We walk a few more steps, and she stops. "Hold here." She raises her arm to the side. "Advance no farther."

Our group stops and the quizzical glances have me shrugging in response.

"There is a powerful warding erected from here to around the far side of the tomb." Boann traces the area with an extended finger. "To go any farther will negate your powers and injure all of you who are mortal."

"Which is everyone except Eva," I say, taking stock of our group. "So, who's here, and what do they want?"

"If it was Mingin or Morgana, the spell would've tripped," Calum says.

"Unless they forced Samuel to remove it," I correct.

"I cannot speak to that," Boann says, "but a great army of men laid themselves out atop the grassy roof of the tomb. They are lying in wait as we speak, hoping for you to step into their trap and lose your powers."

"Which we won't." I turn back the way we came. "Sloan,

you're with me. Bruin, see if you can sense the boundaries of the barrier."

"What's yer plan, *mo chroi?*" Da asks.

"We'll take Dart and the dragons for a run at them. The rest of you, hang tight until we see what we're dealing with. Whatever happens, nobody goes through the warding. We need our powers intact."

Sloan takes my hand and *poofs* us to where the free dragons have gathered on the other side of the river.

"Thanks for coming, everyone." I vault onto Dart's back.

The gray of early dawn is brightening, and I squint at the first signs of sunlight threatening to spill over the horizon. It's happening.

I think about what Boann said the other day.

When rays of first morn's light warm the depths of the sacred tomb, the powers of dark and light will hold their ground or seal their doom.

In a matter of minutes, the sun will rise and fill the inner chamber of Newgrange, and nothing we do will stop it.

I jog to my spike saddle and lock in place as Sloan does the same thing at the spike behind me. "Boann says there's a magical barrier around the tomb and the army of men who erected it are hiding on top of the grassy dome. Our job is to flush them out of hiding and break the barrier so we can get inside the tomb and defend the seal of the Neitherlands."

Utiss and Bryvanay take off with a fire in their eyes at the challenge. I know Dart feels it too because I sense his excitement through our unity bond. "Safety first, buddy. Once we know what we're dealing with, you can let loose."

He pushes forward, his mighty claws ripping through the frozen ground as the force of his strength thrusts us into the air. I call my body armor forward, unsure of what we'll find. Utiss and Bryvanay have taken a wide arc across the sky and are over the farmland on the tomb's far side.

As we approach from the front, they come in hard and fast from behind.

How much force are we exerting? Dart asks me.

Whoever is here, they've taken the Hunter-gods prisoner. You have permission to fry them extra crispy.

I'll tell the others.

As cool as it is when Dart speaks to me through a mental channel, he also shares that with other dragons.

With each *whooshing* pump of Dart's wings, we close the distance between us and the dome.

"Can you see anything, hotness?" I'm squinting and see nothing. Then again, if they hid their barrier, they more than likely hid—

Something powerful hits Dart and topples us back.

An explosion detonates with a violent blast.

My vision fails. My ears are ringing.

The world goes black...

CHAPTER TWENTY

I snap to consciousness...falling through the open air. Wind whistles in my ears and my heart races wildly. I'm toppling head over heels unsure which way is up.

"*Feline Finesse.*" As my spell takes hold, so too does gravity. The orientation of up and down helps. Using my arms to alter my freefall, I get my feet under me. "*Diminish Descent.*"

The falling slows and so does my heart rate.

I blink against the sting of wind and hair lashing my eyes. Cranking my head around, I search for Dart and...

Sloan!

He's unconscious and falling fast.

My body tingles with magical energy and my heart races. The tingling morphs into a burn that erupts into an explosion of my cells. My world tilts on its axis, and the only thought in my head is my need to get to Sloan.

Power ignites within me, and the strong and steady *thrump-pump, thrump-pump*, of wings carries me diving through the sky.

Wings? Holy hell, I have wings. There's no time to dwell on what I've transformed into. Folding my wings back, I dive.

The ground is coming fast—much too fast.

Talons extended, I reach for him, puncturing the fabric of his jacket to grab hold. With everything in me, I fight against his weight and pull upward. The rending of cotton is terrifying. Gripping tighter, I flap to slow our descent. *Bestial Strength.*

Dart's screaming hiss brings my attention to the sky above. My blue boy is racing to get to us, but we're too low for him to help in time.

Come on, hotness, wake up. I flap my wings, lifting, trying with everything I've got. It's no use. We're going to hit the ground.

Come on, hotness.

As the ground rushes up to greet us my hold collapses, and I've got nothing. Sloan is gone, and with the force I'm exerting for upward thrust, I shoot skyward.

It takes a moment to find a balance then I search my surroundings. *Where is he?*

The only explanation for him disappearing is that he woke up, saw the ground, and *poofed* out.

That means he's safe, doesn't it?

I meet Dart on his plummet to get to me, and when he levels off, I maneuver my flight to land on his back.

The change back from bird to woman goes smoothly. When I'm me again, I grab hold of my saddle and access the power of my crown.

Where are you Sloan? I extend my mental inquiry, searching for any sign of him.

Nothing.

Are you all right, Fiona? Dart asks.

I'll be fine. What hit us?

I don't know. I didn't see or sense anything. Then I was thrown back as the sky exploded around me.

Yeah, that's how it felt for me too.

A ghra, I'm here.

The sound of Sloan's voice in my mind brings a rush of relief. Thank you, baby Groot. *Dammit, dude, you scared the crap outta me.*

Sorry. I portaled out, and it took a moment to calm enough to portal back.

As long as you're all right, I'm good. Okay, the dragons and I will try to figure out how to bring down the barrier.

Patty's here now. He has an idea.

I leave them to work on things from their end and give my full attention to the dragons. Utiss and Bryvanay are fire-blasting the top of Newgrange tomb while Saxa and Empress Cazzienth hit it with magic.

Together, they've worn down the illusion masking the presence of the great number of men Boann told us to expect. She was right.

I've got eyes on Droghun and close to a hundred Barghest lying in wait. I relay the intel across the link of the Fianna crown. *The dragons have almost broken through their shielding. In a moment, the necromancer scum will have no choice but to abandon their hiding place.*

We'll be ready, mo chroi.

Sloan, can you portal a team into the tomb to help Samuel and the others?

Not yet. The barrier is prohibitive.

Ask Boann to help. Maybe she can get you guys in.

She's willing to try.

While I wait for them to try things on their end, Dart and I swing around and add to the dragon force. The air is scorching hot from all the dragon fire. It's singeing my eyebrows and skin.

I scan the worried faces of the Barghest below and wonder how hot it is in their little bubble.

Sorry not sorry.

Droghun glares up at the dragons, and the moment he sees me, it's game on. He must know by now that our group isn't going to cross the barrier, so he stops being sneaky and comes at us head-on.

He and four other men raise their arms as the others jump off the tomb and race for our team waiting down the property. Once the army of necromancers is on their way, Droghun and his helpers jump off the lip of the mounded tomb and join the fight.

"Take as many down as you can before they get to our people," I shout to the dragons.

In a surge of power and excitement, the dragons take off in a breathtaking swoop of scales and flame. They're stunning. I feel the power of their wings beating in my lungs and once again, I'm in awe.

Are we joining the fight? Dart asks me.

You are. I'm getting off and heading into the tomb to help rescue the Hunter-gods. Kick ass, buddy.

You too. Dart swoops low over the oval mound, and I jog off his side and drop to the tomb below. My boots slip for a moment in the puddles of the melted frost, but I regain my footing and drop off the ridge of the tomb wall a moment later.

Sloan *poofs* in right beside me and catches my arm. "How about ye don't use the front door?"

I hug him quickly and pull back. "Thanks for not being dead."

"Yer welcome. So? Shall we portal in?"

I'm about to say yes, but my instincts flare, and I think better of it. I hold up a finger and reach out to speak with my bear. *Bruin? What's the word on Samuel and the others?*

They're in the east antechamber. I cut them loose, but they're out of it. Melanippe and Mingin are too focused on the seam to notice they're free, but there are six Barghest in here as well.

So, it is them?

Definitely Melanippe. I'm assuming the man with her is another human puppet hosting Mingin.

More than likely. If we poof in on the south end, can you distract everyone from our arrival?

I can be distracting.

Yeah, you can. Okay, we're coming three, two, one...

Sloan and I *poof* in on the south end of the ritual chamber while Bruin goes Killer Clawbearer on the north end. His theatrics draw the guards to his end of the tomb and give us the chance to materialize and get oriented.

Mingin and Melanippe are lying on their backs beneath the seam of the Neitherlands. By the pentacle circle glowing in the sand beneath them and their state of disembodiment, they're on the astral plane.

Not good. *Rouse Samuel and the others,* I say to Sloan, pointing to the east antechamber. *They're after the seam again, and I need the Hunter-gods to help me defend it.*

What will you do?

I pull out my Dionysus pendant and squeeze it. *Call for backup.*

Sloan *poofs* off as my skin tingles with the signature of Dionysus' power. The Greek snaps into the chamber beside me.

I expect him but am pleasantly surprised to see he brought Eric and Jarod with him too.

"Heirs, you're on the guards. Dionysus, we need to end this seam business once and for all."

He and I rush over to the pentacle circle and lay down to navigate the astral plane.

Do you know how to banish someone to the Neitherlands? Dionysus asks me.

Nope. Do you?

Nope.

So, we wing it. Intention is everything, amirite?

Nope.

I don't have time to think about that. Relaxing my body, I set my mind free and claim my saber-tooth panther form. As a shaman, I am a healer of the realm and can expand my mind beyond the physical plane to ensure that the integrity of the physical and astral planes thrive.

I let my body drift...and jolt to awareness as the energy of Ahren's eagle soars past me on the mystic plane. He brushes me with a feather touch of his wing.

Well done, hotness.

If Ahren's awake, hopefully, Quon Shen and Samuel will follow.

As if in answer to my hopes, Quon Shen's Chinese water dragon *whooshes* by in a great cresting wave. He's the embodiment of fluid motion.

Then Samuel's ebony wolf is there. The great beast glances at me and lowers his chin.

Agreed. This ends now.

Samuel understands the boundaries of the planes better than any of us, and now that he's here, we have our best chance at putting things right.

The five of us advance.

Melanippe's jungle cat turns from where she's working with Mingin to slice open the seam. The throaty growl of her cat is as hissy and vicious as the woman herself. "When will you people learn to stay out of our business?"

"When will you learn we'll never stop?"

The cat launches and I meet her movement, colliding with her mid-air. The two of us crash to the sandy ground of the tomb floor in a tangle of fangs and claws.

Dionysus takes the form of a tiger and joins the fight. The two of us tag-team the Amazon.

At the same time, Samuel, Quon Shen, and Ahren go after Mingin. The man lying on the tomb floor doesn't look familiar, but that means nothing. Mingin is the tainted soul who now possesses his body.

"You'll never win." Samuel reaches toward the seam. They've peeled back two sides of the rift, and smoggy black entities are drifting through the gap

"Honestly, I'm sick of this game," I snap, slashing across her shoulder, my claws tearing at her fur. "Always with the Neitherlands seam. Whoever or whatever you think you'll let out, you're not. We won't let you."

Melanippe's cat grins and a sickening feeling of darkness and dread washes through me. "You won't be around to stop us."

She launches at me with her shoulder, and I brace for impact. It's like getting run over by a speeding truck. I absorb the hit and bite her collarbone. When my feet leave the ground, I take her with me.

We crash into the stone wall and scramble to get to all fours.

I shake my head, clearing the fog from the last hit. She's one helluva fighter, but I prefer fighting her cat on the astral plane rather than the immortal Amazon on the physical plane.

Dionysus has taken a new form. I chuckle as his rhino plows into her, flicking her into the air with his mighty horn. She crashes into the chamber wall and falls limp to the ground.

At the same time, Ahren and Quon Shen land a spectacular hit on Mingin. Thrust backward by the force of a magical blast, he's thrown into the air.

Before he begins to fall, Samuel bombards him with a rapid-fire barrage of magical pulses. "Someone, hold him suspended against the seam," Samuel shouts, shifting back to his human form and raising his palms.

Dionysus shifts into a polar bear and throws his mighty paws toward where Mingin hangs.

Samuel mutters a long string of chanted words I've heard once before. In a vision I had of Mingin's banishment, Fionn spoke them over and over.

Samuel's chanting gets louder and stronger and raises the hair on my neck. The words hang in the air like a song, the cadence creating a magical vibration. The vibration builds, snapping with magical potential.

Ahren and Quon Shen shift back to their human forms and raise their palms and join in.

The hair on my arms stands on end. I reclaim my body and join them, palms raised.

Repeating the chant with them is an exercise in cadence and pronunciations. It's difficult, but I try to stay with them. The power of the vibration builds as the chant takes hold. The intention resonates deep in the marrow of my bones.

This will send Mingin back to where he belongs.

Melanippe screams from where she's scrambling off the floor. She's human again and is shaking with fury.

The body Mingin possesses is convulsing in the air as we forcibly evict the black taint of his soul.

It won't be long now.

The seam has stopped leaking and is sucking escaped souls back into the rift.

Melanippe makes a running leap to pull Mingin down, and I laugh as Dionysus' polar bear clotheslines her and sends her flying without effort.

"Good air, Tarzan."

"Like swatting a fly." He flashes me a toothy, polar bear smile.

Sloan races past me to tackle her. I break off to join him and try to pin her down. It's a fight. Honestly, it's more than a fight. This bitch might be cray-cray, but she's a skilled Amazon warrior.

I get an elbow to the cheek and grunt as my neck cranes around on my spine. "Hurry, boys. We won't be able to hold her long."

A rope of energy joins the raised hands of Samuel, Ahren, and Quon Shen, and in the center of their field of power, Dionysus is holding Mingin's host.

The convulsing stops as the man's eyes flip wide, and a funnel of tainted smog barfs from his open mouth. It's rather gross, in a horror film kind of way, but the seam to the Neitherlands sucks him in like a vacuum, and he's gone.

Melanippe loses her mind and becomes a Tasmanian Devil to

try to hold down. "Can we get a banishment twofer? Then the psychotic lovebirds can be together forever floating around in a smog."

"Sorry," Samuel says, sinking to sit on the ground. "I'm out of power. That tapped me out completely. Maybe in a day or two."

A day or two?

Melanippe bites my wrist where it's braced against her face. Thankfully my body armor is in place, so she doesn't get anywhere. I elbow her in the ribs and resecure my hold. This isn't working.

"Sloan, take us to a Batcave holding cell."

He meets my gaze, and the three of us *poof*. We're standing in Toronto in one of the SITFU holding cells. I push away from her and a split second after that, Sloan portals the two of us outside the cell and hits the containment button.

The red light over the cell door flips green, and the room seals with a satisfying hiss.

"No!" Melanippe screams. "Noooo!"

"Yes." I double over and brace my hands against my knees, heaving for breath. "It's over. You lost, and now your tailpipe exhaust boyfriend is back in the Neitherlands where he belongs."

When my lungs are once again acquainted with oxygen, I collapse against Sloan and hug him. "Score one for the good guys. C'mon. Let's see how Toronto's doing and if we can get a ride back to Ireland."

CHAPTER TWENTY-ONE

The Batcave is bustling when Sloan and I go out to check in. Andromeda has a headset on and is watching the monitors. Maxwell is working on the police computer and cursing about something. Zuzanna and Dan the djinn seem to be coordinating teams to respond to exposure points.

"Hey, how are we doing?" I ask.

Andromeda blinks at me and frowns. "I thought you're supposed to be covering the tomb and the island."

"We are but had to deposit a prisoner into the cells."

"Oh, yeah? Who'd you bring us?"

"Melanippe of Scythia."

She brightens and holds up her palm for a high-five. "Team Light is off to a good start."

"Yeah. She and Mingin were inviting friends to the colliding realms party and decided to jump the starting bell. When we left, Mingin was banished, and the seam was closed."

"Excellent." Maxwell comes over to join us. "Dan, we've got pixies on the Danforth flying over morning rush hour traffic and waving at the commuters."

Dan frowns. "How many commuters?"

"Unknown."

"If they're in cars and exiting the highway, how will we possibly contain that?"

"Also, unknown. Tell your guys to do their best. No doubt we'll have a ton of follow-up wiping to do."

"Well, that can't be good." I point at the screen. It's a Global News bulletin showing a large gorilla climbing the CN Tower in a *King Kong* moment. "Is that a Moon Called problem?"

"I doubt it." Zuzanna frowns at the screen. "More likely a trickster. Garnet laid down the law hard for the next few days. No shifters who enjoy having their limbs attached to their bodies will dare step out of line."

Andromeda taps her headset. "Garnet. We've got a King Kong wannabe climbing the CN Tower and a news helicopter recording it all."

I can't hear his response, but it doesn't matter. Even imagining it is enough to make me laugh.

Funny not funny.

Dionysus snaps in beside me and grins. "Thought you could get away from us, did you?"

I hold out my hand. "Nope. I knew you'd come for us when you finished with the banishment."

"Right you are. Oh, and guess what?" he asks, delighted surprise in his expression. "The host body is remarkably still alive. Samuel will clear his memory, and I'll pop him home."

"Noice. Okay, success out of the gate. Let's keep on keeping on. This is more fun than I thought."

Maxwell turns and scowls. "Fun isn't a word I'd use to describe what's happening, Fi. Not even a little."

I offer them an apologetic smile. "Sorry. We're wrapping up a win in Ireland. We can stay for a bit and help if you need us."

Relief washes over Maxwell's expression. "That would be great. We'll take you for as long as you're not needed back in Ireland."

I nod and turn to Dionysus. "You go back, return Mingin's host to his life, and tell everyone we're helping here for a bit. If anything big happens, you'll have to come and get us because Sloan used up his long-range portaling juice."

Dionysus nods. "Okeedokee, I'll let them know."

Dionysus flashes out, and Sloan and I each grab an earpiece to hear what's going on.

"Wow, what happened to Canadians bein' polite?" Sloan frowns at the monitor wall.

I scowl at the general mayhem of the shenanigans on the screens. "Technically, no one is plotting evil and killing people. This seems to be a lot of fae races wanting to out the world of the empowered."

Maxwell sighs. "Yeah. I understand when you took me on, the intent was to keep the two worlds solidly separate. I'm not sure that's going to be possible now. Even if we're able to wipe and cover up and undo the damage done, this is happening on a global scale. There's no way to know what's getting exposed in other parts of the world."

True story. "So, who makes that call?"

Maxwell shrugs, taps his headset, and returns his attention to the screens. "Yeah, I'm here."

My cell vibrates in my pocket, and I pull it out to read the text Nikon sent.

Hey, Red. Checking in. How's the world treating my peeps?

Sloan and I are at the Batcave. Just brought your favorite Scythian in to lock her down. Mingin banished. Booyah!

Nikon snaps in beside us, and I take stock. He's looking good in black jeans, a t-shirt, and his usual guyliner. A little pale, maybe, but better than the last time I saw him while he was bleeding out. "Mingin's locked away, and you got her? Seriously?"

I hug him, pleased to see the delight dancing in his eyes. "Hey, you. Welcome back to the living. How are you feeling?"

"I'd say close to ninety percent back to normal."

"Which means seventy-five." Andromeda arches a brow at her brother. "Been there, done that. Don't try to play like you're ready to jump back into things."

Nikon makes a face at his sister. "I'm well enough to portal and stand and talk to friends."

"But not much more."

"I already opted out of today's battles."

"Which I'm thankful for." Andy gives in and flashes him a loving smile. "I'm glad you have enough sense to know your limitations."

Nikon holds his hands out to his sides. "With age comes wisdom."

I laugh. "Oh, that reminds me. We need your wisdom. Mother Nature gave us a riddle as one of the three most important things we needed to know going into the Culling."

"A riddle? Do tell. I love riddles."

"It said, 'In the darkest moment of battle and plight, the path to victory is the team for which you fight.'"

Nikon grins. "That's easy. We're fighting for Team Light. The answer is light."

"Right, but how is that the path to our victory?"

He lifts his shoulders and shrugs. "I suppose we have a few days to mull that one over. Thankfully, we're nowhere near our darkest moment of battle."

"Yeah, after a year of training, I'd be pissed if we duffed it right off the tee on day one."

Nikon steps over to the conference table and picks up a cherry Danish. "Not going to happen. Between the preparations we've made and the people we've got in place, Team Light will go the distance."

I think so too.

"What the fuck is that?"

Maxwell grabs the tablet that controls the television screens and turns up the volume of the news coverage.

"—waving signs declaring this the inaugural Fae Pride Parade," the announcer says.

"You've got to be kidding me." I stare at the line of floats pulling onto Bloor Street. "They're putting on a *Fae* Pride Parade?"

"It's got a familiar ring to it." Nikon shakes his head.

"How long have they been planning this? There have to be twenty floats."

Maxwell slides the tablet across the table and throws up his hands. "Fuck me. If they have four days of this planned, there's no way we'll be able to put a lid on this."

I gesture for Andromeda to give me her headset. Securing it over my ears, I move the microphone into place and tap to activate it. "Hey, boss man."

"Fi? What are you doing back? Is everything all right?"

"Mostly, yes. I think we need to regroup at the Batcave when you get a chance."

"What about?"

"I think we need to consider the secrecy of the empowered world as circling the drain and start planning how to address the public's reaction."

There's a moment of silence on the other end of the line. "Is it that bad?"

"I'm sorry to say, it is. Come back in, and you'll get the big picture."

I hand Andromeda back her headset and turn toward the elevators. A moment later, Garnet flashes in, yanks on the glass door, and storms inside, his black slicker flowing out behind him.

Before saying anything, I turn and point at the monitor wall. Between Global News, CTV News, and CP24, there's enough coverage that there's no way Dan's community of djinns can swing things back around to our favor.

"Fucking hell!" The fury of Garnet's lion rumbles in my chest.

"I'm sorry, but I think the secrecy boat has officially capsized."

"It was fucking torpedoed," Maxwell snaps, pulling off his headset and sending it across the table to bump the tablet. "The people we've been trying to protect had no intention of heeding our warnings."

"If this is happening globally, I don't see any way to go back," I say.

Garnet is staring at the monitors, his muscular frame rigid, his fingers curled into white-knuckled fists.

I go over and sit on the table facing him. "It's time to cut our losses and regain control. You and Maxwell need to put your heads together and decide how much the people need to know."

"I think they know most of it." Andy points.

"Not really. It's obvious the cat's out of the bag in some cases, but maybe not all. The world could probably handle the idea of Ostara rabbits, gnomes, and elves, but are they ready for demons, tricksters, and vampires?"

"Yer right, *a ghra*," Sloan says. "If we can isolate exactly how much of the empowered world is exposed, we might be able to blur the lines a little to forestall a mass panic."

Maxwell sighs. "That's a very fine line. Vampires might remain in the shadows here but could be exposed somewhere else. The true fallout to what's happening likely won't become clear for weeks or months."

"That's why we need to change gears," I say. "If the empowered races are so determined to be seen that they're parading down Avenue Road and in front of Queen's Park, there's no way the Guild of Governors or SITFU or any agency will be able to contain them."

Garnet breathes in deep and drops his chin. When he exhales, the growling stops. "All good points. All right, let's shift gears.

Maxwell, it's been a year since we inducted you into our world, but I'm sure you remember your main points of concern. Where do we start?"

"From the perspective of the public or law enforcement?" he asks.

"Your choice."

Maxwell walks over to the whiteboard and starts writing things down. "As far as law enforcement, I'd say, magical criminal behaviors we don't understand. Our right to enforce laws on races with different societal structures and our actual ability to enforce them. Physical danger to humans, dangers caused by community division and prejudice..."

"Prejudice will be a problem because of misinformation," Andromeda says. "Stigmas and stories have been handed down in fairy tales, movies, and media. People already have images in their minds about vampires and werewolves and a dozen other races."

"What about the races behind the faery glass?" I ask. "If this is essentially a fae coming-out party, do they honestly think human citizens will invite centaurs and trolls to walk our streets?"

Garnet frowns. "That brings us back to our initial question about how much exposure has occurred. If it's only the more benign, humanoid races that have already been peoples' neighbors and friends, that's one thing. If this is a complete exposure of the empowered world's dark and dirty, I think that's a different story altogether."

Maxwell's phone rings on his hip, and he frowns at the number. "Deputy Commissioner Maxwell," he says, the phone at his ear. "Yes, sir, I am aware... No, sir, I don't believe so... Yes, I can do that."

Garnet curses, his heightened hearing picking up both sides of the conversation.

Maxwell continues the conversation as he strides into his office and sits at his desk. "My task force is largely on the streets responding to the situation... They are... They have... I can have a preliminary briefing ready for you in an hour... Yes, sir... No. I'll come to you."

He hangs up the phone, pulls two fat binders out of the bottom drawer of his desk, and brings them to the main room. I recognize them as part of the information package Garnet and Andromeda put together when we took him on as our liaison between worlds.

He sets down the binders and taps a finger on the front cover. "All right. We have one hour to decide what we tell the higher-ups and what we hope washes under the bridge. They're pulling together an emergency committee together, and I'm on it."

"That's good," Garnet says. "Having a man on the inside means we can defuse the situation a little."

Maxwell doesn't seem to agree. "And if they realize I've known about the empowered world for a year now and didn't let on? How is that good?"

"Whether they like it or not, you've been instrumental in establishing a positive collaboration with the empowered community."

"Agreed," Andromeda says. "If they try to come at you for it, you can tell them your attorney will kick their asses and won't let up until the day I die. Which, you may tell them, is never."

Garnet grins. "I doubt it'll come to that. Because of the work we've done, we've saved lives, and Canadians have been able to sleep at night because they didn't need to be concerned with the kind of creatures that truly go bump in the night."

Maxwell exhales. "So, are you suggesting we 'fess up about what SITFU is really about?"

"To those in official channels who need to know, yes. To the general public? Not a chance. I think it's essential that the masses know as little as possible."

"I don't disagree, but the horse is already out of the barn. It's too late to close the door." Maxwell flips the front covers of the binders open and frowns at the information he studied so hard to learn. "They're going to know I was part of this."

Garnet shrugs. "I've got broad shoulders. Make me the heavy and tell them I gave you no choice. You either worked within my terms, or we wouldn't work with you. In fact, take me with you to the meeting, and I'll explain that myself."

Maxwell tilts his head as if considering that. "That's not a bad idea, although I'd prefer if they didn't consider you one of the city's most notorious persons of interest."

Garnet grins. "Maybe, when they learn there are creatures worse than me, they'll appreciate me taking a stand."

I chuckle. "If they don't, shift into your lion and make them pee themselves. That would be great."

Garnet flashes me a grin. "You'd enjoy that."

"I would."

"I *wouldn't*." Maxwell gives me a look. "These are both my superiors and my peers. Turning into a lion and making them pee their pants is *not* helpful."

I shrug. "If you don't like my icebreaker idea, I've got nothing."

"That weaselly piece of shit." Garnet is glaring at the television monitor and the coverage of the Fae Pride Parade. Malachi sits on a giant lily pad, waving at the people gathered to stare. He and the water nixies and swamp nixies are having the time of their lives and looking smug in their defiance.

"We can figure out how to put the screws to him later," I say, reading Garnet's mood. "First, we've got less than an hour to scan the news, put together an information pack that doesn't terrify the powers that be, and try to get ahead of this."

Andromeda crosses her arms and looks at me weirdly. "Maxwell's right. As much as we need to give the empowered world a face, Garnet might not be the best choice. A better idea would be someone less intimidating, someone the public could relate to.

You know, maybe the girl next door, or the server at the soup kitchen, or the bartender at your local pub."

Garnet looks at me and grins. "If only we knew someone like that."

I roll my eyes and swallow. "Seriously?"

Maxwell nods. "Honestly, it's a great idea, Fi. You charmed me and swayed me to your cause. I bet you could do it again."

I check in with Sloan, and he shrugs. He'd never tell me what I should do unless he sees a true and clear danger. If he's not fussing, the idea can't be all bad.

"Fine. I'll be your poster child, but not for another three days. In case you forgot, the alliance of the world is hanging in the balance."

Maxwell nods. "Fair enough. I'll lay the groundwork and set up a formal meeting after the Culling has ended. Thank you, Fi. This will work. I know it."

CHAPTER TWENTY-TWO

After a frantic hour of sifting through news stories and deciding what the world might know and not know, Nikon snaps Sloan and me back to Newgrange to regroup with Team Light. The change in scenery is dramatic from what greeted us at the dawn of morning to what is before us now.

Wow. Cleanup on aisle nine.

"Yer back." Da comes over to check in. "Dionysus said ye deserted us in favor of Toronto chaos."

"Not in favor of...but yeah, Toronto is definitely in a state of chaos." I laugh and point at the carnage. "Speaking of chaos, there seems to be plenty to go around today. That's a lot of fried necromancers."

Dillan glances at the swaths of fire-scorched men. "Yeah. Having dragons is an advantage. Either Droghun didn't consider them, or he wasn't prepared to defend against them. Either way, yay us."

Yeah, yay us.

"Did we take Droghun down?"

Da shakes his head. "When it became obvious this was a losing battle, he and a bunch of his men fled."

"I'm sure they'll regroup and be back to make our lives difficult in no time," Calum says.

"I'm sure that's true," Da agrees.

I look everyone over. "What injuries did we sustain? Is everyone whole?"

"We fared well," Da says. "No one sustained anything worth mentionin'. Just basic gashes and some light sprains. Nothin' we weren't able to heal."

"Good, then the first battle is a true win."

Da nods. "It is at that. Now, while we finish cleanin' up, tell me what happened in Toronto."

I join the efforts to sort through the dead and clean up the Newgrange property. All the while, I update Da and the others about what's going on back home.

"Garnet and Maxwell voluntold you to be the face of the empowered world?" Dillan scowls, shaking his head. "I don't like it. There are already enough people gunning for you. The last thing you need is to be *more* in the spotlight."

Da grunts. "Yer not wrong, but neither are Garnet and Maxwell. Fiona has a disarming charm about her. Citizens meetin' her on the street wouldn't consider her a threat or 'other.' She could humanize the empowered community."

"Many of them aren't human, Da," Calum says, dropping a couple of daggers and some guns onto the pile collected. "There's no sense whitewashing reality."

Da and Patty both let out a throaty *harrumph* and look at one another.

"What? You think I *should* whitewash the realities of our world?"

"Absolutely," Da says. "If yer serious about becoming a spokesperson fer the empowered, ye'll need to smile and make all the horrors and savagery of that society dissolve into the background. It'll be yer job to calm the waters whenever something goes wrong."

I think about that as I go back inside the tomb. Samuel is in there with Ahren and Quon Shen.

"How are things in here?" I ask.

Samuel gives me two thumbs-up. "We've spent the past few hours adding patches and strengthening the seam of the rift. As long as it doesn't come under direct attack again in the next three days, I don't think there will be any problem. Mingin is well and truly trapped."

"Good. Mingin's gone, and Melanippe is securely locked away, so hopefully, we're good on that front. Are you three planning to stay and ensure it stays that way?"

Quon Shen sits on the sandy ground and leans back against the stone wall of the tomb. "The three of us are wiped. We'll camp out here and guard the tomb for a few days, no worries."

"Will you be juiced up again by the end so we can banish Melanippe?"

Samuel grins. "You better believe it. I'm looking forward to that more than you know."

I am too, and she only lied and screwed me over for a few weeks. She lied to them and betrayed them for months and months. "Okay, I'll have Dionysus set you up with some food and drink to tide you over."

Ahren nods. "Sounds good. We'll text you if there's any trouble."

I think about that. "Maybe I'll ask one of the dragons to stay and help keep watch. I'd feel better—no offense—and one dragon can do quite a bit."

Ahren laughs, his voice so deep it's crazy. "I don't think anyone could argue that a dragon is a stronger fighting force than us right now. No offense taken."

"Okay, then it's settled. Text me if you need anything or run into any trouble."

"Will do." Samuel drops to sit opposite Quon Shen. "Fi...good luck."

I leave them to recuperate and head out to continue with the cleanup. When I get out there, there's a definite stir among my peeps. "What did I miss?"

Sloan strides over holding out his phone. "Kevin texted us. The groves of the Nine Families are going haywire."

"What does that mean?"

"I'm not sure. Yer father phoned Lugh to get a better idea of what's going on."

The two of us make our way over to where my brothers have gathered to hear Da's conversation.

"Aye, we'll have a look, but it sounds like more of the same... All right... We'll let ye know." Da hangs up and pockets his phone. "Apparently, the fluctuation of fae energy is causin' more irregularities. Evan and Iris called Da about concerns regarding the ambient power surge in their grove. Da called around, and all the groves seem to be affected. He asked that we try to help."

"Is that an emergency?" I ask.

"Not in a battle of good versus evil sort of way, no, but druids are guardians of nature and keepers of the fae, so it's still within our wheelhouse of responsibility to try to help."

"Even if we're the ones who caused the problem?" Dillan asks.

Da gives us a look. "I'd say especially if we're the ones who caused the problem."

"Okay, we'll go visit Evan and Iris and see if we can help with their fae power surge issues, although Myra was pretty sure things would even out on their own."

Da nods. "We can hope that's true. Until then, we'll address each problem as it arises."

I frown at the mess scattered across the landscape between the tomb and the river. "We need to address the fae groves, but we can't leave things like this. Some of us will have to stay and clean up."

"Not at all, cousin." Boann raises a hand toward the destruction. "You have done most of the work. I shall restore my lands."

"Are you sure?"

Boann nods and raises her arms. With a few circling gestures of her hands, the ground churns like it's being roto-tilled from below. Within seconds, the bodies sink beneath the surface, and the ground levels out flat once again. A moment later, the entire span of the meadow sprouts with lush green grass.

"All righty then, thanks for all your help."

Boann nods and smiles. "The pleasure is mine. Off you go to where you are needed next. Be well, cousins. Blessed be."

"Blessed be," we all say as she waves goodbye and glides back toward the river.

When she's gone, I get back on task. "Dionysus, the Hunter-gods are staying here for the duration of the Culling. Can you please outfit them with supplies? Also, can one of the dragons stay to help guard the seam while it's at its weakest?"

"I will stay," Utiss says.

"Awesome. Thank you." With that, we divvy up and *poof* off to check on the sacred groves of the Nine Families of the Druid Order.

The first time Sloan *poofed* me to the Doyles' home was a year ago last September when we came on our family trip to claim our heritage and secure the Fianna treasures from Fionn's fortress beneath the Hill of Allen.

It was the day we met Pip and vowed to help save Nilm from Droghun and the necromancers. It was also the day Emmet and Ciara first crossed paths.

A lot has happened since then.

Sloan, Da, and I arrive in the backyard of their property as the sun drops low on the horizon. According to the app I'm using to track sunrise and sunset, it must be close to four o'clock. It's been a long day already and seems later than that.

"Niall, thanks fer comin'." Evan Doyle strides out of the grove to greet us. "Honestly, I didn't know what to do. I know this is a bad time, but after the devastation to the grove last year, Iris is more than a little protective."

"That's perfectly understandable. I can see why yer concerned. Ye think it's the ambient power level that's causin' that?" Da gestures at the forest in front of us. With the coming of darkness, it's hard to miss that the entire forest emanates a pulsing pink aura.

"Well, that'll be hard to miss as people drive past," Sloan says.

"Aye, that's true. Lugh mentioned that reestablishing Emhain Abhlach would affect the fae prana available to us, but this is a bit much."

"Is it a case of castin' a glamor to hide it from sight, then?" Da scans the grove.

"If it were only the power glow, maybe."

"Ye mean to tell me there's more?"

"Aye, come. I'll show ye."

Evan Doyle leads us into their family grove, and the hair on my arms stands on end. Crossing the threshold of the tree line is like plugging into an electrical socket. My cells ping to awareness and my fae sight triggers without being called.

"Wow. This is a high-voltage grove." I glance around, searching for any sign of their fae. "Where is everyone?"

"That's the rub. At first, we didn't realize how the influx of power might affect things, but over the past two days, it's been hard to miss." He gestures deeper into the trees, and I blink, trying to figure out exactly what we're looking at.

It looks like one of those massive termite mounds that stands twelve feet tall, but at a closer glance, it's a gazillion psychedelic rabbit turds.

"Is that a mountain of Ostara rabbit poop?"

"It is." Iris Doyle steps around the mound from the other side.

"The poor bunnikins have been droppin' their little power nuggets non-stop."

I try not to laugh. It's obvious Ciara's mother is genuinely concerned, and I'm trying to take that seriously. The Ostara rabbit they have here is one of the original creatures from the Goddess Ostara's garden grove. Unlike Flopsy and Mopsy, who are descendants but don't hold the power and magic of their ancestors.

"Did he get into something? A rabbit-lax or something? Maybe too much roughage?"

"No." The scowl that earns me is impressive. It berates me as an idiot and dismisses me as a waste of her time with one crinkled brow. Her daughter has mastered that skill as well. "We don't know what it's about, but it started after you and your siblings meddled with Emhain Abhlach and upset the balance of nature."

I accept that without argument. I've dealt with Ciara enough to know not to start a fight with a Doyle unless I want a drag-out. Which I don't.

"From the outside looking in, it might seem like we meddled, Mrs. Doyle, but believe me, we didn't simply decide to reconnect the island as a conduit of raw prana on a whim. Mother Nature, Manannán mac Lir, Fionn, and Bodhmall all encouraged us to do it, insisting that it was necessary as part of the plan for us to come out of the Culling on the winning side."

"I suppose I shouldn't look a gift horse in the mouth. Yer brother's plan to trap our daughter backfired because of this island business."

"Enough, Mam." Ciara joins us. "I already told ye, Emmet and I didn't part ways because of anythin' other than us wantin' different things and us lovin' each other enough not to want to hold the other back. If ye knew Em at all, ye'd know he'd never plan to trap me. Hell, I doubt he's ever planned anythin' in his life."

I chuckle. "You're not wrong."

Ciara gives each of us a welcoming smile. "Thanks fer comin'. My parents have been in a stew about all this grove business. I told them we'll put a glamor on the glow and give the rabbits somethin' to bunch them up, but that didn't seem to settle the matter."

I shrug. "We said pretty much the same thing."

She winks at me. "See. I was payin' attention. I learned how to think like a Cumhaill."

I take that as the compliment it's meant to be. Wait. Am I getting along with Ciara?

This is a topsy-turvy time.

"Is everything else in the grove normal?" I ask.

Iris lets out an unflattering grunt. "Nothin' is normal. The winnots are blinking like faulty lightning bugs, the sprites are buzzing around wildly like they've taken drugs, and I won't even mention what I caught the elves doing—right out in the open."

I rub a hand over my mouth and try not to let her see my amusement. "I have it on good authority that the prana levels will settle and the surge of power causing the weirdness will subside."

"On good authority from whom?" Iris asks.

"From a fae historian I consulted with about this very issue. Trust me, in time this will all settle down."

"In a few days? Weeks? Can ye be a little more specific about what we're facin'?" Evan asks.

"Honestly, I can't say. This is a new era we're embarking on. If Toronto was any indicator of what we're in for, the secret world of the fae and empowered races has been outed. Get ready for a new normal where people know about magic."

They both look horrified. "Ye don't think things will go back to normal after the Culling?"

"I don't see how that's possible, no."

Ciara chuckles. "Maybe it doesn't matter if our grove glows. Maybe we leave it and fly our fae flag."

Iris flashes her a disapproving scowl. "If yer not helpin', ye don't need to have an opinion."

Ciara grins, unabashed. "Och, Mam, don't get yer knickers in a twist. I was just takin' the piss."

My phone buzzes and I check the incoming text. Da looks at me, and I fill him in. "It seems the other groves are having much the same issues. The fae folks are supercharged and buzzing with energy, and the trees are pulsing with the glow of prana power, etcetera."

Da nods. "Tell them to glamor the glow until we learn more about the state of the world after this is over. As long as no one is *in* danger or *causing* danger, we'll leave it to sort itself out fer now."

"Sounds good to me." I text Da's instructions to the group and leave it at that.

When I finish, Ciara tilts her head back the way she came and walks behind the mound of Ostara poop. I laugh when I check to see if my shield is tingling before I follow her to a secondary location.

It's not.

I meet her around the rabbit manure pile, and she smiles. "I'll not ask ye to pretend yer broken up about Emmet and I not makin' it long-term. Ye must be bustin' yer buttons to see me go."

"Not really. I only ever wanted Emmet to be happy. Despite how we got along, you two matched up better than anyone expected. He's sad and disappointed things didn't work. I'm sad for his loss."

She nods. "That's big of ye, Fi. I don't know that I would've been so charitable if our positions were reversed."

I shrug. "Sloan told me the other day that no one gets to have a say in other people's relationships and he's right. What you and Emmet had was between you two. It lit you up, and I hope you both find that again."

"Thanks, Fi. I believe yer sincere."

Why does everyone sound so surprised when they say that? "I am. Considering we're all Heirs of the Order, I want us to be on good terms."

Ciara lifts her shoulders and shrugs. "I still think yer a pain in the ass know-it-all."

I laugh. "I still think you're a self-important bitch, but hey, I don't want to skewer you anymore."

Ciara laughs. "A distinct improvement."

The two of us fall silent, and the pause becomes awkward. I'm about to excuse myself and rejoin the others when she holds up her hand, and her expression grows serious.

"I love him, Fi. Part of me always will. Emmet was the first person who truly saw the person hiding inside me, and he accepted her, faults and all. I understand we're not a good fit for forever, but the last nine months gave me hope that my perfect man is out there."

"I hope you find him."

She nods. "Me too. So, I wanted to say…it was good to be a Cumhaill fer a while. I admire yer family and the way ye love one another. Give my love to the monkeys, would ye? When they're old enough, give them one of these from their Auntie Ciara."

She hands me a brown sandwich bag folded over at the top. I glance in, and it's full of psychedelic Ostara poops. "We've got plenty, and I like that I've contributed to their druid journey. Pass them around to the others as well. At least then, they won't totally forget me."

I close the bag and wave that away. "Not possible. You're unforgettable. Like a hurricane or a tsunami."

CHAPTER TWENTY-THREE

We take shifts sleeping, our team spread out between the treehouse, Emmet's palace, and Newgrange tomb. Even with Mother Nature telling us the two main focus points for Ireland are the tomb and the island, there are still a few calls to respond to in Dublin and Galway.

Sloan volunteers to head up the response to Dublin with Dillan and Da goes with Tad to Galway.

"I can come too if you want." I blink up from the comfort of my pillow.

Sloan is sitting on the edge of the bed and bends down to kiss me goodbye. "Not necessary, luv. Dublin is my old haunting ground, and I need far fewer hours of sleep. Go back to sleep, and I'll be home when ye wake next."

"If you're sure."

"I am."

I take the out and accept the invitation to get a couple of extra hours of rest.

I wake with a heavy arm hanging protectively over my hip and Sloan standing in the doorway smiling at me. It takes a moment to put the impossibility of that together. Then I twist back to see who's snuggled in behind me.

Dionysus is out cold on top of the comforter and sleeping with a beatific grin on his face.

I chuckle, ease out from under his arm, and shuffle out to the hall to welcome Sloan back. "Hey, how'd it go in Dublin?"

He closes the bedroom door with a soft *bump* and escorts me toward the kitchen. "It was fine. A coven of dark witches took a run at the white witches and tried to overtake their place in the community."

"Is everything all right?"

He nods. "They attempted to take control of the ancestral cemetery the white witches use to connect them to their magic. Dillan and I helped turn the tables. We added to the white witch wardings and managed to take the dark witches down a notch or two in the process."

"Excellent." I rise onto my tiptoes and slide onto a stool at the island. "Then I didn't miss too much."

Sloan pours me a cup of chamomile tea and sets it in front of me. "The question is, what did *I* miss, Cecilia?"

I'm not sure what he means until he tips his head toward our bedroom. "Ye know that song...I get up to wash my face. When I come back to bed, someone's taken my place."

"Cecilia, you're breaking my heart..." I sing a little of the Paul Simon song and chuckle. "Honestly, I have no idea. The last thing I remember is kissing you goodbye. He was probably looking for a place to crash."

"Yer lucky I'm not the jealous type."

I laugh at that. "No. *You're* lucky you're not the jealous type. I don't go for that."

He chuckles. "Point made. I suppose I'm confident enough in yer love that I can weather findin' ye in bed with another man."

"What's this now?" Calum emerges from the bedroom hall with Kevin right behind him. "Fi's sleeping around on you, Irish?"

I roll my eyes and sip my tea. I suppose it's a testament to how well everyone knows me that no one is taking any of this seriously. "I was *in* bed. Dionysus was *on* the bed. Two friends sleeping with clothes and covers in between."

Kevin pulls up the stool next to me. "That's much less interesting."

"Sorry to disappoint. Next time, I'll make sure my sleeping around is racier."

"I'm sorry? What now?" Nikon snaps in, looking confused. "Fi's sleeping around and didn't invite me? I think I've firmly established that I have dibs. Did this happen while I was dead? You shouldn't count a guy out simply because he's dead."

"I'm outtie. Talk among yourselves. Better yet—make pancakes. I'll be out in a bit." I take my tea to go and head back to my bedroom to shower and get ready for another grueling day.

When I step inside my treehouse bedroom, Dionysus is still sleeping, so I pad past the bed and head straight into the washroom to get showered and dressed.

I really do love my life and all the people in it.

My shower is hot and quick, and since I slept with my clothes on in case of an emergency in the night, I put them back on and am good to go.

"Hey, Jane. When did you wake up?"

I meet Dionysus's sleepy smile and grab my brush off the dresser. "Only a few minutes ago. What brings you to my bed, Tarzan? Is everything all right?"

He shrugs. "Eros was being a dick last night, and I had a bad dream. I came to make sure you were safe, and I guess I fell asleep."

I pull the brush through my hair and towel off the ends before they drip down my shirt. "That's fine. We both needed it after the excitement of yesterday. How are you feeling this morning? Any better? Sometimes bad dreams can stick with you."

He pushes up on the bed and sits against the headboard. "It's weird. When I was a kid, my bad dreams were always about me. Me getting strung up and tortured. Me getting struck down by one of my siblings. Me getting stoned and ridiculed by the people Zeus forced to raise me. Lately, when I have bad dreams, they're never about me."

I sit on the edge of the bed next to him. "What are they about now, sweetie?"

"After Mingin and Melanippe took Gran, I had bad dreams about us not finding her on that yacht in time. I dream about you a lot…about bad people taking you. Sometimes it's Nikky and Andromeda, and I can't get to them quickly enough to help them."

I lean forward and hug him. "Oh, Tarzan, you have such a sweet soul. Worrying for others is part of loving people. Sometimes those worries and fears manifest in bad dreams."

"I'm not a fan."

"No. I don't suppose you are. When we were growing up, especially after our mom died, Da always made us give him a happy thought right before we went to sleep. Kinu and Aiden do that with the monkeys too. It helps."

"I'll try that. If it doesn't work, you can expect me to make late-night house calls."

I hug him tightly before easing back. "You know you're always welcome."

He grins. "I know. I like that most of all."

I shuffle back and sit against the footboard so we're facing one another. "Do you want to tell me what Eros said or what your bad dream was about?"

He shakes his head and starts massaging my feet. "More of the same. He's angry because I'm no fun. I spend too much time with humans. I need reminding who I am."

"That's bullshit. You're finally discovering who you are, and he doesn't like it. He's petty and jealous while you become more fabulous every day."

"Thank you. I think so too."

"So, either we don't care what he says, or we try to show him what he's missing. Do you think he'd ever be able to evolve from his selfish dickdom?"

Dionysus shrugs and switches feet. My goodness, the man knows his way around a foot massage. "I don't know. I don't want to disregard the possibility because I was described as a selfish dick more than once myself and look how good I turned out."

I giggle and close my eyes, relishing every squeeze and twist of every toe. "You turned out amazing."

"I did, didn't I?"

The pancakes are ready by the time Dionysus and I head out, and I reclaim my seat at the breakfast bar. Since I left to have a shower, Da and Aiden have joined us, and Bruin, Manx, and Daisy have come up from their companions' den below.

"The gang's all here." Da handles the griddle. "Did everyone get rested up fer day two?"

I nod. "Thank you for taking the early shift, guys. I needed those extra hours."

Da slides the spatula under two fluffy golden-brown discs of perfection and reaches forward to drop them on my plate. "Yer welcome, *mo chroí*. After years of shifts, it's the work of a moment to get up in the middle of the night and be ready fer duty."

I chase a pat of butter over my pancakes with my knife before dousing everything in syrup. "I did not inherit that gene. Sorry not sorry."

"That's fine. We got ye covered." Da hits up Dionysus' plate next. "Eat up, you two. Once yer fed, we're off to the island to check on Emmet and the crew there."

My phone buzzes against the countertop and I open things up to see who needs me. "Nikon? Since you're done eating your pancakes and are ready to roll, would you mind popping back to Queens on Queen to pick up Merlin? He's got the bad juju beacon figured out and needs a ride to the island."

Nikon jumps up from the couch and ruffles Rory's sleep. She grunts and flicks out her wing to clip him in the back of the head. She misses, and Nikon doesn't even notice.

Hilarious.

"Tell him I'm on my way. Meet you there in two shakes." Nikon disappears.

I reach for the jug of juice and pour myself a glass. "Here's to the Time of the Colliding Realms, day two. May the Fates keep shining their favor on us and bring everyone home safe."

"Hear, hear." Da lifts his mug of coffee. "Safe home, everyone."

"Safe home."

After the day two goodbyes and well-wishes end, Dionysus resets the god warding on Gran's and Granda's property, and we snap to Fantasy Island. We arrive in the middle of the grassy land, and I wave at Emmet, the heirs, and the yearling dragons.

Then it strikes me. "Wait. Tarzan, can you portal and use magic here now? Up until now, it's always restricted you to the rocky shoreline."

He snaps out and appears by the tree line of the shifting forest. Then he disappears and materializes on the top of the waterfall cliffs.

A moment later he's back at my side. "It seems the island has accepted me. I think I've gained approval between being a god and taking the oath to connect with the island as one of its protectors."

"Awesome. Can you snap into the hidden city? That would be exciting because then we could visit Emmet without the hassle of navigating the island, the forest, and unlocking the entrance every time we come here."

He snaps out and then is back holding one of the massive peanut butter cookies he brought Emmet for the Brenny celebration. "All signs point to yes."

"Awesomesauce. That's the best news I've heard all day. Yay, you!" I hug him, and when I step back, Nikon has arrived with Merlin. "Yay, you too!"

Merlin chuckles as I grab him for the next hug. "Thank you. Thank you." He hugs me back before holding up a brass pocket watch.

"That's our beacon for the dark ones?"

Merlin nods. "I chose a dark object I already had and imbued it to call out to kindred spirits to draw them here. If I've done my job, once I wind the timepiece and click the plunger to start the watch, it should emit a pulse to draw those already stewing for trouble."

"So, it won't incite anyone who isn't already on the path to be a baddie?"

Merlin shakes his head. "It shouldn't. I specifically set it to call those already in action, intent on gaining a foothold in the Culling's struggle for power."

"*Noice.* Well done. Okay, since we're all here, we might as well see if it works. Let's give it a go."

Merlin winds the dial at the top of the watch and presses the plunger with his thumb. "Here we go."

At first, we all stand as a group and glance around. When nothing happens, I worry. "Did you test it?"

Merlin makes a face at me. "Are you asking if I tested an

enchanted dark object to draw the worst of the darkly aligned to my home before I came here? No, Fi. Call me crazy, but I didn't."

"Well, when you say it like that…" I make eyes at him. "After this is over, I think you should take a few weeks off and hang out with Cazzienth. You're a cranky pants."

Merlin closes his eyes and shakes his head.

"I feel yer pain." Da pats Merlin's shoulder.

Merlin chuckles and opens his eyes. "It'll be fine, Fi. Trust me. I didn't test it, but I did go over the spell more than once and am confident I've got it right. We need to give it a moment. Patience, grasshopper."

Right. I suppose it's not as if they can suddenly feel his spell worldwide. It will take time to build a following. "Sorry. I've been wound up about the Culling for a long time. I didn't mean to take it out on you."

"Not a problem. We're all a little stressed."

True story.

While we wait, I pull out my phone and call Garnet. Thankfully, I don't have Emmet's issue out here. "How are things on the home front?"

"Imagine a flaming bag of dog shit on your front porch. That pretty much covers it."

"Colorful. Other than things being shitty, is my favorite city hanging in there?"

"By a thread. You might want to rethink being the face of Canada's empowered. This is going to suck ass."

"Noted. I'll claim a Scarlett O'Hara moment and think about it tomorrow."

"Tomorrow it is. Anything you need me to do?"

"No. S'all good. I was just checking in."

"Then be well, Lady Druid. My home life and work life will suffer if anything happens to you."

"Aw, I heart you too, Puss. Stay shiny." I hang up before he can ruin our moment and glance around. "What's happening?"

Calum is chatting with Nikon, and they both look over at me. "What do you mean?" my brother asks.

"My shield is tingling, and the hair on my arms is standing on end. Do you guys feel anything?"

They look at each other and up and down the shoreline. "Nope. Nothing," Nikon says.

"What is it, *a ghra?*" Sloan comes over. He's got a strange look on his pretty face, and his attention stays locked on me. "Why do you look like that?"

"Like what? How do I look?"

"Slightly constipated," Emmet says. "Or maybe it's the opposite, and you're cramping up to make a dash."

I make a face at him. "Isn't absence supposed to make my heart grow fonder? Well, it's not working."

I step away from the peanut gallery and over to Merlin. "Is it the beacon I'm feeling?"

"I don't think so. It shouldn't trigger you in any way. I set it for those with a darker alignment."

"Holy crap." Dillan points down the shoreline. "Merlin, I think your old fogey timepiece is kicking in. Either that or aliens are landing, and we're about to be invaded and anal-probed."

Emmet snorts. "Why does everyone think aliens use anal probes? What exactly do you think they'd learn from your ass? No, they use nasal probes. Right up into your cranium to get to the good stuff."

I ignore the mindless chatter of my brothers. My shield is ramping up from a tingle to a burn, and it has everything to do with the weird points where the air is warbling and waving in and out of focus. "What are those? Portals?"

Sloan steps in beside me and frowns. "They look like distortion portals...but there are too many. How could so many be opening at once?"

"I don't know, Mackenzie, but I think we're about to find out."

I activate my body armor and call Birga forward. "I've got a bad feeling about this, boys. Everyone, on your toes."

Heads come around, and I gesture at the point of my concern right as colorful bolts of magic shoot past our heads and a dozen attackers hemorrhage from the distortion portals at once.

"To the dragons," Emmet shouts. All traces of my goofball brother disappear, replaced by the guardian of Emhain Abhlach.

The heirs run to the yearling dragons, and a moment later, they take to the sky. Emmet and Kaida buzz overhead in a blue blur, followed by the rest.

Sloan and I dig in, scowling at the opening portals. There are five, six...no, seven, each with hostile forces pouring onto the beachfront in hordes.

"What is happening?" I ask.

"You wanted a beacon." Merlin erects a forty-foot wall of energy between us and the incoming forces. "I might have made it too strong."

"Ya *think?*"

He shrugs. "On the plus side, your instinct about drawing the Team Dark players here was sound. Look at all the maniacal bad guys that won't rape and pillage innocent villages."

"Yeah, but look at all the maniacal bad guys we now have to face all at once."

Scanning the incoming forces, I try to gauge what we're in for. It's impossible. I don't recognize half of the races to begin to prepare. "What are they?"

"What *aren't* they?" Sloan lifts his finger to point. "Those are banshee, vitterfolk, trolls, djinn, vampires...I don't know what *they* are...."

"They're all here because they felt our call?"

Merlin nods. "Now that they are, they'll want the island's power for themselves."

"Amazeballs."

CHAPTER TWENTY-FOUR

The problem with having a party and putting an open invitation out to the world is that you can't plan how many people will show up. In this case...many more than I expected at once.

*Note to self...*Next time, send out the invite in phases. Yeah, that would likely have been a better idea.

Merlin shifts into his massive dragon form, jumps the energy wall he erected, and runs at the invaders. Nikon, Tad, Sloan, and Dionysus start flashing in and out of vision doing their blitzkrieg melee battle form. I release Bruin, and the two of us dig in.

"How are you feeling, Killer Clawbearer? Are you ready to rumble?"

"Ye better believe it, Red."

The two of us rush forward and greet the group that Sloan called vitterfolk. I know from my training that they're cousins to trolls, but they don't look like it. They're a tall, good-looking group that could pass for humans if it wasn't for their long tails.

We meet them head-on, and Da joins us with his staff spinning. As out of control as the moment is, to have my father spinning his staff beside me is all I need to ground me to get it done.

I told him he was my foundation, and I wasn't exaggerating. With him at my side and our drama sorted out, I feel like we can take on these hordes and send them home with their tails tucked between their legs.

"What do you say, oul man? Care to keep count?"

Da moves with the strength and grace of a man half his age and chuckles. "If ye like, *mo chroi*. Although, I'm feelin' the luck of the Irish flowin' strong today, so there's that."

"Challenge accepted."

Bruin snorts a laugh, stands on his back legs, and calls his body armor. The visual never gets old. And yeah, it slows the attackers down. Not that we need the help. My oul man and I are doing just fine.

The three of us get into a groove and when the attackers thin out, I drop to the ground and press my palm to the sand. *"Tidal Wave."*

Connecting with the heaving body of the Irish Sea, I call the ebb and flow, urging it to grow. *That's it. We're going to protect the island from these intruders. Rise and help me wash them out to sea.*

"Incoming," I say as the water recedes to build. I watch as the shoreline stretches farther out to sea. Then the water rises eight…ten…then fifteen feet into the air as it rushes back toward us.

My tidal wave crashes on the cluster of fighters, knocks them to the rocky sand, and drags them out to sea. The vitterfolk who were still breathing are dazed and in no shape to fight the force of my waves.

For you, Manannán mac Lir. Invaders of your island for you to deal with as you wish.

I have a good idea of how that will go and focus my energy on the battles in progress.

An explosion of magical energy detonates down the beach, and one of the Perry twins is thrown twenty feet into the water.

When he lands facedown and doesn't move, Da turns to check in with me.

"We're fine, Da. Go help him."

He runs off, and Bruin and I assess the battle.

"Where are we needed, buddy?"

The Team Dark visitors might not realize the power they feel is radiating from the island's heart, but I'm sure someone in this crowd will be sensitive enough or informed enough to figure it out.

Whatever happens, we can't let them get direct access to the power of the prana rivers.

"Dragon riders, ho!" Emmet yells, swooping down as Kaida exhales a long stream of flame, torching an army of men with horse heads and glowing green eyes.

Dart, Saxa, and Bryvanay have teamed up with Merlin and are fighting as one hell of a ground troop.

As I watch them engage, Dionysus snaps over to check on me. "Everyone okay over here?"

"Yep. All good, Tarzan. Thanks."

Except something triggers my fae sight, and my malevolence meter redlines.

"Feckin' hell," Bruin says.

I follow my bear's gaze to a portal opening in the sea's shallow waters. An incoming force of centaur guards is racing at us, splashing in the water as they come ashore. Men with cloven feet, hairy chests, and massive ram horns curling against the sides of their heads.

Leading them, mounted on a massive black stallion, is a man with opal-white skin and a head covered with a thicket of silver and gray twigs. His black cloak billows out behind him, the raven feathers fluttering in the breeze of their motion.

"Fuckety-fuck, it's Keldane." A shiver of pure terror races down my spine. If there is one person in the two realms who reduces my confidence into a puddle of goo, it's him.

"Jane, what's wrong? Who's the mossy guy with the abs and the feathers?"

"It's the Unseelie Prince, Keldane."

Keldane's malevolent glare locks on me and his mouth curves in an evil grin. Unbidden, the searing pain of steel piercing my flesh sucks the breath from my lungs. I remember every visceral moment of our last battle…the gaping wound in my chest, my hands slick and warm, the spongy moss under my cheek as I collapsed to the ground.

The world around me spins, and the thundering rush of blood in my ears makes me dizzy.

Dionysus grips my wrist. "Jane? You're scaring me. You look faint."

Contessa McSparkles whinnies in panic. Two trolls have her lassoed and are yanking on her wings. Dionysus looks torn.

"Go, Tarzan. Help her." When he doesn't move, I shake off my panic and straighten. "Go on. I'm fine."

After a moment of hesitation, he breaks away and turns to run. I watch him go, thankful he didn't hear the lie in my voice.

Keldane is racing at me, the long, black raven feathers of his jacket flapping with the speed of his travel. Each time I've come up against him, I've nearly died. The last time nearly killed Dillan and Dart too.

Today, there are too many people I care about.

I blink and glance around. Dillan, Eva, and Merlin are taking on a group of vampires. Jarod and Ciara are facing off with a djinn. Bruin and Manx are holding back a massively ugly troll, and Emmet is angling Kaida so that the pumping of her wings is causing a tidal wave to pour into the two remaining open portals.

How do I defend against Keldane and his centaur army? Then it hits me.

"The shifting forest. Those trees will slow down the centaurs, and Keldane will have to dismount. It's my only chance to beat him."

"Go, Red. I'll do my best to slow them down."

"I love you, buddy."

I turn and beat feet as hard and as fast as I can. The thundering sound of hooves grows louder behind me, but I focus on the line of trees ahead. Fists pumping, I push hard, the muscles in my thighs burning beneath the strain of the pace.

"Look at the spirit in that female. I've missed hunting you, little one." Keldane's voice is unnervingly close and eerily seductive.

I make it to the treeline seconds before the Unseelie prince and his forces. When I glance back, my heart trips at how close they are.

Go, go, go.

I duck into the shadows of the shifting forest and don't stop. As I run, I keep my senses heightened. I listen for the sound of the trees moving to attack. I watch for any sign that I've made an error in judgment.

A hundred yards in, I curl in behind a wide redwood and press my palms flat on its trunk.

Reaching out with my druid connection, I hope the forest recognizes me. I've been here before and pledged my vow to the island.

We're not going to let anyone into the hidden sanctuary. Especially not the men chasing me. I need your help to keep them away.

A small surge of energy greets me, and I think the trees have received my message.

Peeking to the side, I track the approach of Keldane and his men. They're ten feet inside the forest and advancing with more caution than I expected.

Can they feel the forest's magic?

"Turn back while you can, Keldane." I use an echo to make my words bounce from different directions. "You're not behind the faery glass anymore. This isn't your world to command."

His laughter is rich and sultry. It makes my stomach knot that he's so confident. "If you didn't want me to come, why invite me, little one? Have you missed me?"

I glance around, searching for shadows or somewhere to hide. It's mid-morning. The sun is shining brightly and dappling everything around me with golden sunshine. There's nowhere for me to hide.

"Sorry to disappoint you." I scan the branches above. "Never, in all the time we were planning who we'd have come up against, did I think of you."

I press my hand against the trunk of the tree I'm hiding behind. *Now is your time to shine. Please help me.*

This time, the surge of energy is definitely the tree responding. The ground beneath my feet trembles ever so slightly, then the roots and trunks break free from their places in a series of deafening *cracks*.

The trees shift so fast and with such force that they crush three centaurs before the others realize where the danger is coming from.

"Feline Finesse." As a tree whizzes past, I take a running jump and grab a low-hanging branch. Dangling beneath the limb, I lift my feet and hook my heels to pull myself up. Twisting and grunting, I work my way over the branch until I'm in the tree and tagging along for the wild ride.

My tree is booking it.

I brace myself in the "V" of a large branch coming off the trunk and swipe my hair from my face. Steadying myself as we slide, I catch my breath as we shift forward to cut off a centaur's path and change course sideways to crush another.

Boom. Boom. Boom.

The thunder of trees colliding echoes all around and rattles in my chest. Below, dozens of centaurs swing their swords in useless arcs as they gallop this way and that, trying to escape death.

There's no defense against this force of nature using a steel blade. Caught a hundred feet into the depths of the shifting forest, their only option is to retreat…except the trees have no intention of allowing them to leave.

When I've rested from my sprint, I drop and press my hands against the forest floor. I send out my silent request and *Move Earth*.

A gaping crevasse opens in the ground and swallows the fallen centaurs and those too close to get clear of the shifting earth. Thanking the forest for its help, I close the ground and move.

Running on two legs versus four has benefited Keldane. The dark prince is navigating the trees better than the others and sadly hasn't gotten squished.

I don't think it's all dexterity, though.

His magic seems stunted, much like ours was before we connected with the island, but even so, he's not helpless. Keldane with even a fraction of his magical ability is still damn scary.

I run through the trees, my fleet-footed sprint versus his powerful, long strides. He's got almost two feet on me and is an Unseelie prince. The ambient fae magic in the air feeds his cells as much as mine.

"I do love a woman who leads me on a chase. It makes it that much more gratifying to catch her."

I duck behind a wide fir tree to assess my position. *Bruin, if you can hear this, I could use help in the trees.*

I drop to the ground and look under the umbrella of branches hanging low with needles. Keldane is dodging the trees without much difficulty. With his palms up, he seems to have enough power to stop them from crashing into him.

Disappointing.

I really hoped to see him pulped.

Well, the man is partly twig and moss. I suppose I shouldn't be surprised he has power over forest magic.

"Come out and play, little one. Don't be scared. Haven't we always had a good time?"

He pauses, looking the other way. I roll out from under the tree and weave back toward the beach.

"I must have missed the fun part." I throw my voice. "I remember being captured to be kept as your concubine and the time you slashed your scimitar across my chest. I don't remember that being fun."

He chuckles and tilts his head as if trying to filter the sounds to track me. "I suppose we share a difference of perspective."

"I suppose we do."

His stupid twig head turns, and he starts jogging toward me. There's no hesitation in his step. Somehow, he knows where I am.

Dammit. How did he do that?

I tuck in behind the unearthed roots of a fallen tree and gauge my chances of getting back to the rocky beach before he gets to me.

I don't like those odds.

Dropping to my knees, I focus on my intentions. *"Earthquake."* I press my hands flat to the soil and call the tremors to compromise his balance. *"Erupting Earth."* I stare at the hanging tendrils of vines above him. *"Grasping Vine—"*

Rough hands grip deep into my hair and lift me off my feet before my spell takes hold. I scream, shock and alarm warring within me. My scalp burns with the caveman treatment, and I flail behind my head.

"Let me go." I twist, reach, and kick my feet, but I've got no leverage to see who has me or regain my freedom. My scalp is screaming, and tears sting my eyes. "Let me go, asshole, or I'll curse you and fill your mouth with shit and your ears with centipedes."

"I've got the witch, sire," the centaur says.

"I'm not a witch, you moron."

Dangling in the air gives me very little leverage to fight. Still, I'm not defenseless.

"*Faery Fire.*" I call the magical flames to my palms and reach behind my head. The sizzle of flesh is almost as rewarding as the throaty cry of the centaur guard. He drops me, and I scramble to get back on my feet.

Keldane's boot cracks into my ribs and log-rolls me in the air. My head clunks into the trunk of a tree, and if I didn't have my armor on, I would be out cold.

The roar of Killer Clawbearer filters through the rushing waves pounding in my head. I roll to my feet while my bear takes on the centaur I torched.

I scan my surroundings, wondering again about the likelihood of me rejoining my party. My footing is wonky, and my head is spinning.

I won't make it.

The trouble with this magical forest is that it always seems to go on forever. Keldane is moving in fast. Decision made. I turn to bolt when a wall of fur and muscle confronts me.

Shit. It wasn't *one* centaur that made it through the shifting trees to grab me. It was *three.*

I freeze in place, and before I turn to run, strong hands grab my arms and spin me. Keldane has me in his grip and pulls me against his bare chest.

"You led me on a jaunty chase, little one. I'll consider that foreplay."

My reaction to him is visceral—it always has been.

There's something wholly unnatural about the fae prince's power to suck women into his thrall. I can't deny he affects me, but I can control how I respond.

I push my body's natural response to him way down deep and focus on how pee-my-pants scary he can be. "You know, I don't think I've ever seen you with a shirt on. As a prince, couldn't you afford one or do you simply prefer your nipples to be free-range?"

He grins. "Always such a tease. You protest and say you want nothing to do with me, yet here you are, aroused by me once again. You're wondering about the unexplored sexual potential between us. I see it in your eyes."

"Actually, I wondered about you getting jiggy with one of your guards. He was talking about it when I was your prisoner, and I never quite figured out how the mechanics of that worked."

Keldane scowls and lifts me so I'm looking at him eye-to-eye. "It will be my pleasure to show you."

"Pass. I'm a one-man woman, and I'm spoken for."

"Then tell me who he is, and I shall kill him and pave the way for us to be together."

Wow, the butterflies in my stomach all try to migrate south at once. There's no doubt in my mind that Keldane would kill Sloan in a heartbeat.

He leans in close, and I get a whiff of his mossy eyebrows. "Tell me who he is, little one. You deserve nothing less than a prince."

"I…uh, a prince is nice, but my guy is a god. So, there's that. You better set me down before he smites you and all your men."

Keldane's gaze narrows on me. "You lie."

"No. I don't." I reach into my shirt and pull out my pendant. Pressing it, I send up a prayer that this works.

CHAPTER TWENTY-FIVE

Dionysus appears a split second after my thumb presses on my pendant. He takes one look at Keldane dangling me in the air and his entire persona shifts. Gone is my sweet and loveable honorary family member. The man before us is the Greek god of legend. "How dare you."

In the flick of his hand, I'm out of Keldane's grasp, and the Unseelie prince winds up pegged to the trunk of a tree, his feet dangling three feet off the ground. "Let me down."

"Not a chance, twig boy." Dionysus looks me over and frowns. "Are you all right?"

I wrap my arms around him and am more than a little thankful for the support in staying upright. My legs are shakier than I care to admit, but Dionysus is as strong and steady as he's always been. "I'm fine. I was explaining to Keldane that I don't need a prince because I have a god who loves me."

"Forever and always, beautiful."

I slide to Dionysus's hip and keep my arm at his back. As much as I'd love to ask Dionysus to snap Keldane and his men back to the other side of the faery glass and knock them out until the Culling is over, I have a feeling that goes beyond his "protecting my family" loophole of not overstepping his power.

With Eros already making waves for him and the Fates watching him, I can't risk him getting in trouble.

I need to convince Keldane to go back and stay there...but how?

"There's nothing for you to conquer on this side of the faery glass, Keldane. Take the few men you have left and return to your kingdom."

"Who are you to tell me what to do?" he snaps, still dangling from the tree trunk and fighting Dionysus's hold. "You are nothing...a human girl...an insignificant speck next to me."

"I'm certainly not as important or as powerful as you—I don't pretend to be—but I'm not nothing. I'm a protector of this realm."

"This realm is too big for you to claim dominion over. You are one person."

"True, but I have a lot of powerful friends who are safeguarding the world right now."

The malevolence Keldane emits makes my stomach churn and the acrid burn of bile claws its way up the back of my throat. "This isn't over."

"It needs to be over." I hope he can hear the truth in my words. "We've got all kinds of hell breaking loose right now, and I don't have time to bicker. You won't win here. We have gods and dragons and immortals, and we're ready to defend this island's power to the death. Take your men and go home."

The look on his face is murderous. Then again, I suppose he doesn't get shut down often.

Raising a finger, I ensure I have his attention. "If you swear you'll go home, we'll let you down. Deal?"

"Very well. Let me down."

I ease back from hugging Dionysus and nod. "Okay. Let him down."

Dionysus doesn't look pleased, but he does as I ask and

releases his hold on Keldane. Stepping aside, we give him a clear path to his men and a way out of the forest for him to take his leave.

"This isn't over, little one." Venom laces his voice. "You'll regret insulting me like this."

I don't have anything nice to say, so I say nothing.

He strides forward, ducks his twigs under the branches of the closest tree and the tension in the air thins.

Then, right as I'm starting to relax, he changes direction. Faster than a blink, he's rushing us, head down. The twigs on his head morph into blades.

We'll be skewered.

Grabbing Dionysus, I spin the two of us so my armor will take the brunt.

"No!" Dionysus shouts as a wave of power blasts out from him. The force of the energy is incredible, and I'm lucky to be clutching him because he's the only reason I'm still standing.

Locked in his embrace, I wait for the energy to dissipate and my strength to return. When the two of us step apart, I glance around.

Keldane is gone and so are his men. "Tarzan? What happened?"

Dionysus frowns and runs a hand down the front of his shirt. "The last time he attacked you, he got your armor down and almost killed you. I don't deal well with fear. I tend to lash out at whatever makes me afraid."

"I get that. Visceral reactions aren't something we can control. So, what happened to Keldane?"

"Oh, he's gone for good."

Oh, dear. "You obliterated them? Will that get you in trouble? Can you take it back?"

He gives me a sheepish grin. "Impulse murder isn't something you get to take back, Jane."

No. I suppose not. I take his hands in mine. "Will this get you in big trouble? I'm sorry. I never wanted to put you in the hot seat."

He winks, and his brunette curls brush his shoulders as he shakes his head. "It's fine. I was protecting you and would do it again a hundred times over. There will be no kill-shaming. I heart you hard, Red."

I hug him once more and squeeze his hand. "Thank you, Tarzan. I heart you hard, right back."

"I can't lift my arms. Wait…do I still have arms?"

Sloan leans over me, cutting off my view of the bedroom ceiling. "Aye, yer arms are still attached. I'm sure ye'll feel better after a soak in the hot tub."

I chuckle. "That sounds lovely, hotness, but maybe you got clocked on the noggin'. We don't have a hot tub. That's at Stonecrest Castle, and honestly, I'm not sure I'll ever be able to use it now that I know what goes on there with your father."

Sloan rolls his eyes. "I thought we agreed that was the moment never to mention again. No. I'm talkin' about the hot tub Dionysus set up a half-hour ago down by the companions' den right below us."

That sparks some newfound energy. "Seriously? He snapped us a hot tub?"

"A large one. It's a twelve-seater set in a lovely gazebo with fairy lights and a stocked bar."

"You're not supposed to drink in hot tubs."

Sloan arches a brow. "Did ye hear the part about Dionysus bein' the one who came up with the idea?"

"Right, sorry." I raise my hand for him to grab and pull me to sit up. "Next question. How naked are people? Because I am not cool with naked hot-tubbing with my family and friends."

"I asked the same question."

"Do tell. What was the answer? I'm almost afraid to hear."

"It's boxers and swimsuits until midnight and a free-for-all after that."

"Oh, then make sure we set a timer. I don't want to be Cinderella caught late at the ball."

"Already done." He pulls me up to sit on the edge of the bed and hands me a two-piece swimsuit. "You're all set, and all the bits will remain covered."

"Excellent." I take the swimsuit into the bathroom, freshen up, and get changed. "Have Calum, Eric, and Tad gotten back from Cork?"

"Not yet, but Eric texted and said things are under control. A Man o' Green was set upon by three miscreants out to steal his gold. It went badly fer the three. The Man o' Green beat them quite badly with his shillelagh."

"Good. Serves them right."

"Aye, it does, but the three are protestin' that they caught the man fair and square and he's arguin' we're in the wild west of fae laws and refuses to pay up."

"Good for him. This stupid Culling should work in someone's favor. I agree." I grab the fuzzy, monogrammed robes that we got in our rooms when Dionysus outfitted the place and shrug it on. I take a moment in the doorway to admire the scenery.

Sloan studies me and makes a funny face. "Why are ye lookin' at me like that?"

"Can't be helped. Sloan Mackenzie in a bathing suit is worth a moment of appreciation."

He rolls his eyes. "Yer ridiculous."

"Not even a little. If I posted a picture to social media, you'd go viral." I hold up my fingers as if I'm centering him in an imaginary photo. "Yeah, baby."

"Maybe ye should lay back down. Yer delirious and talkin' nonsense."

I laugh at his denial and shuffle over, opening my robe to

invite him in. "I am delirious, but I'm also right. Take me for an evening soak. Then I want to climb right back into our bed."

"As ye wish, *a ghra*. Tomorrow promises to be another long day."

"I'm sure that's true."

I wake with my mind wrapped in a heavy fog of sleep and my shield tingling to life. The air swirls strangely around me, and I realize I'm standing in the middle of a fissure of power.

The blanket of physical exhaustion still has me weighed down in its embrace as I scan my surroundings.

Am I dreaming?

My gaze hardens as I sense the presence of someone powerful in my midst. My heart skips a beat. Then it pounds back to motion at double-time.

I raise my palms and call my armor forward. "Who's there? Where am I?"

I glance down at myself, thankful I got dressed for battle before bed again last night.

Being flashed from my bed to a palace throne room would be worse if I was in my gitch and Sloan's t-shirt. What's happening?

My first thought is Fionn is calling me to get an update on how we're faring during the Culling.

Every instinct in me says this isn't that.

My socks slide over the marble floor of a long, open chamber. As I pad across the room, I focus on the presence I'm sensing ahead. I don't see anyone.

Studying the room as I go, I try to make sense of any of this. The warm, golden walls draped in shades of forest leaves show a palette of green accents: forest, sage, and emerald. The walls are home to a collection of weaponry and artifacts lit by the faint glow of winnots flitting and frolicking along the roofline.

I'm three-quarters across the space when movement draws my attention to a man stepping forward from the cloaking darkness of shadows.

How did he get there? Was he always there?

He steps forward, and the inky blackness of the corner stretches to stay with him. Eventually, he goes too far, and it snaps back in retreat.

The man—an indescribably handsome, tall, dark, and dangerous sort—steps toward me in slow, measured paces. It's a "don't spook the townsfolk" approach I've used myself many times.

"Hello, Fiona. At last, we meet." When he speaks, his aristocracy is as obvious as his omnipotence. Not that I couldn't see that by looking at him.

In a crisp black-on-black suit, shirt, and tie, he's checking all the boxes for *GQ* Villainous Edition.

I release the glamor on my fae sight and rank him through the lens of good versus evil. Surprisingly, he's not as tainted with darkness as I would've bet.

"You are?"

His mouth quirks up to a crooked smile, and he drops his chin. "You don't know? Perhaps I haven't made as much of an impact on you as I've been led to believe."

It clicks into place then, and the hair on my arms stands on end. "Death, I presume."

He nods, looking pleased with himself. "Well, then. Since you got there, I'll assume it wasn't a case of me not being impressive but of you being dim. Doesn't matter. The result is the same."

Did Death just imply I'm dumb?

Why yes…yes, he did.

"Why did you bring me here?"

"The two of us are overdue to have a friendly chat. Here we are, at the halfway mark for the Time of the Colliding Realms, so a conversation about the way of things is in order."

A conversation?

This guy is sleazy slick, and after hearing Evangeline's account of some of their conversations, I focus more on the subtext than what he's saying.

It hits me then. "You're worried. You know Team Light is kicking ass and holding our ground, and you're worried you'll lose."

Though his smarmy smile is locked in place, the tightening of his fingers and the tension around his eyes tells me I nailed that one. "The rebalancing isn't about who wins or loses, Fiona. I would've thought the Goddess of Nature explained that to you. If she didn't—"

"Oh, no. She did. She explained everything. We're all on the same page. You and yours are working to get a stronger foothold for Team Dark, challenging me and mine to hold you at bay and maybe push you back a little further into the shadows."

"Yes, well, it's you and yours I wish to discuss. It was brought to my attention one of my angels overstepped her position and allowed a member of your family to leave his final resting place."

I swallow. No. I don't want to talk about losing Brendan. Even the idea of it squeezes my insides until I can't breathe.

Why can't he leave things alone?

"An acknowledgment of understanding would do you well at this point, Miss Cumhaill. Am I speaking too quickly for you?"

I draw a deep breath. "No. You're asking about my brother, Brendan. I'm with you."

"Excellent. Evangeline claims it was within her purview as the guardian for your family to make that decision. I disagree."

I draw a deep breath and wait for Death's next words, a knot building in the pit of my stomach.

"If anyone is responsible for those kinds of decisions, it is me —and only me."

"She meant well, and she wasn't wrong. The loss of my brother and our need for closure were adversely affecting our family. Considering we were hours away from the beginning of the Culling, that was dangerous. Evangeline acted out of her duty to keep us safe."

He rubs from his jawline down his throat and tests the knot of his tie. "Yes, well, that wasn't her decision to make."

He's not saying anything we haven't expected, and yet, my blood is thundering in my veins.

The shoe is about to drop.

Or, in this case, the Italian loafer.

"Is there a reason you brought me here? If so, I'd prefer you rip off the bandage and get it over with."

"Let's not be hasty. We have only begun to get acquainted."

There's a rhythmic *whir* and *bump* coming from somewhere outside the room, and I glance toward the black void that eclipses the doorway.

The sound steadily grows louder until a guy with the same blond curls and cherubim cheeks as Eva rolls a serving cart into the room. Eva once told us that all the dominions of wing-bearing angels have different colors.

When she was a reaper, her wings were bronze. Currently, because she's training to change her dominion, they're white. If she proves herself and becomes a full-fledged guardian angel, her wings will be gold.

This angel's wings are sage green.

He nods in a polite greeting and heads over to a clothed table in the corner and starts laying out a formal place setting for two.

"What's this?" I ask. "What are you up to?"

"Nothing more than hoping two newly acquainted members of the empowered world can break bread and come to an understanding. Some of the most influential shifts in the lives of men have happened over a shared meal between two parties on opposite sides."

"Yeah, like the red wedding. No thanks. Not a fan."

He looks at me blankly. "You make very little sense. Evangeline often seemed confused about things said in your home. I'm beginning to think it wasn't her being inexperienced or inept."

I'm not sure if I should be more offended for Eva or me. "No. Eva is amazingly astute and skilled."

He shrugs and directs our attention back to the food. "Shall we?"

This whole situation rankles my nerves. Something is not right, and my instincts are rarely wrong. "Many of the most influential shifts in the lives of men were also accomplished by poisoning the opponent. You can't overlook it as a time-honored tradition."

He clucks his tongue. "Fiona, please. Give me more credit. I'm not a thug. I'm a businessman."

"No. You're the ruler of death and the reapers and the power behind Team Dark."

"That doesn't make me untrustworthy."

"Maybe not, but I was raised by a cop and cut my teeth on criminal intent. I can't overlook that you have a strong motive for me not to succeed."

The angel setting us up finishes laying out the dishes, glasses, cutlery, and covered trays. When he straightens, he rolls the cart over to the wall and stands next to it with his wings against the wall and his arms clasped at his back.

Death gestures for us to sit. Not wanting to be overtly hostile, I accept and take a seat.

"I understand your hesitation in trusting me, Fi. May I call you Fi?"

"Most people do."

He bows his head as if me giving him that much is us making progress. "Let's not get twisted up with who's on what side and what that means. We are simply two people having a conversation over Timothy's." He lifts the warming cover off the first tray and shows me the steaming breakfast sandwiches on tea biscuits, the fresh chocolate glazed donuts, and the warm apple fritters.

He lifts the other cover, and there is a steeped apple cinnamon tea, an English toffee coffee with milk, a hot chocolate with whipped cream, and a mini bottle of Baileys.

"These are your favorites, yes?"

Uh-huh, has Eva been reporting in on my takeout fixes? I have no idea what my carb and coffee cravings have to do with anything but whatevs.

"You've done your homework." There's no denying it. My stomach is growling, and I'm fighting my instinct to reach for the hot chocolate and an apple fritter.

"I'm pleased to have it correct. Choose whatever you most prefer, and I will join you. From what Evangeline reports, Timothy Horton's is a countrywide staple to your society."

"It is, although it's either called Tim's or Timmies."

He nods. "Noted. The devil is in the details."

I'm sure. He grins and waits for me to make my selection. I get the feeling breaking bread is a mandatory part of this parlay. Reaching forward, I select the hot chocolate, Baileys, and fritter for a perfect trio.

Death gives me a victorious smile and chooses a ham and egg tea biscuit and an English toffee coffee. "It certainly smells appetizing."

I fuss around with opening the Baileys, take off the lid nice and slow, and dribble-pour the liqueur into the hot chocolate. By the time I'm stirring things up, Death has half-finished his breakfast sandwich.

So, not everything is poisoned, or he's already taken the antidote, or he's immune to his poisons, or I've watched too much television, and there's no poison.

"If we share a meal, will you elaborate on why I'm here and let me get back?"

"Of course. You are the team leader for the Goddess of Nature. She would never let me get away with kidnapping you or harming you to affect my odds. This is merely a meeting of the minds."

Well, that makes sense…in theory.

I don't suppose Mother Nature would allow that. She did say that while the two of them didn't always agree, she considers them partners in maintaining an important natural balance.

With that in mind, I tear a piece of my apple fritter off and bring it to my mouth. Pausing with the cinnamon-sugar bliss at my lips, I wait to see if my shield weighs in with a warning.

When it doesn't, I reconsider my poison theory as possible paranoia.

Popping it into my mouth, I chew for a moment and go back to tear off my next bite. "So, my brother Brendan. You said you wanted to talk about how Eva overstepped. What does that mean?"

Death finishes the last of his tea biscuit sandwich and wipes his mouth with a cloth napkin. He takes a slow sip of the English toffee and frowns as he swallows. "That's very sweet."

"Thus, the toffee."

He arches a dark brow and abandons his cup. Glancing back at the angel with the curls, he tilts his head. "Orion, fetch me my morning cup."

The angel rushes out without pause and my anxiety rachets. Attacking me without witnesses will make it harder for Eva to find out what happened when I don't return home.

"Are you all right, Fi?" Death asks, his head cocked to the side as he studies me.

"Yes, of course. I don't like being kept in suspense. You were about to tell me what you intend to do about Brendan, yet you're not saying anything."

"Evangeline mentioned your family tends to lean toward impatience."

To avoid throat-punching the celestial immortal who holds my brother's fate in his hands, I lick my fingers clean of the sugar glaze coating them and keep my eyes on my fritter. "Eva's a smart girl."

Orion our angel server returns with a clear cup of what looks like a green smoothie and hands it to him.

Without a word of thanks, Death opens the lid to his cup and sips. "Much better. Now, where were we?"

I'm trying not to throat-punch you.

"You were about to tell me your plans for Brendan."

"Oh, right. Only it's not me who will decide your brother's fate."

Hubba-wha?

"No? Then who do I need to be talking to?"

He grins. "What happens to your brother moving forward is solely up to you, Fiona. I'm putting his fate in your hands and giving you a choice."

CHAPTER TWENTY-SIX

After my breakfast chit-chat with Death, Orion escorts me to the hanging gardens. "Please, take a seat on the reflection bench. Your transport back to the surface will be along for you in due time."

I don't get any wiggy vibes off him, so I sit.

The bench is incredibly comfy for a stone slab, and the view is incredible. Lush green vines hang heavy with blooms, water trickles down a picturesque waterfall, and brilliantly colored butterflies flit and flutter aimlessly in the streams of sunlight without care.

I'm almost mesmerized by it all, but before Orion is out of earshot, I turn to speak to him. "Hey, dude. Do you know Evangeline? She used to be a reaper and now is fast-tracking it to become our guardian angel. Maybe she's here? Could you maybe check and tell her I'm here?"

Orion's grin tells me he thinks I'm nuts, and he has no intention of being my messenger.

"All righty then. Good talk."

A moment later, it's me alone with the butterflies. It really is utopian perfection. Deciding to make the most of my moment of peace, I dust off one of my lessons from Sloan and work on my meditation.

Deep breath in, hold, and then out.

After a couple of those, I let my mind wander and try to center myself for the second half of the Culling.

Team Light is kicking ass. Yay, team!

That's the real reason I'm here. Death wasn't trying to get to know his opponent. Big D is scairt and wanted to intimidate me. Nah, it's worse than intimidation....

It's bribery...

No. Ultimatum is more accurate.

My emotions twist up, and I try to swallow past the lump in my throat. Thinking about Brenny and what Death made me do is the opposite of relaxing. I feel like I've let everyone down.

How could I have lived with myself if—

I blink past the tears blurring my vision, push it out of my head, and go back to watching the butterflies.

I sit there for a long while. Although it must be mid-morning by now, my stomach isn't growling. Maybe if you eat an apple fritter in the heavens, it keeps you sated longer. I wonder if it counts against your caloric intake. I'm hoping not.

Not that any of that matters.

What hurts my heart is that Sloan is up by now. He'll be worried, as will my family, and Team Light will be wondering about the day ahead.

Deciding to rush this process a little, I tug out my pendant and smile at Dionysus's cutie face as I press for a help call.

Can a Greek god pop up into the Choir of Angels to pick up a lost friend?

I glance around, waiting...waiting...and nothing.

Guess not.

If he could be here, he absolutely would.

My Tarzan is good like that.

I glance around to see if there's anyone who could maybe call me a celestial Uber. Orion said my transport back to the surface will be along in due time. How long is due time?

I'm on a deadline here, dude.

Settling in, I go back to watching the butterflies dance with the Jurassic-sized flower blooms. Holding my hands up as a measure of scale, I figure they must be a foot across. Cray-cray.

After another long while, my mind drifts again. It's a wonder I don't have to pee. I drank that hot chocolate quite a long time ago and…

Do angels pee?

I get up and wander around the hanging gardens looking for a door with a lady angel on it.

Nope. Nothing.

Despite feeling like I could stay here all day mind-rambling, I'm more determined than ever that this celestial interlude must end. "There has to be someone who can get me back where I need to go."

Before I finish that sentence, something odd tugs at my insides.

"What is that?" It's not like the flutter I get when Bruin shuffles inside me. It's more urgent than that. It's a pull…a calling.

I glance around at the butterflies, but they don't know either. "It's not my shield. It's different. Still, it's nothing good. Something is wrong."

Taking a few steps along the stone wall of the reflection pond, I focus inwardly, searching my instincts.

"It's the island. It's my oath to protect the island telling me there's trouble."

With renewed conviction, I search for someone. "Hello? Is there anyone here who can help me?"

I rush along the winding path back to where we arrived through the main corridor of the building. Only there's no exit. The path meanders back to the reflection bench and the hanging gardens.

"What the fuckety-fuck?" I release my fae sight and call Birga to my palm.

Neither of them responds.

"Seriously? Death, you double-crossing asshole. Get your *GQ* villainous ass in here and get me home. There's no way Mother Nature will go for this shit. Your ass is grass, motherfucker."

As those words echo in the hallowed space, I wonder if dissing the immortal angel who holds my current situation in his hands was the best choice.

My bad.

"Fi, there you are." Evangeline rushes through the greenery, looking harried. "I've been looking for you everywhere."

"Did Orion tell you I need a lift back to the island? I feel it calling. I'm missing something."

"You've missed a lot of somethings."

"What? How much has happened this morning?"

Evangeline scowls and shakes her head. "Fi, you've been gone over twenty-four hours."

"What!" My panicked horror ruffles the butterflies, and they take to the air in a kaleidoscope frenzy of patterns and colors. "How is that possible?"

"Time works differently up here, remember? I've told you that. When I study for an afternoon, I'm away from you for a day or two."

I knew that. "Okay, get me back to Emmet's island, and we'll figure out the other stuff later."

Eva takes my hand, and her magical energy tickles my skin. "Close your eyes, or you'll get dizzy. You need to be in fighting form when we materialize."

No argument.

I close my eyes and pray Death hasn't totally frigged up the Culling for Team Light and me.

Asshole.

Eva and I materialize in the meadow of Emmet's island and my fury flares ten-fold. The place is exploding with magical bolts, gunfire, and clashing blades. There are beasts, Barghest, dark wizards, hobgoblins, and more.

I scan the crowd, taking the attendance of everyone I love. Morgana is on the far shore of the prana river, battling Da, Merlin, Dillan, and Calum, and the ominous black raven clouds that always mark her presence have swallowed the sky.

No Sloan, Dionysus, Brendan...

Oh, Brenny. My brother is gone again, and the reality of that cleaves my heart in two. *I'm so sorry.*

I blink against the flood of emotions trying to take hold and spot Nikon.

He's in a drag-out fistfight with Eros, and—oh, shit—it seems like they've put their friendship on hold for the day.

Bruin roars in the distance. He's taking on a slew of hobgoblins. Either they know he destroyed the Toronto community and want revenge, or they don't and are about to find out who Killer Clawbearer really is.

I still don't see Sloan.

Emmet and Kaida fly overhead with Patty standing at the second spike. He's in his angry leprechaun mode with his weapons vest and is raining a barrage of lucky charms attacks down on the gathered foes.

Orange stars, pink hearts, and green clovers.

Wowzers. Team Light is throwing everything they have at Morgana, and she deflects and dissolves their efforts with little trouble. I stare at the oppressive raven hovering over her, and my shield burns hotter.

And here I stand, in my socks.

I flex my palm and Birga comes to me without fail.

"I need to help fight Morgana. She's the biggest threat."

Evangeline raises her hand and flexes her fist, her scythe appearing in a burst of golden mist. Weapon drawn, she runs toward the prana river, her snow-white wings flaring out behind her.

As gentle as the woman is, the reaper side of our angel is lethal. She culls through the battlefield, lopping heads off all who get in her way.

Birga and I do the same. My girl is pissed about being held back when I called her earlier and even more pissed that we missed a full day and night of battle.

As we work our way across the meadow, I've got one eye focused on the opponent I'm engaging with and the other on the dark queen. "Morgana is still trying to harness more power. First, it was dark souls, and now it's raw prana."

Eva grins, spinning as she extends her strike and sends a hobgoblin's noggin somersaulting in the air. "Merlin believes as long as she's still attached to the raven clouds, part of her banishment curse is still in place."

That's good news.

We make our way deep enough into the pack of hobgoblins for me to team up with Bruin. *Hey, buddy. Sorry I'm late for the party.*

My words incite a rush of relief from my bear. He claws through the two he's facing and turns his broad head my way. *Better late than never, Red. We missed ye somethin' awful. By the way, I'm never sleepin' in my den again. I can't trust ye to be there in the mornin'.*

Totes not my fault but I get it.

He has a chunk of someone stuck on the spears of his skull guard, but I let that go.

I'm heading over to help with Morgana. Keep on kicking ass.
Will do.

Checking in with Bruin does a lot to settle my anxiety about missing day three of the Culling. My biggest panic is still that I can't find Sloan. He's probably here somewhere, and I haven't noticed him with all the commotion.

Yeah. That *must* be it.

Eva and I fight through a few more hobgoblins and make our way to Jarod, Aiden, Tad, and Ciara getting their groove on against a handful of Barghest.

Dayam, Tad's really got the blitzkrieg *poof*-fighting down. He's a magical maniac.

Glad he's on our side.

Aiden flashes me a wink when he sees me. "I told them you'd be back. Love you, baby girl."

"Love you more."

The tussle between Nikon and Eros is the next one in our path to the river. It's not so much a battle but more Nikon and Eros transporting this way and that while Nikon tries to beat the snot out of the god of love and Eros evades most of the hits and is just here for the argument.

I hear a bit of Nikon's and Eros's fight before I get close and my heart breaks. "You did *what?* How could you do that to him?"

Eros's head whips in my direction, and Nikon lands a spectacular right hook that spins Eros like a top.

"Dionysus considers you his friend. If you knew anything about him, you'd know how precious that makes your relationship."

Eros probes his lip and tests his jaw, scowling. "I *am* his friend. That's why I brought his behavior to Zeus' attention. Do you think the God of Thunder wants one of us down here mucking in the wars of men?"

"You thought tattling to his daddy was the right thing to do? Dionysus was happy here. He made himself a home and was carving out a life with people who love him. You're the freaking god of love, yet you haven't got a clue about the emotion."

Eros rolls his eyes. "I don't expect you to understand, human. He's a god. He's so much better than you and your family. I'm not sure what you did to him, but he's better off having his wings clipped and having the pantheon reclaim him."

Better off? My fury boils in my veins, and my hands tremble with its power. "You think forcing him to live among a pantheon of siblings who fear and despise him is better off? To have to play a part for followers who love the drinking and the sex but never took the time to find out what he enjoys doing?"

"It's VR gaming with friends," Nikon spits. "If you're wondering."

Thunder rolls above our heads and I rein in my emotions. "This is a shitty time for you to piss me off, Cupid. The sad thing is, you've got your head shoved so far up your ass, you can't even see how wrong you are."

Dillan shouts behind me. Seeing the raven cloud looming above our heads reminds me there's a war going on, and I'm wasting my time. "You should be ashamed of yourself. You betrayed a friend who even when he was hurt and angry with you, still believed in you."

I point Birga's tip at him and stifle the urge to thrust. "Get out of our war. You don't care about Light or Dark. You're only here to cause trouble. Dionysus needs you to make this right. If you ever cared anything about him, you'll fix this."

Eros' brow arches and he barks a laugh. "I get it now. You're in love with him."

I shake my head. "No. You don't get it. I *love* him. The. End. If you can't see the difference, you're a shit-poor representative for the emotion."

Filled with more frustration, anger, and fear than I can bear, I turn on my heel and continue to the riverbank. Pressing my hands to the soil, I focus my intention and create a land bridge arching over the raw fae power to reach the other side.

"Earth to Stone." When my pathway solidifies, I run across and join the main event.

Occupied as Merlin, Da, and my brothers are, they don't see

me coming until I join them shoulder-to-shoulder. "Hey, sorry I'm late."

My father's head whips to the sound of my voice and the relief in his gaze threatens to trigger the emotions pressurizing my insides.

Not now.

Yes, they're going to blow, but now is not the time.

Da is wearing my crown, and he takes it off and tosses it to me. "Glad to see ye, *mo chroi*. Ye had us worried there fer a bit."

I set the crown in place and take stock as the magic activates. As the fighters of Team Light come online, I check the strength and vitals of everyone I care about.

Except he's not here.

I begin to ask Da about Sloan when a great roar has me spinning toward the river.

A massive, fuchsia-colored serpent breaks through the surface of the prana power and beaches itself on the far riverbank. Last time, I likened the ophidians to a long, fat seal—a forty-foot long, four-thousand-pound seal with twelve stubby legs…and claws…and a jointed jaw with a gazillion teeth.

My evaluation still stands.

One of the large ones breaches first and three more splash through the surface right after. The ground trembles with the impact of their weight falling heavily onto the meadow.

Welcome, ophidians. I hope they can hear me. *We, the guardians of Emhain Abhlach, welcome your aid.*

I sense the moment Merlin's heart rate spikes. His head whips for a glance at the scary hot pink serpents. "Remember the ophidian serpents I told you about?

"They are terrifying."

"Even more than the last time. They're chameleons and take on the color of the prana. When we met them, they were pastel candyfloss. This deep fuchsia tells me they've powered up more than before."

"They were incredibly strong and deadly before," Da adds.

"True story, but the good news is they're also incredibly protective of the prana."

Merlin raises a palm and casts a barrier to shield us from a deflection of Calum's arrows that are bearing down on us. "Then please take a moment to point out who the threats are and ask them nicely not to eat those of us trying to protect it."

"Will do. FYI, they tend to spit prana. If they do, get out of the way."

"Noted."

Evangeline shifts into her dove form and takes to the air. She's a beacon of light against the dark sky, the usual shafts of heaven's light streaming down to follow her flight path and highlight her as a celestial envoy.

Morgana winces against the energy's pure brilliance. No surprise there. The woman probably hasn't seen or touched anything purely good since returning to Tintagel and founding her champions tournament.

Eva cuts through the raven cloud, and it too recoils from heaven's light. It breaks apart and barely reforms in Eva's wake.

I frown and think about Eva's comment earlier. Reaching out on the iron crown channel, I open a conversation. *Merlin, do you believe the raven cloud is a remnant tie binding Morgana to her banishment?*

It's a theory.

I think the cloud symbolizes her gaining strength, but maybe he's right. When I first saw the raven cloud back in Arthurian time, it was ebony black and very well defined as it approached Bathalt on that balcony. Now it's nebulous and stormy gray at best.

What if we step back and the ophidians take a run at Morgana? Da asks. *We're gettin' nowhere. As hard as we come at her, she shuts us down and disarms our attempts. We're using up much more energy than she is.*

I turn toward the prana serpents, and my train of thought jumps tracks. *Is firing raw power at Morgana a good idea? What if she can absorb it somehow like she did with the tainted souls of the Neitherlands? That made her stronger.*

Well, think of something, Fi, because we're running out of steam. I hear the frustration in Dillan's words and try to retrace my thoughts about the cloud.

My instincts tell me there's more to that.

Agonized screaming on the other side of the river has me scanning the falling bodies. The ophidians are shooting streams of prana and hosing down hobgoblins and Barghest.

That's all well and good unless they're also getting our team. *Are you guys clear?*

All clear, Ciara says. *Eric saw what was comin' and Tad got us out of there.*

Excellent.

The strength of the prana's color brings me back to my mental musings. *When the raven cloud was darkest, it had the strongest hold on Morgana. It has all but lost its hold now. Is there a way we can strengthen the tie of her banishment and maybe shove her back into the Neitherlands?*

Merlin has his hands up and contains Morgana's deflections, preventing her from shifting closer to the river.

Samuel knows the most about banishments and the ties that bind, Nikon says.

Yeah. Greek, forget Eros and get the Hunter-gods. I'm putting together a plan.

On it, Red.

I scan the surroundings, wishing I could bounce my thoughts off Sloan. I ache to know where he is but can't bring myself to ask. I need to focus and if something serious happened to him...

Samuel, Ahren, and Quon Shen snap in beside me, and as I welcome them, the iron crown picks them up, and they join the Team Light connected network.

The Time of the Colliding Realms, when the veil is thin, the greatest victory is found when you don't win.

I know, deep in my guts, this is the moment Mother Nature wants me to unravel her clue. If I don't, Morgana will sever her tie with the shadow raven and be free from her banishment.

Brute force isn't working. It takes much less energy to deflect a spell than to disarm it or cast it. With every attack, we weaken, and she bides her time.

We need to strengthen the raven cloud binding her to her banishment.

How do you plan to do that?

By not trying to win. When Samuel frowns, I explain. *Mother Nature told us this event is all about balancing light and dark. If we're building up the darkness to take her, we need to build up the light too. I have an idea for the light. I need you boys to put your heads together with Merlin to figure out how to strengthen the darkness.*

I know nothing about dark magic, Samuel says.

Merlin grunts. *I know a little, but I walked away from dark magic when Morgan le Fay first embraced it and lost herself to the lure of power.*

That's it! Calum lowers his bow and beams at us. *In Fi's half of Morgana's spell book, there were all kinds of spells about strengthening the dark.*

I glance around for Nikon. "Greek, you're up."

"I'm on it." Nikon snaps to where Merlin is standing with his arms extended to hold back Morgana's advance. "Where are we going?"

To the Icelandic lair. Merlin glances at the Hunter-gods. *You'll need to hold her back. I won't bring that book here, and it'll take me time to find what we need.*

Samuel, Ahren, and Quon Shen take Merlin's place as he and Nikon snap out.

"What will we do in the meantime?" Dillan asks.

I think about that. *We need to figure out how to magnify Evange-*

line's heavenly light to force Morgana back into the darkness. Eva? Can you turn up the volume on your beams?

Eva flies down and retakes her human form, dropping to her feet in a graceful flutter of her white wings. *I have no control over my connection with the heavens. The light is simply there and always has been.*

Kaida swoops overhead, and Emmet launches off the blue dragon. He does a damn fine aerial maneuver and superhero lands beside us. *I've got it. Light amplification by the stimulated emission of radiation. We need to make a fucking Eva dove laser.*

"Hubba-wha?"

CHAPTER TWENTY-SEVEN

I'm both dazzled by Emmet channeling Bill Nye the Science Guy and lost to what he said. Light amplification by the stimulated emission of radiation? "Explain, Em. What do those words mean?"

He turns to our father, his focus uncharacteristically tight. "Da, remember my grade nine science project?"

"I remember ye destroyed yer brother's brand-new CD player and I barely kept him from killin' ye."

"Oh yeah, I remember that too. Rude."

Dillan curses and middle-fingers Em. "It was a Bose system, and I saved up all year for it. It cost me five hundred bucks, you dipshit."

Emmet waves away Dillan's words. "You can't put a price on science."

"Fuck that. I can. It's five hundred bucks."

Emmet rolls his eyes and returns the middle-finger salute. "My point is, I know how to do this. We need to make Eva into a dove laser."

"You're not making my girlfriend into a laser. Are you whacked? Scratch that. You are certifiably whacked."

Emmet makes a face and continues, "I'll create an energy mist gathering the island's ambient power. The ophidians can spit a fine spray of prana into it. Those will be our gaseous components instead of neon and helium. Then—"

Dillan grunts. "Who the fuck *are* you right now?"

Da raises his hand. "Dillan, shut yer gob. Yer brother's tryin' to say somethin' important."

Emmet nods. "So, we get the magic prana mist floating in the air, and Eva flies into it. Her heavenly light refracts and expands, exciting the gases. Then, all we need is to focus the energy while Fi gives us a high-voltage pulse, and it's all heavenly beams, sparkles, and rainbows."

Wow, okay, that sounds good in theory, but after a year and a half of these druid adventures, I know it doesn't always work like that.

Still, it's a solid plan…and our only plan.

"Eva? Do you have any objections?" I ask.

Eva shakes her head, grinning. "Sounds like fun."

"Okay, Em. Unless anyone has any other ideas, we're going with dove laser. Go chat with one of the ophidians and see how they feel about the spit the mist part. Maybe they don't have that much control."

"Och, I can help with that," Da says. By my father's expression, he thinks this plan is doable.

That's good enough for me.

"All right, when Em gets back to us with the ophidians' take on things, we'll get this party started."

Everyone seems set on their tasks and that kind of resets everything while we're waiting for Emmet and Merlin to get back to us. The momentary hold gives my mind time to wander and my heart time to worry.

"Da? Where's Sloan? Is it bad?"

My father turns from where he's keeping the pressure on Morgana and frowns. "We don't know yet, *mo chroi*. Wallace says it's too soon to tell what will happen. He put him into a deep healing sleep."

Guilt and despair stab me through the chest. "What happened?"

Da gets knocked back by a burst of energy and shakes his hands. "That's a story fer when we're not fighting the Queen of Darkness. I know it's hard, luv, but try to keep yer focus on the moment at hand."

I haul an unsteady breath through my lungs. *Right.* Sloan's sleeping. He'll be fine. I picture him lying alone at Wallace's clinic, and tears sting my eyes. I blink quickly. Da's right. This isn't the time or place.

Thankfully, Nikon takes that moment to snap Merlin back into the mix.

"Are we good to go?" I look between the two of them.

Merlin shrugs. "We'll soon find out."

When he jogs off around the shielding, I signal Emmet that it's time to start. He finishes speaking with one of the smaller ophidians and gives me a thumbs-up.

Emmet raises his hands to his sides and closes his eyes. The ambient power here is already pervasive, but when he starts to draw the magical energy in tighter, it's almost too much. "Okay, guys. Get ready for prana spit. It's coming your way."

Awesomesauce. "Dillan, if Da has to disperse the prana to mist, you'll have to create an impenetrable sphere to keep Samuel, Quon Shen, and Ahren from getting sprayed."

"On it." Dillan moves into position and takes care of that as the ophidian dips into the river to get juiced up.

The great, pink serpent breaches the surface, stands in the river, and raises his upper body ten feet. Then, he spews the bright pink raw prana into the air.

I give him credit for trying. The spit stream is much finer than their usual volume but it's nowhere near a mist.

That's where Da comes in.

My father has his palms raised and is casting with his focus narrowed on the stream of pink power. Whatever he's doing, it's working. It's like the stream of liquid is hitting a tightly woven screen.

As it contacts Da's spell, it dissipates and becomes the fine mist we need.

Emmet's aura of power is pulsing out from his body in a bright pink glow, and he's once again a Barbie nightlight.

Eva takes a quick run and soars into the sky.

As the striations of heaven's light come down to greet her, I get ready to call lightning to create the high-voltage energy charge.

Samuel, Ahren, and Quon Shen, if this works, when Morgana recoils from the light, switch from defensive to offensive, and force her back into the grasp of her banishment.

Got it, Samuel says. *Good luck, everyone.*

Yeah, good luck.

Eva flaps her wings and hovers in the center of our prana mist cloud thirty feet in front of Morgana. Even without my part complete, once they start focusing the effect, the light refraction starts happening on its own.

I squint as I look up at heaven's light.

It's so bright already.

Morgana falters, turning her head from the brilliance of ethereal grace. If we don't keep her gaze on us while Merlin and the Hunter-gods work the dark end of this, she might figure out our plan and counter.

Someone cover me, I say, the tension of my call to lightning building inside me. *Morgana hates me, and I'm going to get her focused on killing me.*

"Said no one in their right mind, ever," Calum says.

"We've got you, baby girl." Aiden steps in beside me with Calum.

I nod at Emmet and Da, and it all syncs up.

Clan Cumhaill for the not-win.

Calum chuckles. "Again. Who says that?"

"Hey, Morgana, make sure to say hello to your son in hell, bitch." I harness all my frustration and heartache from the day and focus on ending this. "I hope the two of you will be very happy banished in oblivion together."

Morgana's gaze flares as she realizes I've arrived and she switches from deflecting our attacks to initiating her own. "Slayer of sons! We meet again."

"Again…and for the last time. Go back to the hell realm you belong to. You have no business here."

Morgana calls energy to her hands and starts firing at me with all her focus.

Aiden and Calum shield me. Then Tad and Ciara are there to reinforce them, as well.

Satisfied she won't fry me on the spot, I throw my intention toward the prana mist. Instead of the massive lightning strikes I've called before, I temper that down to keep from hurting Eva.

I know she's probably immortal against lightning, but Death is a douche canoe, and after this afternoon, I have no blinders on…or shoes…I hate not having shoes.

Asshole.

He'd like nothing more than to take our family down by a few members.

"Lightning Burst." The energy building behind my call responds without question. It pulses in three quick flashes, igniting the pink fog encompassing Eva's dove.

As Emmet predicted, the lightning bursts agitate the ambient magic, and the prana mist magnifies the fog. Then, the rays streaming from the Choir of Angels explode into light so pure and powerful it hurts for me to look at it.

Morgana screams and recoils, throwing herself back into the air.

The darkness of the raven cloud is almost back to the ebony it once was. Merlin has managed to increase the power of the raven cloud, and the Hunter-gods are strengthening the banishment spell.

So many working parts. So many small actions are needed to make this work.

Please, make this work.

My eyes stream with tears, the brilliance reflecting off Eva's dove too much for me to bear.

She's breathtaking.

The sky is a stark contrast—the powerful dark moving to collide with the purest light.

The two sides surge together, sandwiching Morgana. When they crash with her in the middle, a thunderous boom *cracks* and the magic detonates.

My socked feet leave the ground, and I'm airborne, carried by the force of the collision of power.

Being connected to the magical mist at the time of detonation throws me farther than the others and a sinking realization hits.

I'm hurtling backward into the river of prana, and my powers are offline.

My mind stalls out…

What can I do?

A streak of blue overtakes me, and Dart's talons grab hold. My blue boy plucks me out of my freefall and carries me over the river to the meadow. When we're over land, he drops me into Nikon's waiting arms.

"Gotcha, Red."

I look around, still in shock. Morgana is gone, and the raven cloud is flying off and dissipating. My family and friends are all getting back to their feet.

The fighting is over, and we stand the victors.

"Did we win?"

Nikon sets my feet back onto the ground, his arms still supporting me. Good thing, too. Without him steadying me and keeping me upright, I would ass-plant right here on top of battle death and debris.

"Shit, Fi. You scared me there for a second."

I close my eyes and soak in the moment. "Me too. Thanks for the catch, Greek."

He presses a kiss on my forehead, his heart pounding wildly under my palm. "Mischief Managed."

My soggy socks slide and streak the clinic floor as I run to find Sloan. Nikon snapped me here the moment the battle was over, and still it wasn't fast enough. The first person I come to is the brunette nurse I last saw in the hot tub with Wallace. My mind has shorted out, and I can't think of her name. "Where is he?"

She takes a moment and catches up with who I am and who I mean. "Mr. Mackenzie is with him in his bedroom."

I can't say if I thanked her or not.

Honestly, I don't remember how I got from the main receiving area of the clinic to our Stonecrest bedroom, but the next thing I know, I'm bursting into our suite and racing toward Anne Boleyn.

Wallace closes the book he's reading aloud and sets it on the mattress, barely getting his hands free in time to catch me as I slide into home.

I collide with Sloan's father with an *oof* of expelled air, and I'm coming unraveled. "I'm so sorry."

"It's fine, Fi. No harm done." He steps back, and I climb between the draperies and onto the mattress.

My guy is lying there unconscious and looking as beautiful as ever. He's even smiling the crooked little smirk he makes when he thinks I'm being ridiculous.

"Has he woken up?"

The answer is in Wallace's eyes before he speaks the words. "Not yet. No."

That can't be good. Isn't it a thing that the chances of waking up drop by large margins after the first twenty-four hours? Wait…that might be finding a kidnapping victim. I don't know. I can't think.

I stretch across the bed and lay my chest over his, hugging him. "I'm here, hotness. I'm safe, and I found my way home, and now you need to do the same thing. The Culling is basically over. As soon as the sun goes down, it's a done deal. It's time for you to open your eyes and celebrate with me."

I watch his eyelids for any sign of movement. There is none. His image blurs behind a wall of moisture, and I collapse against his chest. "That's fine. You rest. I love you, Mackenzie. Wherever you are, know that. Then get your perfect ass in gear and come back to me."

I lay over him, absorbing the gentle rise and fall of his chest. In the movies, this is the moment when he reaches up and rubs my back, soothing my sobs.

Only nothing happens.

"Shh, Fi, all right. It's all right." Wallace stands next to the bed with his hand on my back.

After a long moment, I'm steady enough to ease back and sit up. "What's wrong with him? What actually happened?"

I don't know what he sees in my expression, but his expression softens. "Yer father knows the details of what went on. Did ye speak to him?"

"Not about Sloan. I had Nikon snap me here the moment we won the battle. How did he end up here?"

"I only know the story secondhand, but yer father said there was a dark magic uprising in the city. He, Sloan, Calum, and Jarrod went to resolve it and got ambushed. Sloan stopped an altercation the day before, and they didn't appreciate the return visit."

"He told me about the witches in Dublin. He said a coven of dark witches targeted the white witches and they put a stop to it and defended the light."

Nikon leans in with a box of tissues, and I take the hint and try to mop up the mess I've become. "Thanks, Greek." I dry my tears and pull a deep breath. "So, the dark witches were mad we interfered...then what?"

"I'm told the high priestess of the coven hit them with a very powerful, high-level spell. It was a vile, cowardly attack meant to kill them all on the spot."

"Da, Jarrod, and Calum were at Emhain Abhlach fighting. Did they duff the spell? How did it not kill them and why is only Sloan hurt?"

"Sloan took the lead as they approached and if yer da hadn't anticipated what was about to happen, it would've been worse. Thankfully, Niall got a partial shield up before the spell hit. If he hadn't, I expect the four of them would've met their end right there."

"Da didn't mention that."

"No, well, as ye said, there's been no time fer ye to get into the details."

Right. Of course, Da wouldn't be the one to tell me he saved them all from death. That's not what the men in my family do. "So, I assume everyone is trying to figure out the spell and how to counter it?"

"Aye, that's where we are."

"You put him into a healing sleep to keep him strong and comfortable until we figure it out."

"Aye, that's the long and short of it."

"So, are you expecting him to wake up on his own or will we have to revive him?"

"We're hopeful he'll wake up on his own in time."

"And the fact that he hasn't? Is that bad?"

"It's neither good nor bad, Fi. The body takes time to heal, and given the strength of what hit him, we must give him that time. I've been doing this a long time, Fi, and I've rarely seen such a focus of vile energy where the victim didn't die on contact. Sloan is strong and has every reason to fight to live."

"I didn't realize there was another dark witch in Dublin as bad as Moira. I guess we created a void when we took her out."

"Magic is changing. There's a new level of power coming at us since you reconnected the island, and witch leaders channel the power of all within their coven. That makes them more dangerous than ever."

"Do you think that's what happened? Did we enable that witch to be that powerful?"

"There's no way to know. All I can say is if it doesn't dissipate with time, it'll take an incredibly powerful focus of energy to undo the damage done."

I blink and tuck my hair behind my ear. "I'm not sure if you know this about me, Wallace, but patience isn't my best event. I won't even get a participation ribbon."

"Sloan might have mentioned that a time or two." Wallace chuckles and studies me with his doctoring gaze. "Tell me, what happened to you? Are you all right? Is there anything I can do to help you?"

"No. I'm good. Death sucked me up to the Choir of Angels, and I missed a whole day of the Culling. He's a dirty rotten cheater, but he didn't hurt me."

Wallace reaches over and takes my hand. When he squeezes it, his eyes become too glassy for my liking. "Sloan was so frantic about ye missing. When he was here yesterday morning, he was beside himself. He and Merlin had tried a locator spell to find you using yer Claddagh band, but it didn't work."

"I guess there's no cell coverage in the heavens."

"Perhaps not." Wallace squeezes my hand harder. "The way the two of ye love each other and the things ye go through to be together is truly inspiring. I want ye to know that when he said ye'd been taken, Sloan wasn't the only Mackenzie man broken-hearted."

I sit up and lean over to hug him. "I'm fine. This time it's all about Sloan. Although I've told him before, I prefer to be the one bleeding, not the one frantic and holding vigil. This really doesn't work for me."

Wallace chuckles. "I know what ye mean."

"Hey, Red," Manx says, padding into the room. "Glad yer back and yer here."

"I wish we weren't here though…not like this."

"Aye, I know what ye mean." He trots across the suite and leaps onto the bed with feline grace. I lean into him and hug him. "Yer out of steam and yer covered in the muck of battle. Go have a quick shower, and we'll nap until the New Year."

I'm about to shut that idea down, but Manx isn't wrong. "Wallace? Is there anything I need to know or do or not do?"

Wallace shrugs. "Nothing at all. He's sleeping, and there are magic absorption tabs on his vital organs to notify me if the spell worsens. Now we wait."

I scootch to the edge of the bed and jump down. Manx is right. I'm covered in grossness and about to drop. I glance back at my boys. "Save my spot."

Manxy pads in a circle at the end of the bed and lies with his head over Sloan's ankles. "We'll be here."

Wallace nods and tilts his head toward the door of our room. "I'll have a tray of food brought in and will check on ye both in the morning."

"That's fine. Thank you." I hug Wallace, draw a deep breath to rally my strength, and shuffle my soggy feet toward the ensuite.

Shower, clean clothes, bed…that's all I've got left.

CHAPTER TWENTY-EIGHT

After hibernating for a day and a half with Sloan, I can't hide from the world anymore. My phone's been blowing up with messages from family and friends wishing me a Merry Christmas, and despite feeling like someone has hollowed out my heart with a melon baller, I have to pull up my big girl panties and reengage.

"Thanks for coming, Greek." I step in to hug Nikon. "You're my hero. You know that, right?"

The skepticism in his expression says he doesn't. That hurts my heart even more. Stepping back, I take his hands in mine and meet his gaze. "I'm serious. I respect and admire you huge. I'm thankful every moment of every day that you reached out to me on that riverboat, so we could become besties."

He shakes his head. "I'm a thousand percent thankful for you being my closest friend, Fi, but the hero part is ridiculous. You're the one battling the big bosses, and at most, I'm there to facilitate change of venue moments."

My eyes widen. "Then you don't see our relationship like I do."

"No. I'm sure that's true. There's no need to blow smoke up

my ass though. I'm good."

"Seriously? Have you ever known me to say something I didn't believe?"

He tilts his head from side to side and rolls his eyes. "Well, no. If anything, you're a little too honest for your own good."

"Exactly, so look into my eyes and hear the truth of my words. You *are* my hero, Nikon Tsambikos. In my world, a hero isn't someone who can fly or who has laser vision and can lift a bus. A hero is someone who, despite not having superpowers, stands in the path of danger and harm because it's the right thing to do."

I take my finger and draw an imaginary X across my heart. "You are my hero because you stand by me in the darkest moments, never doubt me, you love my family as your own and have died to keep them safe, you live by a code of honor, you're the one who catches me when I fall from a dragon *and* the one who hands me a box of tissues when my world is crumbling."

"Wow, Fi…that's a lot."

"That's how I see you."

He looks down and frowns. "You give me too much credit. I'm not nearly as selfless as you think. I'm here because I want to be, and you wouldn't admire me half as much if you knew why."

I reach forward and lift his chin so I can meet his gaze. "Do you think I don't know you're in love with me? I see you, Greek. I know your heart. It's big and beautiful and yes, right now, I'm the one who fills it, but you had me in there for centuries before we even met."

His face twists. "You knew?"

"Of course." He tugs his hands, but I don't let go. "Love is never something to regret or feel embarrassed about. I'm honored you love me. It's such a privilege to have you care for me."

He exhales a sad sigh. "You've been in love with Irish since the day we met."

"True story, but that doesn't mean I don't have room in my

heart for you too. It's just a different kind of love."

"I get it. Sloan is a stand-up, great guy, and he loves you with every breath he takes. I'd love him too if I were in your shoes."

I laugh, glad he holds no resentment toward Sloan.

Horror clouds his eyes, and he pales. "Do you think he knows?"

Considering Sloan's two primary disciplines are Health and Spiritual, I have no doubt he does. "Sloan knows what kind of man you are, and he knows where the two of us stand. I guarantee you that he doesn't judge you for your feelings."

Nikon shakes his head. "Still, I'll have to apologize. I mean, there's a line guys don't cross…"

"You've never crossed it." I cup his jaw with my palm. "No apology necessary. People love who they love. Now that your world has opened, and Hecate's hold on you is over, you'll find your perfect partner."

He chuckles. "You said that once about Melanippe."

"I'm not wrong often, but when I am, I tend to go big." Stepping forward, I wrap my arms around him and set my ear to his chest. "I love you, Nikon. You are my friend, my family, my hero, and a safe place when the world comes at me. I never want that to change."

He presses a kiss to the top of my head. "It never will. You're stuck with me."

"Good because whether you believe it or not, I need you in my life a lot more than you need me."

His chest bounces against my cheek with his laughter. "You're crazy."

"I've been told." I ease back and am relieved to see his anguish has dissolved. "You *are* my hero, Greek. I'm so lucky to have you in my life."

"Ditto. Thanks, Fi, for loving me back."

I shrug. "Easy-peasy. What do you say we get going? People to see. Bitches to banish."

Nikon laces his fingers with mine. "Hells, yeah. I'm looking forward to this."

Nikon snaps us first to the secret encampment in the Bavarian Alps to pick up two guests, then to the SITFU headquarters on the tenth floor of the Acropolis building in Toronto. The four of us materialize outside the elevators, and I lead the way through the security protocols on the double doors.

"There she is." Garnet comes out of his office. "If it isn't the face of the empowered world finally coming home to address the dumpster fire that is our life."

He's only half-joking, and I feel bad for tapping out. "I'm sorry, boss man. I've left you all in the lurch, I know. That wasn't my intention."

"Ignore him, Fi." Andromeda casts Garnet a withering glare. "You get to take a beat to regroup. How's Sloan? Any improvement?"

I shake my head. "Merlin's been trying to unweave the spell, but it's the level of power that caused the damage that's the problem. Supposedly it was a perfect storm kind of moment with the spell, the caster, the surge in the world's prana, and the magic of the Culling."

"I'm sorry, hon, but if I've learned anything about your family in the past year and a half, it's that you Cumhaills always find a way."

"True story. Everyone's trying to figure out how to replicate that power level without triggering the original spell to kill him. We're being cautious."

"As you should be." Garnet drops his chin. "As much as I want to encourage you to take all the time you need, I have to be the asshole in the room."

"I get it. I won't leave you hanging."

"I appreciate that."

With that sorted, I introduce the two eight-foot-tall, five-hundred-pound yeti we brought with us. "Garnet and Andromeda, this is Kimne and Deene. Melanippe and Mingin invaded their compound, kidnapped their young, and killed their queen. I promised them I would keep them informed about their capture and banishment. This is me keeping my word."

"It's a pleasure to meet you." Andromeda gestures at her office as her sister steps out. "You might remember our sister, Politimi. She stayed within your compound some time ago."

Where Nikon and Andromeda have the warm Mediterranean complexion, golden hair of the Greek gods, and smooth lines, Politimi has dark hair and eyes, pale skin, and angular features. "I wanted to say hello and offer my condolences on the loss of Queen Thorra. She was a strong and intelligent female. I was honored to call her my friend."

Kimne bows his head. "Few outsiders ever gain the respect of our people. Our queen spoke of you fondly. I shall take your words and share them with the others."

"I am pleased."

When that seems to be wrapping up, I take control of the conversation once again. "FYI, I told Kimne and Deene they could have a moment alone with Melanippe before we transport her to Newgrange."

Garnet arches an ebony brow. "A moment alone? For what purpose?"

Deene draws a slim-bladed dagger from the sheath at her hip and smiles. "To shove this into her chest."

Garnet looks from them to me. "Explain."

I shrug. "It's an immortal blade. They say it will render her unable to fight or escape. Their laws demand they kill their enemy in a life debt to honor their queen. Since Melanippe is immortal, rendering her incapable of escaping her banishment is as much as I could offer."

Nikon, Andromeda, and Politimi give the dagger a wary glance. I don't blame them. I'm sure it's not often they've come across something that could negate their immortality.

"It shall happen." Kimne meets Garnet's gaze. "We are not asking permission. We are thanking you for the opportunity."

The growl of his lion is nothing he can control. He is an alpha, and Kimne meeting his gaze and telling him how things will play out doesn't go over well.

I should know…he growls at me all the time.

"Kimne isn't challenging your authority here, Garnet. The yeti simply want to honor their queen as their customs demand. Then they will return to their compound."

Garnet swallows and I wait for his gold eyes to return to amethyst as he tethers his beast. "Fine, but we're not opening the cell, and they aren't getting anywhere near the Tsambikos with that dagger. I will flash them into the cell myself. The rest is up to them."

Kimne nods. "These are acceptable terms."

Garnet lifts his gaze and stares up at my yeti friend. "I assume Fiona explained to you that Melanippe is an Amazon warrior. She won't simply allow you to dagger her."

Kimne nods. "There would be no honor for our queen if she did."

"All right then. Let the games begin."

Garnet looks tiny next to Deene and Kimne. If I were in better humor, I would take a few candid pictures to chuckle over later. Sadly, I don't have it in me.

As it turns out, neither does Melanippe.

Garnet flashes the yeti duo into the cell, and they are much more dedicated to staking Melanippe than she is to protecting herself.

Sadly, I can relate.

Having your love taken smothers the fire inside.

In any case, after a few thumping backhands and a couple of impressive ground-smashing throwdowns, Deene plunges the dagger into the center of Melanippe's chest, and the Amazon warrior falls still.

Kimne straightens and lifts his chin. "We are ready."

Garnet takes a moment to examine Melanippe to determine she is truly incapacitated. Then he hits the security release on the cell. "All righty then, kids. Take her away."

I admit, I'm not thrilled about a dagger that incapacitates immortals, and I'm even less thrilled it's five feet away from Nikon, but the Greek is a trooper as always and snaps us to Newgrange without hesitation.

"Samuel, Ahren, and Quon Shen, you remember Kimne and Deene, yes?" I say as we join them in the tomb's main ritual chamber.

Kimne bows his head. "It seems there is a measure of closure at this moment for a great many of us."

Samuel gestures for him to lay Melanippe in the center of the pentacle circle they've prepared beneath the seam. "Agreed. There definitely is. Shall we?"

He lays Melanippe on the sandy stone, and I take my place on the pentacle circle. The two yeti envoys kneel on either side of her. They spoke to Samuel and asked to be the ones to hold her down during the banishment.

Whatever soothes your wounds.

I glance at the empty point of fire, and my heart aches for Dionysus. We haven't seen or heard from him since Eros tattled to Zeus and he was repo'd to the Greek Pantheon.

Samuel takes his time casting the bubble of protection around us, and when that's ready, he nods at Kimne. The yeti pulls the dagger free.

It's pathetic, really, that she's reduced to this.

Melanippe, the great and powerful Amazon warrior is broken and hollow. She doesn't fight. She stares up at the seam and seems at peace with passing into the Neitherlands.

Maybe I feel a little broken myself, but I genuinely hope she finds her happiness with Mingin—just not on this plane where they can hurt people.

The banishment continues for another ten minutes before her body arches toward the ceiling. She lets out a blood-curdling scream and falls still.

It all seems a little anticlimactic. Or maybe I'm in a funk. Yay team!

Nope. I'm definitely in a funk.

When it's all said and done, I hug Samuel, Quon Shen, and Ahren and wish them well. Their task is now complete, and they are anxious to get back to salvage what's left of the lives they had before this Hunter-gods business began.

"Keep in touch, boys." I wave as they get ready to leave. "If you ever need anything, you know where to find me."

"In the middle of the latest clusterfuck." Quon Shen laughs.

Ha! He's not wrong. "Laters."

When the goodbyes are complete, Nikon gestures at Melanippe's body lying on the ground. "What are we supposed to do with her?"

"Nothing at all." Kimne slides the immortal dagger back into the hole in her chest. "It will be our pleasure to take her body back to the compound to dispose of. Many of our community need closure as well, especially our young."

I check with Nikon, but neither of us seems to have any opinion on that.

"Hey, if you want the body of the crazy woman who tormented your family, have at it. We certainly don't need it."

Nikon nods. "Let me take you home…and if you don't mind, can you keep your immortal blades away from my sisters and me?"

Kimne bows his head. "You have our word. The Tsambikos immortals have ever been friends to our people and will remain that way."

Deene scoops the vacant shell of Melanippe's body off the tomb floor. "Thank you for today. You gave us your word and honored us with our chance to fulfill our duty. I might have been wrong about you, human."

Coming from her, that's high praise.

I take Nikon's hand and grip Kimne's wrist. "Let's get you home. There's something I need to tell my family to fulfill my duty."

When we get back to Ireland, I find Gran's and Granda's property deserted. No one in their house, Da and Shannon's house, or the treehouse. "Where the hell is everyone?"

Nikon shakes his head and pulls out his phone. "My cell's dead. So, if there's a message, I didn't get it."

I pull out my phone, and there is more than one notification waiting. "Emmet invited everyone to the palace for a belated Yule celebration."

Nikon takes my hand. "Is that where we're going?"

"Can we stop and get Sloan? I know he's not awake, but I can't bear the thought of facing a family event when he's lying alone in our bed."

"Of course. Hey, maybe the island's extra power might help his recovery. Wallace said we need to power-boost him, right?"

"Right. That's a good thought. Let's swing back to Stonecrest and get Sloan and his dad. Wallace deserves a night out for Yule too."

Twenty minutes later the four of us snap into the great room of Emmet's palace, and I release Bruin to socialize.

It's bittersweet to see everyone here. Kinu and the kids, Kevin and Bizzy, Liam and Shannon, Gran and Granda…Everyone we fought to protect all week.

Instead of being happy, seeing them breaks my heart for those who aren't here: Sloan, Dionysus, and Brenny.

Da is the first to notice our arrival. "Wonderful, ye got the message. Come. We've been waitin' on ye. We've missed ye the past two days."

I know they have.

I couldn't face the holiday celebrations. Coward that I am, I hid behind Sloan's condition because I wasn't ready to face them.

Granda rushes over to clear the cushions off one of the couches and Wallace lays Sloan down. Gran grabs a throw blanket and fusses over him while I continue to sink into the quicksand of my grief.

"That bad, is it?" Da brushes his finger against my damp cheek.

I meet my father's worried gaze. "I'm afraid it is."

That seems to suck the cheer out of the room.

All eyes turn toward Sloan, and I shake my head. "It's not Sloan. There's no change there. He's still taking his sweet time sleeping it off."

"Then what is it, *mo chroi?*"

With all eyes on me, I figure I've put this off long enough. "I owe you all an apology. It's my fault Brenny's not here with us tonight…or will be ever again."

Da's russet brows pinch tight as his gaze narrows. "I don't understand. We always suspected Death would reclaim Brendan. That's not yer fault, luv."

I swallow against the lump of emotion blocking my throat. "It is, actually. Death took me to the Choir of Angels for a reason. He offered to reverse Brendan's death and give him back to us to resume his life."

I meet my brother's gazes, and my tears fall in earnest. "I

wanted to say yes. I did. Everything in me wanted to erase the pain of losing him for all of us."

"There was a cost to it." Da's gaze grows harder with every moment. "It was a carrot dangled in front of ye. What was the trade-off to make it happen?"

"Mostly my pride." I swipe my cheeks. "He wanted me to go back and fight, but maybe remember I owed him one. Maybe I didn't have to fight so hard. And maybe our team didn't have to stand so firmly against the darkness of his."

Da chuffs. "That's not yer pride, luv. That's yer honor. There's a big difference between the two."

Dillan curses. "It wasn't a choice at all, baby girl. You realize that, right? It was blackmail."

I shrug and pull in a stuttered breath. "It was, but I still had a choice because the minute I turned him down, he sent a reaper, and Brendan was lost to us. Mother Nature told me we didn't have to win. Maybe I should've considered it. Maybe we could've regained the ground we lost over time, and we'd still have Brenny."

"Och, ye can't play that game, my luv." Da pulls me against his chest. "Take it from the man who lost himself doin' that very thing. Maybe if I hadn't brought my work home, he wouldn't have wanted to be a cop. Maybe if I hadn't spoken on his behalf, he wouldn't have gotten on Guns and Gangs. Trust me, *mo chroi*, I've played that game the past year, and there's no way to win. All ye'll do is drive yerself mad and lose sight of everything else that matters."

I'm still hugging Da when my brothers start to pile on, and the family hug takes hold.

Emmet kisses my temple. "You made the right call, Fi. If Brenny ever found out he got his life back at the cost of letting the bad guys win, he would've kicked your ass and never forgiven you."

"Damn straight I would," Brendan says behind us.

CHAPTER TWENTY-NINE

Our family hug breaks apart, and we find my brother standing in the middle of the room with Mother Nature and Eva. He looks whole and healthy and not nearly as dead as you expect a dead guy to look.

"You're here," I gasp, running to hug him. "I'm so sorry. I couldn't save you."

"Of course, you couldn't. Don't be stupid."

I choke, half laughing and half crying at such a Cumhaill retort. "Okay, I needed that."

Brenny gives me a bone-crushing squeeze, and I don't care that I can't breathe. "Emmet is right. I would never want my freedom at the cost of any of you or the world's safety. It wouldn't be worth it."

"Ye knew that, didn't ye?" Da smiles. "Yer instincts are keen. Somewhere beneath the grief of thinkin' ye cost yer brother his second chance, ye knew the price was too high."

"That doesn't mean I wasn't tempted or didn't regret my decision."

Brendan winks at me. "I get it. For a chance to keep me

around, I think most people would find it tempting to sell their soul."

I laugh. "Yeah, you're pretty great and so humble."

"I know it. Did I ever tell you about the time when I stepped into a spray of bullets to save a woman and her little girl?"

I press my cheek against his chest and close my eyes. "I might have heard about that."

"I heard about it too," Mother Nature says.

The Clan Cumhaill huddle breaks up, and we turn our attention to the goddess in the room. "I'm sorry Death tested you, Fiona. It wasn't kind, but from where I stand, you made the right choices at every turn. That says a great deal about you, but also a great deal about your father and your family."

I glance at my brothers and my father. "Yeah, they're pretty great."

She nods. "And have dedicated their lives to justice and safeguarding the innocent long before learning about your empowered heritage, I hear."

I'm not sure who she heard it from, but whatevs. She's the divine mother. She must have little birdies to tell her things. "Yes, heroes one and all."

"There has to be a reward for that, doesn't there?"

Da shakes his head. "No, ma'am. The reward is in the doin' of the deed itself and livin' a life to be proud of. That's thanks enough."

"That's true, but still, since Death offered Fiona a deal regarding reinstating Brendan's future, I figure I'm within my rights to do the same."

The whole room freezes and my heart starts hammering double-time in my chest. "What kind of a deal, milady?"

"While I can't offer him his old life back because I won't risk altering the course of things already set in motion, I propose that Brendan live here, on this enchanted island with Emmet. The hidden city is waking and having two lawmen here is not only wise but likely necessary."

Emmet blinks. "You said the city was quirky. You never mentioned needing policing."

Mother Nature's smile tells us nothing. "Brendan's reinstatement here would alter nothing of the human world or the balance. Your family would have him back, and he would be free to live and do all the things he planned to do, but only if he remains here within this pocketed realm."

I turn and look at Brendan, my entire body shaking. "Would you? Can you live here with Em, and we have you back?"

"Hells yeah. Sounds good to me." Brendan meets Emmet's gaze and holds up his fist for a bump. "What kind of rent do you charge to live in your golden dildo?"

We all bust up and break into another round of Cumhaill hugs. First with the seven of us, then adding in everyone else.

As the festivities continue, I walk Mother Nature across the room to thank her without all the fanfare and hoopla. "You've given us such a gift. From the bottom of my heart, I can't tell you how much this means to us."

"It is my pleasure, Fiona. I wish your family well."

"Thank you. I, uh, hate to be presumptuous but I have to ask about Sloan. He got hurt in the Culling. Dark witches tried to kill him." I glance at where my guy is lying alone on the sofa.

Mother Nature takes my hand, and I know by the look on her face, she's not going to fix him magically. I try not to let my disappointment show, but I'm not a good actor. "Do you remember when Emmet fell into the prana and turned into a kangaroo?" she asks.

I swipe my cheek and blink past my tears. "Yes."

"I told him not to lose heart, that everything will happen as it is meant. He needed to be patient."

There's that word again.

I pull in a labored breath. "Are you saying this is part of Sloan's journey?"

"I am."

"He'll come out of this at some point?"

Mother Nature smiles and squeezes my hand. "Have faith, Fiona. The world is a magical place and getting more magical every day. Everything he needs is here on this island. In time, it will all come together."

Lady Divinity leaves us to our celebrations, and I hook my arm with Eva's. "Were you, by chance, the little birdie who told Mother Nature what Death did?"

Dillan's attention sharpens. "Babe? Did we get Brendan back because you advocated for us again as our guardian angel?"

Her blonde corkscrew curls swing as she shakes her head. "Not as an angel, no. I spoke to her as your girlfriend and a friend to the family. It wasn't right that Death tried to leverage your brother's life against Fi's ethics. She is a special girl, and I knew how much that hurt her."

If it's possible to see someone fall further in love, I'm blessed to witness it. Dillan's warm and gooey center isn't something he exposes often, but those of us closest to him know it's there.

For Eva, it's always close to the surface.

"You are a very special girl too, angel." He winks and pulls a black velvet box out of the pocket of his jeans. Dropping to one knee, he opens the ring box and holds it up for her to see. It's a set of silver bands much like the ones Sloan and I wear.

"Every time I think I can't possibly love you more, you prove me wrong. Whether you're a reaper or a guardian or a girl I met at a housewarming party, I want you at my side, Evangeline of the Choir—forever and always."

"Forever and always," Evangeline repeats, her dimples punctuating her wide smile.

"Be mine forever, angel. 'Til death do us part."

Eva chuckles. "Not even then. Who are we kidding? I know people."

Dillan barks a laugh. "So, is that a yes?"

"Oh, goodness, yes," she gushes, sticking her hand out for him. "I want to wear your ring and be yours forever and behead bad guys with you and have your babies and everything else."

I glance around, happy to see that Calum is recording this on his phone and everyone is here to witness their moment. Well, almost everyone.

I leave the family crush and go over to the couches. Sitting on my knees beside one, I lay over Sloan's chest. "Dillan just asked Eva to marry him, hotness. Don't worry. Calum recorded it, so you can see it when you wake up. The point is, you're going to wake up, Mackenzie. Mother Nature said so."

I hug him and chuckle. "She also said I have to be patient. You know how bad I am at that. So, save me from myself and—"

"Auntie Fi, why's Uncle Sloan sleeping through Christmas?"

I ease back onto my heels and wipe my tears with my sleeve to talk to Jackson. "Remember how I told you this week was important because we had to fight bad guys and make things safe for all the people who aren't lucky enough to have magic?"

"Ya-huh."

I gather Sloan's hand in mine and take comfort in his warmth. "Well, Uncle Sloan got hurt by a bad lady witch, so his da put him into a magical sleep to help him rest while he gets better."

"Like Sleeping Beauty? She prickled her finger and went to sleep."

I grin. "Exactly like that. But, just like Sleeping Beauty, someday soon, the spell will break, and he'll wake up."

"Did you try kissing him? That worked for her and Snow White too."

To play along, I rise on my knees and give it a try. When I pull back from my kiss, Jackson leans in and frowns. "Are you sure you did it right?"

I laugh. "Pretty sure. I think he needs more time."

"Will he wake up by my birthday?"

Considering Jackson's birthday is in the summer, I sure hope so. "We have to wait and see. Mother Nature said to be patient."

"I don't like patient. Mommy says that all the time."

I chuckle. "I'm with you, buddy. Being patient is hard work."

The excited gasps from my gathered family have us looking over to see what we're missing. I can't see for the people in the way, but the air above the group is glowing with golden mist. I straighten, taking Jackson's hand as we head over.

Stepping shoulder-to-shoulder with Brenny and Liam, I blink at the man pimped out in the white suit. He's got the same ethereal grace and beauty as Eva, but the power coming off him is incredible.

"Who's the suit?" I whisper to Liam.

"I think he's an archangel and Eva's getting some kind of promotion."

"I can't see," Jackson complains.

Liam reaches down and props Jackson on his hip. "Let's try to be quiet, buddy. The angel man is talking."

"—your heaven's light to force back the darkness and protect your charges. However unconventional the solution, it was effective. To acknowledge your efforts, it is my pleasure to welcome you, Evangeline, to my domain. From this day forward, a guardian you shall be."

The man in the white suit touches Eva's forehead with the tip of his finger. It's an *E.T.* moment because his finger is glowing with power.

When that glowing digit connects with her skin, her eyes roll back, and her wings flare out behind her.

When Dillan first brought her home, her wings were the

metallic bronze of the reapers. Death took that away from her when she declared her intention to change dominions and replaced them with plain white.

I think he intended the white wings to be a point of shame and reflection. Eva didn't see them that way.

She saw the purity of the white wings as a clean slate full of potential. Now, they're the shimmering gold of the guardians.

She flexes her arms and a rush of power snaps in the air, her wings expanding to their full span behind her.

The archangel lifts his chin and smiles. "Welcome, child, to my dominion. May the dedication and honor you've shown thus far continue to make your brothers and sisters proud."

Eva clenches her right fist in front of her chest, grips it with her left, and bows. "I won't let you down, my lord."

"No. I don't believe you will." The archangel casts a curious glance over our group. "Is this the family Death appointed you to protect?"

Eva grins. "It is, my lord."

He chuckles. "Humans, animals, immortals, empowered, and not. Quite an eclectic bunch."

"This is the Clan Cumhaill. They are a beautiful family—my family," She holds her hand out for Dillan. My brother links hands with her and steps beside her.

The archangel seems even more amused by that. "I return you to your celebrations. Evangeline, report for reassignment at the new moon."

"Thank you, my lord."

When the angel in the crisp white suit snaps out, we all stare at one another, dazzled.

"Who was that, babe?" Dillan asks.

"That was Gabriel. He is the heavenly messenger and rules over the guardians. *And* my new boss. I did it."

Dillan faces her and cups her face in his hands. "We never doubted you for a second, angel. Congratulations."

Cue another round of Cumhaill celebration.

Liam plugs his phone into a portable speaker, and Shakira's *Hips Don't Lie* starts blasting.

Brendan jumps into a word-for-word serenade, and my grandparents, Nikon, Eva, and Wallace get their first view of my brother in his element.

Holy hell, it's good to have him back.

CHAPTER THIRTY

"Miss Cumhaill, thank you for coming in." The man at the head of the conference table stands as I take off my coat and hand it to Nikon. Maxwell and Andromeda are already seated and other than them, there are nine others including the speaker welcoming me.

"My pleasure. I'm sorry it wasn't sooner."

The speaker is a military man, born and bred, and gestures at the empty seat to his right. "Deputy Commissioner Maxwell explained to us that your husband was injured in the events of last week. Our thoughts and prayers are with you both."

"I appreciate that and have it on good authority he'll make a full recovery."

"On whose authority would that be, Fiona?" Andromeda asks the question, knowing the answer already.

Okay, so we're going that route. All righty then.

"Mother Nature," I say. "She visited our family two days after the Time of the Colliding Realms and assured me Sloan would revive given time."

Maxwell winks from across the table. "I'm glad, Fi. He's a good man."

"He is, thank you." At each seat, there is a nameplate, a closed folder, a pen, and a glass of water. I take a sip of water and meet the gaze of each of the heads of law enforcement who have gathered. "All right, ladies and gentlemen, I'm sure you have a million questions for me. I know I did when I learned about the empowered world, so fire away. Ask me anything, but I apologize now. I'm told I tend to speak too honestly at times."

The man who greeted me, Brian Tunde, CAF, opens his folder and glances at his notes. "Mr. Maxwell has done his best to downplay the events of last week as a solitary event, assuring us we've seen the worst of things. As a Director for the Canadian Armed Forces, I don't have the luxury of simply taking him at his word."

"That's understandable."

"If you will, please explain exactly what happened last week and why. If the empowered world has existed all along, why did things detonate the way they did?"

I spend the next hour explaining the Time of the Colliding Realms and the balance of things. It's mostly a flowing narrative of events, but the representatives from the different enforcement factions of Canada—armed forces, RCMP, policing, border patrol, diplomatic protection, and House of Commons—interject when they need clarification.

"Do you share Mr. Maxwell's sentiment that the worst is over, Miss Cumhaill?" Marlo Gaines, Ministry of Natural Resources asks.

"The worst of it, absolutely. The thinning of the veil is a cyclical thing, but the event that just ended only happens once every thousand years."

"What do you anticipate going forward?" Garish Basu of the RCMP asks.

"Honestly, I don't know. Largely, the disruptions we saw in Canada were one of two things. Either they were sects trying to gain a little power in a time that allowed for them to color outside the lines or they were the sects who are simply tired of living unknown and unseen in a city they consider their home."

"I can think of a dozen ways that would've been better if they simply wanted to let the world know they existed," Tunde says.

I chuckle. "Oh, I'm with you. Fae Pride Parade? That was crazy. Still, the majority of the fae sects in the city are harmless and have been forced into the shadows for centuries. Like my da says, 'Ye can only push a beachball under the water fer so long before it pops up and splashes yer face.'" I deliver the wisdom of Niall Cumhaill with my best Irish accent and smile.

"You say the majority of the empowered sects are harmless and yet—"

I hold up my finger and stop the woman from the embassy. "No, I said most of the fae sects in the city are harmless. Many members of the empowered world are not. Wizards, vampires, djinn, hobgoblins, necromancers, banshee, vitterfolk, they are not harmless."

"Which is exactly why someone like Garnet Grant and the Guild of Governors exists," Maxwell says. "They have been policing their own for centuries and doing it well enough that no one knew the difference. It makes sense to leave that system in place and not try to meddle in things we don't yet understand."

Tunde shakes his head. "You're talking about people who could take down a building with a look or a jet with a gust of breath or blow up a subway by throwing energy from their palms. How can you suggest we do nothing?"

I raise my hand to stop Maxwell's response. "He's not saying you do nothing. He's saying that for the time being, leave Garnet and our Guild of Governors in place to handle things and we can bring you up to speed on the empowered community.

"The worst possible thing you could do is start treating every empowered person as a weapon pointed at you. If you do that, you're enacting a self-fulfilling prophecy, and they will turn on you."

Andromeda nods. "For the most part, the fae and many of the empowered sects just want to live their lives. When things spill over into the community, SITFU is already in place, and we intercede. Bringing DC Maxwell into our confidence became necessary last year as sects began posturing for the Culling. That's over now."

I swallow and set my water glass down. "Andromeda is right. There is a good chance things will settle down now, and the public never needs to know the extent of the magical world around them. If things escalate, fine, maybe the policing agencies and military get involved, but it's too soon to hit the panic button."

Mr. Tunde gives me a placating smile. "No offense, Miss Cumhaill, but how old are you?"

"Twenty-four."

"While you are charming, well-spoken, and I understand why Mr. Maxwell wanted you to be the one to interact with the response council instead of Mr. Grant, I'm not sure your sweet smile qualifies you to make those decisions."

"One of the first things you need to learn about the empowered world, Mr. Tunde, is never to judge a book by its cover. I'm more than a twenty-something girl with freckles. Did Garnet shift and show you his lion?" I already know he did.

Several of the people around the table blanch.

"Well, who do you think took him down when a vampire used him as a weapon against the city?"

Mr. Tunde frowns at me. "You and what army, Miss Cumhaill?"

I shake my head and call faery fire to my palm. "No army, sir. Only me. Would you care for a demonstration?"

After the meeting with the response council ends, Nikon snaps Maxwell, Andromeda, and me back to the Batcave to give Garnet the lowdown.

"Well done, Lady Druid." Garnet grins. "You had them in the palm of your hand."

"You sound awfully sure of that, boss man. Did you guys already report in?"

Andromeda shakes her head and removes the Lakeshore Guild pin from the lapel of her suit jacket. "No need. Garnet had eyes on us the entire time."

Garnet accepts the return of the mini camera. "I don't trust people I don't know and especially people who are already trigger-happy and looking to shut us down."

"So, if things got out of hand, were you planning to flash in there and take them out?"

"It would've been my pleasure, but since everyone behaved, they live another day."

I chuckle and accept my coat from Nikon. "Well, until the next dumpster fire burns, I'm still considering this the holidays. Call me if you need me...no wait, I'll be at Emmet's island, and I won't get the message inside the city."

"Nikon's been coming home at night," Andromeda says. "We can always send you a message through him."

"Good enough."

"How is magical island life going?" Garnet asks. "Myra says you hope the added ambient power will help Sloan recover."

"That's our hope. So far, he's still sleeping, but it's been nice to hang out with Brendan. Also, Dart and Contessa McSparkles enjoy the freedom to fly with the other dragons. It's been a good couple of days to refill the well after the last year."

Garnet nods. "Then be off. Enjoy your family celebration and know that we're sending Sloan our best wishes for a swift recovery."

I hug Garnet and reach up on my tiptoes to kiss his cheek.

"Thank you. All my love to you and your girls. Once Sloan's out of danger, we'll do a dinner and drinks night."

"I'll tell them. They'll be thrilled."

Stepping back, I take Nikon's hand. "To the golden dildo, please."

Nikon chuckles. "What the hell were they thinking when they designed that tower?"

"No idea. Maybe that one day people would need a good laugh?"

"Yep. That must be it."

Nikon and I snap back to Ireland and join the crowd in the great room. Once again, we seem to be the last to arrive, and the party has begun without us.

Brendan and Emmet have taken to their brotherly duty of being guardians of Emhain Abhlach almost as seriously as their duty to host family events.

Since neither of them is to leave the island, Clan Cumhaill must come to them.

"Welcome, little sister," Dillan says, his silver top hat slightly askew. "You two are six shots behind us."

I widen my eyes at Nikon. "Do *not* feel pressured to catch up."

"No pressure." Nikon laughs, unwinds his scarf, and tosses his jacket on the chair by the door. "I hear I'm behind on the boozing. Someone catch me up."

I roll my eyes and go over to the couch where Sloan is lying peacefully. Manx is curled up on the rug, and Wallace is sitting with a book reading to them.

"How are my Mackenzie men this evening?"

Wallace closes the book and offers me a tired smile. "We're doing as well as can be expected, I suppose. How was your day in the city?"

"Long. I'm looking forward to dinner. I'm starving."

Gran and Granda come over to hug me, and I thank them for spending time with Sloan and the family.

"Och, luv, it's our joy to see yer brothers so happy."

We talk a bit more. Then Granda helps Gran don her sweater.

"Are you leaving?"

Gran nods. "We are. I'm missin' my wee home, and as much as I want to be here fer every moment with ye, I need some quiet time as well."

"I totally get it. Without Brendan, quiet was all we had the past months. I think we'll drink in the cacophony a long while yet before we grow tired of it."

"We couldn't be happier about it," Granda says. "Have some savage craic fer yer Gran and I, will ye?"

"Honestly, I think I'll curl up on the couch with Sloan until dinner, and we'll turn in soon after."

I turn to Wallace and touch his arm. "You are welcome to stay, always, but you look tired, and I'm not going anywhere for the next couple of days. Why don't you go home, take some time for yourself, and maybe call your decorator friend? We can regroup in a couple of days for New Year's Eve. You're all coming, right?"

"Wouldn't miss it," Granda says.

Wallace meets my gaze and looks torn. "Are ye sure ye wouldn't mind if I take off?"

"Not at all. I'm looking forward to the two of us spending an evening together. I have a lot to tell him about my day and in this state, he's a really good listener."

Wallace chuckles. "I'm sure that's true. All right. If yer certain."

"I am." I hug them all and say our goodbyes.

"Nikon, son. Can we get a lift home?" Granda asks.

His question gets lost in the noise of male laughter.

I press my fingers between my lips and whistle. "Greek, before you're snapping impaired, we've got three to beam home."

Nikon jogs over, touches his nose with his finger a few times, and winks at me. "I'm good. I'll be right back. Don't let them start beer pong without me."

When they're gone, I pull back the blankie, climb onto the couch, and snuggle against Sloan's side. "Hey, hotness. How about we take it easy for a bit? I missed you today and could use some downtime."

Fiona? Can you come down to the meadow? There's something Saxa and I would like to discuss with you.

I wake with Dart's voice still in my mind and sit up, discombobulated. *Buddy? Were you just talking to me?*

I was. Will you come down to the meadow? Saxa and I want to speak to you.

Sure. Yeah. I'm on my way. I sit up and flip the blanket back. "I'll be back, hotness. Save my spot."

Getting to my feet, I search the room, looking for Nikon. I don't see him, but Tad's there with the heirs.

"Hey, Tad. Can you do me a favor and *poof* me down to the meadow? Dart and Saxa want to talk to me."

He sets his plate of finger foods down on the mantle and wipes his hands on his ripped designer jeans. "Sure thing. Happy to."

I glance back at who's here. I don't know how long I was asleep, but I seem to have missed the dinner bell. "What time is it?"

"Half-seven."

I laugh. "Oh, I thought for a moment I slept the whole night away."

"Nope. Just a power nap."

I glance around and find Kevin checking on Bizzy asleep on a chair in the corner. "Kev, can you keep one eye on Sloan for a bit? Dart wants to talk to me. I'll be right back."

He gives me a thumbs-up, and I take Tad's hand and squeeze. "Thanks for the ride, McNiff."

He shakes his head. "No need to thank me. I'm at yer service."

We *poof* down to the meadow, and I find my blue boy there with Saxa. "Hi, guys."

"Did I wake you?" Dart bends to look at me. "I'm sorry, Fi."

I rub the center horn on his snout and wave off his concern. "Not a problem, buddy. I crashed with Sloan on the couch. I'm good."

"How is he?" Saxa asks. "Has there been any improvement?"

"Not yet, but Mother Nature told me to have faith."

"We were thinking about what else she told you," Dart says. "Can you tell me again, as close as you can remember?"

I think about that for a moment. "She said the world is a magical place and getting more magical every day. Everything Sloan needs is here on this island. In time, it will all come together."

The two of them look at one another, and I know by the focus that they're speaking privately.

"Want to let me in on the conversation?"

"We have an idea," Dart says, his tone tentative. "It's Saxa's idea, really."

The sun glistens off Saxa's canary yellow scales, making her look even brighter than usual. "I'd like to bond with Sloan. Dragons have a great deal of magic, and I think that if we formed a union bond, I could help him fight the spell that holds him in stasis."

I'm speechless, my mind still stuck in a sleepy fog.

"I believe when Mother Nature said everything he needs is on the island, she meant not only the power of the island itself but the power of a dragon bond."

I finger-comb my hair and scratch my head. "You rejected bonding with a rider your entire existence. Do you want to form a union with him?"

"I rejected the kind of riders that dominated the dragons of my time. I've watched how you and Sloan ride Dartamont. You respect him as an equal and consider his feelings and needs."

"Of course. We love him."

"Exactly. If you think you and Sloan could love me in the same way and give me the freedom to be not only his mount but a being with my own strengths and wishes, I believe it would be a good match."

I swallow, my mental hamster spinning to catch up. "I have no doubt Sloan would cherish you as much as I do Dart. If that's your only concern, I would be thrilled to welcome you into our family for the long term."

It doesn't skip my attention that her bonding with Sloan would also give him longevity. That has been a secret dream since I learned I wasn't going to age and die as expected.

Still, with her relationship with Dart and knowing who Sloan is, it's a great solution.

"How do we make it happen?"

"I would take him with us into our den. Dragon lairs are a magical place, and within the privacy of our space, Dart and I will perform several arcane incantations. We will take very good care of him, but I will need you to trust me."

"You need to take him? I can't be there?"

"I'm sorry, Fiona. There are some things dragons consider sacred. Our rituals are one of them."

Dart edges forward and nudges me. "You can trust us, Fi. You know you can."

I search my instincts. The only hesitation I have is not being able to care for him and be with him. "When do you want to do this?"

"As soon as you are ready to bring him here to me."

I turn to Tad, and he's already nodding. "Got him. Back in a flash."

When Tad's gone, I move over to face Saxa. "Are you sure

about the bonding? I don't want you to do anything you're not sure about. If it's only about Sloan, we'll figure something else out."

She shakes her head. "That's how I know it will be fine. Thank you, Fiona, for always giving me a voice. I swear to you, I will do everything in my power to bring him back to you."

Tad *poofs* back with Sloan in his arms and Kevin, Nikon, and my brothers along for the ride.

"Do I lay him on your back?" Tad asks.

"That will be fine," Saxa says.

I rush over to kiss him goodbye before he goes. "This will work, Mackenzie. Just think, when you wake up, we can go dragon-riding together. That will be fun, eh?" I don't want to let him go, but after breathing him into the depths of my lungs, I kiss him again and nod. "Okay, let's get him settled on her back."

CHAPTER THIRTY-ONE

For two days, I wait, sleeping in fits and spurts, dreaming I hear Dart calling me at night and standing on the grand balcony, staring out at the meadow all day. I gave my other half to the dragons. Was that reckless? Crazy? Did I act without thinking?

"Hey, baby girl." Brendan drapes his arm across my shoulder and squeezes me. "Staring won't make it happen."

"I know. I feel sick. At least when he was on the couch, I could hold him and talk to him. Now…he's just gone. I don't know what's happening. Is he cold? Does he wonder where I've been?" I stare into my brother's bright green eyes. "What if I made the wrong call?"

"Second-guessing won't help. You believe in the power and the magic of dragons. So, just believe."

I draw a deep breath in and exhale. "I know, you're right. I just…"

"Love him. I know. We all get it." He chuckles and tilts his head toward the card game unfolding on the table. "Come take your mind off things for a bit. We're playing Asshole."

"I don't know that I could concentrate."

He snorts. "Concentrate? Did you hear the part when I said we're playing Asshole? It's not rocket science, baby girl."

I chuckle and let him tug me inside. "Fine, but no one can ridicule me. I'm fragile. Consider me a china flower."

He arches a brow, and we both start laughing.

"Too much?"

"Yeah, a little bit."

"Hey, Fi," Dillan says, shuffling at the table. "Do you want to be dealt in?"

"I suppose—"

The signature of his magic snaps in the room before he arrives. Straightening, I search until—"Tarzan!"

I run around the table and jump, wrapping myself around Dionysus like a crazy koala. After thoroughly hugging him, I give him a big, sloppy kiss on his cheek. "I've been so worried about you. Are you all right? Can you come home now?"

His smile melts so much of the chill I've felt the past few days. "It's New Year's Eve tomorrow, isn't it? Didn't you say I was in charge of the New Year's afterparty?"

"I sure did. Oh, my goodness I've missed your face. Welcome home."

Dionysus hugs me again, and a huge tension in my chest eases. "I missed your face too, Jane. Thanks for the warm welcome."

I let my legs dangle back to the floor and stop hanging off him. "How are you here? Was Zeus awful? Did Eros fix it? Tell me everything."

That's when his façade cracks. I see the hurt and exhaustion of his ordeal, and I realize I'm pushing. "Never mind. All that matters is that you're here and you're safe."

My brothers come over, and there's a long line of back-slapping manly hugs.

"It's good to have you home," Calum says.

"Our lives aren't as interesting without you, Greek," Emmet

adds.

"You are the spice of our lives, dude," Dillan says.

"Thanks, guys. It's good to be back. What did I miss?"

We spend the next hour and a half telling him about the final battles of the Culling, about Sloan and the dragons, about Brendan getting to stay with us, and about Dillan and Eva getting engaged.

"Look at me. I'm Cupid." He winks. "My parties are magical."

"They sure as hell are," Dillan says.

"You've never been to one of my soirees, Brendan." Dionysus grins. "Tomorrow night, I will throw you one."

Brendan doesn't know what he's in for. "Sounds good, but it'll have to be here. I'm on island arrest."

Dionysus shrugs. "The venue doesn't matter. It's the activities that make the event. Emmet and I have already been working on remodeling one of the portrait galleries into a fun fest backdrop. Tomorrow night, you can prepare to be amazed."

"I look forward to it. Truly. It sounds like a lot of fun."

"Och, a guy sleeps fer a week or two, and the world keeps partyin' on like nothin' happened."

I follow the deep and delicious Irish lilt to the balcony's entrance and scream.

I run to him, arms out and tears streaming. "Are you real?" I hiccup, crying against his ear. "No, don't tell me. If this is a hallucination or you're a trickster, I don't want to know. Let me enjoy it."

Sloan's arms are tight around my ribs as he chuckles against my ear. "Yer ridiculous, Cumhaill."

"Yeah, but that's why you love me, right?"

"Somethin' like that." He eases back and brushes his fingers over my forehead and down my temple, moving my hair out of my face. "I heard ye, by the way. All those hours I laid there, I couldn't respond, but I heard it all."

I waggle my brows and laugh. "Uh-oh, did I say anything I

shouldn't have?"

"I believe ye told me to get my ass in gear and find my way home to ye."

"Actually, I told you to get your *beautiful* ass in gear. Emphasis on the beautiful."

He claims my mouth, and the kiss is far too intimate for the company in the room, but for once I don't care. I love this guy, and I don't care who sees it or knows it or gets their retinas burned out by watching it.

After days of anguish, my world finally sits right on its axis.

I ease back breathless. "Anne Boleyn, right now."

"You boys are in serious trouble now."

It's twenty to twelve, and time for the annual Cumhaill New Year's Eve resolution assessment. Last year, we added Sloan but had a hole in our family because we had Brenny's predictions from the year before and no Brenny. This year, not only do we have my brother back, but we also have Sloan, Dionysus, Nikon, and Eva to include in the family resolutions.

Calum and Kevin start the rhythmic hammering of fingers against the ancient table in the great room of Fantasy Island. I rip open the envelope sealed on December thirty-first of last year and pull out my sheet of paper.

"I, Fiona Kacee mac Cumhaill solemnly swear that in the year to come, I will drink less, exercise more, and love Sloan Mackenzie more every day. I don't need to convince Da to let me have a cat this year because I have Manx, and now that I know I'm meant to be a druid, I will be the best-damned druid that the empowered world has ever seen. Suck it, bad guys."

Calum's eyes widen. "Wow, Fi, you nailed it."

Da nods in agreement. "I agree with yer brother, *mo chroi*. I think ye get full points."

"Does she really?" Emmet makes a face. "I feel like those were all pretty safe. Drinking less and exercising more have been her go-to pledges for the past five years. Love Sloan…boring and not measurable. Best druid ever? Again, I vote vague."

Dillan snorts. "You're just salty because you said you would make a huge collar and get a commendation."

Emmet makes another face. "Yeah, but being the king of my island and policing an enchanted city is an upgrade."

I hold up my list. "Come on boys. I nailed it."

"We'll put it to a vote." Dillan snatches my page out of my hand. "You don't get a point for drinking less."

Emmet laughs. "No. You don't."

"I do exercise more."

"Fine, but Dillan and Sloan got perfect scores, so you're already out of the running."

"Tough crowd." I laugh.

Calum snorts. "Agreed."

Dillan sends my sheet sailing. "Bam. Drop the mic, bitches! All right, Irish, it's down to you and me."

Sloan looks sideways at me. "What does that mean, *a ghra*? I'm afraid."

"It means you're in the sudden death, Cumhaill elimination round."

"Having spent the last week hovering on the brink of death, I think I win."

Dillan makes a face and waves that away. "Nice try. You can't play the ole 'witches hexed me to die, but I clawed my way back to life' card."

"I don't know, D." Emmet casts a glance around the table. "I think maybe he can."

Brendan lifts his drink and nods. "Having spent the last year on the other side of the death thing, I think Irish has a point. After all, if he hadn't come back, none of us would be here celebrating."

Dillan flips Emmet a middle-finger salute and flops back in his chair. "Yer all a bunch of bleeding-heart girlies."

I laugh. "*Rude.* As one of the girlies at this table, I object to your sexist remark."

Sloan rolls his eyes and finishes his drink. "It's almost time to ring in the New Year. We need to make our predictions fer this year's envelope."

I hold up the masterpiece of art Jackson, Meg, and Bizzy contributed to the event this year. After everyone comments on the gifted genius of our offspring, I point at the pad and pen each of us has before us. "Everyone has five minutes to write down four predictions for next year and seal them up."

Sloan grabs his paper and leaves the room.

Emmet busts out laughing. "Once again, Irish goes the secrecy route. Amateur!"

"Who won the event from last year, Barbie boy?" Sloan calls.

I bust up laughing. "That's it, baby. Don't apologize for your process."

I pick up my pad and tap the end of my pen on the paper. I, Fiona Kacee mac Cumhaill do solemnly swear that this year, I will…

"Two minutes, assholes." Brendan laughs as he scribbles on his pad.

With the tip of my pen madly moving over my notepad, I jot down the first four things that come to mind. Reading them over, I snort. "Okay, I love my coming year."

Emmet grins. "Good. That makes two of us."

I stuff my paper into the envelope, tuck in Emmet's, and wait, watching the others: Kev and Calum, Dillan and Eva, Brendan and Liam, Da and Shannon, Nikon and Dionysus, Aiden and Kinu, Gran and Granda. At the sound of the bell, Sloan jogs into the room, folds his, and adds it to the pile.

I collect them all, stuff them into the envelope, and hand it to

Da. He passes his hand over the artwork and seals it. "The end. Until next year."

"Until next year," we repeat, raising our glasses.

"Red, it's time." Bruin hollers from the balcony.

Scrambling up from the table, we grab our drinks and race outside to watch the dragons give us a fire in the sky tribute for the New Year.

"Countdown time!" Kinu shouts, grabbing Jackson and bringing him out to see. Meg tried to stay up, but she crashed with Bizzy and the twins.

I squeal, rushing to get to Sloan so the two of us can look over the railing together. The dragons are swooping in the air, blowing fire as Merlin's fireworks spell starts letting off the first charges.

"A castle!" Jackson shouts, pointing. "A dragon!"

I laugh at the pyrotechnic masterpiece exploding into colors in the sky. "Best fireworks evah!"

Sloan wraps his arms around me, and I feel the power of Saxa's dragon in him. We haven't had time to digest everything that happened the past week or what it means. Yes, the world's prana levels are rising and causing unexpected magical fallout. And yes, the empowered world has been officially exposed, but at this moment, none of that matters.

I take in the crowd and can't help but smile. Bruin and Manx drink whiskey from their roasting pans with Daisy and Doc. Dart and Saxa are dancing in the sky with Dart's siblings. The monkeys are curled up and asleep in the bed we set up in the corner. My family, by blood and by choice, are here with me.

Through the trials of becoming the woman I know I'm meant to be, I managed to scrape through in one piece with the help of my family and friends.

Everyone is alive and well.

Life is good.

Love is better.

EPILOGUE

The brass bell over the door chimes as I enter the bookstore and...don't enter it. "What the fuckety-fuck?"

The place is packed.

In the year and a half I've worked at Myra's Mystical Emporium, we've never had a rush of more than four or five customers in the store at one time.

Today it's standing room only.

"What the hell is this?" I glance over my shoulder at Sloan, and he looks as confused as I am.

"Is she havin' a sale and forgot to tell ye?"

I laugh. "Somehow, I don't think so." I tap the broad shoulder of the linebacker blocking my entry. "Excuse me. Sorry, yeah, can I get inside? I work here."

There's a shifting of bodies, but nothing improves. It'll take me half an hour to get to the back desk.

Turning to Sloan, I take his hand. "Can you *poof* us into the kitchenette? I doubt the back room is this densely populated."

He glances at the people walking along Queen Street and frowns. "What? Now? From here?"

"We can duck down the alley if you want, but this is the new world, after all. Magic is real."

Sloan's frown deepens, and I sympathize. It's been a tough few weeks since the Culling and having the privacy of our empowered world exposed still feels wrong.

"I know how you feel, but it's fine. This is us, right? The new normal."

"The new normal where nothin' is normal at all."

He's not wrong.

The tingle of Sloan's wayfarer magic rushes over my skin, and a moment later we've *poofed* into the privacy of the back room.

"Much better." I take a beat and relish the moment of respite. After drawing a breath, I'm ready to face whatever is happening in the store.

The muffled voices of more than a hundred people excitedly shouting over one another are threatening to bust through the door.

Poor Myra…the Emporium is her Zen temple.

Yanking the door open, I take in the chaos and push into the mix. Getting to the back desk from the kitchenette is a straight shot of twenty feet.

Myra is racing around behind the antique display table with a little bear cub curled up at her feet. Imari doesn't like crowds, and the stress of her daughter feeling stressed is probably a large part of why my dear friend looks like she's ready to crumble.

It's not a good look for her.

"Hey, girlfriend." I step in to help. "What the hell is this?"

Myra turns to me, her vertically slit eyes glassing up as she sees me. "It's too much. That's what it is."

"I get you. I'm here to help. How about Sloan takes Imari to play with the monkeys and we'll call in reinforcements to deal with things here?"

"That would be wonderful. Thanks, duck. I haven't had a chance to get to my purse to call for help."

I crouch and pass my hand over Imari's fluffy round ears. "Hey, baby girl. Would you like to get out of here? Uncle Sloan will *poof* you to Jackson's house to play for a while. Would you like that better?"

The little bear uncurls, and I lift her into my arms to snuggle her close. When I pass her to Sloan, she tunnels into the seam between his arm and his ribs.

Poor little cub.

"Maybe stay a few extra minutes to make sure she's all right. Tell Kinu what happened so she can keep an extra watchful eye on her."

Sloan cuddles her closer, strokes a soothing hand over her fur, and frowns at the crowd. "Are ye sure yer best to stay? I can get all three of ye out of here."

"No, only Imari. Whatever's happening, Myra won't abandon her store to this crowd. Come back soon and bring the boys if they're around."

Sloan scowls at the crowd once more, then takes Imari back into the kitchenette and they're gone.

"Okay, so what the hell is happening?" I ready myself to take on the masses.

"You know how I spelled my shop so no one except the empowered can find it and only if I have something they need?"

"Yeah."

"Well, from what I gather from speaking to customers the past half-hour, these are people who have latent empowered genes suddenly coming into their powers. They range from thrilled and excited to panicked and furious, and they all want answers. The spell translates that into needing something my bookshop can provide."

"Amazeballs." I scan the faces of the mob and take that in. "You think they're all here for Empowered 101?"

"So far that's what I've come up with."

Everyone is shouting and reaching and clasping books in

their arms. It's bedlam. Giving up on Sloan being able to round up a couple of my brothers to get here, I pull out my Team Trouble pendant and press the call for backup.

Jumping onto the desk, I stand above the crowd. I press my finger and thumb together under my tongue and let out a whistle that could shatter glass.

The cacophony cuts off, and the room of newly empowered rowdies quiets.

"Hello, everyone. I'm Fiona. I get that many of you are overwhelmed, and you've come for answers. We'll do our best to get you sorted, but you need to calm down. How many freaked out because you don't know what has woken up inside you?"

About sixty people raise their hands.

"How many are freaked out because you think you *do* know what's woken up in you?"

Another thirty or so raise their hands.

"How many of you have no idea why you're here, but you simply felt a draw to come?"

That accounts for most of the rest.

The air charges with a surge of power and Garnet, Anyx, Zuzanna, Dionysus, Nikon, Dillan, Calum, and Sloan start appearing behind me.

"All right. Here's what we're going to do. Who here thinks you might be Moon Called or another type of animal shifter?"

When hands go up, I continue, "Can those of you with your hands raised see this lovely blonde couple behind me? This is Anyx and Zuzanna. They will meet you in the other part of the store by the leather couches. Quietly and courteously move to join them, and they'll help you figure out what's happening."

The crowd jostles a bit to let those people out of the crush. When things have mostly settled down, I raise my hand to go again.

"Who has manifested some kind of magical ability they don't understand and don't know how to control? Maybe sparks from your fingertips or the toaster exploding when you touched it or something weird that keeps happening?"

Cue a round of rising hands.

"All right. This is Dionysus—yes, *the* Dionysus of myth and legend. He and my brother Dillan will meet you on the second level of the shelving at the back. That's where the section on magical races is."

Again people break off, and the group is starting to be a little more manageable.

"Is anyone feeling overwhelmed by raw power or violence? Don't hide if you have dangerous impulses. A lot is happening in the magical world right now, and we're here to help. No judgment."

A dozen hands go into the air, including the linebacker from the door.

"This is Garnet Grant. You might as well meet him now because he's the head honcho for Toronto's empowered folks. He is now the captain steering your ship and wants to help you tether dangerous tendencies. Meet him inside the doorway to the other part of the store near the Tarot cards and crystals."

I scan the forty people I have left, trying to figure out what I've missed.

"Is anyone suffering from physical mutations or alterations they don't understand or know what they're leading up to?"

About a dozen people raise their hands. "Okay, perfect, Nikon and Sloan will meet you at the front of the store by the entrance and window. Go ahead and make your way there."

Sloan and Nikon vanish.

That leaves us with about thirty people left. "If I haven't covered something you relate to, or if you're part of the crowd that doesn't know why you're here, move in closer, and Myra and I will do what we can to get you sorted out."

Myra holds my hand while I jump down from the desk, then

kisses my cheek. "This is why you are the fae liaison and my favorite employee."

I laugh. "I'm your only employee."

"I was smart to hire you. Well done, duck."

It takes all morning and half the afternoon to get through the people who had crammed themselves into Myra's bookstore. Every time we think we're at the end of the crowd, the brass bell rings again, and another rush floods in. Still, in the end, the flow ebbs.

"Well, that was a fun day with friends." I flop onto one of the leather couches at the Batcave.

Garnet gives me a sidelong glance as he strides toward his office, his scowl firmly locked in place. "My wife and daughter were mobbed. We need to figure out what the fuck has gone wrong with the world and fix it."

I close my eyes and think about that while Dionysus chats quietly with Dillan. It's so good to have my god of good times back. He hasn't opened up about what happened when he got recalled to Olympus, but something is bothering him.

I'm looking forward to nut-punching Eros the next time I see him.

Nikon and Calum flash into the entrance with their arms full of pizzas and beers. Dillan jogs over to open the doors for them. "Welcome to the prana post-panic party, boys."

Nikon takes in the scene and chuffs. "This is the worst party ever."

I chuckle and sit up. "We've been tasked to figure out what's gone wrong with the world. Garnet wants us to fix it."

Nikon busts up laughing. "Fix the whole world? Wow, okay, our lion leader has lofty goals."

"It can't only be the reconnection of Emmet's island upping access to prana," Dillan says.

"What makes you say that, D?" I hold my hand up and Dionysus pulls me to my feet.

"Well, think about it. If the island's connection to the raw prana of the Cistern causes this much magical mayhem, it would've exposed the empowered world long ago."

"I don't know that I agree." Nikon sets the pizzas down on the table. "Life was much simpler in centuries past. Populations were smaller and more dispersed. It was easier to stay out of the public eye if you didn't want something to be known. Maybe it affected this many people proportionately, but they were better able to hide it."

I swing past the offices on the way to the table, signaling to both Garnet and Maxwell that the food has arrived. "In my mind, the biggest difference between then and now isn't population density or dispersion. It's that now, because of the Internet, television, and global awareness, everything ends up public knowledge."

Dillan shakes his head while flipping back the lids of the boxes, searching for the pizza he wants. "It's not public awareness or the Internet that brought a hundred and fifty panicked citizens to the Emporium today. Something magically mysterious is afoot."

"Thanks, Sherlock." Chuckling, I grab two slices of Hawaiian and a bottle from the case of beer. "So, if we don't think it's the re-established connection with the island, what's our theory?"

"I'm afraid I might know." Merlin comes through the double doors to join us. He tosses Calum a USB drive and points at the monitor wall. "If you will."

Calum hustles over to the computer, plugs in the drive, and fires up the wall of screens.

Sloan jogs into the office, back from taking Myra to pick up

Imari and escorting her home to Garnet's compound. "What did I miss?"

"Nothing yet. Merlin's about to explain his theory on the world's current state of mayhem."

Merlin takes off his wool trench coat and tosses it over the back of one of the chairs at the conference table. "It's bugged me since everything went to hell."

"What has?" Garnet storms out of his office looking even pissier than when he went in.

"The awakenings. The power it takes to activate latent fae genes is considerable but can be explained in small occurrences by tracking a significant event."

Butterflies of guilt flutter around in my belly. "Like reconnecting Emmet's island and boosting the world's ambient power?"

Merlin nods. "Exactly. Before the Culling began, Imari's unicorn sprouted wings, and young Jackson's wayfarer gift awoke. We expect things like that when turning up the power dial. A magical shift occurred, and there was a magical impact."

"But?"

"But they're empowered beings imbued with magic who simply upped their game. Contessa McSparkles was already a magically conjured unicorn, and Jackson was a druid and able to communicate with animals and nature."

Garnet chuffs. "So, you're saying there's a big difference between leveling up the power they already exhibited and actually 'becoming' empowered."

"A massive difference."

Images start popping up on the screens, and I take a bite of ham and pineapple bliss. I groan as I chew—Hawaiian pizza. So good. So, so good.

Sloan stiffens, staring at the images on the screens.

I don't know how to process the visuals.

"What the hell are we looking at, dude?" Dillan folds two slices into each other for a double-decker.

It looks like footage from a post-apocalyptic sci-fi thriller: major roadways overgrown with invasive vines, griffons circling crumbled skyrises, people opening portals on city streets, coming and going as if it's normal.

"The question is, what will it be?" Merlin says. "During the Winter Solstice and the four days of the Culling, the veil was thin, and the power levels were in flux. I understood the leveling up happening then, but the alarming percentage of the population having a magical awakening since then didn't make any sense."

"Until you figured out what?" Garnet growls at the footage of empowered people running wild in the street and overrunning human citizens.

"I had a hunch, so I summoned a time-jump demon to take a little hop—"

"You summoned a *demon?*" My shock sends a chunk of ham down the wrong pipe, and I choke. Holy hell…a demon?

I try to absorb that tidbit while I cough and sputter.

Merlin flashes me a placating smile. "A lesser demon. Time-jump demons can be summoned for a one-off task and returned to purgatory without consequence. Not all demons are Asmodeus, Fi."

I cringe at the mention of his name. "And Asmodeus is not the composer."

"No, not Amadeus." Sloan chuckles.

"Back to the fucking point," Garnet snaps.

Merlin nods. "Right. So, I tasked the lesser demon to hop ten years into the future, take some footage of the state of the world, and hop back."

"This is our world in ten years?" Sloan asks.

"It is."

"Is that a volcano in San Francisco?" I point at an image of a conical black mountain in the same frame as the Golden Gate Bridge.

"This is more than the thinning of the veil between worlds." Sloan scowls.

Merlin nods. "It is. And it's more than the reconnection of Emmet's island to the Source power."

The warning growl of Garnet's lion brings us to the end of his patience. "Spit it out."

Merlin casts a glance at Garnet. "I think the veil is down. Not thin. Not breached. I think something happened during the Time of the Colliding Realms that brought the barrier between the magical world of the empowered and the non-magical world completely down."

I swallow, my mental hamster spinning out on that one. "What does that mean? Can we get it back up?"

"I have no idea, but if the peek into the future is anything to go by, there was no hope to keep the empowered world a secret. We're looking at a new normal none of us is ready for."

"That's my take on things too," Maxwell says directly behind me.

I jump and turn, patting my chest. "Dude, you scared the bejeezus out of me, and I just stopped choking. How long have you been standing there?"

"Long enough to realize your job as a liaison to the empowered world just got complicated." He drops three files on the conference table and slides them out so they're all lying flat. "I've got urgent requests from the Montreal PD, the New York Port Authority, and the Rome Historical Society for you and your team to help with what's going on in their cities."

I flip the cover open of the first file and blink. "Wait, what? I thought I was going to be the liaison for Toronto empowered concerns—maybe Ontario. How did this become a global gig?"

Maxwell shrugs. "That's the beauty of going viral on the

Internet, Fi. You're the face of the fae freak show and how to handle what no one knows how to handle."

Garnet's scowl couldn't get much darker. "Just because they ask doesn't mean we have to oblige. We can tell them to go fuck themselves and find someone else."

That would be easier, but my instincts won't let me walk away. "No. This is new to everyone. If I can help other agencies in other cities figure out what's happening in their streets, I don't mind trying."

I take in my family and friends and know I'm asking a lot but… "It's not something I can do on my own."

Calum lifts his beer in salute. "Go, Clan Cumhaill. All for one and one for all."

Dillan nods. "Fuck, yeah. It's time to Musketeer the shit out of this crazy new world."

I check in with Sloan, and he smiles at me. "We'll take it one disaster at a time, *a ghra*, as always."

Dionysus drapes his arm across my shoulder and kisses my cheek. "We're with you, Jane. Whatever you need and wherever that takes us."

Nikon is the last to weigh in. He winks and extends his hand between us. "All mischief shall be managed."

I set my hand on his, and the others follow suit. Connected as we are, my heart swells with love and pride. It doesn't get any better than this. "Stay tuned world. Things are going to get interesting, and Team Trouble is on the job."

THANK YOU

Thank you for reading *A Danger Destroyed* and sticking with us to the end of the Chronicles of an Urban Druid. While the story is fresh in your mind, and as a favor to Michael and me, please click HERE and tell other readers what you thought.

A quick star rating and/or even one sentence can mean so much to readers deciding whether to try a book, series, or a new-to-them author.

Thank you.

If you want more of Clan Cumhaill, continue with book one of the Case Files of an Urban Druid and claim your copy of Mayhem in Montreal.

CASE FILES OF AN URBAN DRUID

Welcome back to the whacked and weird world of Fiona mac Cumhaill.

In the past two years, I leveled up as a kick-ass urban druid and became the leader of the Fianna Warriors my ancestor Fionn mac Cumhaill needed me to be.

The thing is—four months ago everything changed.

The veil between realms came down.

With dormant genes waking, the dominant races jockeying for their place in the hierarchy, and the world around us pulsing out of control with power, my position as the Fae Liaison of Toronto has gotten off to a chaotic start.

Is anyone really surprised?

In her second series, **Case Files of an Urban Druid**, Fiona brings you more druid adventure, family shenanigans, and mythical tales of magic and mystery.

Claim your copy today!

AUTHOR NOTES - AUBURN TEMPEST

FEBRUARY 21, 2022

We did it! Fifteen books in eighteen months and the Chronicles of an Urban Druid series is complete. Thank you for being here and thank you to LMBPN for the stellar system that got my stories out to the world.

Yay team!

The way I see it, the first series was Fi learning about her heritage and her powers, gathering her family and friends, and now she's ready to launch into the world and have some wild and wacky adventures.

Enter the **Case Files of an Urban Druid.**

This next series will have the same cast of characters and now that the big bad of the Culling is over, and the world has gone crazy, more of the loveable antics that make these characters so much fun.

I've been taking notes of the fan suggestions: Yes, Nikon needs to find someone fabulous. No, Michael won't go for a harem with Sloan and Fi…lol, but *I* love the idea. Of course, we need more of Dionysus being outrageous. Yes, I'm going to put together a family tree or character list for the front pages so you can remember who's who. A great suggestion that Jackson could develop wayfarer powers. Yes, a later series of the next generation with Imari, Meg, and Jackson as a dragon rider would be tons-o-fun!

Keep the ideas coming. Who's your favorite character? Do you want to know more about something/someone we crossed paths with? Is there a spin-off idea you want to read? I've got a couple of ideas but would love to hear from you.

Feel free to drop us a line: UrbanDruid@lmbpn.com

Don't forget to check out book one in the Case Files of the Urban Druid series, *Mayhem in Montreal*.

Slainte Mhath,
Auburn Tempest

AUTHOR NOTES - MICHAEL ANDERLE

APRIL 4, 2022

London, England
Thank you for not only reading this book but these author notes as well! Before I go into any of my personal…issues… I want to thank you for following us w/ the Urban Druid series, and I really hope you join us for the Case Files of the Urban Druid.

You know, where more shit happens and we have more fun ;-)

Dammit – I'm too old for this shit…
So, I'm in London getting ready for the London Book Fair. This will be the second major book event (not including 20Booksto50k™) I'll have spoken at since COVID restrictions eased.

The problem(s) started when we arrived at the airport at noon on Saturday in Las Vegas for a 3:05 departure. It seems our first flight (through Dallas) was already going to be late, and we absolutely would miss our connecting flight.

The bastards!

Long story short, we waited at the airport for three hours before we got to talk to American Airlines Executive Platinum people. The queue was hours long for the callback.

While we were stuck at the airport, there were all of these bright, flashy things called… Slots? Yeah… Slots.

It became the most *expensive* time in the airport for me, ever.

We finally got the return phone call which put us on a 11:00 PM flight to New York. That led us to a 10:05 AM flight in New York to London and Bob's your uncle. Except now I've had lousy sleep on two flights, and I'm hungry as hell. One not-so-wonderful pizza and way too many cherry sours later, I'm fidgeting like a puppy on a sugar high.

I can't sleep.

3:30 AM comes by (local time), and I finally doze off to wake up in fits and starts. The light shows behind the curtains, and neither myself nor my wife gets up.

I finally roll out of bed and look at my iPad to see the damage. 3:30 PM … oh…crap.

I have an 8:00 o'clock AM in the morning. It's 11:15 PM at night at the moment, and I'm hoping I get some sleep.

I need to get on stage in 12 hours, and I'm hoping to be coherent.

So, it's 11:15PM. I'm in London, I have no shades, and I'm jetlagged.

You know? *I'm just too old for this shit…*

I hope you have a fantastic week or weekend, and talk to you in the next story!

Michael

AUBURN TEMPEST - URBAN FANTASY ACTION/ADVENTURE

Find Me
Amazon, Facebook, Newsletter,
Web page – www.auburntempest.com
Email – AuburnTempestWrites@gmail.com

Auburn Tempest - Urban Fantasy Action/Adventure
Chronicles of an Urban Druid
Book 1 – A Gilded Cage
Book 2 – A Sacred Grove
Book 3 – A Family Oath
Book 4 – A Witch's Revenge
Book 5 – A Broken Vow
Book 6 – A Druid Hexed
Book 7 – An Immortal's Pain
Book 8 – A Shaman's Power
Book 9 – A Fated Bond
Book 10 – A Dragon's Dare
Book 11 – A God's Mistake
Book 12 – A Destiny Unlocked
Book 13 – A United Front

Book 14 – A Culling Tide
Book 15 – A Danger Destroyed

Case Files of an Urban Druid
Book 1 - Mayhem In Montreal

Misty's Magick and Mayhem Series – Written by Carolina Mac/Contributed to by Auburn Tempest
Book 1 – School for Reluctant Witches
Book 2 – School for Saucy Sorceresses
Book 3 – School for Unwitting Wiccans
Book 4 – Nine St. Gillian Street
Book 5 – The Ghost of Pirate's Alley
Book 6 – Jinxing Jackson Square
Book 7 – Flame
Book 8 – Frost
Book 9 – Nocturne
Book 10 – Luna
Book 11 – Swamp Magic

If you enjoy my writing and read sexy/steamy romance, my pen name for the books I write in Paranormal and Fantasy Romance is JL Madore. You can find me on Amazon HERE.

ABOUT AUBURN TEMPEST

Auburn Tempest is a multi-genre novelist giving life to Urban Fantasy, Paranormal, and Sci-Fi adventures. Under the pen name, JL Madore, she writes in the same genres but in full romance, sexy-steamy novels. Whether Romance or not, she loves to twist Alpha heroes and kick-ass heroines into chaotic, hilarious, fast-paced, magical situations and make them really work for their happy endings.

Auburn Tempest lives in the Greater Toronto Area, Canada with her dear, wonderful hubby of 30 years and a menagerie of family, friends, and animals.

CONNECT WITH THE AUTHORS

Connect with Auburn

Amazon, Facebook, Newsletter

Web page – www.auburntempest.com

Email – AuburnTempestWrites@gmail.com

Connect with Michael Anderle and sign up for his email list here:

Website: http://lmbpn.com

Email List: http://lmbpn.com/email/

https://www.facebook.com/LMBPNPublishing

https://twitter.com/MichaelAnderle

https://www.instagram.com/lmbpn_publishing/

https://www.bookbub.com/authors/michael-anderle

OTHER LMBPN PUBLISHING BOOKS

Sign up for the LMBPN email list to be notified of new releases and special deals!

https://lmbpn.com/email/

For a complete list of books published by LMBPN please visit the following page:

https://lmbpn.com/books-by-lmbpn-publishing/

www.ingramcontent.com/pod-product-compliance
Lightning Source LLC
LaVergne TN
LVHW091709070526
838199LV00050B/2330